MORE THAN WORDS CAN SAY

ALSO BY ROBERT BARCLAY

If Wishes Were Horses

MORE THAN WORDS CAN SAY

ROBERT BARCLAY

DOUBLEDAY LARGE PRINT HOME LIBRARY EDITION

WILLIAM MORROW
AN IMPRINT OF HARPER COLLINS PUBLISHER

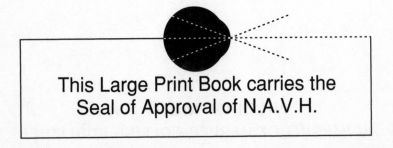

This Large Print Book carries the
Seal of Approval of N.A.V.H.

For my parents, Harry and Muriel.
I couldn't have done it without you.

MORE THAN WORDS CAN SAY

Prologue

As the young woman sat on the front porch of her cabin, her heart ached. Unable to sleep, she had left her bed and come here to gaze out over the moonlit lake she so loved. It had been her hope that the soothing waves might coax the sandman nearer, but so far, that had not been the case.

A black leather journal lay in her lap, its next empty page waiting to accept her troubled thoughts. To be sure, she had written other journal entries since coming here to spend the summer alone. But to her great dismay, each one had been more heartrending than the last. Worse yet, the one she was about to create would surpass even the sadness of its predecessors.

At last, she unscrewed the cap from her fountain pen, and she began to write:

Friday, August 7, 1942, midnight

This wonderful cabin is quite unused to seeing heartache. Instead, it has always been a place to which I could come and happily forget all about the world. But now a terrible war is raging, the same awful struggle in which so many other countries have been desperately fighting for years but finally engulfed the United States just nine months ago. So now heartache and worry exist even here, instead of the happy and joyous feelings that had heretofore always filled these humble rooms. Even so, the war is but one factor in my grief, rather than the entire cause. Because most of my heartache, I must admit, is a product of my own making . . .

Before now, I had always loved being here. And for as long as I can remember, I had believed that I always would.

But so much has happened to me during my brief summer stay that I can no longer be certain of those long-held sentiments. Part of my anguish is due to the fact that this terrible war has taken my loving husband far from me, so that he might finish his military training. And then he will go on to lead others like him in the killing of our enemies, leaving me alone and causing me to wonder if he will ever return . . .

Pausing for a moment, she put down her pen and then turned to gaze down the sandy, moonlit shoreline. A recently built cottage stood there in the darkness. Although no lights shined through its windows at this hour, she knew that he was there. She could almost feel his presence, beckoning her to go to him. As tears began filling her eyes, she again bent to her task . . .

As I look out at the lake, the intense quiet of this place only deepens the sense of guilt that has been growing in my heart since the day I first met him. I should go home, I know; back to Syracuse, where

I would not be so easily tempted. But if I did return to my previous life, would it still hold the same meaning for me? Or would the pain of being without him cause me to rush back? Sadly, I fear that it would be the latter . . .

I know that I should leave here and do my very best to forget him, but I cannot. Because so long as he remains, my heart won't let me. And so, I sit alone on my porch at midnight, watching the waves and wondering where the fates will eventually lead me. As I look at the sky, the clouds seem unusually bright this night, highlighted as they are by a magnificent full moon. Are all of the world's lovers like them, I wonder? Are we too just clouds of constantly changing nature, randomly colliding with one another in a turbulent sky?

On finishing her soul-searching entry, the distraught young woman closed the journal. And this time when she cried, her tears came without end . . .

1.

Early June 1999
Syracuse, New York

"Congratulations," Allistaire Reynolds said. "Despite the tragic circumstances, of course."

Yet again, Chelsea Enright nodded incredulously. "Thank you," she answered. "I think . . ."

Allistaire leaned back in his chair. He was an attractive man in his early sixties, with a full head of gray hair and a matching, neatly trimmed mustache. The sleeves of his white dress shirt were rolled up, and a navy suit jacket hung informally from his chair back. A lifelong antiques hound, he had tastefully decorated his law office with a selection of Americana that gave the room a homey, lived-in look.

"Your grandmother Brooke had me amend her will on the day that you were born," Allistaire explained. "Although she never said why, she wanted you to have the cottage rather than your mother. And for other reasons that she never divulged, after her car crash she never went back."

"I'm grateful to Gram, but I'm not sure about what to do with a cottage," Chelsea said. "I was aware that she owned it. But I've never seen it, and my inheriting it is a big surprise . . ."

Allistaire shrugged his shoulders. "I understand," he answered. "But before you pass judgment on a place that you've never even seen, let me explain a few things."

His lawyerly persona now surfacing in full, Allistaire leaned forward and laced his fingers atop the desk.

"As you probably know, your great-grandfather James first owned the cottage," Allistaire said. "He was the one who had it built, back in the 1930s. Then, in 1943, while your grandmother was still in her in her midtwenties, she had her car accident. Because of the war and having to care for your grandmother, your great-grandparents became too busy to get up there very often. When they died, your grandmother of course inherited the place, but she never returned there. Because of her handicap, she requested that this firm serve as her property manager. The first lawyer who handled it arranged for all of the cottage expenses to be sent here, where they were paid from Brooke's escrow account. That remains the case today."

Pausing for a moment, Allistaire took a sip of coffee and collected his thoughts.

He soon continued. "Anyway, sometime around 1946 or 1947, your great-grandparents thought it prudent to hire a young handyman to help look after the place. He's of French origin and quite ancient now, but believe it or not, he still does a pretty good job. Knows the property like the back of his hand. He oversees any needed repairs, keeps me updated, things like that. When the first attorney retired, your grandmother became my client, and I've taken care of all her affairs since then. Even though they never met, the caretaker served your grandmother steadfastly for all that time.

"Also," he added, "before her recent death, Brooke had the cottage's appliances and electrical service upgraded, along with the phone service. She realized that she wasn't getting any younger, and she wanted to know that when you inherited the place, it would be livable—or sellable, should you wish. She even had a dishwasher installed, but otherwise, nothing about the property has changed. It must be an antique-hunter's dream! Long story short, the place has been uninhabited for over sixty years, and now it's yours."

Allistaire gestured toward a thick file that lay atop his desk.

"Everything's in there," he said. "Repair bills, Brooke's will, tax receipts, deed, escrow account statements, your codicil—the works."

While staring blankly at the folder, Chelsea shook her head. "I still don't get it," she said. "That cottage should have gone to my mother."

Allistaire smiled again. "Perhaps," he answered. "But Brooke was a sharp old gal. She must have had some good reason for willing it to you, rather than to Lucy."

"But I'm not sure that I can afford to keep it," Chelsea answered. "The taxes, the maintenance . . ."

"Don't worry about all that," Allistaire answered. "There's enough escrow money—which, by the way, is now also under your control—to cover the expenses for a long time. And there are additional funds set aside in Brooke's will, should you need them. Plus, the property is completely unencumbered."

"So I can sell it, if I want?" Chelsea asked.

As Allistaire leaned back again, his chair hinges squeaked pleasantly. "Sure," he answered. "But you should at least go and look at it. Who knows? You might like it."

Chelsea doubted that, because she had never been the outdoors type. She didn't particularly like hiking or boating, the only place she had ever caught a fish was in her supermarket basket, and her most adventurous experience with wild-life had been raising Dolly, her beloved golden retriever.

While Chelsea considered his advice, Allistaire admired her. She was a tall, sin-gle, and attractive woman of thirty-three. Chelsea was a respected and tenured art teacher at a local Syracuse high school, and she loved her work. Though he was a confirmed bachelor, whenever Allistaire saw Chelsea, he sharply lamented their insurmountable age difference.

For his part, Allistaire Reynolds had long been a partner at Grayson & Stone, LLC, and he had handled the Enright family's affairs for decades. The Enrights were wealthy by Syracuse standards, and as is so often the case with people of substance, they had suffered their share of thorny legal issues.

"Okay," Chelsea said. "So I've inherited Gram's cottage. I know that it's some-where up in the Adirondacks, but that's about all."

Allistaire opened the folder on his desk

and took from it a weathered envelope, which he handed to Chelsea.

"Maybe this will help," he said. "Provided you had reached the age of thirty, your grandmother stipulated that immediately after her death, you should be given this letter in private. That's largely why I asked you to come here today. I wasn't made privy to what the letter says, but perhaps it will provide some answers about all this. It's been in this firm's possession for a long time."

As Chelsea stared at the yellowed envelope, she correctly surmised that it was a product of a different era. In her unmistakable penmanship, Brooke had addressed it with an old-fashioned fountain pen. Curiously, it read, *"To My New Granddaughter."*

"I suggest that you read it now," Alistaire said. "And with your permission, I should probably read it too. There might be something in there that affects my duties in all this." Smiling, he produced a letter opener and handed it to her.

Her grief suddenly returning in full, Chelsea slit open the yellowed envelope.

Inside she found two sharply folded sheets of her grandmother's personal stationery and a small, nickel-plated key. Like the envelope, the pages had been written upon with a fountain pen:

My Dearest Child,

Forgive me for how I address you in this missive, but you were born just today, and your parents have yet to christen you. If you are reading this, I am at last gone from this world. Do not mourn me unduly, for my life was full— far more so, in fact, than you ever knew.

By now, you realize that you have inherited my property on Lake Evergreen. You may trust in everything that Allistaire tells you, but for reasons that will eventually become clear, you must not allow him—or anyone else— to read this letter. For now, all I can tell you is that I have willed the cottage to you, rather than to your mother, because I am hoping that when you grow older, your capacity for forgiveness will be the greater one. Your mother knows that this is to happen, but she is unaware of the true reasons.

Because you are reading these words in the distant future, I cannot possibly know what twists and turns your life has taken or in what manner you have chosen to live it. Should you wish to sell the cottage, you have my blessing. Nevertheless, you must not relinquish ownership before you follow the instructions that I am about to describe. Only then, my dear, should you decide whether to keep it or to let it go. Please also know that as the years go by, I will do my very best to be there every step of the way, watching you, guiding you, and mentoring you.

Although it will be many years before you become a woman, I already sense that there will grow a strong bond between us—perhaps even greater than the one I already share with your mother. Regardless of what you may have heard, be assured that Lake Evergreen is a wonderful place. Because of personal reasons, I have not visited my cabin for many years, nor will I ever do so again. But that is all right, because it has now become yours. And, as you will soon learn, it was best that the cottage has lain undisturbed until this day, when you are at last old enough to understand.

Travel to Lake Evergreen soon, my dear granddaughter, and be sure to go there alone. When you arrive, go to the guest bedroom and move the bed aside. You will notice three certain floorboards, easily identifiable because their joints are scratched and worn. When you remove them, you will find an old tin box; its lock can be opened with the key you now possess. Inside the box are some additional things that I wish to bequeath to you. And like the cottage, only after much consideration should you decide what to do with them.

Whatever decision you choose to make, I'm sure it will be the right one. My soul has been bothered these many years, but I hope that placing this letter and my beloved cottage in your care will finally grant me a measure of peace. Lastly, my child, know that my thoughts and prayers go with you.

Your loving grandmother,
Brooke Bartlett

Stunned, Chelsea refolded the pages. Despite her overpowering grief, she knew one thing. She would trust in her grandmother's instructions and follow them to the letter. After collecting herself, she placed the letter and the mysterious key back in the envelope.

"May I also read it?" Allistaire asked compassionately.

Her grandmother's written warning still fresh in her mind, Chelsea shook her head. "No," she answered.

"Are you sure?" he asked. "There might be something in it that—"

"No," Chelsea said insistently.

Although taken aback, Allistaire relented. "Very well," he said. "Do you have any instructions for me?"

Chelsea looked down at the envelope for a time, thinking. "Leave things as they are for now," she said. "After the funeral, I'm going to Lake Evergreen. When I get back, we'll talk again."

"Please inform me before you go," Allistaire requested, "because Jacques and Margot will want to greet you. You'll need their help at first."

"Who?" Chelsea asked.

"Jacques Fabienne and his wife, Margot," Reynolds answered. "They're your grandmother's—or should I now say *your*—caretakers."

Chelsea placed the precious envelope inside her purse and stood to go.

As Allistaire shook her hand, he said, "I hope that you find your answers."

"So do I," Chelsea answered. *Whatever they might be . . .*

2.

On leaving Reynolds's law office, Chelsea got into her Mustang convertible and lowered the top. She then headed away from downtown and toward Fayetteville, one of Syracuse's most upscale suburbs. As she drove, her hands started shaking again. This time, however, it was less a result of her grandmother's passing and more because of the mysterious letter and key that lay inside her handbag. In an attempt to calm down, she took a deep breath and eased her death grip on the steering wheel. Doing so helped a little, but nothing could fully stem the sense of

unrest that had come with Brooke's unexpected message from the past.

Her grandmother's death had hit Chelsea harder than she could have ever
imagined. The funeral was scheduled for
tomorrow, and she dreaded it. Chelsea's
other three grandparents had also passed,
but the death of "Gram" had been especially devastating. The tragedy had rattled Chelsea to her very core, causing her
to finally shed the youthful sense of im-
mortality that everyone seems to harbor
for a time.

Today was June 1, but as far as the
weather was concerned, summer had of-
ficially arrived. As with most upstate winters, the previous one had been harsh and
uncompromising, causing Syracusans to
emerge from their hibernations like sleepy
bears, stretching and blinking in the sun's
unfamiliar warmth. The trees were at last
showing their leaves, softball leagues were
forming, and it seemed that everyone was
smiling again. It was a lovely time of year,
and had it not been for her grandmother
Brooke's death, Chelsea would have been
happy too.

The only child of Lucy and Adam Enright, Chelsea had enjoyed a rather privileged upbringing. Her father owned several large auto dealerships, though he spent little time at them these days, preferring instead to oversee things from his downtown corporate office. Still a robust man, depending on the season he could be found bird or deer hunting, skiing the local slopes, or attacking the golf course at his country club.

To her father's disappointment, Chelsea had never expressed any interest in the family business, preferring instead to receive her MFA and teaching credentials at Syracuse University. Teaching helped to fulfill her, and she enjoyed having her summers free. Because of Brooke's inherited wealth and Adam's financial success, Chelsea's mother, Lucy, had never worked, instead immersing herself in the Syracuse social scene. She was a fixture at fashion luncheons, charity group meetings, and her much-beloved bridge club games.

Ironically, Chelsea's family's social standing had seemingly cursed her love life more than it had helped it. She oftentimes wished that she could meet a good man who had never heard of the Enrights, but the longer she remained in Syracuse the more discouraged she became. Although Syracuse claimed nearly one hundred fifty thousand residents, it seemed that everyone already knew everyone else. Moreover, news and gossip traveled with the speed of light—especially when it concerned the relatively wealthy.

Putting her thoughts aside, Chelsea at last guided her convertible up a long knoll and onto a huge circular drive, where she parked among the host of cars already there. Since her grandmother Brooke's death, the Enright house had been bombarded with friends, relatives, and the food everyone had brought. At first glance, today appeared no different.

Before getting out of her car, Chelsea took the key her grandmother had included with the letter from her purse and hung it on her cherished silver necklace, also a gift from her grandmother. She then safely tucked both treasures back inside her blouse. Having Brooke's mysterious key lying directly over her heart felt right, somehow.

Knowing that she would need to redo

her hair and makeup, she gazed at her face in the rearview mirror. Her wavy, dark red hair was long and parted on one side. High cheekbones, large green eyes, and a sensuous mouth completed her lovely portrait. Today she was clothed in tan Ralph Lauren slacks, a white silk blouse, and shiny brown pumps.

As Chelsea walked across the driveway, she admired the lovely home in which she had been raised. Built entirely of stone, it closely resembled a small English manor house. Professional gardeners maintained the immaculately trimmed lawn and colorful landscaping, and the house sat atop a hill, allowing for a magnificent view. When Chelsea's parents divorced, Adam had graciously transferred full ownership to Lucy.

Until she started teaching, Chelsea had lived here all her life. She had loved growing up in this wonderful place and although she now owned a perfectly lovely town house of her own, every time she visited, she was reminded of how much she missed it. After crossing the brick driveway, she opened one of the stately double doors and walked inside.

As expected, she encountered a subdued atmosphere. Appropriate music was softly playing and there were many visitors, most of whom she recognized. They seemed to be about equally divided into those who were glumly milling about by themselves and others who were congregating in mournful little groups. While making her way across the foyer and into the kitchen, Chelsea was compassionately greeted by many of them and she responded in kind. The kitchen was also busy and hugely overloaded with food. For some reason, casseroles seemed to be the most popular offerings. She sighed a bit as she stared at it all.

I'm sure that my mother and father appreciate all this, she thought. *But I could never understand why people always bring so much food to those whose terrible grief has totally robbed them of their appetites . . .*

On seeing that a makeshift bar had been set up on the kitchen island, she poured two fingers of single-malt scotch. She took an appreciative sip before walking on into the living room.

By almost any standard, the Enright living room was immense. Its greatest attributes were an emerald-green rug, dark colonial furniture, and a huge marble fireplace. After making the rounds of those who had congregated there, Chelsea stepped out onto the equally large sunporch that adjoined the living room's far side. Here, she hoped to find some solitude.

Floor-to-ceiling windows overlooked both the swimming pool and the tennis court, and beyond the sloping hill, there lay a wonderfully expansive view of Syracuse's southeastern side. Taking refuge in one of the many overstuffed chairs, she swallowed another welcome sip of scotch. For a time, she wished that she could simply melt away into the chair cushions and become invisible to all who might wish to offer up yet more depressing condolences. She hadn't seen her mother yet, but that would happen soon enough.

A few moments later, Lucy's two shih tzus happily arrived and began nuzzling Chelsea in an urgent quest for food.

Her mother had named them Rhett and Scarlett, and although they were not Chelsea's type of dog, she liked them well enough.

When she reached down to pet Rhett, a familiar voice said, "God, how I dislike small dogs! I don't know why your mother got them, but that's Lucy for you. Give me a big old gundog every time. Speaking of which, how's Dolly these days?"

Chelsea looked up to see her father, Adam, standing beside her chair. "She's fine, Dad," she answered.

Adam Enright bent down and kissed his daughter's cheek. "And Syracuse's most eligible bachelorette?" he asked. "How's she doing?"

Chelsea rustled up a little smile. Seeing her father always brightened her mood, no matter the circumstances.

"When I meet her, I'll ask," she answered. "Have you been here long?"

Adam shook his head. "I just arrived." He pulled a chair closer and sat down. "How are you holding up, kiddo?"

"I hate clichés, but I'm doing about as well as can be expected," she answered.

"Yeah, me too," Adam answered.

"And Mom?"Chelsea asked.

"She's still devastated," Adam answered. "But I always knew that would be the case. They were practically joined at the hip."

Chelsea nodded. "Yes . . . ," she said sadly.

Chelsea looked lovingly at her father. He was a tall, fit man in his early sixties with short gray hair, deep blue eyes, and a strong jaw. He had been her rock while she was growing up, and Chelsea thought he looked especially handsome today in a black polo shirt, gray slacks, and cordovan loafers.

Adam and Lucy had divorced while Chelsea was in college. With no daughter left to raise, they had slowly and quietly grown apart, he with his ever-expanding businesses and she with her ever-widening social obligations. There had been no adultery, no fighting, no real animus of any kind. Their loss of intimacy having been more insidious than sudden, it was as if they had simply given up on loving each other. Then one day Adam had quietly left the house, and in her own way, Lucy understood.

Adam had enjoyed several relationships since then. But although Lucy had
received many offers of companionship,
she had chosen to remain alone. Chelsea had never known why, save for the
possibility that her mother still lived in
the past and was unable to move on. Or
perhaps the men that Lucy had met
since her divorce hadn't been appealing enough, especially after having been
married to a man as vibrant as Adam. In
any event, unlike many children of divorce,
Chelsea could honestly say that she still
loved her mother and father equally. And
for that much, at least, she felt lucky.

"So how was school this year?" Adam
asked.

"Okay," Chelsea answered. "Plus, I
make really big bucks as an art teacher."

"Speaking of which," Adam said, "have
you reconsidered my offer?"

Chelsea shook her head. "Thanks, Dad,"
she answered. "But I really don't want to
work for you. I like my summers off too
much."

Adam chuckled quietly. "I know," he
said. "Even so, I'd be immensely happy
to assign you absolutely no responsi-

bilities and grossly overpay you for completely ignoring them."

Chelsea smiled at her dad. Then she again remembered her grandmother's letter, and she cautioned herself against mentioning it. Even so, she was brimming over with questions that Adam might be able to answer.

"It wouldn't work out just now, anyway," she added. "Shortly after the funeral, I'm going away for a few days."

"Oh?" Adam asked. "Where to?"

"Apparently I've inherited Gram's old cottage on Lake Evergreen. I need to go and see it, before deciding whether it's worth keeping."

It took a few moments, but Adam finally remembered. "Good Lord . . . ," he said. "You're quite right. I'd totally forgotten about that. And congratulations, I suppose . . ."

Chelsea's eyebrows lifted questioningly. "You *suppose*?" she asked.

Adam nodded. "Well, yes," he answered. "God only knows what kind of shape the place is in by now."

"Allistaire says that it's been well maintained over the years."

"Could be," Adam said. "I wouldn't know."

"So you were aware that I'd inherit it?" Chelsea asked.

"Sure," Adam answered. "But it's been so long now that I'd forgotten."

"Did you ever go there?"

Adam shook his head. "I've never even seen the place. By the time your mom and I were married, the cottage had been closed for nearly twenty years."

"Do you know if Mom has any pictures of it?"

"I have no idea," he answered. "But even if she does, by now they're so old that they'd probably make the place look a lot better than it really is. Would you like me to come along and help you check it out? I'd be glad to do it."

Chelsea almost agreed before stopping herself. She would need privacy if she were to properly follow Gram's instructions. Even so, she briefly lamented the lost chance to be with her father for a few days.

Chelsea shook her head. "Allistaire told me that a caretaker has been looking after the place," she answered. "He and his wife are supposedly going to meet me there and show me the ropes."

"Well, if you find that you need any-thing, call me and I'll drive up. If not, come and see me when you get back, because I'll be eager to hear all about it. And now, I'm going to get a stiff drink and find your mother. I'm sure she could use some support. In our own way we still love each other, you know."

Chelsea kissed him on one cheek. "I know, Dad," she said.

With that, Adam headed off toward the kitchen. Hopeful that he might provide them with some food, Rhett and Scarlett eagerly scampered along after him.

While taking another sip of scotch, Chelsea again looked out the broad pic-ture windows, thinking. Since her grand-mother's death two days ago, she had been trying to summon up some cour-age and store it away in her heart, against the awful day when she would again lose someone she loved. Perhaps then she could call upon those carefully preserved armories of strength and use them as shields against her pain. Then she shook her head a little. Was she deluding herself? Probably, she realized, but it was a pleasant fantasy to nurture.

Brooke had known many people in Syracuse. She had also been well recognized for her charity work and was a driving force on the board of the Everson Museum of Art, an avid painter right up to the day of her death. Her donated works hung in many local homes and cultural facilities. And it was from her that Chelsea had acquired her own love of art and painting. In the end, Brooke died in her sleep, passing from this world in much the same way that she had lived in it— quite peacefully, and without being a bother to anyone.

To her surprise, just then Chelsea thought she heard Gram's comforting voice, whispering to her from afar. That wasn't really the case, of course. Even so, she could clearly remember the many times that Gram had advised her as she was growing up. Gram was always there, always kind, always ready to help with any concern. If Chelsea didn't seem to grasp her answers, Brooke would usually say, *"When you're older, you'll understand."*

How odd, Chelsea thought as she again

focused her gaze outside. *That's much the same thing that she said in her mysterious letter . . .*

As she thought more about it, her fingertips unthinkingly sought out the little key that lay underneath her blouse. This time, touching it came automatically. And for some reason she had yet to understand, she found the gesture oddly reassuring.

Chelsea finally arose and walked to the far end of the sunporch. It was here that Brooke had sat and painted. The easel still stood where it always had, with its back toward the windows. An incomplete landscape rested on it, waiting to be finished by an artist who would never return. Just as likely to remain orphaned, Brooke's various painting tools lay on a nearby table.

Brooke once told Chelsea that her interest in painting had begun shortly after her last visit to Lake Evergreen. She had hired a teacher to come to the house and instruct her, Brooke had also said, until she had developed a style all her own. But when Chelsea had innocently asked Brooke whether her final visit to the lake had had anything to do with her wanting to paint, a sad look had overtaken Brooke's face. She then politely told Chelsea that her reasons had been personal and that she didn't wish to speak of them.

Chelsea picked up one of the brushes, remembering. Its wooden handle felt warm, as if her grandmother had just held it. She sadly closed her eyes, realizing that it was the sun that had blessed it, rather than her grandmother's touch. She put the brush back down, wondering what would become of such cherished mementos. Just then, someone touched her shoulder.

"Hi," Lucy said softly.

Chelsea turned and gave her mother a long, meaningful hug, as if some of the strength she had been storing away might somehow be imparted to her in this hour of need. When at last she stepped back, Chelsea was disturbed by what she saw.

Lucy hadn't slept in two days, and dark circles lay beneath her bloodshot eyes. Her usually perfect makeup looked haphazard and wrong, from being so frequently reapplied between crying spells. Although her short gray hair was in place and she was suitably dressed, an over-whelming sense of grief showed through her every attempt to appear normal. When her tears erupted again, she did her best to wipe them away.

As Chelsea searched her purse for a tissue, her fingers brushed against Brooke's aged letter, reminding her of both its message and its warnings. Much the same way that she had kept it a se-cret from her father, she must now also do the same with her mother, she knew. She had never been guarded around her parents, and she didn't enjoy being that way now. But she had resolved to follow Gram's wishes, so when the tissue came out of her purse, the precious letter stayed behind.

"How are you doing, Mom?" Chelsea asked.

Lucy's faint smile seemed forced, man-ufactured. "As best I can," she answered. "It's just so hard, you know? We lived together for ages . . . and now I'm rattling around in this big house all by myself. It's so quiet at night, after everyone has gone home . . ."

Then Lucy looked carefully around as

if she were appraising her home, rather than admiring it. "Do you think that I should sell it now?" she asked Chelsea. "With Mother gone it seems so big, so empty . . ."

Chelsea sighed and shook her head a little. Less than an hour ago, she had asked Allistaire Reynolds that very thing about Gram's cottage. *Death has an odd way of forcing us into making choices,* she thought. She put a comforting arm around her mother's shoulders.

"I think that you're getting ahead of yourself," Chelsea answered. "There'll be lots of time to consider that. And we'll talk to Dad about it, too. He always knows what to do."

Lucy's next effort to smile proved no more genuine than before. "I don't suppose that I could ask you to stay with me for a few nights?" she said. "I could really use the company."

And just how do I answer that? Chelsea thought. *Should I obey the secret wishes of my grandmother or the more immediate needs of my mother?*

It had long been Chelsea's opinion that Lucy's brittle and rather martyr-like personality was a result of never having had to work at a "real" job, among "real" people. As far as Chelsea was concerned, Lucy's charities, black-tie balls, and bridge club didn't count. Because of her late father's wealth and Adam's success, Lucy had never worked a day in her life. As Chelsea had grown into adulthood, she had come to suspect that it was precisely this insulation from the real world that had shaped her mother's personality. Rather than produce a sense of superiority in Lucy, it seemed that the privileged isolation she had experienced her entire life had somehow created a sort of silent inferiority in her makeup. Lucy had always been a good person, Chelsea knew, but never a great mother. And because of that, it had been Adam to whom Chelsea had always been the closest. But she loved her mother, and she hated seeing her in so much pain.

"I'll tell you what," Chelsea said. "I'll stay with you for a few days, but then I have to leave town for a little while. Would that be okay?"

Chelsea went on to explain her meeting with Allistaire and how she was going

up to Lake Evergreen to view the property. To help cushion the blow of her leaving, she then fibbed a little and told Lucy
that Allistaire thought it best if she went
there soon. She didn't like doing it, but
she was trying to walk a fine line between helping her mother and obeying
the wishes set forth in Brooke's mysterious letter. When Chelsea finished, Lucy
nodded.

"Three or four days will be enough, I
think," Lucy answered. "I'll probably be
better after that. By then, I could probably use some time alone, anyway."

Sighing, Lucy wiped her eyes again.
"Oh . . . by the way," she said. "Mother
wanted you to have something else."

"What is it?" Chelsea asked.

Lucy walked shakily toward an end
table, where she picked up an old black
notebook. She walked back over to Chelsea and handed it to her.

"It's Mom's recipe collection," Lucy
said. "You're a far better cook than I, and
she was always reminding me that it would
be better off in your care. As was the case
with so many things, she was right."

Chelsea looked at the old notebook. It was so fragile that it was practically falling apart, with an old rubber band around its middle holding it all together. Although she hadn't seen it for years, she remembered it. Just as she had painted nearly every day of her life, Gram had cooked nearly every day of her life. Sloping ramps had been built in the kitchen so that she could wheel her chair onto them and work at the proper height. Chelsea had never read any of the recipes the notebook contained; the most she knew about them was that they were all supposedly of Brooke's own devising.

"Thank you, Mom," Chelsea answered. "I'll always treasure it."

"I know you will, honey," Lucy answered. "I know."

At last, Lucy seemed to buck up a little. "And now," she said, "let's go and rejoin your father. We both need his strength right now. And we'll see if we can eat something. God knows there's enough food!"

Glad to see that her mother had at least partly rejoined the land of the living, Chelsea smiled.

"Sure, Mom," she said. "I'm glad that Dad's here, too."

Without further ado, the grieving mother and daughter went back into the house and slowly made their way across the spacious living room.

3.

Later that night, Chelsea juggled her keys and a paper bag containing some leftovers for Dolly while simultaneously struggling to unlock her town house door. It wasn't going well, and a thunderstorm was fast approaching. Just as the first drops fell, she at last made her way inside and switched on the lights.

Not surprisingly, Dolly sat waiting for her. Dolly was a gorgeous, light-colored golden retriever with big, brown eyes and a warm heart. On seeing Chelsea, she barked and happily jumped up, innocently adding to her mistress's predicament.

"Yes, I know you're hungry," Chelsea said. "Don't worry—I've got something special for you tonight."

After finally placing her items atop the foyer table, Chelsea tousled Dolly's ears. "Haff you been goot?" she asked. "Because eef you haven't, vee haff vays awff makink you talk!"

"*Woof!*" was Dolly's ubiquitous reply.

Chelsea released Dolly into the backyard, then she unwrapped the plate of meatloaf she had selected from the bounty at her mother's house and she set it on the floor. When Dolly returned she immediately tore into the food, her tail wagging furiously as she nosed the plate hither and yon.

Hoping to assuage some of her tension and grief, Chelsea took a long, hot shower. She then donned a bathrobe, put her wet hair up in a towel turban, and poured a glass of Bordeaux. She carried her wine to the living room sofa, where she could watch the gathering storm through the windows. After lighting several candles, she dimmed the lights, reclined on the couch, and took a welcome sip of wine.

The rain was coming harder now, the

heavy drops forming silvery rivulets on her windowpanes and curiously distorting everything that lay beyond them. Dolly soon appeared and jumped atop the couch. Just then, another lightning bolt flashed across the night sky, followed by a strong thunderclap. Unlike many dogs, Dolly was never frightened by storms.

Chelsea took another sip of wine and again looked out the window. Even as a child she had always loved rainstorms— the way they smelled and how they always made everything seem clean and new. Then her thoughts turned inward, and she closed her eyes for several moments. Her beloved grandmother was gone, and the mere thought of Brooke's passing still stabbed unrelentingly at her wounded heart.

Almost immediately, she began to cry. Perhaps her tears came so suddenly because she was at last alone. Or maybe the death of her grandmother had finally settled into her soul. Whatever the reason, she let her tears flow freely this time, causing her emotional surrender to somehow feel both good and bad.

She had worshipped her grandmother,

and valiantly attempting to withstand this huge loss was nearly more than she could bear. For the last two days, she had steadfastly tried to be the same capable woman that she had always been. But when darkness at last fell and she was alone, her disguise quickly crumbled, just as it had done tonight. Even when she tried to be tough, the unbearable sadness bled through her carefully crafted façade. It appeared in her face, in her mannerisms, and in her reticence to believe that her grandmother was really gone.

The funeral was tomorrow, and she hugely dreaded laying Gram to her final rest. Like most people, Chelsea believed in attaining closure. But this time her heart rejected it, because it would mean that her beloved grandmother was truly gone for good. Sighing, she did her best to compose herself.

She fully realized that most people thought she just glided along in life as the privileged daughter of an equally privileged family. But her real friends knew that Chelsea had always been something of a scrapper and quite willing to go her own way, if need be, to follow her heart.

Yes, she could have taken the easy road and gone to work for her father. She smiled a little as she recalled Adam's comic but heartfelt offer of employment. Many would have gladly taken that path, she knew. But she hadn't wanted a soft, unchallenging life of nepotism. In her heart of hearts, she had long felt the need to prove herself all on her own.

Despite its civilized nature, Lucy and Adam's divorce had shattered Chelsea's world.

When Adam left the house for good, Chelsea had been shocked and she cried for days.

In some ways, the divorce had been more difficult for her than for anyone else. But by now Adam and Lucy's parting had matured, its raw nature replaced with a more socially presentable patina. So much so that whenever the three of them were together, it almost seemed like they were a true family again.

To her credit, Chelsea had never placed blame or taken sides. Not only because she loved them both, but also because of the quiet and largely civilized way in which Adam and Lucy had finally separated. During that difficult time, it had been Gram who encouraged Chelsea to pursue her MFA. It had been painting, plus her great love of children, that had led Chelsea to become an art teacher.

Chelsea had loved those halcyon days when Gram had so patiently taught her. Eventually Chelsea's painting style would find its own path, differing rather sharply from Gram's. Some would later say that Chelsea's works even outshined Brooke's, but Chelsea never agreed. To her, Brooke's paintings were among the best she had ever seen. Chelsea still loved to paint, but these days she had time for it only during her summer breaks. While continuing to gaze out the rain-streaked window, she took another sip of wine.

In addition, Brooke had always hoped that Chelsea could find someone worthwhile to love, someone who could make her feel whole and cherished. But sadly, Brooke died knowing that there was no one special in Chelsea's life. With that memory on her mind, Chelsea's thoughts inexorably turned toward her unsuccessful love life.

She had experienced her fair share of

romantic liaisons. But so far, no man had held much real interest for her, causing the few relationships into which she had entered to be short-lived. Truth be known, she wished that she could meet a genuine man's man. She certainly didn't desire some overly macho brute. But she did want someone who was confident in his masculinity, someone who would ultimately care more about her than he did his golf game or the cut of his suit. And with each passing day, she increasingly doubted whether such men still existed. She had been disappointed again and again over the years, and some of her girlfriends said that she was being too picky.

So far, no man had broken her heart to the point of desperation, but none had rescued her from her loneliness, either. Although she was only thirty-three, she increasingly felt as if the prospect of finding someone who would both love and understand her was dwindling with each passing day. Even so, she refused to "settle," as some of her female friends had done. True enough, they had gotten married. But Chelsea could oftentimes detect a sense of sadness in their eyes that had much to do with what their futures might have been had they held out for true love. Knowing that each woman's heart was similar yet also different, Chelsea had never been judgmental about the life decisions that her female friends had made. But she felt sorry for some of them, and she refused to take the same course.

Sadly, her soul mate hadn't arrived. She had never believed that one plus one equaled two in a healthy and loving relationship. Instead, she had always held tight to her conviction that one-half plus one-half equaled one. But her other half remained a ghost, an apparition of her own making who caused her mind to yearn and her heart to suffer. Much to her own disappointment, she was a single woman in her thirties who lived with her dog.

Tired of reliving her problems, she extinguished the lights and candles and walked into her bedroom. After drying her hair and removing her robe, she slipped gratefully beneath the cool, crisp sheets. Dolly soon wandered in and jumped atop the bed. Lightning again illuminated the night sky, followed by another strong bang of thunder. Like usual, Dolly seemed oblivious to it. As Chelsea's eyes gained heaviness, once more she lovingly touched the mysterious little key that lay upon her chest.

A few days from now, she thought as the dark tunnel of sleep approached. *A few days from now, I'll go and see Lake Evergreen. I wonder what it's really like . . .*

4.

Four days later, Chelsea found herself navigating the mountains and valleys of the Adirondacks. The sun was high, and the passing scenery was lovely. After another half hour or so, she would turn onto Rural Route 30 North and then search for Schuyler Lane, the narrow dirt road that encircled Lake Evergreen.

She had consulted a road map to learn that the nearest town from Lake Evergreen was Serendipity, New York, some twelve miles farther north. She had also learned that Serendipity boasted all of 12,793 people. Small, certainly, but also large enough to provide whatever extras she might need during her brief weekend stay.

Along with Dolly and one suitcase, she had brought an AM/FM radio and a CD player. Allistaire had warned her that even if there were a radio there, it probably wouldn't work. He also said that there would of course be no television. Chelsea had also brought along the old recipe notebook that Brooke had bequeathed to her. Although she had yet to examine it, she might try preparing one or two of them, she reasoned, if the mood struck.

Chelsea had borrowed a new Explorer from one of her dad's dealerships to use for the trip and was relying on Allistaire's handwritten directions. Allistaire had also arranged for Jacques and Margot Fabienne to meet her at around three P.M., so they could help her open the cottage and also drop off a few staples. So far, she was ahead of schedule.

Chelsea was enjoying the Explorer, despite its unaccustomed size. She had doubted the need for such a big vehicle, but her father had insisted. Besides, he had said, dogs get antsy on country drives, especially gundogs. A few years ago, Adam had trained Dolly to hunt game birds with him. Why have a retriever, he argued, that couldn't retrieve? Chelsea had smiled at that. She didn't hunt or fish, but she had no problem with those who did. And where she was headed, she reasoned, that attitude was probably a good thing.

Chelsea glanced at the rearview mirror to see that Dolly did in fact seem restless. Chelsea had left one of the rear windows down so that Dolly could occasionally stick her head out and allow the rushing wind to ridiculously buffet her face. Someone once told Chelsea that dogs did that because they loved having their highly acute senses of smell bombarded with so many new and unusual scents.

But who really knows? Chelsea thought as she concentrated on the road again. *And Dolly isn't telling. . .*

Like Chelsea had predicted, Brooke's funeral had been huge, depressing, and seemingly endless. The Enright house had then again overflowed with people. For the rest of the day, Chelsea had endured yet more sober conversations, crying, and purposeful hand-wringing. In Chelsea's opinion, Lucy had ensured that Gram's service was far too ostentatious. Although Gram had been well-to-do, there hadn't been a pretentious bone in her entire body. Chelsea also knew that rather than approve of her grandiose send-off, Brooke would have most certainly laughed at it.

While driving along, Chelsea tried to remember what she knew of her family history. Brooke's father, a man named James Ashburn, had become wealthy in his own right. He had quit school early and started out by selling newspapers, come rain or shine, on one of Syracuse's busy downtown street corners around the turn of the century. Then later, like many other young men of his era, he saw action during World War I. On his safe return home, he became a tenacious reporter for the same paper that he had so eagerly hawked as a young boy.

Striving tirelessly, he ended up owning not only the newspaper but also much of the surrounding business property as well. But because of her father's manic work ethic, Brooke hadn't seen much of him while she was growing up, so she had been raised largely by her mother, Gwendolyn. Like many hard-boiled newspapermen of that era, James had been a voracious drinker and smoker. When a heart attack suddenly took him in his midfifties, Gwendolyn wisely sold all of James's holdings, ensuring that neither she nor her daughter, Brooke, would want for anything.

Brooke had married the first man she fell in love with, not an uncommon occurrence in her day. William Bartlett was a handsome and respected editor on James's paper. Soon after they were married, the Japanese bombed Pearl Harbor. Feeling an irresistible call to duty, "Bill" immediately quit the paper and enlisted in the army, hoping to become a war correspondent. James offered to use some of his considerable influence to keep Bill out of the war, but Bill adamantly refused. Although Brooke understood, when he left for basic training, her farewell to him had been tearful and heart wrenching. Tragically, Bill died in the war. But Chelsea didn't know the particulars, because Brooke never wanted to talk about it.

Putting her family history aside, Chelsea smiled a little as she again touched her shirt and felt the key that lay beneath it. The closer she came to the cottage, the more she was dying to know what lay inside the hidden tin box.

She soon came upon a dirt road leading off to the right, and she stopped the Explorer. There she saw an ancient, weather-beaten road sign. It was little more than a pair of battered two-by-fours that had been nailed together and pounded into the ground beside the intersection. Its hand-painted letters read SCHUYLER LANE.

After consulting Allistaire's directions for what would be the final time, Chelsea tousled Dolly's ears. "This must be the place, girl," she said. "Pretty swank, huh?"

As if convinced that they had at last arrived, Dolly barked eagerly.

Chelsea smiled. "I know, " she said. "Truth is, I'm getting curious, too." She then made a left-hand turn and started guiding the Explorer down the narrow dirt road.

Schuyler Lane was lovely. True enough, it was just a simple dirt road, with a dividing line of scruffy grass down its center where tire treads didn't roam. Overhead there lay a dark canopy of maple branches, born from the dense woods that lined either side. The branches seemed to have made a pact to stretch toward each other above the road and marry in the middle. They gave the lane a shadowed and romantic look, causing Chelsea to smile a bit more as she traveled on.

Soon the lane split in two; one branch went east, and the other headed west. This was where it divided so as to encircle the lake, Chelsea realized. She consulted Allistaire's directions again and saw that she needed to go west.

As she traveled farther, she occasionally caught shiny glimpses of a lake on her right and of a few cottages that also flashed, phantom-like, through irregular gaps among the trees. At last she came upon an old sign that had been nailed to a tree, its hand-painted letters worn and faded from the passing years. It still said ASHBURN, the last name of Chelsea's great-grandfather.

Chelsea took a deep breath and turned right onto a private drive of sorts that headed northward toward the lake. Here the maples gave way to stands of fresh-smelling pines, and the ground's dense, green covering was gradually surrendering to one more sparse and sandy in nature. Just then she saw the old cottage, and she drew a quick breath.

It was larger than she had envisioned. Its back side faced the road, and it had been sturdily built of shaven logs that were stained dark red. The peaked roof was made of dark shingles; a squat stone chimney rose from its center. There was a main structure with a smaller wing attached to its right-hand side. A few windows graced this side of the building, all of them covered over with boards that had been painted to match. Against the back wall there lay a great pile of stacked firewood, its bounty partly covered with an old tarp. Evergreen trees dotted the ground around the cottage, their tall branches swaying lightly in the wind, their clean, fresh scent riding on the summer air. From what Chelsea could see, Jacques and Margot had yet to arrive.

Down the slope leading away from the cottage lay Lake Evergreen, the mid-afternoon sun bouncing off its surface, its waves dancing lightly with the rising and falling breeze. When Chelsea gazed across the lake, she realized that it was larger than she had imagined, its opposite side lost in a summery haze.

Chelsea got out of the Explorer and opened a rear passenger door for Dolly, who eagerly sprang from the SUV as if she had been imprisoned inside it for days rather than hours. Chelsea instinctively knew why Dolly had suddenly become so happy and boisterous. At home, she had only a small yard in which to run. But here, Dolly had a huge range of new adventures lying before her, each one awaiting her eager exploration. To be on the safe side, Chelsea attached a leash to Dolly's collar so that she couldn't go bounding off and become lost.

With Dolly desperately straining at her leash, Chelsea walked toward the cottage. The west side held a door, two boarded-up windows, and little else. Farther along, there was a short flight of steps leading up to a long porch that lined most of the front side. Here too, every window was covered.

On the east side of the property there

stood another building. Nearly the size of the cottage, it too was built of logs that had been stained red, and its windows were also covered. Part of it extended out over the water and rested on concrete pylons. This was the boathouse, Chelsea realized. Down at the shoreline, a long wooden dock extended into the water. Curiously, an old mailbox was attached to the far end of the dock by means of an upright two-by-four.

Chelsea had to admit that she was pleasantly surprised. As Allistaire had said, the place was old but in very good condition. Whoever Jacques and Margot were, they had done a wonderful job during their many decades of service.

Chelsea then walked Dolly down toward the lakeshore some fifty feet away, whereupon Dolly started thirstily lapping up lake water. To Chelsea's amazement the shore was one of pure sand, rather than of rocks and mud like other New York lakes she had visited, and it stretched all the way from the water back to the cottage, its uniformity broken only by a few patches of defiant beach scrub. Reaching down, she took a handful of the sand to find that it was fine and soft, much like the saltwater beaches she had visited. She then cast her gaze about the shoreline. The lake appeared to be round, but the view from where she stood could be misleading.

After slipping off her sneakers, she rolled up her pant legs and led Dolly out into the water a bit. The lake was rather warm, the sand beneath her feet soft and forgiving as the short, restless waves pleasantly brushed up against her calves. Aside from the warmer water and the less aggressive waves, it was not unlike standing in the ocean. And also like the ocean, the gradient was very gentle. Clearly, the entire property was far more enticing than she had expected.

A few moments later, a phrase from her grandmother's letter sprang to mind, causing her to smile. *"Regardless of what you may have heard, be assured that Lake Evergreen is a wonderful place . . ."*

Still standing in the water with Dolly, she again cast her eyes up and down the sandy shoreline. She saw no dwellings toward the east, but when she looked westward she discovered another lake-shore cottage, standing about forty yards away. Although a black Jeep Wrangler was parked nearby, no one seemed to be about. A long wooden dock extended into the lake, and tied up at the dock was an aluminum fishing boat, bobbing gently with the waves. Farther out on the lake a red and white, high-winged floatplane tugged gently at her moorings, her snub nose facing obediently into the wind.

I wonder who lives there, Chelsea found herself thinking. Then she looked at her watch. *Two P.M. I got here early, it seems. Even so, I wish that Jacques and Margot would hurry up. I'm eager to see the inside of the cottage, and—*

Suddenly Dolly let go a vicious growl, and she started straining at her leash again. To Chelsea's horror, Dolly's teeth were bared, and she was now pulling so hard at her leash that Chelsea could barely keep from being dragged.

"What's the—" Chelsea said. And then she saw the problem.

Another dog was standing down the beach, near the cottage with the floatplane. It looked like an English setter, but Chelsea couldn't be sure. What she could be sure of, though, was that Dolly and the other dog had suddenly discovered each other, and they clearly weren't happy about it.

Before Chelsea could do anything, Dolly's worn leash snapped and the two dogs charged one another. As Chelsea watched helplessly, they quickly became embroiled in a vicious dogfight. Still shoeless, Chelsea dropped the broken leash and ran toward the warring dogs. When at last she arrived, she unthinkingly tried to separate them. But as she did, the setter bit her hand. Chelsea yelped and backed away as the two dogs kept at it.

Just then she heard someone cry out, and a man rushed from the cottage. He was shirtless and holding a large plastic bucket in one hand, and a dog leash in his other. To Chelsea's surprise he dashed right past her and the fighting dogs and then charged straight into the lake, quickly filled the bucket with lake water, and ran back.

As he passed Chelsea, he angrily

shouted, "Get the hell out of the way!" While Chelsea quickly stepped aside, he threw the entire bucket of water onto the two entangled dogs.

The man apparently knew about dogs, because the effect was immediate. Shocked by the water, Dolly and the setter quickly backed off from their fight. The man then dropped the bucket to the beach, quickly snapped a leather leash onto the setter's collar, and dragged him aside. Not knowing what else to do, Chelsea grabbed Dolly's wet collar and did the same. After taking a couple of deep breaths, the stranger looked straight into Chelsea's eyes.

"Chelsea Enright, I presume?" he asked.

"Yes," she finally answered. "But how did you know?"

"Jacques and Margot told me that you were coming today," he answered. "But I didn't think your arrival would be so dramatic."

Chelsea was mortified. She had meant to replace Dolly's leash for some time but hadn't. Clearly, this was not how she had wished to meet her new neighbor.

"I'm so sorry!" she said. "I didn't know this would happen! Dolly usually isn't like that!"

To her great relief, the man finally smiled. "That's okay," he said. "But right after we sequester the dogs, we've got to tend to you."

"Huh?" she asked.

He pointed at Chelsea's right hand. "You're bleeding," he said.

Amid all the excitement, Chelsea had forgotten all about being bitten. There was a jagged gash at the base of her right thumb, and blood was running from it. Now that things were calmer, the pain suddenly set in.

"Come with me," the man ordered as he beckoned toward his cottage. "We've got to get you fixed up."

"What about the dogs?" Chelsea asked. "We can't let them go at it again."

"I know," he answered as he began leading the black and white spotted English setter forward. "Come on, Jeeves," he said. "You've eaten enough people for one day."

Before reaching his cottage, he turned and looked back at Chelsea. "Bring your retriever in after me," he ordered, "but keep your distance. Dogs are a lot like kids. Until they learn to play nicely, they belong in separate rooms. And by the way, has your retriever been spayed?"

"Yes," Chelsea answered.

She watched as he mounted the porch steps with his dog and started opening the screen door.

"Excuse me," Chelsea said, "but I didn't get your name."

The shirtless man turned and looked back at her. "It's Yale," he answered. "Brandon Yale."

Chelsea nodded as she began leading Dolly toward the cottage.

Okay, then, she thought. *Brandon Yale it is. . .*

5.

While keeping a safe distance behind, Chelsea led Dolly up the steps, across Brandon's porch, and into his kitchen. As Chelsea looked around the inside of his cottage, what she saw of it appeared quaint and nicely decorated.

"Put your hand over the sink," Brandon said as he sequestered his wet English setter in a bedroom down the hall. "You're bleeding all over my floor."

While Chelsea did as he ordered, he walked back and approached Dolly carefully. Chelsea still had hold of Dolly's collar with her good hand, but she doubted that she could fully control her if she acted up again.

"Now, be a good girl," Brandon said quietly as he squatted down and looked into Dolly's wary eyes. Still soaking wet, she showed her teeth again and let go a soft but meaningful growl. Brandon smiled at her and stood up.

"A hard case, huh?" he asked. "We'll fix that."

He went to the refrigerator and rummaged around for a few moments. When he returned, he held a piece of leftover fried bacon in one hand. He carefully held the bacon out toward Dolly.

"Here's a peace offering," he said to her. "I never met a dog yet that didn't love bacon, and I'll bet that you're no different."

Dolly growled a bit more, sniffed warily at the bacon, and then snatched it from Brandon's grasp. While she chomped on it, Brandon said to Chelsea, "You can let me have her now."

"Are you sure?" Chelsea asked.

"No," Brandon answered. "But it's my guess that the bacon tastes better to her than I would."

As Brandon took Dolly's collar, Chelsea let go. To Chelsea's surprise, Dolly acquiesced.

"Atta girl," Brandon said to Dolly. "Now, come with me."

To Chelsea's even greater amazement, Dolly obeyed straightaway. After Brandon placed her in another room and shut the door, he walked back again.

"How'd you do that?" Chelsea asked. "She's never that good with strangers." Suddenly the pain from her hand struck again, and she winced.

"Simple," Brandon answered. "Dogs and bacon is a match made in heaven. Now then, let's have a look at you."

After washing his hands, Brandon carefully examined Chelsea's wound.

"This won't need surgery," he said, "but you're in for some stitches. First, though, we've got to get it clean." He turned on the faucet, waited until the water ran cold, and then looked into her eyes. "Sorry," he said, "but this is going to hurt."

He quickly placed Chelsea's wound directly under the running water and held it there, causing her to yelp. When he had finished cleaning the wound, he wound a clean towel around her hand.

"Do you drink alcohol?" he asked unexpectedly.

"Yes," she answered.

"Is bourbon okay?" he asked.

Chelsea nodded eagerly. "Right now, anything will do!"

Brandon walked across the kitchen, where he opened a cupboard door and produced a bottle of Canadian bourbon. He poured some into a glass and put it before her.

"Don't go away," he said. "I'll be right back."

While taking a welcome sip of the bourbon, Chelsea took another moment to examine Brandon's country-style kitchen. Although it was clearly more functional than beautiful, it managed to exude its own sort of appeal. Her mind racing, she shook her head.

What have I gotten myself into? she wondered. *And who is this Brandon Yale person who's trying to patch me up? Should I let him? I should probably be on my way to a hospital. Do they even have one in Serendipity? And who names his dog "Jeeves"?*

Brandon soon returned with a squat, black leather bag. While he was gone, he had slipped on a black T-shirt to go with his faded jeans and thong sandals. When he placed the bag on the kitchen counter, Chelsea saw that it bore a gold-plated identification plaque that read BRANDON YALE, MD.

"So you're a doctor?" she asked.

Brandon nodded. "Thus the letters *MD*," he said teasingly. "Now, tell me— when was your last tetanus shot?"

"Two Thanksgivings ago. I sliced my-self, rather than the turkey."

Brandon laughed a little. "Okay," he said. "Allergic to anything?"

"No," she answered.

As Brandon opened his bag, a thought struck Chelsea. "What about rabies?" she asked anxiously.

Brandon shook his head. "Jeeves was the one that bit you, right?"

"Yes."

"Then it's okay," Brandon answered. "Jeeves doesn't have rabies any more than I do. But if it'd been anybody else's mutt, I'd make you take the shots."

He soon produced a hypodermic and began filling it from a small bottle.

"What's that?" Chelsea asked warily.

"A local anesthetic," he answered. "Unless, of course, you'd rather do this au naturel."

Chelsea quickly shook her head.

Brandon nodded and administered the shot. Almost at once, Chelsea's pain began to subside.

"Thank you," she said.

Brandon smiled. "No need," he answered. "I'd do the same for any shoeless city slicker."

Beginning to feel more at ease, Chelsea again sipped some bourbon. "So tell me," she said, "what kind of doctor still carries a medical kit around with him?"

"The kind who still makes house calls," he answered while searching his bag again.

He soon produced a bottle of hydrogen peroxide, which he opened. Brandon poured some directly into her wound. To Chelsea's relief, it didn't hurt. Using her free hand, she again tasted the very good bourbon.

"So, now what?" she asked.

Brandon snorted. "You certainly ask a lot of questions," he answered.

"Well, it's my hand, isn't it?" she asked back. Then she laughed a little. "And besides," she added jokingly, "how do I know that you're not some sort of country-fried quack?"

Brandon rummaged around inside his bag again. "Oh, I think you're safe enough," he answered. "To the best of my knowledge, Harvard Medical School doesn't produce many quacks."

"Harvard?" she asked. "Really?"

"Yes," he answered.

"I can't begin to imagine how many jokes you must have suffered."

"You mean about the 'Yale' guy who went to Harvard?" he asked back. "Yeah, you can say that again."

He soon closed her wound with seven precise stitches. When he finished, he dressed her hand with a fresh bandage.

"There you are," he said. "All set and ready for company. I used dissolving stitches, so they won't have to be removed. Come tomorrow, I'll check it again. But I don't have any oral antibiotics here, so I'll have to give you a shot."

"Oh, god," she answered. "Do you have to?"

"Yep," he answered. "Jeeves doesn't have rabies, but he's still a dog. I don't even want to think about where his mouth has been."

Smiling, Brandon produced another clean hypodermic. "So where would you like it?" he asked. "In your arm or your backside?"

One corner of Chelsea's mouth turned up wryly. "My arm will do nicely," she answered.

Brandon gave her the shot and then closed his bag. For a moment or two afterward they simply stood there, each unsure of what to say next. At last Brandon washed his hands again, and he casually shoved them into the back pockets of his jeans.

He was good-looking, she decided, in a craggy sort of way. Not what one would call classically handsome, but striking nonetheless. Despite his scholarly profession, there was something of a wild and untamed quality about him. He appeared to be about her age, and he was tall and muscular. His dark hair was a bit on the wavy side, his eyes were blue, and his jaw was strong. A mysterious hint of an old scar lay on his right cheek, and adding to his rugged good looks was his rather short, aquiline nose. A discreet glance at his left hand told her that he wore no wedding ring.

"Well, I think you'll live," he finally said to her as he poured a bourbon for himself. "By the way, when are Jacques and Margot due to arrive?"

Suddenly remembering, Chelsea checked her watch. It was a bit before three P.M.

"They'll be here any minute now," she said. "I should probably go back to my place and wait for them."

Brandon shook his head. "There's no need," he answered. "We can see them drive up from my porch."

They went to Brandon's long, screened-in veranda and sat down on two old rocking chairs. Chelsea had a nice view of the lake and of the red and white floatplane moored offshore. She pointed at the plane.

"Is that yours?" she asked.

Brandon nodded. "I've been flying for about ten years now. Aside from it being fun as hell, I also use the plane to make house calls. And sometimes, I land in a lake and drop a fishing line out the pilot's window."

Chelsea looked around again. "So this house is also your office?" she asked.

Brandon laughed. "Lord, no," he answered. "I don't really have an office. I'm an ER doc at the Serendipity hospital. But sometimes, people call me here and ask if I can come to see them. I usually drive, but if it's some distance away and they're on the water, I use the plane. The idea started out small, then word got out and it grew to the point where I could now probably do that full-time, if I wanted. But I'd likely starve to death! Many of the folks that I visit have no insurance and can't afford to pay me, so I let them slide. Or sometimes, they give me whatever they have. Last week I returned home with several chickens in the back of the plane. They were crated up, of course, but they still made a helluva mess."

Chelsea's eyes widened. "Chickens,

really?" she asked. "What did you do with them?"

Brandon looked at her and smiled. She was starting to like his smile, she realized.

"I'm pretty good with a scalpel," he answered. "If you don't believe me, go look in the freezer."

"Okay, I get it," Chelsea answered. "So, do you live here all year 'round?"

Brandon shook his head. "No one does. There are eighty-some cottages on this lake, but so far as I know, not one of them is winterized. Besides, living out here in the winter would be impossible. They don't plow the roads, and the mail service is by boat, which of course stops when the lake freezes over. During the winter, Jeeves and I live in my house in Serendipity."

Chelsea took another sip of bourbon, thinking. *No winterization, the local doctor sometimes gets paid in chickens, they don't plow the roads in the wintertime, and the mail is delivered by boat.* Lake Evergreen was starting to make Serendipity sound like a major metropolis.

Brandon causally propped his feet up on an old, wooden coffee table that sat before them.

"So tell me about yourself," he said. "It isn't every day that I get a visitor."

Chelsea provided him with a quick thumbnail sketch. She then also explained about her grandmother's death and how she had inherited the cottage.

"I'm sorry about your grandmother," he said. "Jacques and Margot told me that she died. I never knew her, but they are always saying how wonderful she was. Even though they never actually met her, they talked on the phone. The truth is, Jacques is so old now that for the last few years, I've been the one doing all the heavy lifting at your place. But don't tell him that you know, because he still considers it his baby. They've spent the last two days, from dawn to dusk, getting the cottage clean and ready for you."

Chelsea was quite surprised to learn that Brandon had been helping to maintain her cottage. *What a sweet gesture,* she thought.

"I didn't know about your contributions to the cause," she said. "Can I pay you something for all of your trouble, plus your medical services?"

Brandon made a throwaway gesture with his free hand. "Nah," he said. "Just invite me over to dinner one night, and we'll call it even."

"You've got a deal," she answered.

Then her thoughts turned again to her cottage and the mysterious tin box that had induced her to come here.

"So you've been inside my place, I gather?" she asked.

"Sure. Not the boathouse, though. For some reason, Jacques has always been pretty secretive about it."

"So what's the inside of the cottage like?" she asked eagerly.

"Well," Brandon said, "it's—"

Just then they heard a horn blow, and they turned to see an old Ford pickup arrive at Chelsea's place.

"That's them," Brandon said. "I'll come along, because whether Jacques wants to admit it or not, he'll need my help getting things done. But first, I'll let the dogs out."

"Won't they just fight again?" Chelsea asked.

"Maybe, but they've got to declare a

truce eventually," Brandon answered. "Might as well be now."

He strode back down the hall, let Dolly out, and told Chelsea to take her by the collar. Then he opened another door and took hold of Jeeves's collar. After a time, he slowly led Jeeves nearer to Dolly.

At first, Chelsea feared another snarling row as the dogs glared menacingly at each other. But after some hugely inappropriate sniffing, tails finally wagged, so Brandon and Chelsea let the dogs go. In mere moments they were eagerly standing side by side before the porch door, begging to be let outside.

"Ah . . . ," Brandon said. "And so it begins."

"I'm impressed!" Chelsea answered. "But I can't let Dolly run loose! She'll get lost!"

"Not when she's off with Jeeves," Brandon said. "He always comes home."

"Does Jeeves always return because he loves you so much?" Chelsea asked.

Brandon laughed again. "A nice thought," he said. "But mostly, I think it's because this is where he gets fed."

At first, Chelsea was hesitant about letting Dolly loose. But so far, Brandon had been right about the dogs, so she decided to trust his judgment.

"Okay," she said. "You can let Dolly go, too." As Brandon made for the screen door, Chelsea asked, "Why did you name your setter 'Jeeves'?"

Brandon stopped and turned around. "That's simple," he answered with another smile. "He's an English breed, and he does what he's told."

When Brandon opened the screen door, the dogs charged from the cottage and began happily bounding down the sandy shoreline, as if they had been best pals for years. Brandon turned back toward Chelsea, and he smiled.

"Dolly 'n' Jeeves," he said. "Has a certain ring to it, don't you think?"

Despite her worry about Dolly getting lost, Chelsea was forced to grin, too.

"Yes," she answered. "As a matter of fact, I do."

As Chelsea accompanied Brandon toward her cottage, she again surreptitiously touched the key hidden beneath her shirt, wondering . . .

6.

With the arrival of her caretakers, Chelsea became even more consumed with the thrill of the unknown. Like one's first walk toward a new lover's bedroom, approaching her cottage offered both excitement and promise.

What will be inside the tin box? she wondered. *And will knowing make me happy or sad?*

While Chelsea reclaimed her sneakers, Jacques and Margot Fabienne got out of their battered pickup. Jacques, a great Gallic bull of a man whose strong, fleshy facial features bore a respectful expression, wore a dog-eared carpenter's bib over an old blue shirt, and work shoes that had also seen better days. An honest-to-goodness black French beret sat atop his head. His face bore a series of craggy lines and wrinkles that seemed a road map of the many places he had been and the things he had experienced. As Chelsea approached, he respectfully removed the beret from his shiny, bald head.

Margot was tall and whippet slim, with short, haphazard white hair that looked like she cut it herself. Her eyes were deep green and when she smiled, the wrinkles at the corners of her mouth and eyes gathered pleasantly. She was simply dressed in a black shirt, a pair of women's tan trousers with a wide leather belt, and sensible shoes. In her hands she held a ceramic Dutch oven. The slight aromas escaping from around its lid were homing signals to Dolly and Jeeves, causing the dogs to gather wishfully at Margot's feet and hopefully thump their tails. While smiling down at them, Margot whispered something in French.

With a smile on his face, Brandon went

to Jacques. When he gave Jacques a hug, he couldn't get his arms around the great Frenchman.

"*How are you, Jacques?*" Brandon asked in French.

His use of a foreign language surprised Chelsea a bit, causing her to raise an eyebrow.

Jacques smiled before answering. "*I am good for someone so old!*" he replied in his native tongue. He then gave Chelsea another glance before looking back at Brandon. "*The new owner is beautiful, is she not?*"

Brandon smiled back at him. "*Indeed!*" he answered. "*But I suddenly find myself hoping that she doesn't speak French!*"

While Brandon and Jacques laughed, Margot cleared her throat and shot both men a sharp look of reproach.

"We will speak only English before the new owner, you two," she said sternly. "We agreed, remember?"

"But you just spoke French yourself, *non*?" Jacques protested.

Margot gave Chelsea a wink. "That was different," she said. "I was talking to the dogs."

Chelsea liked Margot at once, and she smiled at how this slight, aged woman had so quickly put Brandon and Jacques on notice. But Chelsea also realized that for virtually anyone else, doing so would be a nearly impossible task. Brandon and Jacques seemed to be stalwart, independent souls, men who didn't imagine themselves subject to much and, for better or worse, seemed largely unconstrained by many of society's rules. Chelsea wasn't used to being around such men, but she was finding that she enjoyed it. And although she hadn't understood a word of what Jacques and Brandon had said, like many women, she liked hearing it in French, nonetheless.

Chelsea gave Brandon a questioning look. "So you speak French too, I see," she said.

Brandon nodded. "Yeah, but I still mangle it pretty badly," he answered. "Over the years, Jacques and Margot have been kind enough to teach me. Many have been the nights when we shared a bottle or two of wine while they immersed me in the subtleties of their native language. But sometimes, all I really got immersed in was the wine. Then they'd laugh themselves silly, while I slurred my words and said ridiculous things like, 'That bathtub looks good on you!' Anyway, I still don't read or write it much, but I can speak it pretty well, and that comes in handy up here."

Still holding his beret before him, Jacques approached Chelsea. Although his fingers were the size of sausages, his handshake was gentle.

"It is a pleasure to meet you, mademoiselle," he said. Then his expression sobered. "We were so dismayed to hear of your grandmother's death . . . Madame Brooke was a true lady, and she will be missed. We will do our best to serve you like we served her."

At the mention of Gram, Chelsea felt another wave of grief rush through her. But this time her pain was tempered with a strong sense of gratitude for the Fabiennes and everything that they had done for Brooke.

"Thank you both," she answered quietly. "We buried her yesterday . . ." She again glanced at the container Margot held. "And what have you there, may I ask?"

Margot smiled. "Coq au vin," she answered proudly. "It's my own recipe. We also brought some crusty bread and red wine to go with it. They will come in handy on your first night, no?"

"Thank you very much," Chelsea said. "As it happens, I love coq au vin."

Brandon laughed at her rather mangled pronunciation. "Given the way that Margot makes it, coq au vin is two things," he said. "First of all, it's chicken stewed in wine sauce."

Chelsea smiled again. "I already know that," she chided him. "But what's the second thing?"

"French heaven on earth," Brandon answered.

Jacques produced a key ring from one of his pockets and walked to the cottage. After opening the screen door, he turned back toward Chelsea.

"The moment has finally come," he said. "After so many years, a member of Madame Brooke's family will at last go inside."

Before unlocking the door, he thought for a moment. Then he walked back to Chelsea and contritely handed her the keys.

"Perhaps mademoiselle should do the honors?" he asked. "After all, it is your place now, *n'est-ce pas*? Please forgive my presumptuousness, for old habits die hard."

Chelsea nodded and took the key from him. Her hand trembling slightly, she inserted the key in the lock and turned it over. As she pushed open the door, its old hinges squeaked pleasantly.

Until this moment, she hadn't known what to expect. Before coming here she had asked Lucy if there were any pictures of the cottage, but Lucy didn't know. For lack of any better information, Chelsea had envisioned some primitive shack that was barely livable. But after seeing the cottage's well-maintained exterior, she had become hopeful.

At last she went inside, followed by Margot. While Jacques and Brandon busily removed the outside window boards, the afternoon sunlight came streaming in. Almost as if she were viewing a slide show, Chelsea watched the various rooms present themselves one by one.

She was standing in the kitchen, where everything, both old and new, positively glistened with cleanliness. The walls were of knotty, polished pine. An old potbellied stove sat in one corner, its narrow black chimney ascending through a high ceiling made of rough-hewn timbers. Allistaire had been right about the appliances, Chelsea realized. Each had indeed been replaced; even the stainless steel sink and faucets looked new. Although the black and white checkerboard floor appeared original, it too was spotless. The old wooden cabinets and countertops were slightly warped from age but seemed serviceable enough. While Margot set the new oven on "warm" and placed the coq au vin inside it, Chelsea walked on into the living room.

Where the kitchen had been an odd mishmash of generations, here only the past prevailed. Both the floor and walls were built from pine, lending the room an unexpected lightness. The living room was rectangular, with one of its longer sides facing the lake. The peaked ceiling was high, and like that of the kitchen, it too had been quaintly fashioned from old beams and rafters. A chandelier made from artfully entangled deer antlers hung from the ceiling's center beam, and an old dining table with six captain-style chairs was positioned along the left-hand wall. To Chelsea's right lay the bathroom door, and just beyond that was the door to the mysterious guest bedroom to which Brooke had alluded in her letter.

On the left side of the living room stood a beautiful fireplace that had been fashioned entirely of rose quartz rocks. Chelsea had never seen its like, and the effect was striking. On the slate mantel stood an unfinished portrait of Brooke that had presumably been started sometime before her tragic car crash. A massive leather sofa, its surfaces elegantly cracked here and there with age, sat before the fireplace. A huge vintage radio stood against the wall on the fireplace's right-hand side, and on the other side there stood an old rolltop secretary and a matching chair. Just left of the desk was the door leading to the front porch.

The far end of the living room held double doors that invited entrance into the master bedroom. Taking the bait, Chelsea walked in and looked around. Here, too, everything was vintage. A large picture window looked out upon the sandy shoreline, the boathouse, and the shimmering lake beyond. A mahogany, king-sized sleigh bed faced the window, as did the matching dresser. A paned skylight in the ceiling let in the afternoon light while also revealing some evergreen branches above it, swaying gently in the breeze.

Still trying to hide her excitement, Chelsea walked back through the living room and at last entered the guest room. It was a small space with a single latticed window, a shiny brass bed, and a lone maple dresser with matching mirror. As Chelsea tried to discreetly peer under the bed, she realized that without actually going down on her knees, she would never identify the three special floorboards that Brooke had mentioned in her letter. The longer she stood looking, the more she wanted to go after them right there and then.

While she remained lost in thought, Brandon approached. Crossing his arms over his chest, he leaned against the doorjamb and grinned at her.

"So, what do you think?" he asked.

A bit startled, Chelsea turned to face him. Doing her best to forget about the box, for a few awkward moments she found herself at a loss for words.

"I honestly don't know what to say," she finally answered. "In its own special way, this is one of the loveliest places I've ever seen."

"Have you visited the porch yet?" Brandon asked. "It's great."

She followed Brandon across the living room and out onto the porch. It was deep and long, its right-hand side ending at the joint where the living room's front wall met the master bedroom. The inward-slanting screened windows provided a marvelous view of the lake. Some old rocking chairs and cocktail tables sat there, and candled hurricane globes hung at regular intervals on the back wall. From here one could hear the sound of the waves and feel the refreshing breeze as it winnowed its way through the screens.

She then shook her head unbelievingly, much the same way she had done in Allistaire Reynolds's office only four days prior. On first learning that the cottage had become hers, she had been quite willing to sell it sight unseen. But now that idea seemed remote. She was falling in love with the place, and she knew it.

"I'm simply amazed," she said to Brandon. "I never guessed that it could be so wonderful."

Without answering, Brandon quietly walked to one of the screened windows, where he stood looking out at the lake.

"It is, isn't it?" he at last replied softly, as if he were speaking only to himself. "And it's even better when you have someone to share it with . . ."

When he didn't turn around, Chelsea went to him and gazed quizzically into his eyes. After a few moments, he at last returned from his personal reverie.

"Are you okay?" she asked. "For a moment or two, it was like you had gone off alone somewhere."

He smiled apologetically. "Sorry," he answered. "I was just thinking about someone I used to know. It happens, sometimes . . ."

Just as Chelsea was about to respond,

Jacques and Margot joined them. Jacques smiled broadly and placed his meaty fists akimbo.

"So, mademoiselle," he asked. "Does your vacation home meet with your approval?"

Chelsea laughed a bit. "Are you serious?" she asked. "What could be better than this? I have so much to thank you and Margot for! Without you two, by now this place would be in ruins."

She almost thanked Brandon too, before remembering his warning from before. She would do so later, she decided, after the Fabiennes had left.

Jacques shot a wink at Margot, who smiled back knowingly. "But there is more," he said to Chelsea. "You still haven't seen the boathouse."

Chelsea smiled. "True," she said. "But no boathouse in the world could be as lovely as this cottage."

"No, boathouses are seldom lovely," Jacques answered. "But yours holds a special surprise that I think will please you very much."

Chelsea raised her eyebrows. "What is it?" she asked.

"To answer that," Jacques said, "mademoiselle must accompany me there."

Ever more curious, Chelsea looked at Brandon. "Do you know what he's talking about?" she asked.

"Haven't got a clue," Brandon answered. "Like I said before, Jacques has always been secretive about it."

"True, *mon ami*," Jacques said to Brandon. "But now it is at last time for that secret to come out. So follow me, you two, and you shall see."

Jacques and Margot led them off the front porch, then across the sand and toward the boathouse. As she neared, Chelsea realized that it was larger than she had first thought, causing her to wonder why one would need an accompanying building so spacious.

After unlocking the door, Jacques turned back toward Chelsea and Brandon, and he smiled. Saying nothing this time, he unceremoniously opened the door and walked in. Because he and Brandon had already removed the window boards, there was no need to turn on the lights.

The boathouse was cluttered with all manner of appropriate things. An old aluminum rowboat lay upside down atop two sawhorses. A workbench lined one side of the room, and hand tools of nearly every description hung on the wall above it. Nests of tangled fishing line, old lures, antique rods and reels, and a couple of still-deteriorating fishing baskets also clung to the walls. The air smelled of grease, motor oil, and the distant past.

Although the room was cluttered, Chelsea remained at a loss about the special surprise Jacques had mentioned. Hoping for an answer, she cast another quizzical glance at Brandon, but he only shrugged his shoulders.

And then she saw it. There was a solid wooden door in the far wall, allowing entry into what she knew must be the other half of the boathouse. With only a smile, Jacques handed her a silver key chain. After walking across the room, Chelsea unlocked the other door and crossed the threshold. Brandon followed her, as did the Fabiennes. Once inside, Jacques switched on the lights.

This other room was windowless. In the middle of the floor, a boat lay in a heavy steel cradle that hung from the ceiling. In the floor directly below the boat lay twin, closed doors that presumably opened up and over to lay flat on the floor on either side, thus exposing the water below. A series of electrical wires ran from a motor on the far wall to a wall switch. Chelsea could easily deduce that when the switch was activated, the cradle would gently lower the boat down onto the waves below it.

The boat itself was covered over with an old canvas tarp. Wasting no time, Jacques and Margot walked over and pulled off the tarp. As they did, Brandon gasped.

"My God, Jacques!" he said. "She's beautiful! How long has she been in storage like this?"

As if he were showing off his first newborn child, Jacques beamed with pride.

"Since the day the cottage was closed for good," he answered. "She hasn't seen the light of day since. The engine was prepped for long-term storage, and twice a year I have polished her wood and chrome and conditioned her leather. She still looks good, no? There are few remaining like her."

Then he turned and looked at Chelsea. "And now, mademoiselle," he said softly, "she's yours."

Although Chelsea knew nothing about boats, even she realized that this was something very special. As she neared it, she became entranced. Clearly, this craft was a product of a more elegant age.

"It's amazing," Chelsea said. "I've seen boats like this only in magazines."

"I'm sure that's true," Jacques boasted, "because they've become so rare. She's a 1941 Chris-Craft. One of only three hundred seventy-one made that year. Because of the scarcity of raw materials during the war years, no more were built until 1946. And soon after that, boat makers began using fiberglass. Your great-grandfather bought her new and had her shipped here. Madame Brooke loved her, and she went out in her nearly every afternoon. After her accident, she ordered me to carefully put her in storage to await another day, and so I did."

Wide-eyed, Chelsea circled the boat. The graceful craft was sixteen feet long; her shiny mahogany hull, topside, and chrome trim positively gleamed. There was a cockpit both fore and aft, each of them fashioned with plush leather seating and able to accommodate two persons. In between them was the housing for the inboard engine. The steering wheel was huge and boasted a chrome horn ring, like that of an antique car. Her long, pointed bow was elegant and built for slicing through the waves, and a two-part, low-slung glass windshield lay before the driver's cockpit. When Chelsea walked around the gracefully tapered stern, she smiled. The name of the boat had been painted there in gold lettering.

"*Beautiful Brooke . . . ,*" Chelsea murmured, almost to herself.

"Your great-grandfather named her after his only child," Jacques said. "If the mademoiselle would like, I know a shipwright in Serendipity who can activate her again. I could tow her to his shop, where he would do all the work. It would probably be pricy, but he's the only one I trust to do it right."

While still staring at the beautiful boat, Chelsea nodded. *Beautiful Brooke* was far more than just some marvelous antique. In her heart, Chelsea somehow knew that this craft would prove to be just as much a link to her grandmother's mysterious past as would the cottage itself, or whatever lay inside the tin box. Although she had never been the outdoors type, she suddenly wanted to enjoy this boat, to experience it just as Brooke had done those many years ago, when she had still been a healthy and spirited woman. But there was more to it, Chelsea knew. To her continuing astonishment, with every passing moment she was feeling more and more a part of this wonderful place.

"Yes," she said. "Please arrange it."

Jacques nodded. "Yes, mademoiselle," he answered.

Margot looked at her watch. "It is becoming late, *mon cher*," she said to Jacques. "Time for us to go."

After everyone left the boathouse, Jacques handed all of the keys to Chelsea. Then the four of them unloaded the groceries that the Fabiennes had brought, and they stored them away. Margot gave Chelsea a quick tour of the kitchen, showing her where she could find things. Finally, Jacques gave Chelsea their home phone number and a small packet that contained all of the paperwork on the lovely old Chris-Craft.

At last, the Fabiennes stood ready to go. As Jacques respectfully removed his beret again, a rather sad look overcame his face.

"If there is ever anything you need," he said, "you have but to call us. And you have a good neighbor in Monsieur Brandon, who can also help with things. In the meantime, I will contact you about picking up the boat."

"And if you like the coq au vin," Margot added, "I'll be happy to teach you how to make it."

With the Fabiennes about to leave, Chelsea felt her heart unexpectedly swell. Although she had known them for less than two hours, this stalwart old Frenchman and his equally indefatigable wife already seemed like family. She stepped forward and kissed each of them on the cheek.

"That would be lovely," she answered. "Au revoir."

At last the Fabiennes got into their old truck and headed for home. As the dust settled on the road, Chelsea turned back toward Brandon.

"What wonderful people . . . ," she said. Brandon nodded his agreement. "And now, mademoiselle," he said in a near-perfect imitation of Jacques's accent, "is there anything more that I can do for you tonight?"

"No," she answered quietly as she searched his blue eyes. "You've done so much already . . ."

She then took another moment to again examine this man, this new neighbor of hers who until only hours ago she had never known existed. He seemed so totally in his element here, she realized, standing on the beach in his jeans and T-shirt, with Jeeves obediently by his side and his dark hair being lightly ruffled by the breeze. So confident, so at home in this remote and captivating place. She wanted to thank him properly for all his help but was unsure of how. Just then she heard his stomach growl, and she knew.

"Tell you what," she said. "Why don't you come by for dinner later and help me eat some of that coq au vin Jacques and

Margot brought? You won't even need to bring the wine."

Brandon smiled. "I thought you'd never ask," he replied.

Chelsea thought to herself for a few moments. "See you in a couple of hours, then?" she asked.

"Sounds good," he answered.

Smiling to herself, Chelsea turned and walked toward her new cottage.

7.

Now that Chelsea was at last alone, her desire to find Brooke's hidden tin box became overpowering; it had been the real reason why she had asked Brandon to wait for two hours before coming back over. She hurried to the guest bedroom and shoved the big brass bed to one side.

When she looked down at the floor, she saw the three scratched floorboards. But they refused to succumb to her fingernails, causing her to realize that she needed something tougher with which to pry them loose. She went into the kitchen, where she grabbed up a strong knife and a flashlight, then she returned to the guest room. When she inserted the knife blade into the cracks between the floorboards and pried them up, they lifted easily. She carefully shined the light down into the darkness.

The cottage had no basement, only a dirt foundation. Lying there was not the tin box she had expected to find but a small leather valise, the kind that people used long ago, with leather straps that buckled around its outside to keep it securely closed and travel stickers pasted upon it, speaking of the various places it had seen. She peered around some more with the flashlight to make sure that there was nothing else down there, then she grabbed the old valise and manhandled it up through the hole.

Despite its age, the valise was in relatively good condition. Although it was damp down there, no animals had been able to bother it. While hoisting the valise up onto the bed to take a better look, she heard something slide around inside it and her heart skipped a beat.

She found the identification tag and eagerly wiped it clean. As expected, it read BROOKE BARTLETT. The two brass buckles securing the leather straps were badly rusted, but she was able to free them up and undo the straps. With breathless anticipation, she opened the valise and looked inside.

At last, there it was—the old tin box that Brooke had promised. With trembling hands, Chelsea removed the box and set it on the bed. It was rusted and battered but intact. An old padlock secured the hinged lid.

She removed the necklace from around her neck and took the little key from it. Because the key was in so much better condition than was the box, they seemed to have come from different times, perhaps even different worlds. Chelsea tried inserting the key into the padlock, but at first it refused to go. After some determined finagling, she finally succeeded.

And now, she thought. At last she turned the key and opened the box, inside of which she saw a small, leatherbound journal. Beside it lay a yellowed manila envelope. Chelsea then gently carried both items to the dining room table for a better look.

The journal was black, its surface bearing web-like cracks that had been honestly earned over the passage of time. The name *Brooke Bartlett* was engraved on its cover in gold leaf. Some of it had flaked off in places, causing Gram's name to appear strangely disjointed. The old envelope was sealed. It too bore Brooke's name, written in her familiar penmanship.

With trembling hands, Chelsea first picked up the envelope and opened it. It contained about a dozen old black-and-white photographs, each yellowed and dog-eared but still discernible. Chelsea began viewing them one by one. To her disappointment, nothing had been written on their back sides.

Every picture showed Brooke during happier, healthier days. She looked to be in her midtwenties, and it appeared that all the photos had been shot here at Lake Evergreen. Some were of Brooke only, while others showed Brooke and a man. Most had been taken outdoors, but a few had been shot inside Chelsea's cottage.

Brooke had been pretty, Chelsea realized. Tall, and with what appeared to be long, auburn hair, she had possessed a good figure and welcoming eyes. The man was unusually attractive and looked about Brooke's age. He had a strong jaw and a slight widow's peak in his wavy, light-colored hair. In one photo his hands were thrust into his pants pockets, and a lit cigarette dangled from between his grinning lips. Then Chelsea realized something. The man in the photos with Brooke wasn't her grandfather.

Chelsea had never seen any pictures of Brooke during her grandmother's younger days, so viewing her standing upright and in the full flower of her youth was both jarring and wonderful. There was something uniquely mesmerizing about these photos, these fascinating snippets of the past. Chelsea felt drawn into the pictures, as if she were actually being transported back in time to meet a much younger and more vivacious woman. These scenes were from a far different era, and her grandmother seemed an equally different woman from the one Chelsea had known.

Finally, she looked at the last one. It showed Brooke sitting in a chair, her chin held a bit high, her arms settled serenely at her slim waist, her smile demure. She was dressed in a short-sleeved shirt and pleated women's slacks, reminding Chelsea of the sort of things that Katharine Hepburn sometimes wore during her younger days. In the foreground there sat a man with his back to the camera. The tip of his cigarette could be seen extending slightly past his right cheek, its smoke curling gently into the air. In his right hand he held a brush that was caressing the canvas, and in his left a painter's palette.

Chelsea then carried the old journal out onto the porch, where she sat in one of the rockers and eagerly began reading her grandmother Brooke's first entry:

Wednesday, June 3, 1942, 5:00 P.M.

I've been alone here at Lake Evergreen for three weeks now. As I sit on the porch the stars are out, and the night creatures are singing. My dog, Ike, lies on the floor beside my rocking chair and this new journal rests in my lap. At long last I've begun writing in it, as I promised myself I would do. I think that I'm going to enjoy writing but will probably do so only when I have something noteworthy to record. And as is the case with most diarists, I will also probably come to wish that I'd begun doing so long ago. Plus, I hope that the great sense of quiet here will help to make my musings meaningful. It seems an odd thing, being concerned about the quality of a text that no one else will ever read . . .

Earlier this evening, the radio announced that nine B-17 Flying Fortress bombers from the Seventh Air Force attacked a Japanese fleet of forty-five ships, just south of the Midway Atoll. It's so good to know that we're at last taking the fight to the enemy! But although the war news reaches even here, there is an overriding sense of peace in this place that simply can't be found back home in Syracuse. Because I see other people infrequently, unless I'm reading a newspaper or listening to the radio, sometimes it's like the war doesn't exist.

For here, the waves of Lake Evergreen still rush the shore whenever they choose, the offshore breeze sways to and fro at its own behest, and the trees wave in the wind of their own accord, just as they all would do if the world were still at peace. It's almost as if time has no meaning in this calming, magical place, and I'm so glad that I decided to stay the entire summer. Recent events have been momentous, and I need some peace and quiet in my life just now . . .

The new cottage next door has at last been built, and the owner moved in today. The cottage lies about fifty yards or so down the beach, on a tract of adjoining land that Father sold last year. Father was originally going to keep that land, but with the coming of the war he decided to let it go. He says that the owner is a man named Butler. Father has met him, of course, but I hadn't yet. And so, after giving him a chance to get settled, I took a little housewarming gift over to him . . .

While humming pleasantly to some Glenn Miller coming over the radio, Brooke Bartlett again consulted her handwritten recipe book. She had begun it last year, shortly following the bombing of Pearl Harbor. Everyone, it seemed, needed a way to cope after that dreadful day, and entering her culinary concoctions in this little book had become hers. She very much enjoyed creating her own dishes and obsessively tinkering with each one until it was just right. As the war became an increasing part of her life, she had seized on the idea of naming her delicacies after Allied war leaders and American movie stars who were well-known for aiding the cause. It was late afternoon, and she was making one of her favorite pies to take to her new neighbor.

Once again running her eyes down the handwritten page, she found where she had left off. She had already baked the graham cracker crust. Then she had mixed the cream cheese, milk, lemon juice, and vanilla, and slowly poured the mixture into the crust. Now would come the topping. She pitted the cherries and cooked them in a saucepan with water for ten minutes. Then she added some precious sugar and cornstarch and let the mixture cook until it thickened. Although sugar was dear these days, she wanted to make a good first impression on her new neighbor.

Earlier today, from out her kitchen window she had watched as several moving men carried furniture into the neighboring cottage. They were gone now, but she had yet to see the new owner.

It's of no matter that I haven't seen him yet, Brooke thought with a smile. *I've never known a man who didn't appreciate a well-made pie.*

After letting the mixture come to room temperature, she gently spread it across the top of the cream cheese and placed the pie in the refrigerator to cool. She then stepped outside and went around the back of the cottage to her little victory garden, where she snipped two mint leaves, which would serve as the pie's crowning touches. Preparing that pie had made her especially happy, because during the last six weeks, she had had no one to cook for besides herself.

Finished at last, Brooke cleaned the dishes and poured a glass of iced tea. After walking into the living room and turning off the radio, she went out onto the porch and sat in one of the rocking chairs. Ike, the black and white English springer spaniel she had fondly named after General Eisenhower, followed along dutifully and slumped down beside Brooke's chair. She had gotten Ike as a source of companionship, soon after her husband, Bill, joined the army.

While sipping her tea, she looked out across the waves. Her father's new Chris-Craft bobbed lightly at anchor, and the wind ruffled the colorful beach umbrella she had secured in the sand. She loved being at Lake Evergreen and had always taken comfort in the fact that only her immediate family had ever enjoyed this cottage. Although Brooke was no snob, she found the sense of exclusivity appealing. To date there were only four other cottages on the lake, including both hers and the new one next door.

Despite the isolation, her father was still betting that would change. Ten years ago, a friend of his had told him about Lake Evergreen and its possibilities for development. And so James, always searching for an opportunity, came to see for himself and immediately bought two

tracts of lakeside land from a local contractor who had planned on building
cottages there but who was still down on
his luck from the Depression.

Soon after, James ordered the building
of his cottage and boathouse on the very
desirable stretch of beach over which
Brooke's eyes now gazed. Although it
was to have been his home away from
home, his devotion to the newspaper
kept him from visiting often. But Brooke
and her mother had already spent many
summer days and nights here talking,
laughing, cooking, and enjoying all the
peace and solitude that this lovely spot
had to offer.

The apple hadn't fallen far from the
tree, it seemed, because Brooke majored
in journalism in college. It was an unusual
choice, when so many women were study-
ing such traditional fields as teaching and
nursing. Then again, many people found
Brooke to be an unusual woman. Following graduation, her father suggested that
she come and work for him. She interned
in various departments so she could understand the newspaper business, and in
the end she finally became the paper's

head librarian. It was an absorbing job, because it fell upon Brooke to decide which pieces were worth archiving and which were not. She loved the work, and she took to it like a duck to water.

In the spring of 1941, Bill Bartlett unexpectedly entered Brooke's life. Tall, charming, and two years her senior, he was an editor for a small, downstate paper who had come to apply for the recently vacated city editor job. Impressed by the young man, James had hired him on the spot. During his first visit to the paper's library he had met Brooke, and they were immediately smitten with one another.

Their courtship was a happy, whirlwind affair and their June wedding was Syracuse's social event of the season. After their honeymoon they took an apartment. While Bill was being mentored by Brooke's father at the paper, Brooke and her mother searched for a first home for the newlyweds. But just as they were about to close on a newly built house, the Japanese bombed Pearl Harbor and everything changed.

Bill enlisted, hoping to become a war correspondent. If one's civilian career was in demand in the army, there was a good chance that one would be assigned to similar duty. After finishing his basic training at Fort Polk, Louisiana, he had been accepted into the three-month officer's training program at Fort Benning, Virginia. He was nearly done with that training and although Bill's letters brought Brooke great relief, she always feared what might happen to him once he was sent overseas.

With Bill gone, Brooke threw herself into both her work at the paper and supporting the home front. If Bill was willing to risk his life, then she too should be doing her best. And so she organized scrap collections, conducted blood drives, and participated in several other forms of volunteerism, all while still working full-time. But her greatest burden was constantly wondering whether her husband would survive the war. As a result of burning the candle at both ends, Brooke had become thin and pale, causing her parents to insist that she take some time off from everything.

At first she had resisted the notion, until she considered going to the cottage. This visit to Lake Evergreen would be different, she decided, because she would spend the entire summer there alone. And once rested, she would return to her job and civic duties with even greater zeal.

Brooke felt quite at home here, all by herself. Even so, she sometimes became lonely. In order to fight that feeling she would occasionally drive into Serendipity for dinner or to take in a movie at the small cinema there. She had recently seen a film called *This Gun for Hire* with some newcomer named Alan Ladd, and right there and then she had decided that he would become a major movie star.

Leaning back in her chair, she sighed and took another sip of tea. She missed Bill desperately. He had been her rock, her lover, her best friend. She needed him both mentally and physically, and his continued absence stabbed at her heart. She was a young, healthy woman, and like so many women whose husbands had gone off to war, she had needs that weren't being fulfilled.

She of course knew that some military wives were finding illicit satisfaction in the arms of civilian men. But she loved

Bill far too much to ever betray him. Some wartime wives were already asking their husbands serving in faraway lands for divorces and because it was so detrimental to morale, Congress had recently passed a law that made it far more difficult for military wives to petition for divorce. No matter to her, Brooke realized, because she could do no such thing to Bill. When the war ended, he would come home to a loyal and loving wife.

Despite her own faithfulness, however, she couldn't help worrying about his. How often was he granted leave, she wondered, and where did he and his friends go, when they could? And if so, would he . . . ?

In an attempt to quash her doubts, Brooke closed her eyes and shook her head. No, she decided. He would not betray her. Short as it was, their time together had been wonderful. And besides, she and Bill had a plan. One day, Bill would run the paper. And they would have children—in their perfect world, one boy and one girl. That had been their dream, anyway, until the coming of the war. And when Bill returned they would take up their plan again. *If* he returned, she reminded herself.

The war, she thought solemnly. *Everything is always about the damned war. Right down to how much sugar I can use in my pies . . .*

After taking a deep breath, she stood from her chair to go and change her clothes. The pie would be ready soon, and she wanted to look presentable when she met her new neighbor . . .

A short while later, Brooke was carrying her sumptuous offering across the sandy beach. She had chosen a yellow sundress and a pair of matching Mary Janes. She was glad to see that Mr. Butler's gray Packard coupe was still there, but when she mounted the steps and rapped lightly on the porch door, no one opened. She knocked again and waited a bit longer, but still there was no response.

Curious, she walked around the far corner of the house, looking for its owner. There, she saw a man kneeling in a freshly turned victory garden, planting seeds. From what Brooke could tell, he was tall and slim. His tan work shirt and matching trousers seemed a bit baggy on him. He was planting each seed lovingly, as if it were a small treasure.

At last, Brooke cleared her throat. "Uh . . . excuse me?" she said.

When he arose, he did so with a bit of difficulty. As Brooke looked at him, she realized that he was about her age and somewhat taller than she had first supposed. A smoldering cigarette dangled from between his lips. Before answering her, he took it from his mouth and stomped it into the sand.

"Hello there," he said simply. His voice carried a masculine sort of huskiness that she found appealing. "I didn't hear a car drive up, so you must be my new neighbor, right?"

When he smiled again, his grin had a bright, almost incandescent quality that Brooke immediately liked. As he pulled off his work gloves and stuffed them into his back pockets, he took a quick glance at the pie.

"And besides," he added, "with sugar being so precious these days, who else would be bringing me dessert?"

Brooke walked closer and held out one hand. "I'm Brooke Bartlett," she said. "You bought this tract of land from my father, James."

He took her hand and shook it firmly. "Ah, yes," he answered. "Your dad sure knows how to run a hard bargain, I'll give him that. I'm Gregory Butler, but please call me Greg."

"Greg . . . ," Brooke answered.

He was a very striking man, she thought. His height and leanness gave one the impression that when God made him, the only raw materials the Almighty had left at his disposal were muscle, bone, and sharp angles. He seemed confident and quite at ease with himself. His longish, wavy hair was light brown, with blond highlights that shined in the late afternoon sun. She also noticed that he had a right clubfoot, which explained why he had difficulty rising from the garden. His kind-looking eyes were the softest shade of gray. Deep dimples graced either side of his mouth when he smiled, and a slim, dark mustache graced his upper lip. He looked rather like Errol Flynn, Brooke decided.

"What are you planting?" Brooke asked.

"Coneflowers," he answered. "Are you familiar with them?"

Brooke nodded. "They're in the daisy family, right?"

"Right," Greg answered. "When these come up, they'll be violet. And once they get started, they grow wild. I'm not sure that they'll take in this sandy soil, though."

"I thought that maybe you were planting a victory garden," Brooke said.

Greg smiled and shook his head. "Truth is, I don't need one," he answered.

As Brooke handed him the pie, he thanked her.

"It looks delicious," he added. He then held up an index finger. "May I?" he asked.

Brooke nodded. "Sure," she said.

After dipping his fingertip gently into the pie, he tasted it. "God, that's good," he said. "And it's chilled!"

Brooke beamed. "Right," she answered. "It's my own recipe."

"What's it called?" Greg asked.

"Churchill's Cherry and Cream Cheese Pie."

A curious look overcame Greg's face. "Excuse me?" he asked.

"I name all my own recipes after war leaders and such," she answered.

Greg grinned. "Just ours, presumably?" he asked. "I mean, I hope that the daughter of upstate New York's largest newspaper owner isn't naming her food after our enemies! No 'Hitler Ham,' I take it?"

Brooke laughed broadly. "No!" she answered. "Even though he is one!"

As Greg smiled again, the corners of his eyes wrinkled pleasantly. "We need to get this into my refrigerator, don't we?"

"Yes," Brooke answered. "The sooner, the better."

"I just made a pot of fresh coffee," Greg said. "Would you like some?"

Brooke was surprised by that, and the look on her face said so. "You made a whole pot just for yourself?" she asked. "Where'd you get it all from?"

Greg gave her a sly wink. "I know a guy . . . ," he said, and left it at that.

As Brooke followed Greg inside, she saw that his cottage was quite pleasant. Some unopened boxes lay here and there, indicating that Greg was still in the process of getting settled. Because new furniture was scarce these days, he had furnished the interior with used items that lent the place a comfortable, already-lived-in look. After following him into the kitchen, Brooke put the pie into the refrigerator.

"So how do you take your coffee?" Greg asked.

"Black, thanks," Brooke answered.

Greg poured two steaming cupfuls. After putting some cream and sugar into his, he joined Brooke at the small kitchen table. As if it were the last cup she might ever enjoy, Brooke sipped her coffee.

"I haven't had any this good in a long time," she said, "regardless of how you got it." She then took another sip of the very good coffee. "And if it means drinking some of this wonderful stuff once in a while," she added, "then even J. Edgar Hoover won't be able to drag the truth out of me. And besides, I love to cook. Might I borrow some sugar from time to time?"

"Sure," he answered.

Brooke looked around again to see that several large, black-and-white framed photos already hung on the kitchen walls. They were all landscapes and had been expertly shot. Each of them was signed *"Gregory Butler."*

"Your photographs are lovely," she said. "Are you a professional photographer?"

"Yes," Greg answered. "But my photography alone doesn't pay the bills. I'm also a portraitist in oils. Between the two, I just make ends meet. I'm here for my first summer to work mostly on the photography. But I also brought my painting things, in case a job pops up. And I'll be converting one of my bedrooms into a darkroom, so that I can develop my photos here. Come this fall I'll take all the developed shots home and then deliver them to the New York City gallery that consigns my work."

"So is that where you live?" Brooke asked.

Greg nodded. "Greenwich Village, to be exact," he answered, "among all the other starving artists."

Brooke sipped her coffee again. "Misery loves company?" she asked.

As Greg thought for a moment, Brooke suddenly worried that she might have misspoken. After all, she reminded herself, she had only known this man for about ten minutes.

Greg selected a Chesterfield from a gunmetal cigarette case lying on the table. Before lighting it, he raised his eyebrows.

"Do you mind?" he asked.

"Not at all," Brooke answered.

"Thanks," Greg replied.

He lit the cigarette with a matching lighter and took a welcome drag.

"Well," Greg said while exhaling the smoke out his nostrils, "it's really not so much about the money. It's more that like minds always seem to congregate. Kind of like those American expatriates who gathered in Paris during the twenties. Novelists . . . painters . . . poets. You know—itinerant artists like me!"

Brooke laughed a little. "You don't look very Bohemian," she said.

"Well, I'm not, really," he replied. "In fact, I was raised in Watertown. That's how I know my way around up here. I learned photography from my dad, and then I attended art school in New York City. After that, I settled there."

"And this cottage?" Brooke asked.

"My mother died when I was young, and I lost my dad two years ago," he answered. "I used my small inheritance to build this cottage, because I wanted to own a summer place where I could work in peace. I'm sort of a loner by nature, I guess. This first summer is my trial run, so to speak. If it works out financially like I hope, I'll spend all my summers here, taking photographs, and my winters in New York, painting portraits. Down there, there are no great wilderness scenes to photograph like up here. Conversely, up here there's little call for portraits. So I'm hoping to alternate between the two, depending on the season. I didn't get drafted because of my clubfoot."

"I'm sorry," Brooke said. "Does it bother you?"

Greg shook his head. "Not really," he answered. "I was born with it, so . . ."

After letting his words trail off, Greg set

his half-consumed cigarette in an ashtray and took another sip of coffee.

"Are you married?" Brooke asked. "Do you have a family of your own?"

"No," he answered.

"At the risk of sounding forward," Brooke said, "I'm surprised that an attractive man like you is still single."

Before answering, Greg looked down at his expressive hands for a time. They appeared strong, with prominent knuckles and veins. *Artist's hands,* Brooke realized. *The sort of hands that can create beauty out of nothingness . . .*

"I guess the right woman never came along," he answered quietly.

Silence reclaimed the kitchen for a time as they sipped their coffee, each wondering silently about the other.

"And you?" Greg finally asked. "Your dad mentioned that he had a daughter working at his paper. What brings you up here all by yourself?"

Brooke provided him with a thumbnail sketch of her and Bill, and also explained her reasons for coming to Lake Evergreen this summer. When she finished, Greg picked up his cigarette again and sat back in his chair.

"It must be tough," he said, "having your husband away like this. Do you hear from him much?"

Brooke sighed. "Because he's a college graduate, right after he finished his basic training at Fort Polk, they put him straight into officer's training at Fort Benning," she answered. "He's almost done with that now. And he writes as often as he can. But even if I got ten letters a day, they still wouldn't be enough . . ."

No sooner had she spoken the words than her never-ending worry suddenly assaulted her heart again, and she sadly looked down at the floor. For the last six weeks there had been no one to talk to like this, and doing so now was surprisingly cathartic. But even though she hardly knew this man, there was already something about him that said her emotions would be safe in his care. At last, Brooke cleared her throat.

"And the mail is so slow," she added, "because of the army censors. Just because he's safe right now, that doesn't mean he won't come to some harm after he ships out to England. That's where he thinks he'll go, anyway. Three months ago, a friend of mine got a card from her husband in the morning mail and then a death notification telegram from the War Department that same night."

With the return of that harsh memory, Brooke started to break down more fully. Silence again reigned between her and Greg for a time as she tried to collect herself. Her eyes were tearful, and she was shaking slightly. Understanding her plight, Greg politely remained quiet and gave her all the time she needed. He nearly reached out and touched her hand, then thought the better of it and offered her a handkerchief instead.

"Sorry," Brooke said while dabbing at her eyes. "It happens, sometimes."

"It's highly understandable," Greg answered. Then he gave her a little smile. "Would some of Churchill's whatchamacallit pie help cheer you up?"

Brooke shook her head. "No appetite," she answered. "It's always the same when I get this way. It doesn't happen often, but when it does . . . Anyway, I should be going."

Greg smiled and patted her arm. "Before you leave . . . ," he said.

He stubbed out his cigarette in the ashtray, then he arose slowly, in that awkward but rather endearing way of his. After searching through one of his moving boxes he produced a full bag of sugar and another of roasted coffee beans. To Brooke's surprise, he handed them to her.

"You didn't get those from me," he said.

At last, Brooke smiled. "Thank you so much!" she answered. "Does this make us partners in crime?"

"You bet," Greg answered. "Thank you for the pie, Brooke. Should you need help with anything, just ask. And please come back over any time you want. Believe it or not, I can be a pretty good listener."

Brooke nodded. "I already believe that," she said. At last, she stood. "Well, good-bye, then," she said.

"Bye . . . ," Greg answered.

As Brooke forlornly carried her precious bags back toward her cottage, Greg stood on his porch and watched her go. She had removed her shoes and was slowly walking through the shallow waves, as if they provided some sort of soothing remedy for her emotional pain.

How lovely she is, Greg thought. *And yet, so alone. Another disturbing sign of the times in which we all find ourselves . . .*

As he lit another cigarette, something he couldn't quite explain made him watch Brooke go until she was out of sight.

. . . and I certainly didn't distinguish myself with that first visit!" Chelsea read further. *"Greg seems like such a nice man, and there I was, crying up a storm at his kitchen table the very first time that we met. I must think of some way to make it up to him. I didn't mean to break down like that . . . but sometimes I miss Bill so much that I just can't help myself. And I'm so tired now. Time for bed, it seems. Tonight I'll sleep like the dead, despite all my worries . . ."*

8.

On reaching the end of Brooke's first entry, Chelsea looked out over the waves of Lake Evergreen, thinking. She wanted to read more, but after checking her watch she realized that Brandon would arrive soon.

Although her hand hurt a bit, she set the dining table and fed Dolly. At last she poured a glass of Margot's wine and returned to sit on the porch and await Brandon. Soon Chelsea's thoughts went back to the carefully written words of her late grandmother, which had finally returned to the light of day after nearly sixty years.

Chelsea had found Brooke's first journal entry heartwarming yet also a bit unsettling. Heartwarming in that it seemed wonderful to "hear" Brooke speak again, and to "see" her going about her life as a much younger woman—a woman whom Chelsea had of course never known. But it had been unsettling, too, because of how much Brooke missed her husband. And also because of how hard and lonely those times were for women like her, whose men were off fighting the war. Perhaps most important, Chelsea was coming to sympathize with Brooke's plight during a time in her grandmother's life about which she had heretofore known so little. Sighing lightly, she took her first sip of the excellent wine that the Fabiennes had brought.

And I have a feeling that this journal has much more to tell me, she thought. *But what will those things be?*

Just then Chelsea heard someone shout, causing her to gaze down the shoreline. Brandon and Jeeves were racing down the length of their dock and heading toward the lake. Brandon wore only swim trunks, and when he and

Jeeves reached the dock's end they both leaped into the water. Brandon had taken a bar of soap with him, and he began washing himself with it. While Jeeves swam happily around in little circles, Brandon submerged for a few moments, then he surfaced again, laughingly rubbing his face.

A bit later they scampered back to their cottage. As Chelsea watched Brandon go, she felt an unexpected tug on her heart. Although the feeling surprised her, she found it pleasant.

A man and his dog . . . , she thought. *Some things in this world never change . . .*

But what she had just seen was more than a simple case of "a man and his dog," she soon realized. It was another example of Brandon living the way he wanted. Here, she was starting to understand, the rules were oftentimes whatever one made them.

She then cast her gaze out across the waves again. The sun had nearly finished setting against the opposite side of the lake, giving one the impression that it was being literally engulfed by the waves. It was a beautiful thing, making Chelsea wonder how many times Brooke had also sat here and enjoyed this same spectacle.

It seemed to her that whenever Brooke visited Lake Evergreen, she had been whole and happy, with most of her life still ahead of her. Then Chelsea sighed again as she compared this lovely image to the other day at her mother's house, where she had sat alone on a different porch, staring glumly at her grandmother's abandoned things.

Chelsea again felt for the necklace beneath her shirt and the little silver-plated key that now hung from it. She guessed that it was here at Lake Evergreen where Brooke had always been her most vibrant, her freest, and her happiest. And during the few short hours she had been here, Chelsea could already sense those same feelings starting to overcome her, too. As she took another sip of wine and her jazz CD played pleasantly, her thoughts again turned to Brandon.

In his own rugged way he was certainly handsome; even the mysterious scar on his cheek seemed to somehow suit him. And he was intelligent, obviously. He wore no wedding ring, but that didn't mean he wasn't involved with someone. From what little Chelsea knew about him, he seemed honest and caring.

But appearances can be deceiving, she reminded herself. *And the best men are usually taken, anyway. Harvard Medical School, no less . . . Impressive . . . How does a Harvard-educated doctor end up in Serendipity, New York, making house calls from a floatplane? I'll bet that's an interesting story . . .*

Just then Dolly let go a soft growl. When a brisk knock came on the screen door, Chelsea jumped a little.

"Permission to come aboard?" someone asked.

Relieved to see Brandon, Chelsea smiled. "Permission granted," she answered.

"Can Jeeves come in too?"

"Sure," Chelsea said. "What kind of dinner party would it be without the Jeeves 'n' Dolly show?"

As Jeeves and Dolly approached one another, yet more tense and inappropriate sniffing ensued before they finally settled down.

"They'll get over that in a few days," Brandon said.

Chelsea snorted a little. "That would be nice. It's pretty indiscreet!"

Brandon was wearing worn jeans, a white shirt with rolled-up sleeves, and old boat shoes. Although his thick, damp hair had been brushed back, it was already starting to drift down over his forehead again. Chelsea also noticed that he had brought along a six-pack of Canadian ale and a pair of beer bottle cozies.

"Thanks, but you didn't have to do that," she said. "We've got the Fabiennes' wine, remember?"

"I know," Brandon answered as he carried the beer into the kitchen and loaded it into the refrigerator. "Just being neighborly."

When Brandon didn't soon return to the porch, Chelsea began to wonder what was taking him so long. Just as she was about to call out to him, she heard him laugh uproariously. She turned and looked into the kitchen to find Brandon leaning against the counter and reading Brooke's old cookbook. When she unpacked, Chelsea had left it on one of the countertops.

"What's so funny?" she called out.

Still laughing, Brandon brought the cookbook and some wine out onto the porch, and he sat down.

"God," he said. "Your grandmother certainly was a card, wasn't she?"

"What are you talking about?"

"You mean to say that you don't know?" he asked. "You've read this, right?"

Chelsea shook her head. "Actually, no," she answered. "I've owned it for only a few days, and I haven't had the chance to look at it yet. What's so funny?"

Brandon handed the cookbook to her. "Take a look," he said. "Brooke must have written it while she was up here during the summer of 1942."

Her curiosity piqued, Chelsea opened the old book. On the first page, Brooke had written:

Brooke Bartlett's Wartime Recipes for Total Victory!
Summer 1942
Lake Evergreen, New York

Chelsea turned the page to find a list of original recipes and the corresponding page number where each one could be found. Again, everything was handwritten in black fountain ink. As Chelsea scanned the list she too couldn't help but laugh, while also suddenly remembering the homemade pie that Brooke had described in her first journal entry.

The notebook included such other original creations as Patton's Pork Chops, Eisenhower's Eggs Benedict, Roosevelt's Roast, and MacArthuroni and Cheese, to name but a few. Chelsea then turned to the page for something called Montgomery's Mutton to find that a recipe for it actually existed and that it sounded quite good. At last she set the old book down on the table between her and Brandon.

"See what I mean?" Brandon asked.

"Is this the sort of thing that happens to your mind if you stay here long enough?" Chelsea asked laughingly.

Brandon smiled. "I don't know," he answered. "But I can tell you two things, for sure."

"And what are they?" Chelsea asked.

"Your grandmother was certainly someone I would have enjoyed knowing," he said.

"And the other?" Chelsea asked.

"The MacArthuroni and Cheese sounds incredible," he said.

While the quiet reigned once more, they sipped their wine as the waves lapped at the shore, and the sun continued its nightly vanishing act. Some stars started blinking through heaven's increasingly dark canopy, and the night creatures began their nocturnal warblings. As far as Chelsea was concerned, the rest of the world no longer existed. Then she remembered Brandon's earlier comment that day, when they had first come out here. He had cryptically mentioned thinking of someone and how it sometimes happened to him.

"Someone" and *"sometimes,"* Chelsea thought. *Who is that person, I wonder?* After considering it for a few more moments, she decided to leave it alone for now. *Maybe later,* she thought, *after we know one another better. But there is something that I'm dying to know . . .*

She turned and looked at him. "Forgive me if I'm being forward," she asked. "But I presume that you're not married, right?"

To Chelsea's mild surprise, Brandon's

expression darkened a little. "That's right," he finally answered. "Never have been."

Despite his slight melancholy, Chelsea decided to risk asking another question. "Anybody special in your life right now?" she inquired gently.

After shaking his head, Brandon took another sip of wine. "No," he answered. As if unsure, he paused for a moment. "And what about you?" he asked. "Is there anybody special in your life?"

One corner of Chelsea's mouth turned up into a little smile. *Turnabout is fair play,* she thought.

"No, there isn't," she answered. "So tell me," she said, deciding that it was a good time to switch the subject, "how long have you owned your cottage?"

"For ten years now," he answered. "I bought it from an old, lifelong bachelor who had become too ill to enjoy it anymore. He was a portraitist, I'm told. Because he was dying and had no heirs, he sold the cottage furnished. Most of the stuff was too beat-up to keep, but I did hold on to some of the nicer things. And from what the Fabiennes told me, your great-grandfather built this cottage way back in the thirties, right?"

Chelsea nodded. "He was a Syracuse newspaperman who died young," she answered. "This was supposed to be his place to get away from everything, but he was a workaholic, and he never got up here much. Then the war started and as you can imagine, it was even more impossible for him to leave. As best I know, Brooke spent at least one of her wartime summers here alone."

"I'm sure that I would have enjoyed knowing her," Brandon said.

Chelsea nodded. "Everyone did," she answered. "Soon after her husband, Bill, shipped out for England, Brooke gave birth to my mother, Lucy. But six months after Lucy's birth, Brooke's car was viciously struck by a drunk driver, pinning both her legs beneath the dashboard. Blessedly, Lucy was not with her. The other driver died immediately, and Brooke was condemned to live out the rest of her life in a wheelchair. Despite Brooke's misfortune, not once did I ever hear her complain or rail against God for having done such a terrible thing to her. Instead, she decided to concentrate on what she could do, rather than what she could not."

Pausing for a moment, Chelsea took another sip of wine and gathered her thoughts.

"As best I know," she said, "with her mother's help, Brooke then focused all of her attention on raising my mother. She also began to paint and cook. Later in life, she became something of a force in Syracuse's various social circles. But to everyone's surprise, after her accident she never revisited this cottage. No one knew why and she never said, which made her attitude all the more odd, because with help she could have surely returned. And although she refused to revisit the cottage, she also refused to sell it."

"She sounds like she was something of a dynamo," Brandon said, "despite having been in a wheelchair."

"Yes," Chelsea answered softly, remembering. "That she was."

Brandon was easy to talk to, she was learning. There was something calm and confident about his behavior, his speech, the way he moved. And he never seemed pushy or self-absorbed, like some other men who had been overly eager to impress her. He seemed to live on a timetable of his own choosing, with priorities to match. And the more she saw of him, the more endearing he became.

"So shall we eat?" she asked. "I don't know about you, but the smells coming from the kitchen are driving me crazy."

Brandon quickly grinned at her. It was good to see him smile again, she realized.

"Sure," he answered. "But I'll take care of things. You rest that hand of yours."

As they went into the kitchen, the dogs followed and hunkered down hopefully near the potbellied stove. Brandon took Margot's dish from the oven and placed it on a trivet. When he removed the lid, the enticing aromas fully escaped at last, causing the dogs to take full and proper notice. He then cut the bread and plated the coq au vin.

As Chelsea took her first bite, her face lit up. "*Oh . . . my . . . God . . . ,*" she said softly. "It's amazing. The best I've ever had."

"Yes," Brandon answered. "Just like the two people who brought it."

Chelsea took another sip of wine to find that it went perfectly with the chicken. "So what's their story?" she asked. "I know that my great-grandfather hired them sometime after Brooke's accident, but that's about it."

Brandon wiped his mouth with his napkin. "They were both born and raised in France," he said. "After they married, they emigrated to Quebec and finally settled in Serendipity. Jacques started doing odd jobs, and he answered the caretaker ad that Brooke's father had placed in the paper. The rest, as they say, is history."

After a time, Chelsea finished her meal and sat back in her chair. The rich French wine was starting to take effect, emboldening her a little. After such a long and momentous day the sensation was welcome, but her injured hand had begun throbbing again.

"So tell me," Chelsea said, "what's Dr. Brandon Yale really like?"

Brandon smiled. "Well," he said, "he's not perfect, certainly, but most folks seem to think he's a pretty good guy. He likes bourbon, hunting and fishing, flying around in his plane, and watching old movies. And he likes to try to help people when he can, such as opening up old cottages for new neighbors."

Chelsea smiled to herself. *And so a picture starts to emerge . . .*, she thought.

"May I ask you another question?" she said.

"Sure."

Chelsea placed one elbow atop the table and rested her chin in her uninjured palm. "How'd you get that scar?" she asked.

Brandon shook his head and snorted slightly. "Before college, I joined the army and became a ranger," he answered. "My folks weren't well-off, and it helped to pay the tuition. That's also where I learned to fly. Anyway, I wish I could say that I got this scar from some special ops mission, but I can't."

"So how did you get it?" she asked again.

Brandon let go a rather chagrined smile. "I got drunk one night, while on leave in Wyoming," he answered. "On my way out of the bar, I stumbled straight into one of the saloon's swinging doors. Knocked me right on my butt. Pretty embarrassing for a ranger."

Chelsea couldn't help but laugh. "Well," she said, "at least you're honest."

Brandon laughed a little. "My friends had to pick me up and load me into my car. No man left behind, as we rangers say!"

"We seem to be quite out into the boondocks here," Chelsea said. "Is there anyplace nearby where I could pick up a few things, without having to drive all the way into Serendipity?"

"As a matter of fact, yes," Brandon answered. "There's a combination diner and sundry shop about two miles west of here on Schuyler Road. A lady friend of mine named Jenny Beauregard owns it. Some of the retired locals gather there every morning for coffee and gossip. The store part doesn't carry a lot of things, just the necessities. But the food and coffee are good, and the place might save you a longer trip one day. Sometimes I stop there and get a cup to go while I'm on the way to the hospital."

"Thanks," Chelsea answered. "I'll remember that."

Chelsea sat back in her chair and looked at him. She was beginning to like this man, she realized. Just then Chelsea's injured hand bit her again, and she winced slightly.

"You go back onto the porch and sit down," Brandon said. "I'll clean up the mess."

"Are you sure?" she asked.

"Yeah. In fact, it'll be kind of a treat for me."

"Why?"

"Because this cottage of yours is quite possibly the only one on all of Lake Evergreen that has an actual, working dishwasher, that's why," he answered.

After Brandon had cleaned things up, he again joined her on the porch, as did the dogs. Night had fallen in earnest, and Chelsea was becoming tired. But at the same time she was enjoying his company, and she wasn't eager to see him leave.

"I should go home," he said.

"Are you sure?" she asked rather

quickly. Then she caught herself, wondering if she had sounded too forward, too interested. *The wine,* she realized.

"Yeah," he answered. "And besides, you look like you could use some rest."

Just as Brandon was about to leave, he realized that he had nearly forgotten something.

"Before I go," he said, "do you remember the beer that I brought? Well, I actually had an ulterior motive. Watch this!"

Before Chelsea could ask what he was talking about, Brandon looked down from his chair and shouted, "Jeeves! Fetch!"

"*Huh?*" Chelsea asked.

Brandon winked at her. "Check this out," he answered.

To Chelsea's amazement, Jeeves immediately bounded up from the floor and scurried into the kitchen, where he skidded to a stop on the linoleum floor directly before the refrigerator. From where they sat, Brandon and Chelsea could easily turn and see. Although Chelsea hadn't noticed before, at some point during the evening, Brandon had apparently tied a kitchen towel to the refrigerator door handle. Jeeves promptly bit into the end of the dangling towel. Then he squatted down on his haunches and yanked the refrigerator door open, the various items in the door shelves rattling noisily.

My God . . . , Chelsea thought. *I must be seeing things . . .*

Brandon had placed the beer bottles on the lowest shelf, where Jeeves could reach them. Cocking his head at a sharp angle, Jeeves gripped one of the cozy-protected bottles between his jaws and he removed it. To Chelsea's added astonishment, Jeeves then used his rump to push against the refrigerator door, shutting it. Proud as proud could be, with his tail wagging high, he strutted back onto the porch and promptly dropped the cold beer onto Brandon's lap. If it were possible for a dog to grin from ear to ear, Jeeves was doing it.

Never before in her life had Chelsea been so at a loss for words. For several moments she sat dumbfounded, wondering if what she had just experienced was some sort of hallucination.

"Are you *kidding* me?" she fairly shouted. "I've heard of dogs fetching slippers and the morning paper—but a *beer*?"

"You saw it here first," Brandon answered as he set the beer on the coffee table. "I'd have never believed it either, if one of the hospital surgeons hadn't taught his dog to do it. The first time I saw it done was at one of his poker games, and I reacted just like you. Then he showed me how to train Jeeves. But you've got to be patient, because it takes months. And you always have to use a beer cozy to protect the dog's teeth. I taught Jeeves last winter. As you might imagine, when the snow falls in Serendipity, there isn't much to do."

Then he paused and smiled into her eyes. "Gives a whole new meaning to the term *man's best friend* . . . ," he added.

Chelsea didn't want to embarrass herself by laughing so hard, but she just couldn't help it. Never in her life had she ever seen anything so wonderfully preposterous. Moreover, like her father, she had always loved dogs. If she and Brandon could teach Dolly to do it, she would have one-upped her father for all time. At last, she regained control of herself.

Today has truly been one for the books,

she thought. *A wonderfully surprising cottage, Gram's wartime journal, and a beer-fetching dog* . . .

"Do you suppose that you could teach Dolly for me?" she asked Brandon. "If you knew my father, you'd realize that it would forever put me in your debt."

"Happy to try," he answered, "but I can't promise that we'll be successful."

For a time they again sat there on the porch, saying nothing and looking at each other. As the waves drifted ashore from the darkness beyond, they made a consistent, comforting sound. At last, Brandon stood.

"Now I really have to go," he said. "I've got an early day tomorrow. Try to keep your bandaged hand out of the water, and I'll come by tomorrow night to check on it. Oh, and although it isn't really dangerous around here, you should keep your doors locked at night. And *never* put your trash outside the cabin. Instead, I'll help you drive it to the dump every so often."

"Why?" she asked.

"Bears," he answered.

"*Bears?*" she asked incredulously.

"Yep," Brandon answered.

Chelsea stood to see him out. After opening the porch door and letting Jeeves go, he paused for a moment and looked into her eyes.

"It's nice to finally have a neighbor," he said. Then he smiled a bit, the corners of his eyes wrinkling handsomely. "Especially such a pretty one," he added quietly.

Yet again, Chelsea felt something tug at her heart. "Good night," she said in return. "And thanks again for everything."

Chelsea then watched Brandon and Jeeves stroll back down the moonlit beach until they finally disappeared into the darkness. She felt a bit tired, but her curiosity about Brooke's journal remained high, and she was dying to know more. And so, rather than retire, she took the old journal to the couch, where she settled in with the last of the Fabiennes' excellent wine.

On opening the journal to the next entry, she eagerly began to read . . .

9.

Friday, June 5, 1942, 10:00 P.M.

As I write these words in my journal, Greg has just departed my cottage and gone home. We spent the late afternoon and most of the evening together, both on the lake and here at my place, where we shared dinner. I must say that I'm finding him to be a very charming man. And because of that, I'm still having a difficult time understanding why he isn't married. He has so much to offer a woman, it seems . . .

But these are strange times, and they

have made for equally odd personal lives. Just the same, I was able to become more acquainted with him today, and I must say that I find his company very appealing. And I must also admit that now, as I sit here alone on my porch, I'm surprised by how much I miss his company . . .

"Thank you for this!" Greg shouted happily at Brooke, trying to be heard above the roar of the Chris-Craft's energetic motor. "I haven't gone fishing in ages!"

Brooke smiled and then turned the boat's steering wheel a bit, adjusting their course.

"Neither have I!" she shouted back. "Since the war started, my dad hasn't gotten up here much. He's the one who taught me and who always took me out!" Then she turned toward Greg for a moment and smiled as she watched the wind torment his light-brown hair.

"And besides," she added, "although I've gone fishing alone once or twice, it's always better to have someone along! Don't you agree?"

Greg smiled broadly. "Absolutely!" he answered.

It was late afternoon, two days since they had first met. By now the sun had begun its nightly descent, the sky was clear, and a light wind bothered the surface of the lake. It had been Brooke's idea to take Greg fishing, partly because she had wanted to go, and partly as a way to thank him for the sugar and coffee he had so graciously given to her. It was her plan to catch a couple of fish today and to serve them to him as tonight's dinner. Preferably some walleyes, she hoped, because they were the best eating.

But first, we've got to catch them, she thought.

Greg had enthusiastically accepted her invitation. He loved to fish, he said, and had done a lot of it around here during his youth. But because money was tight, he had yet to purchase a boat and motor. And so just before five o'clock, the two of them had set off across the waves in search of their evening meal.

Brooke was wearing tan shorts, a simple white shirt with the sleeves rolled up, matching sneakers, a white tennis visor, and sunglasses. Greg was dressed the same way as when Brooke had first met him: a tan work shirt with matching trousers and a pair of no-nonsense work shoes. Today he also sported a pair of aviator sunglasses, which Brooke found appealing.

As she piloted the boat farther out into the lake, Brooke pursed her lips, thinking. She had to admit that catching some fish for dinner was not her only motive for being out here with Greg, because she could presumably catch the fish without his help. Rather, her reasons had been more complicated. To her own surprise, she had very much wanted to see Greg again. He had been on her mind for the last two days, and because of that, she had felt even more alone than usual. But now that he sat beside her in her father's speeding runabout, she felt happy again.

But am I too happy about this? she wondered. After thinking about it for a few moments, she shook her head knowingly. *No,* she thought. *We're neighbors, after all. And what could be more normal on Lake Evergreen than two neighbors out trying to catch their dinner?*

When they were about one hundred yards offshore, Brooke cut back on the throttle, then she turned and looked at Greg. He seemed so comfortable and happy, sitting there beside her in the front cockpit.

"So, what do you think?" she asked him. "Are we far enough out?"

Before answering, Greg lit a cigarette and looked around. "I'd say it's about right," he answered. "Did you plan on trolling or jigging?"

Brooke looked at the sky. It was still clear, with little chance of rain. The sun would be down soon, and the chances of catching something would improve.

"Trolling, I'd say," she answered. "Seems the right sort of night for it."

"I agree," Greg answered as he left his seat and went astern.

Back there on the floor lay all their fishing things: two rods and reels, a tackle box, a net, a worm box, and a wet burlap bag that Greg had brought along. Brooke didn't understand the need for the bag, but she had yet to ask about it.

While Greg began preparing the rods and reels, she asked, "So what's the wet bag for, anyway? That's a new one on me. Even my father never brought one of those along. And when it comes to fishing, he knows just about everything."

"The answer's simple," Greg said. "The easiest way to keep fish fresh out here is inside a wet burlap bag. If you rewet the bag with lake water from time to time, you can keep 'em fresh damned near all day."

"Really?" Brooke asked. "I've got to admit, that's one I didn't know."

Greg smiled as he took another drag on his Chesterfield. "Well," he said, "it certainly helps my ego to know that there's *something* about fishing I could teach you."

Brooke laughed. "There are many such things, I'm sure," she said.

Greg looked at her and snorted. "I'm not," he said laughingly.

While Greg opened the tackle box, Brooke set the boat on a course that ran parallel with the shoreline. After cutting the throttle back to trolling speed, she watched as Greg baited one line with a worm harness, a pair of lead weights, and two live worms. He then secured an artificial lure called a Canadian Wiggler onto the other rod's line. Brooke approved of his strategy.

"You're doubling our chances, right?" she asked.

Greg smiled. "Yep," he answered. "Once we know what they're biting on, we'll make both baits the same." He then handed the worm-baited rod to Brooke. "*Bonne chance,*" he said.

Brooke smiled back at him. "I didn't know that you speak French," she said.

Greg winked at her. "Just enough to get by," he answered. "It comes in handy when trying to procure such things as sugar and coffee beans for the pretty neighbor lady."

Understanding his meaning, Brooke laughed a little. Then, as the boat meandered along, she cast her line into the water and let it out slowly, allowing the lead weights to submerge the bait. After letting out enough line, she settled back onto her seat to wait.

Greg also cast his line. As the boat puttered along, the two of them looked at one another and smiled knowingly.

There was something quite marvelous about fishing, Brooke had always thought, something that she couldn't put her finger on. Perhaps it was because there was so much solitude out here on the water. Or maybe it had to do with so greatly enjoying times like this with her father, as he had taught her. Whatever the reason, she had never really cared that much whether she caught any fish. Bringing in a catch was better than coming home empty-handed, of course. But to her way of thinking, just being out here was always reward enough.

Although Greg and Brooke still did not know that much about each other, they conversed little as the time passed, the boat slowly plied the waves, and the sun settled ever lower in the sky. That's just how it was with fishing, Brooke knew. And Greg seemed to understand that, too. There was no need to be chatty or gregarious, for being out here wasn't about those things. Moreover, it seemed to Brooke that they were becoming more comfortable in each other's company. And whenever that was the case between two people, talking wasn't always needed.

Just then Greg got a hit on his line and he immediately jerked his rod tip skyward, trying to set the hook. As his rod bowed down again, he smiled.

"Got one!" he shouted. "Come and grab the net!"

After quickly reeling in her line, Brooke set down her pole and rushed astern. Net in hand, she watched Greg as he carefully reeled in the fish.

His technique was very good, Brooke realized. Time after time he patiently lowered the rod tip while taking in more line, only to carefully lift it again and begin the process anew. Soon a very nice walleye appeared alongside the boat, its slick body reflecting multicolored hues just below the surface of the water.

"Okay, now," Greg said. "Get ready, 'cause here he comes!"

Just as the fish broke the surface, Brooke smoothly netted it. With the fish still wildly flapping about in the net, she quickly set the net on the floor of the boat.

"Well done!" Greg said. "Now let's get this hook out of him."

Greg removed the flapping fish from the net, then used a pair of pliers to free the hook. He held the fish up and smiled.

"A good one!" he said. "About three pounds. Do we need another?"

Brooke smiled back. "Well," she answered, "it's still early. And besides, we can't go home with you one-upping me this way! So let's stay out a bit longer, okay?"

"Okay," Greg answered as he thrust the walleye into the wet burlap bag. He then replaced Brooke's worm harness with a Canadian Wiggler, and they eagerly returned to their fishing.

An hour and a half later, Brooke was happily whistling along to some Tommy Dorsey playing on her radio, while at the same time she expertly filleted the two good-sized walleyes she and Greg had caught. As she did, she smiled and shook her head a little. Greg had been right about that burlap bag. It had kept the two fish nice and fresh, all the way home.

Greg had gone back to his cabin to wash up and to retrieve a bottle of white wine that he said he had been saving for a special occasion. Because it had been so long since he had tasted fresh walleye, he said, tonight's dinner would surely be special enough to warrant opening the wine.

After finishing the task of filleting, Brooke paused and thought for a moment. She wanted to make this dinner special, somehow. It had been some time since she had cooked a full meal for anyone other than herself, and she wanted everything to be just right. She was hoping to do something novel with the fish fillets, but she wondered how.

After rifling through her cupboards and pulling out a few varied ingredients, she believed that she had concocted an answer. She wouldn't fry them, she decided. And so she started improvising, which always made her the happiest whenever she cooked.

While preheating the oven, she combined some melted butter, crushed Ritz crackers, grated cheese, and small portions of basil, oregano, and garlic powder in a mixing bowl. She then dipped the fillets in some of the leftover butter, covered each piece with the crumb mixture, and put them into the oven to bake.

Just as she was setting the table, Greg returned with the wine. He had changed into a white shirt with navy slacks, causing Brooke to remark how nice he looked. After thanking her, he opened the bottle and poured two glasses of the already chilled wine. Smiling broadly, he gently clinked his wine goblet against hers.

"To the fruits of the sea," he said.

Before taking her first sip, Brooke smiled back at him. "I couldn't agree more," she answered. Then she laughed a little and added, "And to think that for once, Gregory Butler is eating a dinner that wasn't entirely supplied by surreptitious means!"

Greg laughed a bit in return. "Actually, that isn't altogether true."

"What do you mean?" she asked.

"Well," he answered, "there is the matter of this rather good Chardonnay . . ."

Brooke nodded knowingly. "Let me guess," she said. "You know a guy."

"Yeah," he said, smiling. "Several, actually . . ."

Brooke smiled back. "I'll bet," she answered.

Just then Greg narrowed his eyes a bit, and he glanced around Brooke's little kitchen.

"What's that wonderful smell?" he asked. "I've noticed that you're not frying the fish, so you must be baking it, right?"

Brooke nodded. "It's a new recipe I just invented. I hope that it'll be good! Sometimes my culinary contrivances are very tasty, and sometimes they're not." She then handed her personal recipe book to Greg. "I've also taken to writing them down in that," she added. "Who knows—maybe someday one of my descendants will find it useful!"

Remembering the Churchill's Cherry and Cream Cheese Pie she had given him, Greg laughed as he scanned her handwritten recipes. "So what are you going to call this newest dish?" he asked.

Brooke thought for a few moments before taking another sip of the very good wine.

"Well," she answered, "I don't want to be redundant, but how about Winston's Baked Walleye? Sounds about right, doesn't it? Provided it passes muster, of course."

Greg laughed and lit a cigarette. "Yes," he answered enthusiastically. "I think that it does."

"Good," Brooke said. She then picked up a wooden mixing spoon and brandished it threateningly, as if it were some sort of weapon. "Now that that's settled, you go and drink and smoke yourself to death out on my porch," she ordered him. "I don't much like men messing up my kitchen when I'm cooking, and I'm not done yet."

Greg laughed a little. "Okay, okay, I'm going. Just let me know when things are ready, and I'll rejoin you."

While Greg waited on the porch, Brooke sliced up a couple of fresh lemons. She also prepared a green salad with olive oil, Parmesan, and balsamic, and then she began preparing some risotto, over which she would also sprinkle the remaining Parmesan.

As she worked, Greg sat contentedly in one of the rocking chairs on the porch and looked out over the waves. It had been a long time since a woman had cooked for him, and having one do so now was certainly a treat. After sipping some more wine and taking another luxurious drag on his cigarette, he shook his head slightly.

God, she's wonderful, he thought. *Her husband Bill's a lucky man. She's not only beautiful and intelligent, she's also a damned good cook. All of which make me wish that I'd met her first. . .*

When he heard the telltale tinkling of glass, silverware, and plates, he realized that she had begun setting the table. He smiled, knowing better than to ask whether he could help her. For he now understood just how much that little kitchen and everything about it was her own special domain, and he liked that about her. He had also very much enjoyed fishing with her, and he had to admit that he had never known a woman who fished so well or who liked doing it so much. In many ways she seemed ideally suited to Lake Evergreen, he realized, even though she had had a privileged upbringing and was the daughter of one of Syracuse's wealthiest men.

Just then she called him to dinner,

breaking his personal reverie. And so he rose from his chair in a rather awkward of his and then joined her at the table.

Everything looked wonderful, and he said so. The fish seemed baked to perfection, the salad was crisp, and the freshly prepared risotto was still steaming. After they sat down, he looked at her and smiled. As if she had been doing it all her life, she first prepared a plate for him and then one for herself. Only then did she sit down across from him.

When Greg took his first bite of the fish, his face lit up. To his happy surprise, he had never tasted anything quite like it.

"Damn!" he said. "This is wonderful! This settles it! Winston's Baked Walleye is definitely worthy of a place in your recipe book!"

After Brooke took a tentative bite of the fish, she nodded. "I think you're right," she answered. "And what about the risotto and the salad?" she asked. "Are those okay too?"

As he enjoyed one of the best meals of his life, Greg nodded happily. "Absolutely," he answered. "With food this good, and your cabin so close to mine, you may never get rid of me!"

Brooke was unsure of what to say. She was beginning to genuinely like this man, this handsome artist who had so unexpectedly entered her life. In many ways he was quite unlike the other men she had known, including her husband, Bill. Just then the memory of Bill overtook her heart again, as did the lingering sense of sadness she always experienced every time she thought of him or whenever she received another of his heartfelt letters. Sighing slightly, she put down her fork.

The change in her was not lost on Greg. Although he still did not know her well, he believed that he was beginning to understand her moods, her needs, and that special sense of fearful melancholy she always seemed to carry regarding her husband. It was Bill, Greg realized, of whom she was now thinking, rather than him. For the first time since knowing her, he reached out and touched her hand. To his surprise, doing so came naturally to him, almost automatically. And to his further contentment, she did not pull away.

"Are you thinking about Bill again?" he asked her.

"Yes," she answered sadly. "I'm sorry, sometimes I just can't help it. I don't mean to ruin our dinner, honestly I don't. It's just that sometimes my thoughts of him take over, and there's nothing I can do about it."

Greg instinctively rubbed her hand a bit, the same way he might do to comfort a crying child or an ill person. To him, the gesture had no greater meaning than simply trying to calm her. Or so he had thought at the time, he would later realize. . .

"That's quite all right," he said gently. "No one could expect you to feel any differently. If you did, you wouldn't be human."

"Thank you for understanding," Brooke said. Then he saw her smile just a bit through her sadness. "You somehow always seem to make me feel better," she said. "And you're such a good listener, too. All I can say is that I'm glad it was you who became my new neighbor, rather than somebody else."

"Thank you," he said. "That means a lot to me."

They then returned to eating their dinner, this time in relative silence. Greg knew that Brooke didn't really feel like talking, and for his part, he was content to simply be in her presence and to enjoy her marvelous cooking.

At last they began tentatively chatting about this and that, the same sort of things, he supposed, that most Americans probably discussed at the dinner table during this time of war. As if there were some tacit agreement between them, they spoke no more of Bill or of Brooke's sadness in missing him. When they had at last finished eating, Greg sat back in his chair, looked at her, and smiled.

"Well," he said, "you can certainly cook! Assuming that an army travels on its stomach, if all of our boys had you cooking for them, we'd take Berlin and Tokyo in no time."

At last, Brooke smiled fully. "Thanks," she said. "It's been a while since I had a man to fuss for. I enjoyed it."

"As did I," Greg said softly.

After they cleaned up the dishes, Greg made some fresh coffee. He poured a cupful for each of them, whereupon they went out onto the porch and sat down.

The wind had risen a little, causing white-caps to form on the surface of the lake. The scent of evergreen rode the night air and the sky was still cloudless, allowing thousands of stars to sprinkle the heavens. It was wonderful, Greg thought. Just as the woman sitting next to him was wonderful, as well.

"Does it ever bother you?" Brooke asked.

Greg turned and looked at her, her profile lovely in the moonlight. "Does what bother me?" he asked back.

"How privileged we are," Brooke answered. "Sometimes I feel guilty about being here in this beautiful and serene place, while so many others all around the world are fighting for their very lives. When it comes Bill's time to fight, and I cannot know from day to day whether he's still alive, I sometimes wonder if I'll be able to endure it. I also wonder if I'll be able to return here again before the war ends and enjoy all these innocent pleasures that seem to make me feel so guilty."

Greg nodded. "Yes," he answered, "I

know what you mean, and it sometimes bothers me in a way that you may not understand. Because of my foot, I could not enlist. I cannot be with them, as an otherwise healthy man should be. Yes, it bothers me. It bothers me a lot."

Suddenly worried that she might have offended him, she reached out and touched his hand.

"I'm so sorry, Greg," she said. "I didn't mean it that way. You have no choice in the matter, I understand that. And I also know that if you could be out there with them, you would be."

"Thank you for understanding," Greg replied. "Not serving is something that I wrestle with every day of my life. Perhaps when this damned war is over and the survivors come back home to us, I'll feel like I'm a part of everything once again."

Sighing slightly, Greg shifted in his chair. He didn't want to go back home yet. But it was growing late, and he now felt a need to be alone, to think about the time he had spent with her today and the things they had said to one another. When he stood from his chair, Brooke understood and followed suit. And then, to his pleasant surprise, she took both of his hands into hers.

"I fully realize that I don't know you very well yet, Greg Butler," she said. "But I already have the feeling that deep down, you are a very good man."

"Thank you, Brooke," he said. Then he gave her a little smile. "It's been a long time since I had food that good."

"In that case," Brooke said, "we'll have to do it again very soon. So tell me, can you hunt as well as you fish?"

Greg laughed. "I'll see what I can do," he replied. "I have a feeling that no matter what kind of game I brought to you, you could turn it into something marvelous."

Brooke only smiled. "Good night, Greg," she said.

"Good night," Greg answered softly. "And thanks again for not only the meal, but also for the wonderful company."

As he walked back down the moonlit beach toward his cottage, about halfway there Greg Butler stopped, turned, and looked back at Brooke's little cabin. The lights were still on and he could easily imagine her in the kitchen, cleaning up the final odds and ends of their dinner together. As he stood there watching, he lit another cigarette, its glowing end bright in the evening's darkness. Then a thought came to him, and he sighed.

Living next to her all summer is going to be wonderful, he thought. *But it will also be terrible, because she's someone I could very much come to care for. And because of that, I must always remember that she belongs to another. But will I succeed in that effort?*

As he took another drag on his cigarette, he looked up at the stars and shook his head.

Only time will tell, he thought.

On finishing Brooke's second entry, Chelsea closed the old book and then placed it on the coffee table before the fireplace. Her mind lost in thought, she sat there for some time before finally giving in and going to bed.

10.

Late the following afternoon, Chelsea lay atop a lounger, which she'd placed just short of the waves' furthermost reach, so that they slid to and fro beneath her. The beach furniture she had seen in the boat-house was dilapidated beyond use, so Brandon had lent her the lounger, plus a beach umbrella that was supplying some welcome shade.

The white, one-piece swimsuit she wore was comfortable, as were her matching sun hat and sandals. Dolly had been fed and she was off somewhere with Jeeves, the two of them no doubt searching for something to chase. Chelsea had also taken her first real swim in the lake as best she could while also trying to keep her bandaged hand dry. Afterward she had lain on the dock and let the sun and wind dry her.

She put down the magazine she had been reading and then she turned and looked out across the water. Save for the occasional pleasure craft, things were quiet. The breeze was pleasant, and the waves were light. A perfect summer's day, it seemed, for contemplating the nature of the universe. And right now, her universe was Lake Evergreen.

She had called her mother earlier this afternoon to let her know that she was all right and to try to get an idea of how Lucy was holding up. As Chelsea had feared, Lucy still sounded brittle and frail. She had expressed a modicum of interest in Chelsea's trip, but when Chelsea tried to explain how marvelous the cottage proved to be, Lucy hadn't cared, and she immediately reverted into martyr mode. With a heavy heart, Chelsea had at last said good-bye. It was clearly going to take a lot of time before Lucy felt whole again, if she ever did.

While leaning back in her lounger, Chelsea lowered one bare foot and allowed it to be caressed by an incoming wave. Living like this could soon become habit forming, she realized. Was it wrong of her to be enjoying herself while her mother so desperately mourned? There was no clear-cut answer for that one, she decided. Besides, she had resolved to obey her grandmother's wishes.

She no longer intended to sell the cottage; of that much, she was now certain. In fact, she was considering spending her entire summer there. With a little help from Allistaire Reynolds, it could easily be arranged. Her mail could be forwarded via the mail boat, and she could use direct deposit for her paychecks. However, if she stayed, she would need more clothes. She could go home and fetch them, or, she supposed, buy some new ones in Serendipity. The selection probably wouldn't be great, but she certainly didn't need anything fancy to wear up here, either. Best of all, if she stayed, she would have lots of time to take up her painting again. Perhaps Serendipity might even have an art shop where she could get the things she needed.

But such housekeeping issues were minor. Ultimately, her decision about whether to stay rested on but two things. One of them was the still fully undisclosed nature of Brooke's private journal. And the other, she was starting to realize, was Brandon Yale.

She turned and gazed down the beach toward Brandon's cottage. It was a gray, clapboard-sided affair that appeared to be about as old as hers. His Jeep was gone, leading Chelsea to believe that after lending her the beach furniture, he had gone to the hospital. He must have struck some sort of deal with the hospital administration in order to have such freedom, she guessed. However, given the informal nature of everything up there, she wasn't surprised. Besides, how in all good conscience could they reject a native-born son who had become a Harvard-trained doctor?

As she turned back toward the restless lake, she again thought about Brandon. He was a very pleasant man, she knew, but she also guessed that he could be reticent. Because he remained something of a puzzle, Chelsea couldn't help but wonder about that. So far, the only evidence of any taciturn side had been yesterday when he had looked wistfully out at the lake, and then again, just before dinner. Partly because of that, Chelsea's personal interest in him grew larger by the moment. He intrigued her and she very much wanted to understand his hopes, his dreams, and his needs. Most of all, she wanted to know whether he had such an interest in her. Nevertheless, she had no idea how to bring the two of them closer. And then, an answer appeared.

She could tell him the entire story, she thought. If he agreed, they could further examine Brooke's journal together. Perhaps if she shared the experience with him, he might open up more. She fully realized that because she still didn't know what the journal had to say, she might be taking a risk. In addition, doing so might violate the spirit of Gram's intentions, which bothered her a bit.

But at the same time, Brooke's letter had said that Chelsea could handle these things as she wanted. And despite how little she might know about Brandon, her heart of hearts said that she could trust him. Plus, ever since she'd first read Gram's letter back in Allistaire's office, another need had been growing inside her. The more she explored the journal, the more she realized that she wanted someone with whom to share its mysteries. And, she remembered, Brandon had already said that the previous owner of his cottage had been a portraitist. Was Gregory Butler the one who had started the portrait of Brooke that still sat above the fireplace mantel? And if so, might Brandon somehow have a stake in all of this, too?

Just then, she heard a car, and she turned to see that Brandon had come home. At once Dolly and Jeeves appeared, barking out their greetings. After laughing and tousling their ears, Brandon waved to Chelsea and went inside his cottage. He would come and see her soon, she knew, because he had promised to check on her hand.

Still wondering what to do, Chelsea abandoned her lounger and walked back to her cottage to await him.

11.

After changing into some dry clothes, Chelsea poured herself a beer, then grinned widely at the amazing memory of Jeeves actually fetching one for Brandon last night.

Now, she thought, *if we could only teach Jeeves how to cook, we'd have it made . . .*

Then she realized something, and it took her aback.

"We" . . . ? she thought. *Is that what I'm already thinking—that Brandon and I constitute a "we"? You'd best slow down, girl . . .*

Just then, she heard a knock on the

screen door. Brandon stood there, his medical bag at the ready.

"Come on in," Chelsea said.

"Thanks," he answered.

Brandon looked nice, Chelsea thought. He was dressed in navy slacks, a matching dress shirt, and more formal shoes.

"Want a beer?" Chelsea asked. "My delivery isn't as spellbinding as Jeeves's, but I'll happily get you one anyway."

He set his bag atop the counter. "Yeah," he answered, "that'd be great."

After sipping their beers, at Brandon's suggestion they went and sat at Chelsea's dining table.

"Now then," he said, "let's get another look at this hand of yours."

Brandon rolled up his sleeves and gently removed the bandage. After checking Chelsea's wound, he nodded his approval.

"It looks good," he said. "I'm not going to replace the bandage, though."

"Why not?"

"Because wounds heal faster when exposed to the air," he answered. "The same goes for bites like yours. But you mustn't overuse your hand, and I still want you to keep it dry. Do you need another shot for the pain?"

"No, it's better now," Chelsea answered. "When a girl is in distress, it's great to have a neighborly doctor nearby."

And there it was again, she suddenly realized as she searched his face. The quiet, almost maudlin side about him that seemed to suddenly surface from time to time. Chelsea had originally believed her comment to be quite benign. But when Brandon's expression had so quickly sobered, she realized that she had unwittingly touched a nerve. *Another part of the puzzle?* she wondered.

"Thanks," he finally answered.

It was at last time, Chelsea decided, to take the plunge. "There are some things that I'd like to show you," she said. "Would you mind staying a bit longer?"

"Of course not," he answered. To her relief, he finally smiled again. "Besides, I've got a beer to finish."

"Excuse me for a moment," Chelsea said.

She walked out onto the porch and then returned with the journal and the photos, all of which she set on the table. After perusing them a bit, Brandon gazed questioningly into her eyes.

"Okay, I'll bite," he said. "What's all this about?"

As Chelsea told him everything, he listened with great interest. When she finished, Brandon sat back in his chair.

Then, for the very first time, she dared to reached out and touch one of his hands. Perhaps she did so because she was starting to understand how much she really cared for him. Or maybe it was because she was considering sharing Brooke's journal entries with him, and her heart felt the better for it. Whatever the reason, when their hands met it felt vitally significant to her, as if part of the invisible barrier between them had suddenly come down.

After collecting up the photos, Chelsea asked Brandon to accompany her into the living room, where she gestured toward the painting.

"You mentioned that the man you bought your cottage from was a portraitist," Chelsea said. She again pointed to the man in one of the photos. "Could that be him?" she asked.

After several moments of looking, Brandon nodded.

"His name was Gregory Butler," he said. "And yes, he's the same man from whom I bought my cottage. He looks much younger here, of course. But it's him, no doubt about it. He had a clubfoot, poor man."

Brandon then looked up at Brooke's unfinished portrait again. "And," he added quietly, "it seems that he's also the man who started this portrait. He must have been Brooke's neighbor up here. And he would have been her only one."

"What makes you think so?" Chelsea asked.

"Because there were so few cottages on this lake at that time," Brandon answered. "And because Butler also had his cottage built for him back in 1942, if what you say about Brooke coming here to spend the summers alone during the war years is correct, then yes—they had to be neighbors."

He then thought quietly for a moment. "Just as you and I now are," he added.

As Brandon's words echoed the last journal entry that Chelsea had read, she suddenly felt her connection to him deepen. It was a sensation that she welcomed.

"And Greg had a clubfoot, you say . . . ," Chelsea mused, "even though it can't be seen in any of these shots."

"Yes," Brandon answered.

"Which explains why a man of his age wasn't in uniform," Chelsea answered.

"You're right," Brandon answered. "He couldn't have passed the physical."

"And you said, 'His name *was* Gregory Butler,'" Chelsea added. "Is he dead?"

"Yes. Five years ago. He was a long-time smoker who died of lung cancer. When he went into the hospital for the last time, I looked in on him sometimes, but we never became close."

"I wonder who took these . . . ," Chelsea mused.

"Gregory might have," Brandon answered. "The camera could have had a timer and been mounted on a tripod."

Chelsea looked at all the photos once more. There always seemed to be some sort of unspoken connection between Brooke and Gregory, something that intimated more than just neighborly friendship. Her heart suddenly in her throat, Chelsea turned and looked back at the old journal lying on the dining table.

All of the answers are in there, she realized. *I can feel it. It's almost as if Gram is calling out to me from the past, desperate to tell me everything . . . But will her journal reveal secrets that I'll regret learning? Were Brooke and Gregory Butler more than just friends? And if so, then what of her husband, Bill?*

Knowing that Chelsea was struggling with her emotions, Brandon remained quiet. Given that he had actually known Greg Butler, he too was being drawn into the mystery. But of greater importance, he realized that Chelsea was fearful of what she might discover, and he sympathized with her.

Still uncertain, she looked back into his eyes. Her eager, impetuous side wanted to read every bit of the journal this very moment, no matter how long it might take, and to let the chips fall where they may. But the more romantic part of her nature demanded that she read it little by little while savoring it and gradually absorbing whatever it had to say. As she stood

there looking at Brandon, she again considered whether to do so with him or
alone.

Given her growing feelings for him,
sharing the journal with Brandon was the
most tempting. And perhaps most important of all, if the diary proved to be
truly disturbing, she believed that she
could rely upon him for emotional support. But would Brandon really want to
spend so much time with her? Or might
he think that this was just a ruse designed
to keep him near? Worse yet, would her
highly personal request cause him to turn
away from her? Proposing this idea would
be a risk, she realized. But if he agreed,
it would be worth it. It also meant that
most times they could only delve into its
mysteries at night, after he had returned
from the hospital.

At last, she decided to include him, if
he would agree. But something else was
bothering her, and it showed on her face.

"Do you suppose we could talk a little?" she asked.

"Is there something wrong?"

Chelsea nodded. "Maybe," she said.
"You see, I've sort of been putting two

and two together with these pictures, and . . ."

"I know," Brandon answered. "So have I. And the possibility must be disturbing for you. Tell you what—I'll fix us something stronger than beer, and we'll discuss it."

Chelsea let go a small but grateful smile. "Thank you," she said. "I was hoping that you'd understand."

"And how about I make a fire?" he asked. "We can sit on the sofa and talk there."

While Chelsea waited on the couch, Brandon brought their drinks and readied a fire. The Fabiennes, making his job easier, had already brought newspaper, kindling, and a few logs inside. Soon there were flames jumping and crackling in the lovely rose quartz hearth, and between the fire and the bourbon, Chelsea began to feel some welcome comfort seeping into her bones. Brandon then joined her on the couch. For a while, they said nothing to one another, each of them content to simply sit side by side and watch the dancing flames. After a time, Chelsea looked down at her glass, thinking.

What happened to you here, Gram? she wondered. *Did you come to this wonderful place expecting to be alone but find that you were falling in love? And if so, what did you do about it? Did you and Gregory also sit on this very couch, just as Brandon and I are doing now? Did you fall willingly into his arms? Or did you resist him, knowing that it would be wrong? Was he kind, was he understanding, was he—*

Brandon gently touched Chelsea's shoulder. "Hey," he said. "Is anybody in there?"

Chelsea took a deep breath. "Sorry," she answered. "I was just thinking." Then she paused and again sipped the smoky-flavored bourbon. "About a lot of things . . ."

Brandon nodded thoughtfully. "If I'm about to offend you, I apologize," he said. "But do you really think that Brooke and Gregory . . . ?"

"I don't know," Chelsea answered. "With both of them gone, reading that journal is the only way to find out."

"Are you sure that's what you want?" Brandon asked. "You might learn that

that old journal actually belonged to Pandora, rather than Brooke . . ."

"Maybe," Chelsea answered. "But yes, I will read it. And for two reasons. First, I need to know."

"And the second reason?" Brandon asked.

"Because Brooke asked me to," Chelsea answered quietly. "What I don't know, though, is why. Especially if she . . ."

Finally deciding to take the plunge, she turned and looked into Brandon's eyes.

"Will you do something for me?" she asked. "I know that it's a lot to ask, but I'm hoping that you'd be willing to read the journal along with me. At first, I couldn't wait to read it by myself. But now I'm not sure that I want to go it alone. I know that this isn't your concern. But perhaps we could explore a bit of Brooke's journal each night . . . maybe taking turns reading it aloud to one another. As a way to pay you back, I'd happily make dinner for us every time. Please, Brandon . . . it would mean so much to me."

Brandon searched her lovely face. *God,* he thought, *a man could get lost in those green eyes . . .* To better collect his thoughts, he returned his gaze to the fire.

Chelsea was trusting him, he realized. Enough so that she was willing to bare her beloved grandmother's past with him—a past that might well prove disappointing and hurtful. He could easily understand her wanting someone with whom to share the journal's secrets. But what struck his heart the most was that she wanted to do it with *him*. Letting go a deep breath, he decided. Just as Chelsea was becoming more special to him by the moment, so too would be their coming understanding of Brooke's journal entries, wherever they led.

"Of course I will," he answered. "We'll learn the tale together. And in return, I'll gladly take you up on your offer of dinner every night. Regardless of what we find in the journal, that part of it sounds wonderful. Maybe we could even re-create some of the old recipes in your grandmother's notebook."

"Thank you," she said earnestly. She then went to the dining table and retrieved the journal, which she handed to him.

"I've already read the first two entries," said. "So if you would, I'd like you to now read them, too."

"All right," he answered.

After a time, Brandon closed the old journal and set it back down on the coffee table.

"And so they meet . . . ," Chelsea said quietly.

"Yes," Brandon answered gently. "And they go fishing together. All of which still sounds like pretty innocent stuff to me."

"I know," Chelsea answered as she again looked down at the old photos lying beside her on the couch. "But there's something about these pictures that . . ."

Turning, she looked into Brandon eyes. "Thank you again for doing this with me," she said. "It means more than you know."

"You're welcome," Brandon answered. "Besides, after reading those first two entries I must admit that I've become hooked on Brooke's story too, and why she wanted you to know it so badly. And like I said, I'll be here for you, no matter where her journal might take us."

Smiling, he put two fingers beneath

Chelsea's chin and gently lifted her face to his. As he searched her eyes, she felt a sudden wave of emotion roll through her.

"But right now," he said, "I want something else."

Chelsea's mind raced. *A kiss?* she wondered.

"What is it?" she asked, her voice breaking again.

Brandon grinned. "Dinner," he answered. "You promised me, remember?"

Although she was disappointed, Chelsea couldn't help but laugh.

"Yes," she said. "I remember. But it can't be Brooke's MacArthuroni and Cheese, because I don't know how to make it yet. Will bacon and eggs do? And after we eat, do you suppose that we could read another of Brooke's journal entries?"

"That'd be perfect," Brandon answered.

As Chelsea arose and walked into the kitchen, Brandon placed another log on the fire.

12.

After finishing their dinner, Chelsea and Brandon settled down on the fireplace sofa. Not only was Chelsea eager to discover what the next entry said, she was now also looking forward to doing so with Brandon.

She handed the journal to him and smiled. "Would you like to do the honors?" she asked.

"Sure," he answered. After taking the journal from her, he thumbed to the third entry and began reading loud:

Tuesday, June 16, 9:00 P.M.

Today was a most pleasant one. I took Greg into Serendipity for lunch and to meet Emily Rousseau, a dear friend of mine. Her father owns and runs a little French restaurant there. Not only did we have a good time, it gave me another opportunity to get to know Greg better. It seems that the more I'm around him, the more I'm coming to like him. There's a sort of calmness and certainty about him that I must say I find appealing . . .

As Brooke and Greg stood before the little restaurant, Greg smiled. The place had a tricolor awning that hung out over the street. Dark green wooden columns graced either side of the door, and behind its prettily etched windows were low brass rails, from which hung white lace curtains. Curiously, each of the windows sported an image of a light-blue, hand-painted rooster that tickled Greg's artistic side and made him chuckle. Brooke opened the door and ushered him inside.

As he entered, Greg very much liked what he saw.

Somewhat longer than it was wide, the Blue Rooster boasted a shiny, black and white checkerboard floor. The 1920s-style white, tin-lined walls were adorned with ersatz pilasters, each one topped with an ornate fluted crown. Booths of dark leather lined either side wall, the tops of their adjoining seat backs adorned with shiny brass rails. Wrought iron tables for four with white lace tablecloths took up the remaining floor space, and frosted globes that hung from the high ceiling supplemented the sunlight coming through the front windows. Its source a mystery, soft accordion music wafted through the room, and each table and booth held a vase filled with delicate violet flowers.

Most of the customers were women, Greg noticed as Brooke guided him toward one of the booths. As they went, more than one intrigued female turned and watched him.

Their rapt attention was not lost on Greg. Once he and Brooke were seated, he stared at Brooke and said, "God, I feel like a rooster in a henhouse!"

Brooke laughed as she removed her hat and gloves. "Well," she answered, "in truth, I must admit that not many men come here. And with so many fellows off fighting the war, good-looking ones like you are in short supply. Anyway, the Blue Rooster has always been sort of a women's place, if you know what I mean." Then she smiled and gave him a wink. "Maybe I should have brought along an umbrella or something, to shoo away all of your lusty admirers!"

Greg laughed and lit a cigarette. "If it gets that bad," he said, "just shoot me instead!" Then he looked around a bit more. "So where's this girlfriend of yours?" he asked.

Brooke also scanned the restaurant and finally spied the person for whom she was searching. When she pointed her out to Greg, he realized that she was one of the waitresses.

"So that's Emily Rousseau?" he asked.

Brooke nodded. "She works here for her father, Henri, who owns and runs the place. Emily is married, but so far, she and her husband have no children. My mother and I first visited this place a couple of years ago, and we both fell in love with it. That was when I met Emily, and we've been close friends ever since."

While he watched Emily work, Greg took another drag on his cigarette. Like Brooke, Emily was tall and she had a nice figure. Her dirty-blond hair was rather long. For work purposes, Greg surmised, just now she wore it up. Her eyes were blue, and she smiled a lot as she worked the tables. She was so at ease with everyone that it appeared she was on at least speaking terms with most of them. As she went about her duties, her energy level seemed limitless.

Greg returned his attention to Brooke. "She seems to know *everybody,*" he said.

Brooke nodded. "Serendipity is a very small town."

Greg smiled. "True enough," he said.

Just then, Emily noticed them, and she hurried straight over. After eagerly taking a seat beside Brooke, she gave her a big hug.

"Hello, *ma chère!*" she said, her voice

carrying a telltale French accent. "It's been a while!"

"I know," Brooke answered. "It's good to see you, too."

Then Emily gave Greg a discerning look. *"And who do we have here?"* she asked in French. *"My, but aren't you the handsome one! I thought that Errol Flynn lived in Hollywood, but here he is, at Le Coq Bleu!"*

Greg smiled. *She's so full of life,* he thought. *And she apparently assumes that I didn't understand her . . .*

"Thanks for the compliment," Greg answered in French.

Emily's cheeks blushed slightly. "Whoops," she said. "It seems that I just got caught."

Brooke laughed. "No fair speaking French, you two!" she admonished them. "But if I had to guess, I think that I got the gist of what you were saying!"

Greg crushed out his cigarette in the table ashtray and stretched out his hand. "Greg Butler," he said to Emily. "I'm Brooke's new neighbor out at the lake."

Emily happily shook his hand. "Ah, *oui,*" she said. "Every time I've visited

Brooke's cottage, I've noticed how well your place was progressing. So it is at last done, and you have moved in?"

"Yes," Greg answered, "and I love it there. I'm a painter and a photographer."

Emily looked at Brooke. "It must be nice to finally have a neighbor after all this time, *non*?" she asked. "And an artistic one, too?"

Brooke looked at Greg, thinking. "It is," she finally answered. "And he actually fishes as well as I do."

Emily laughed. "Then the two of you were made for each other!" she said.

When Brooke's expression suddenly sobered, Emily realized her faux pas and she quickly placed one hand over her friend's. "I'm so sorry, *ma chère*," she said earnestly. "I know how much you miss Bill, and I didn't mean to imply that—"

"It's okay," Brooke answered. "It's just that I've become so lonely in his absence. Until Greg moved in next door, I was actually considering going home early."

"But Bill's officer's training will be finished soon, *non*?" Emily asked. "And maybe then he will get some leave and come visit you before he ships out."

Sighing, Brooke comfortingly rubbed one arm. "I can't say," she answered. "I don't know much about how the army works. All I know is that I miss Bill terribly, and I'm already sick and tired of this damned war."

Emily nodded. "As are we all," she said. "But America just got in, and we still have a long road ahead of us, I fear . . ."

Silence reigned among the three of them for a time as they each searched for something more pleasant to discuss. But whenever the war was mentioned, time seemed to literally stand still in a dark and macabre way. At last, Emily broke the silence.

"So, what would you like to eat?" she asked.

Brooke finally smiled a little at Greg. "Have you ever tried a *croque-monsieur* sandwich?" she asked. "Emily's father, Henri, makes them with Gruyère."

Greg nodded. "I love them, but I haven't had one in a long time."

"Okay, then," Brooke said to Emily. "We'll have two of those, and I'll have an iced tea."

"Ditto on the tea," Greg replied.

"Oh, and before I forget, Papa has a new side dish," Emily said.

"What is it?" Brooke asked.

"Seasoned, deep-fried pickle slices."

Brooke smiled wryly. "How interesting," she said. "Now, how come I never thought of that?"

"I don't know," Emily said, laughing. "But I'm sure that Papa would let you give them one of your made-up names, if you want."

"I might just take him up on that," Brooke answered.

"Okay, then," Emily said. "I'll be right back with everything."

As Emily hurried away, Greg watched her go. "Adorable . . . ," he said.

Brooke nodded. "And one of my very best friends," she said. "Her father built this place with his own two hands. Have you ever been to Paris?"

While lighting another cigarette, Greg shook his head.

"Well, if you had, you'd know how close to an authentic Parisian restaurant this place really is," Brooke answered.

"Of that I have no doubt," Greg answered. "And hopefully, that famous city will soon be crawling with American soldiers, rather than Nazis."

When Brooke's expression darkened a bit once more, Greg shook his head. "I'm sorry," he said. "It seems that I just keep sticking my foot in my mouth. Or clubfoot, as the case may be . . ."

Brooke nodded. "No apology needed," she answered. "The truth is that if I'm going to have a husband fighting overseas, I'd better get used to the idea. And besides," she added with a bit more authority in her voice, "this maudlin attitude of mine isn't what Bill would want."

"I'm glad to hear you say that," Greg answered. Then he gave her another of his nearly incandescent smiles. "And I'll bet that when you were at your happiest, you were a real handful."

At last, Brooke smiled fully. "So I've been told," she answered.

A few moments later Emily brought their food, and they ate for a time in silence. "You're right," Greg said. "No offense to your cooking, but this is one of the best things I've ever had. And thanks for introducing me to Emily. She's a great gal."

Just as they were finishing their lunches,

Emily came back over. "Thank you," Greg said. "And the deep-fried pickle slices were amazing! I'll be sure to come back here, I promise you."

"And we thank you," Emily said. Then she gave him a short, mischievous smile. "Try not to break too many hearts this time when you walk back to the door, *oui*?" she asked. "After all, it isn't every day we get a movie star in here."

Greg laughed. "I'll try to keep that in mind next time," he said laughingly.

"And please come out to my cottage sometime soon, won't you?" Brooke asked Emily. "It's been a while since you visited."

"*Mais certainement!*" Emily answered.

With that, Greg paid the bill, then he and Brooke left the restaurant. Sure enough, just as many female eyes watched him leave as had watched him arrive . . .

"*And so, Greg has made his first visit to the Blue Rooster,*" Brandon read aloud. "*And as I said before, it was a lovely day. We had taken my Cadillac into Serendipity, and before leaving for home Greg offered to drive, and I agreed. And so, we put the top down and drove back through the lush, green countryside to Lake Evergreen. And even now as I write this, I'm not sure what possessed me to do so, but when I laid my head upon his shoulder, it somehow seemed right."*

Brandon closed Brooke's journal and set it down on the coffee table.

"Was that the end of the entry?" Chelsea asked.

"Yes," Brandon answered.

"Does the Blue Rooster still exist?" Chelsea asked.

"Yes," Brandon answered, "as a matter of fact, it does. Emily Rousseau owns it. She's a very old woman now, and something of an institution in Serendipity."

"Do you suppose we could go there sometime?" Chelsea asked.

"Sure," Brandon answered. "I'm familiar with Emily. And although we can't know whether she and your grandmother stayed in touch all those years, I'm sure she'd love to meet you."

Suddenly feeling the need to be closer to Brandon, Chelsea scooted over a little. She then said nothing for a time as she watched the flames dance in the lovely rose quartz hearth. Emily Rousseau was someone she very much wanted to meet, and she hoped that she could do so soon. Because of all the citizens of Serendipity, Emily might be the only remaining one who could tell her about her late grandmother.

Brandon ended up staying for another hour while the two of them talked and watched the mesmerizing flames. And when at last he did go home, while standing on the porch and watching him walk down the sandy beach, Chelsea felt yet another tug on her heart.

13.

Why isn't she responding? Brandon wondered desperately. *What on earth should I be doing that I am not?*

He again checked the vital-signs monitor and saw that both her heart rate and blood pressure were still falling. It was Brandon's job to keep this woman alive until the surgeon was prepped. But he was clearly losing the battle, both for her and for himself.

To his surprise, she suddenly opened her light-blue eyes and looked straight at him. At first, she began to smile. But as she came to fully understand her surroundings, a look of abject terror overcame her. She started to say something, but before the words could come out, she lost consciousness again.

She knows . . . , Brandon thought. *She knows where she is and that I'm trying to save her . . .*

Blood covered his latex gloves, and sweat poured into his eyes. Several nurses aided him, their faces a series of taciturn masks as the life inexorably drained from the badly injured woman. Every time he tried to help her, it seemed that he couldn't work fast enough. And every time he tried to think of something else to help save her, it was as if all of his training had somehow abandoned him. He felt useless and inconsequential as his patient struggled to stay alive.

Then he watched in horror as the final bit of breath rattled from her lungs. The telltale sounds coming from the monitor soon became a steady tone, and the electronic life line went flat. Because they had known this woman, several of the nurses started to cry. And then, quite extraordinarily, he heard the bizarre sound of a dog, plaintively whining . . .

Brandon suddenly awakened and lurched upright in his bed. Outside his bedroom window, the sun was starting to rise. His chest was heaving, and he was drenched with sweat. The nightmare had come again, he realized. Jeeves stood anxiously by the bedside. As he laid his muzzle atop the covers and worriedly gazed at his master, his whining began anew.

Brandon sighed and shook his head. Before reaching down to give Jeeves a comforting pat, he ran his fingers through his damp hair.

"It's okay, boy," he said to Jeeves. "Just another one of those nights."

He tossed the covers off his naked body, put on a robe, and shuffled into the kitchen. He always prepared his coffee the night before and set the timer to start before he awakened. As he took his first sip of the life-giving brew, the warm mug felt good in his hands. After letting Jeeves outside, he went out onto the porch and sat down. Although the sun was still rising, his pilot's instincts said that the day would be fair, with a slight wind coming off the lake. Good flying weather, he realized, but he wouldn't be flying today.

He hadn't suffered his recurring nightmare for a while, and he had been hoping that it had at last abandoned him. But now he knew differently. His real-life failure to save that woman had haunted him incessantly for more than three years. And shortly thereafter, the tragedy had begun invading his sleep as well. The nightmare didn't resurface often, thank God. But when it did, it rattled his very soul.

Just then the phone rang, interrupting his thoughts. He shuffled back into the kitchen to answer it.

"Hello?" he said.

"Brandon," a female voice answered, "it's Claire."

Claire, he thought. *So kismet exists, after all . . .*

"Hello, Claire," he said. "Is everything all right?"

"No," she answered. Her voice sounded frightened, worried.

"What's wrong?" he asked.

"It's Rachel. She's sick."

"How so?"

"She's coughing, and she feels warm to me."

"Can you bring her to the emergency room?" he asked.

He believed he already knew the answer. But because visiting Claire was something he would rather avoid, he had needed to ask.

"No," Claire said. "Pug never came home last night, and I'm alone, without the truck. He's probably off drunk again. Can you come?"

Silence reigned on the phone line for a time as Brandon closed his eyes. "All right," he finally answered. "I'll leave soon."

"Thank you, Brandon," Claire answered quietly. "And God bless you."

As Brandon hung up the phone, a lone tear ran down his scarred cheek.

14.

Still half-asleep, Chelsea again heard an odd, unrecognizable sound. It was loud, causing her to roll over angrily and wonder why the infernal noise wouldn't just stop and leave her alone. Then the strange clatter came again, this time growing into a continual racket so strident that it seemed to drill straight through her. Determined to discover the cause of the noise, she clambered out of bed, threw on a robe, and with Dolly in tow, shuffled out onto the porch.

She looked at the lake to find that the mysterious sounds had been coming from Brandon's floatplane, as its engine had been starting up. The attractive red and white aircraft was preparing to take off. She watched with sleepy interest as Brandon turned the plane into the wind and pushed the throttle to the max.

The roaring plane was soon speeding across the waves, and then it lifted free of Lake Evergreen's watery grasp. It was an interesting sight to see, causing Chelsea to wonder about whomever Brandon was visiting this time. As the plane banked into an easterly climb, Chelsea watched until it vanished from sight.

Perhaps it was only wishful thinking, but she thought she smelled freshly brewed coffee, so she walked into the kitchen to investigate. To her happy surprise, her new coffee machine was burbling pleasantly. *Brandon,* she realized. He must have prepared it for her after doing last night's dishes. *Bless you,* she thought as she gratefully poured her first cup. She then heard Jeeves whining just outside the kitchen door, so she let Dolly out to join him.

As Chelsea took another sip of coffee, she fully realized how lousy she felt. She and Brandon had killed that entire bottle of wine last night, and some of the Pinot's effects were still with her. Moreover, her wounded hand was throbbing again. After taking another welcome drink of coffee, she went into the bathroom and eagerly slipped out of her robe.

One of the cottage's greatest attributes was its huge, old-fashioned porcelain bathtub. It was pure white with clawed feet, a goose-necked spigot, and knobbed faucet handles. Doing her best to keep her wounded hand dry, Chelsea drew a hot bath and lay in it for nearly an hour, letting the warmth seep into her bones.

On finally feeling more human, Chelsea realized that her appetite had resurfaced. She wanted some breakfast, but her head still ached a bit and she didn't feel much like cooking for herself. Then she remembered the diner that Brandon had mentioned last night, and she decided to visit it. And so, after grabbing up her car keys and her purse, she set off to find the place . . .

Fifteen minutes later, Chelsea found the diner. Although it looked old and isolated, it was busy. Alongside it lay a series of lakeside docks, complete with gas pumps for car fuel, boat fuel, and perhaps plane fuel. Various kinds of boats were tied up, indicating that people also came here by water. About fifteen vehicles, most of them pickup trucks, were haphazardly parked in the gravel lot.

The diner was a true American classic—one of those wonderful old stainless steel affairs that Chelsea had always loved, with a long stretch of windows running across its front side and a pair of chrome doors at its center. A large sign hanging over the doors read BEAUREGARD'S. When Chelsea approached the front doors, she smiled as she saw a sign reading SORRY, WE'RE OPEN! As she opened the door and walked in, a little brass bell attached to its top cheerfully announced her entrance.

Inside, the 1950s still reigned. Unlike newer "vintage" diners, this was the genuine article. A row of red leather booths lay alongside the front windows. Fifties-style tables and chairs stood on the floor between the door and the counter. An ancient, bubbling Wurlitzer jukebox stood in one corner playing some classic Elvis, and the small sundry shop Brandon had mentioned lay on the far right side of the room. The interior walls were also stainless steel; the floor was red and white checkerboard linoleum. Several uniformed waitresses were in evidence, all busily going about their duties. Typical of most diners, the grill lay on the opposite side of the counter.

Most of the customers were older men, picking at their breakfasts while they shared the latest doings. The welcome aromas of strong coffee, fresh baked goods, and frying sausage lingered in the air, causing Chelsea's appetite to sharpen further. Like so many things about Lake Evergreen, she immediately liked this place.

Deciding to sit at the counter, she spied an empty seat next to an obviously near-sighted old man, holding today's newspaper about two inches from his nose. As she settled onto a stool, a woman behind the counter sauntered over. About the same age as Chelsea, she had short blond hair, a pert figure, and deep dimples. Despite the early hour, her apron already showed the telltale signs of hard work. As she crossed her arms over her chest, she gave Chelsea a knowing smile.

"You ain't from around here, are you?" she asked, the southern accent in her voice quite noticeable.

Chelsea smiled back. "That's true," she answered. "But how did you know?"

"Well," the woman answered, "for one thing, you've never been in here before, and I know *everybody*. Then there's the still-shiny shoes, the brand-new Explorer parked outside, and the Ralph Lauren purse," she answered. "To me, all those things scream 'city girl.'"

Chelsea liked her immediately, and her smile said so. "You don't miss much, do you?" she asked. "Are you the owner?"

"Yep," the woman answered. "You want some coffee?"

Chelsea nodded vigorously. "Black, please."

The woman poured some fresh coffee into one of those marvelous porcelain mugs that only diners seem to use, and she put it down before Chelsea.

"I inherited this joint from my daddy,"

the woman said as she busily wiped the countertop. "He built it in '54. You don't see many real ones like this anymore. Truth is, it was cheaper to just keep everything the way it was, rather than remodel it. Turned out to be a good decision, 'cause if you wait long enough, damned near everything comes back into style eventually." She smiled and offered a hand. "Jenny Beauregard," she said, "at your service."

Chelsea shook her hand. "I'm Chelsea Enright," she said. "So you're a friend of Dr. Yale."

"How'd you know that?" she asked.

"Brandon mentioned you and this place during dinner last night," Chelsea answered. "I own the cottage next door to his."

"So you're the one," Jenny replied. "I shoulda guessed. Last time he was in, Brandon said that somebody from Syracuse had inherited the neighboring cottage and was finally gonna come open it up."

"That's me," Chelsea said. "I have to admit that at first, I was skeptical. But after I saw it, I was hooked."

Jenny gave Chelsea a knowing wink. "Not to mention Brandon," she said.

Chelsea blushed a little. "Well, yes," she answered. "He seems like a really nice man. How do you know him?"

"We went to high school together," Jenny replied. "Then he joined the army, and afterward he went off to that fancy college and became a doctor. Truth is, we're lucky to have him back."

Chelsea lifted her bandaged hand. "Tell me about it," she said.

"How'd you get that?" Jenny asked.

"I was bitten by Jeeves, the Beer-Fetching Wonder Dog."

Jenny laughed again. "Yeah, I've seen Jeeves do that trick, too!"

"Are you from someplace down south?" Chelsea asked. "I can't help but notice your accent."

"Nope," Jenny answered. "I was born and raised up here. But my parents were from Georgia, and when you grow up around a mama, a daddy, and three older brothers who all talk this way, some of it's gotta stick. Matter of fact, I'm a direct descendant of General P. G. T. Beauregard, the Confederate hero of Bull Run."

"Sorry," Chelsea said apologetically, "but I can't say that I've ever heard of him."

Jenny smiled and made a throwaway gesture with one hand. "Don't worry about it," she answered. "Nobody up here ever does. So, do you want some breakfast?"

"Yes, but I don't know what. Could I see a menu?"

"Sure thing," Jenny answered.

She reached under the countertop and produced a menu, which she handed to Chelsea. As Chelsea scanned the breakfast selections she found that many were recipes from the deep South, including such things as hoecake, grits, southern fried steak, and pecan-encrusted French toast. As Chelsea's happy confusion grew, the expression on her face was not lost on Jenny.

"How about lettin' me decide for you?" Jenny answered. "If anybody knows what's good here, it's the owner."

Chelsea was intrigued. "Okay," she answered. "Surprise me."

Jenny turned and barked out a few words to the short-order cook, who quickly set to work. After attending to a couple of other counter customers, Jenny returned.

Soon after, Chelsea's breakfast arrived. But when she looked down at the plate, not everything there was recognizable. She saw plenty of scrambled eggs and bacon, but lying next to them was some sort of messy-looking side dish.

I did tell her to surprise me, Chelsea thought. She looked back into Jenny's smiling eyes.

"Uh . . . what's that?" she asked while pointing her fork at the food in question.

"Homemade biscuits with white pork-sausage gravy," Jenny said. "My own secret recipe."

"For *breakfast*?" Chelsea asked.

"*Especially* breakfast," Jenny answered. When Chelsea took her first tentative bite, she grinned. This was nearly as pleasant a surprise as Margot's coq au vin.

"Wow, that's good," she said. "Who knew?"

Jenny gave her a wink. "If you look around," she answered, "damned near everybody."

"Can I ask you something personal?"

Chelsea said in between bites of her breakfast.

"I suppose," Jenny answered. "Given how you've taken to my biscuits and gravy, we're practically sisters."

Chelsea laughed a little. "Are you married?" she asked. "Got any kids?"

"Nope on both counts," Jenny answered. "I was married once, but he turned out to be a real snake. Cheated on me with every available skirt he could find. We got divorced two years ago."

"I'm sorry," Chelsea said.

"Don't be," Jenny answered. "I'm better off without him. It's like my late daddy always said—'everything's a matter of perspective'!"

"Maybe you're right," Chelsea said.

"Why did you wanna know?" Jenny asked.

"Well," Chelsea said, "aside from Brandon, I'm pretty much alone up here. It'd be nice to have a woman to talk with. Maybe you could come out to the cottage sometime. We could eat chocolate, drink wine, and commiserate about our love lives." Then a conspiratorial smile overtook her face. "And perhaps discuss Brandon a bit more . . . ," she added.

Jenny grinned. "You got a deal," she said. "Sounds like fun!"

While the two of them laughed, another customer entered the diner and looked around. When Jenny heard the bell atop the door ring, she looked across the room, just as she always did. Almost at once, her face fell.

"What's wrong?" Chelsea asked.

"Somebody just came in who I could live without," Jenny answered. "And damn if he ain't already noticed you sitting here. You're too good-looking, that's what it is. Makes you stick out like a sore thumb. Truth is, pretty newcomers ain't in great supply around here."

A man claimed the bar stool on Chelsea's left. Given Jenny's warning, Chelsea didn't turn to look at him. She didn't have to, because he was doing enough gawking for both of them. She felt his attention strongly, and the sensation was jarring.

"Jenny . . . ," the man said dully, his eyes still looking Chelsea up and down.

"Pug," Jenny answered back.

Chelsea surreptitiously checked the

man's reflection in the mirror on the wall opposite the counter. As best she could tell, he was about her age. He seemed rather short, his blondish hair was wayward, and it appeared that he hadn't shaved in several days. He wore a black and white checked shirt, carpenter's pants, and work boots. Had he been better groomed, he might have been passable, Chelsea decided. As he sat there beside her, he seemed to be having trouble staying atop his stool. Worst of all, the way he stared at Chelsea was making her more uncomfortable by the second.

"What do you want, Pug?" Jenny asked. "Looks like you're on another bender. Or still hung way over from the last one, at least."

"Coffee . . . ," he said thickly, his eyes still locked onto Chelsea. His voice was low and gravelly, like he smoked a lot.

Jenny served him some coffee.

"So who's this?" he asked, still looking at Chelsea.

"None of your business," Jenny answered.

"Aw, now don't be like that," Pug answered. Some of his words were slurred, and many of the others weren't coming out quite right, either. "Besides, maybe the lady would like to answer for herself," he added. Smiling, he edged a bit closer to Chelsea.

"You're pretty," he said.

"You're not," Chelsea answered.

Pug laughed. "What's the matter, precious?" he asked. "Are you too good for the likes of me?"

Chelsea finally turned and gave him a hard look. She could smell the scent of stale liquor on his breath. His nearness repelled her, but she held fast.

"Mind your own business," she said.

Pug smiled crookedly. "So who are you?" he asked. "Maybe we could go for a ride on my Harley sometime."

"A ride?" she asked. "With you?" Chelsea shook her head. "You know those warning signs for kids that they have at amusement parks?" she asked.

Pug's face screwed up with confusion. "Yeah, so what?"

"Well, take the hint," Chelsea said.

"Huh?" Pug asked.

"Okay, I'll spell it out for you," Chelsea said. She then held out one hand and raised it a good six feet above the floor. "You have to be at least this tall to ride this ride."

"That ain't funny," Pug answered angrily.

Just then, the old man sitting beside Chelsea put down his paper and turned to look at them. "I hear tell she's the one inherited the old Ashburn place," he said.

Jenny's face suddenly fell. *Damn,* she thought. *That's a bell we'll never unring . . . Why the hell did he suddenly have to put his two cents in?*

"Shut up, Jeb," Jenny ordered. "This ain't your business, and you know it."

For some inexplicable reason, a look of rage suddenly overtook Pug's face, and he glared hotly into Chelsea's eyes.

"So you live next to that bastard Brandon Yale?" he demanded.

Chelsea turned away and said nothing more, which only enraged Pug further.

"Now, listen to me, you conceited bitch—"

Before Pug could finish his sentence, Jenny slammed a baseball bat down onto the countertop so hard that every plate, cup, and piece of silverware atop it jumped. As the entire diner went silent, the atmosphere became thick with tension.

"Jesus, Jenny!" Pug said. "Weren't no need for all that!"

"Seemed like it to me," Jenny answered back. "Now you get the hell out of here. And you too, Jeb. Coffee's on the house."

After giving Chelsea another lascivious look, Pug finally staggered out. With his newspaper folded under one arm, Jeb followed. Once they were gone, some of the patrons cheered and clapped, telling Chelsea that Pug and Jeb were well-known around here.

Chelsea looked down to find that her hands were shaking. At last, she let go a sigh of relief.

"Whoa . . . ," she breathed. "Does that sort of thing happen often around here?"

Jenny shook her head as she hid the bat back under the counter. "Course not," she answered. "Pug's a special case, is all, and not one to let work interfere with his drinking. Jeb's not nearly as bad. But he loves to instigate, 'cause he's got nothing better to do."

"*Pug?*" Chelsea asked.

"Yeah," Jenny answered. "As in *pugnacious*. One of our teachers pinned that on him early, and it stuck. His real name is Earl Jennings. And by the way," she added, "I loved your bit about riding this ride. Never heard that one before."

"Why does he hate Brandon so much?" Chelsea asked.

Jenny sighed and scrubbed her face with her hands. "Well," Jenny said, "you didn't hear this from me, but the truth is that Brandon's got a few demons."

"He does?" Chelsea asked.

"For sure," Jenny answered. "And that sonofabitch Pug is one of them."

15.

Brandon reduced the power to the Cessna's engine, then he gently nosed the floatplane lower. There were some light clouds in the area, and he wanted to get beneath them to improve his line of sight. Because Claire Jennings lived on the water and her home was some distance away, Brandon had chosen to take the plane. Soon he broke through the mist, and he smiled.

After leveling the Cessna at three thousand feet, he readjusted the fuel-to-air ratio a bit and set a south-by-southeasterly course. Finally he settled in to watch

the various lakes, rivers, roads, and hills—
each a conspicuous landmark to an experienced pilot—slip effortlessly beneath
him. Brandon loved flying, and he was
good at it. The army had taught him well.
He had an instrument rating, which meant
that he was licensed to fly in bad weather,
with only his gauges to guide him. Such
advanced skills, however, wouldn't be
needed today.

He always enjoyed traveling to see his
"special" patients, as he sometimes liked
to think of them. Almost always they were
people who had no way to get to Serendipity. Many had no transportation and
were without anyone to take them. Some
poor souls were totally incapacitated.
And others—like Claire Jennings—were
simply stranded and afraid.

Although he was rarely paid for these
trips, Brandon had always found reward
enough in the simple doing of them. He
never experienced such great personal
satisfaction when treating people in an
impersonal office setting or in a frantic
emergency room. In their own homes, his
patients always seemed to appreciate
him more. They listened more earnestly

to his advice and had ample time not only to ask about his welfare but also to inquire about the latest Serendipity gossip. Many treated him to a home-cooked meal or offered some other small token of their gratitude. After graduating from medical school he'd had his pick of positions, but when it came time to decide, he realized that the money and prestige associated with loftier posts actually meant little to him. And so he had happily returned to his hometown of Serendipity, to put his talents to use.

Brandon looked for the cluster of small lakes that would indicate he was on the proper course. After a couple more minutes of searching, he spotted them. They lay about six points off to the west and ten miles or so away. They were his last major landmarks before beginning the descent toward Devil's Pond, where Claire Jennings lived.

Banking the plane slightly to port, he headed for them. His final course was set now, and he could afford to relax a bit. As the emerald hills and silvery lakes of the Adirondacks passed beneath him, Brandon's thoughts soon fell upon Chelsea

Enright, the lovely neighbor woman who had so unexpectedly breezed her way into his life.

Given how long the old Ashburn cottage had been abandoned, he had all but given up on the prospect of anyone ever opening it back up. But he had always imagined that if someone did, the new owners would likely be a family with kids, or an elderly couple wanting a place in which to spend their remaining summers. And so, when the Fabiennes told him that a single woman had inherited it, he had been surprised. And very pleasantly so, once he met her.

Although he liked Chelsea very much, he still didn't know a lot about her. There could be no denying that she was beautiful and intelligent. Plus, she had a spunky attitude that he found very attractive. He smiled as he remembered tending to her wound. What was it she had said? Oh, yes—she had intimated that he might be "some sort of country-fried quack." She had grit, he realized, but she also seemed gentle and caring.

But as Brandon thought about things some more, he frowned. Yes, he was interested in Chelsea. Very much so, in fact. But there was something holding him back—something that he had been trying to overcome for the last three years, but to no avail. And going to visit Claire Jennings this morning would only reopen those old wounds. He possessed a guilty sort of pain that had been thrust upon him against his bidding—one that had lodged so deep in his soul that he was starting to doubt it would ever leave.

He was acutely aware of its catalyst. But at the same time, he had no idea how to banish it from his thoughts, his dreams, and his heart. He wanted it gone so that he could get on with his life. But what woman could love so broken a man as he? Even with such a potent incentive as Chelsea Enright now in his life, he still felt powerless to change things. Just then he saw Devil's Pond looming up ahead, and it forced his mind back to the task at hand.

The name *Devil's Pond* was misleading, because it was easily the size of Lake Evergreen. It lay east to west in an oblong shape and was surrounded by high hills. If the wind was northerly or southerly, it made for difficult water landings because it forced the pilot to land across the lake, rather than along it. Luckily, today's weather obliged.

As Brandon descended, he saw the Jenningses' isolated trailer up ahead, nestled in among a stand of pine trees. Dropping the power a bit, he nosed down and buzzed the trailer. He did this for two reasons: to see for himself if Pug's old pickup was in fact actually gone, and to let Claire know that he had arrived. As he made another pass, he saw that Claire had left the trailer and was walking toward the Jenningses' ramshackle dock. Brandon then circled around again and began his landing procedure.

Carburetor heat on . . . speed reduced . . . flaps down . . . fuel mixture adjusted for the final time . . . airspeed indicator reading just above stall speed . . . steady, steady . . .

With the lake surface looming larger by the second, he lifted the Cessna's nose slightly and let her settle. Just as the stall warning buzzer went off, the twin floats hit the waves once, twice, then the plane finally leveled and began taxiing across the waves. Brandon gave the engine a quick shot of power so as to help turn her, then he steered her toward the dock and cut the engine, letting her glide nearer. As he approached, Claire helped to guide the plane alongside.

Brandon grabbed his bag, opened his door, and stepped out onto the port-side float. From there, it was an easy jump to the dock. Claire was already tying up the plane. As he neared her, she let go a rather tepid smile.

"Hi," she said quietly.

Brandon gave her a hug. Doing so felt good but also hurt at the same time.

"Hi back to you," he said. "It's been a while."

"Yes," Claire answered.

Saying nothing more, she and Brandon began walking toward the trailer.

16.

Just as Brandon remembered, the area surrounding the Jenningses' place was a disaster. The weeds were ankle high. An old Chevy truck with its hood up had sat idle for so long that vegetation had grown straight up through its cannibalized engine compartment. A ragged clothesline, heavy with wet and mended wash, lay bowed between two trees. What remained of the stone walkway to the trailer was cracked and broken, and the screen door hung slightly askew, as if begging for someone to come and fix it. Inside a doorless, dilapidated shed, Pug's old black Harley leaned tiredly on its kickstand.

Brandon shook his head. *Some place for a handyman,* he thought.

As he strode up the fractured walkway, he sighed. He hadn't been inside the Jenningses' trailer often, but each time he had, it had been a mess. And no wonder, given that Pug was an alcoholic. Brandon had long felt sorry for Claire. Although she was a good woman, living with Pug was nearly impossible. Still, she tried. Because Pug had been off drinking all night, Claire had been given a chance to tidy things up, and for once the inside of the trailer seemed largely presentable.

As Brandon walked into the living room and looked around, Claire followed him.

"Where's Rachel?" he asked.

"This way," Claire answered as she began leading him down the single hallway.

There wasn't much in Rachel's room, but at least it was clean. A dresser, a chair for Claire, and a child's mobile hanging from the ceiling were the only noteworthy items. Three-year-old Rachel lay in the crib, crying. Her face was red, and it was immediately clear to Brandon that she was in distress.

Brandon handed his bag to Claire, then he walked over and lifted Rachel from her crib. Rachel muttered *"Da-da?"* but on realizing she was mistaken, she started crying again. As Brandon held her close, she soon quieted. Feeling a bit upstaged, Claire gathered her robe closer and stared down at her ragged house slippers.

"You're always so good with children," she said. "Better'n me, for sure. How d'you do it?"

Brandon turned and looked at her. "I have no idea," he answered, "but it certainly helps in my line of work."

Claire had once been pretty, with the prospect of a happy life lying before her. But even at her young age of thirty, those days seemed distant. She was too thin by far. Her sallow face revealed years of struggle and hardship, and she had long, rather scraggly brown hair. Whenever Brandon saw her—which was seldom these days—she always seemed beaten, downtrodden. *And again, why wouldn't she?* Brandon thought.

When Claire had gotten pregnant soon

after high school, she and Pug were married. She lost her first child, a boy, during his delivery. Pug had always wanted a son, and the child's death threw him into a long-standing depression that nearly destroyed their marriage. Soon after, he started drinking more heavily.

Despite that loss, what he saw as his greatest personal tragedy came some years later, causing his subliminal rage and sense of blame to become permanent parts of his character. Rachel's birth had also occurred around then, and it had helped a bit to ameliorate things for a time. But soon after—and fueled by yet more alcohol—Pug's frenzied sense of anger returned for good. It was a tale with which Brandon was all too familiar, because he had been such an integral part of it.

Brandon looked at Claire again. "I need to put her down on a bed," he said.

Claire nodded, and they left the room. The master bedroom had the same sort of forlorn, thrift-store look about it. Brandon gently placed Rachel on the bed, while Claire put his bag down beside her.

He took Rachel's temperature to find

that it was 101 degrees. Using a stetho-scope, he listened to her lungs, heart, and abdomen. After examining her eyes, ears, nose, and throat, he nodded to himself and put his instruments back into his case.

"What is it?" Claire asked.

"The flu, most likely," he answered. "But it's her fever that concerns me most. We need to make sure that it doesn't become something worse, like pneumonia. Do you own a thermometer?"

Embarrassed, Claire shook her head. Brandon reached back into his bag and produced a spare one.

"You can keep that," he said. "I assume you know how to use it . . ."

Claire nodded. "What else should I be doing for her?"

After giving Rachel a low dose of Tyle-nol, Brandon handed the bottle to Claire.

"Give her one of those, with food, as instructed on the bottle," he said. "Her fever should break soon. If it isn't gone by this time tomorrow, call me again. And make sure that she gets lots of fluids."

"Thank you," she said. "I only wish that I could pay you something."

"You know better than that," he answered.

Claire picked Rachel up, and she and Brandon walked back down the hall. When Rachel realized that she was back in her crib, at last she fell asleep. Brandon and Claire returned to the sparse kitchen, where they sat at a cheap dinette table with four chairs.

"Want some coffee?" Claire asked.

Brandon nodded. "That'd be good," he answered. "I didn't have the best night, either."

Claire stood and poured two cups of coffee. As she did, Brandon sadly watched.

She could have been so much more, he thought. *And she should have been. Funny how instead of unfolding for us as they might, our dreams sometimes only get in the way. . .*

As Claire brought the coffee to the table, Brandon felt his concern for her and for Rachel start to get the better of him. While trying to control his rising anger, he abruptly shoved his chair back and stood up. He walked to one of the kitchen windows and glumly stared at the ever-present mess lying outside.

"What's wrong?" Claire asked.

With his back still toward her, he said, "Why the hell don't you divorce him?"

"I can't."

Brandon turned around and glared at her. "Why not?" he demanded.

"For one thing, I got no money," she answered. "And even if I did, where would Rachel and I go? How would we survive? Hell, Brandon, I can't even pay you for today . . ."

As much as it saddened him to hear it, he couldn't disagree. But seeing her and Rachel imprisoned here like this still tore at his heart, because even now he felt partly responsible.

"I could help you, if you want," he offered. "Money, a place to live . . . It's the least I could do, considering . . ."

Claire shook her head. "That'd be crazy, and you know it," she answered. "If Pug found out, there's no tellin' what he'd do. He still hates you bad as ever. Your helpin' me might end up making things worse for everybody. And God knows I don't need nothin' worse to come along."

Brandon sighed. As much as she and Rachel meant to him, all he wanted to do right now was to climb back into his plane and get away from here—away from the heartache, the squalor, and the scathing memories.

"I have to go," he said. "Remember to call me if Rachel doesn't improve. If I need to, I'll come back. Pug or no Pug."

"What about your coffee?" she asked.

"Sorry. Another time, maybe."

Claire stood and embraced him. "Thank you for coming," she whispered. "You're the best man I know. And I feel so bad about what happened three years ago. I know that you tried . . ."

His nightmarish memories suddenly revisiting him, Brandon closed his eyes. When he opened them again they were wet, and he wiped them with one sleeve.

"Sorry again," he said. "That still happens, sometimes. Help me push the plane off?"

"Sure," she answered.

A bit later, Brandon was again taxiing the Cessna across Devil's Pond. As the plane gathered speed he glanced out his side window and saw Claire standing on the dock, waving good-bye. Soon the plane was climbing into the sky and winging its way back to Lake Evergreen.

Good-bye, Claire, Brandon thought. *And thank you for forgiving me. Now if I could only forgive myself. . .*

17.

"Thanks for this," Brandon said to Chelsea. Fully satisfied, he put down his fork and gave her a broad smile.

"I've never tasted Eisenhower's Eggs Benedict before," he said, laughing, "and I must admit that it's wonderful. I've always been a huge fan of the dish, and I never thought that it could be improved upon. But I must say that in her own way, Brooke certainly accomplished that."

Chelsea smiled back at him. Brooke's Eisenhower's Eggs Benedict was made with a sausage patty instead of Canadian bacon, and the hollandaise sauce included bits of diced mushroom. Chelsea had served it along with some hash browns made with diced green pepper and onion. It had been her first attempt at preparing one of Brooke's wartime recipes, and doing so had made her feel even more connected to both the bygone era in which they had been created and the woman who had created them.

"Why, thank you, Dr. Yale," she said. "This is my first crack at making them—no pun intended—and I must agree that they did come out well. But the credit goes to Brooke, not me. Anyway, it's nice to have you here tonight and to be sharing another meal with you."

Brandon leaned back in his chair and smiled again. "And to also share another of your grandmother's journal entries, right?" he asked.

"Yes," Chelsea admitted. "That too."

"Would you like some help clearing the table?" Brandon asked.

Chelsea shook her head. "No," she said, "I'll get this. But could you start a fire?"

"Will do," Brandon answered. "First, though, I'll need to bring in some more wood."

While Brandon was around the back of the cabin gathering wood, Chelsea started cleaning up the dishes. As she did, she smiled to herself. She had always enjoyed cooking and had particularly enjoyed preparing her first of Brooke's wartime recipes. The Eisenhower's Eggs Benedict had been a big hit with Brandon. And soon now they would share another of Brooke's journal entries—something else that she greatly enjoyed.

By now she very much liked Brandon, this handsome and rather enigmatic doctor next to whom she lived. Although it was clear he had some secrets, his supposed maudlin side never seemed to surface too often or too harshly. And that, Chelsea was beginning to realize, was one of the things that intrigued her the most. Despite whatever personal demons might taunt him, Brandon always seemed a strong, calm, and sympathetic man. And as she came to know him better, it was those very traits that further convinced her she had done the right thing when asking him to explore Brooke's journal with her.

Before leaving Beauregard's, Chelsea

had tried asking Jenny what she meant about Pug Jennings being one of Brandon's "demons." Jenny had been reluctant to answer, saying only that it would be best if Brandon explained these things to her himself. Because she and Jenny had just met, Chelsea didn't press the issue. She also knew that her relationship with Brandon was still too new to risk asking him about such sensitive things herself. So she had decided to wait and see if the time would come when he might offer them up of his own volition.

As she finished tidying up the kitchen, Chelsea looked out the open, paned window that lay just above her sink. The sun had set about an hour ago, and it was proving to be a lovely night. There was no wind, which meant that she could easily hear the night creatures singing and the waves of Lake Evergreen as they caressed the sandy shoreline. The sky was cloudless, the stars were bright, and she felt very much at ease this evening.

But then she thought about Brooke's journal again, and she sighed slightly. She had yet to discover why Brooke had wanted her to read it or how she would feel about it when she had finished. Only time would tell her, she knew, as she and Brandon explored the rest of it.

His arms loaded with wood, Brandon came up the porch steps, followed by Dolly and Jeeves. As he began preparing a fire and the dogs hunkered down in one corner of the living room, Chelsea poured the last of the coffee into two mugs, retrieved Brooke's old journal from the porch, and walked on into the living room.

Once the fire got going, Brandon joined her on the sofa and took a sip of coffee. "And so, are you ready?" he asked.

"As ready as I'll ever be, I guess," Chelsea answered as she tucked her legs up under her.

"Would you like to do the honors, or shall I?" Brandon asked.

"It's my turn, I think," Chelsea said as she searched through the journal. On finding the fourth entry, she began reading aloud:

Sunday, July 5, 1942, 3:00 P.M.

Another month has passed and yesterday was the Fourth of July, the first since America's entry into this awful war. Even though I'm spending the summer here at Lake Evergreen, where every-thing seems so still and peaceful, this first such Fourth has touched me, even here. I cannot know what yesterday was like in Syracuse or in any of America's other cities. But if it was anything like here, this normally celebratory day must have also carried with it a rather sad and uncharacteristically fearful tone. I'm sure that the bands played, the crowds cheered, and the red, white, and blue could be seen fluttering everywhere. But I have no doubt that beneath all that supposed good cheer, there also lay an incredible sense of worry and concern about whether this wonderful nation of ours will continue to exist and how many more such halfhearted Fourth of July celebrations must pass before we all know our futures . . .

And to that end, I was handed a sur-prise last night. It was an experience that affected me deeply—not because of what was said, but rather because of what, at the request of another, was left unsaid. And its tenor remains with me

even now, a full day later, as I write
these words . . .

As the evening wind kept trying to disturb
her hair, Brooke retied her scarf. She and
Greg were in her yellow Cadillac convertible with its top down, heading into Serendipity. It was about eight P.M., the sky
was clear, and the wind rushing by the
open car was cooling. Greg was driving,
and as the big Cadillac's twin beams shone
brightly down the country road and the
dashboard lights highlighted Greg's
handsome features, Brooke found herself
looking forward to this evening.

He had asked her this morning if she
wanted to come with him, and although
she was at first unsure, she had finally
accepted. She had been momentarily
concerned about what the people in Serendipity might think. Then again, those
whom she knew were fully aware that her
husband was away in the army, and they
probably also knew by now that Greg
Butler had become her new neighbor.

But we're still likely to cause some com-
ment, just the same, Brooke thought as

they entered the outskirts of Serendipity. *And I'm going to let that be their problem, rather than mine. It is, after all, a fund-raiser for the war. And there's no reason that Greg and I, like everybody else who will be going, can't enjoy ourselves.*

They were headed to the high school, where there was to be a Fourth of July fund-raising dance for the USO. And although the gymnasium wasn't a swanky venue, it had been beautifully decorated.

As they entered the large room, Greg put a twenty-dollar bill into the kitty that was being tended to by a pretty young WAC, who thanked him profusely. Given the times, it was a handsome contribution indeed. When Brooke asked him about it, he shrugged his shoulders and lit a cigarette.

"I realize that it's probably more than most are donating," he said. "But given that I can't enlist, it seems the least I can do."

"Thank you for bringing me here tonight," Brooke said. Then she couldn't help but again think of Bill, and she sighed a little. "And I also thank you for the contribution you just made."

With that, Greg seemed to buck up a little. "A small price to pay, madam, for accompanying such a beautiful woman to this event."

After Greg escorted her to one of the many little tables for four that had been arranged around the perimeter of the room, Brooke sat down with him and took it all in. A stage had been set up at the far end, upon which a ten-piece band was playing popular tunes. Red, white, and blue bunting seemed to hang everywhere, as did the American flag with its forty-eight bright white stars. There were also war posters that castigated American citizens for talking out of turn and others that showed Uncle Sam imperiously pointing his index finger at the viewer and demanding that they either buy yet more war bonds or immediately join the army. Another proclaimed, WEAR THE FIGHTIN'-EST WINGS IN THE SERVICE! FLY WITH THE MARINES! while the one hanging next to it shouted out, MAN THE GUNS! JOIN THE NAVY!

Although Brooke and Greg had arrived early, she guessed that there were already at least two hundred people there, most of them couples who were dancing and drinking the night away. Most of the women wore dresses and gloves, and the men wore single- or double-breasted suits. Greg was wearing a dark gray double-breasted, a white shirt with a blue tie, and a gray fedora. Brooke had chosen a white dress with matching pumps and gloves. There was also a smattering of men and women here in uniform who, Brooke guessed, were recently enlisted citizens of Serendipity come home on leave. Because the Fourth of July had landed on a Saturday this year, the timing for this event had been perfect.

"Would you like a drink?" Greg asked as he removed his hat and set it on the table.

Brooke nodded. "I'd love a sidecar," she said, "provided they know how to make it. It's been ages since I had one."

Greg stood up, crushed his cigarette out in the ashtray, and gave her a wink. "Good choice," he said. "And if they don't know how, I'll teach them!"

Brooke laughed. "Of that, I have no doubt!"

Just then, Emily Rousseau and her husband, John, approached Brooke's table. Brooke saw them coming, and she smiled.

"Hello, you!" Emily said. "I didn't know you'd be here!"

"Hi, Emily," Brooke answered happily. "Coming here tonight was Greg's idea. And I must say that I'm glad! I honestly didn't think it would be this nice!"

"Yeah," Emily answered. "It looks great, doesn't it? I'm hoping that we can raise some decent money for the USO."

Brooke then turned and looked at John. "Good to see you, too," she said.

"And you," John answered. "Damn, but you're a vision in that white dress! Betty Grable's got nothing on you!"

Just then Greg returned with the drinks, whereupon Brooke introduced him to John. "Pleased to meet you," Greg said. "Want to join us?"

Emily gave Greg a wink. "I thought you'd never ask!" she said.

"I heard some news on the radio today," John said while sitting down, raising his voice above the music. "It seems that the Flying Tigers have been disbanded. They did a helluva job, though. Shot down more than three hundred Jap aircraft and lost only fifty of our own. Now, if things were only going that well in Europe . . ."

With John's talk of the war, Greg saw Brooke's expression falter a little, and he gave her a smile. "Enough of all that," he said to Brooke. "Shall we dance?"

Brooke nodded. "Yes, thanks," she answered. But as Greg escorted her into the midst of the whirling couples, a concern crossed her mind. "Forgive me for asking," she said, "but are you sure . . . ?"

Greg took her into his arms and nodded. "Well, I'm no Fred Astaire," he answered with a wink. "But if you'll stick close, I'll do my best to see to it that we get around the floor and back without creating a scene."

Brooke smiled. "You got yourself a deal," she answered.

Just then the band finished the tune they had been playing and started up again with "Stardust," a song that had been made wildly popular last year by Artie Shaw.

When he heard it, Greg smiled. "Perfect . . . ," he said.

As Greg led her around the dance floor,

Brooke found his dancing to be better than she had expected. Not perfect, certainly, but she soon realized none of that mattered. All that mattered was that she was with him, and she quickly became swept up in the moment. Brooke was a very good dancer, and despite Greg's rather awkward style she followed him effortlessly.

As the band played on, Greg held her a bit closer and Brooke did not object. And then, a few moments later, something happened, something that would change this night for Brooke and that she would never forget.

She watched as an attractive young army officer in uniform walked up behind Greg and tapped him on the shoulder, asking if he could cut in. Before replying, Greg searched Brooke's face for an answer. But Brooke had none, stunned as she was by seeing a man who looked not unlike her husband, Bill, standing before them in his crisp new uniform and asking for a dance. When Brooke did not reply, Greg decided that he had little choice but to grant the soldier's wish.

As Greg retreated and Brooke's new

partner took her into his arms, she became deeply affected by his presence.
No man in uniform—not even Bill—had
ever held her. And as the dashing officer
began to lead her about the floor, she
found herself suddenly wondering what
her beloved Bill was doing, so far away,
at this very moment.

The officer smiled at her. "Thank you
for this," he said quietly.

Still nearly at a loss for words, Brooke
said, "You're welcome . . . May I ask
where you're from?"

To her surprise, the officer shook his
head. "Please," he said, "would it be all
right with you if we didn't talk?"

His answer surprised her. "Why not?"
she asked.

Although the captain smiled back at
her, his expression was tinged with a bit
of sadness.

"Well, you see," he said, "I'm shipping
out soon. And you have absolutely no
idea what it means to a man like me to be
in the arms of a woman like you, even for
so briefly, just before I have to go away.
And so, if it's all right with you, can we
just enjoy this moment for what it is? Be-

cause for me, well . . . I can't be sure that one will ever come again."

Brooke found herself so affected by the young captain's heartfelt remarks that all she could do was nod. And as he skillfully guided her across the floor, she again found herself thinking about Bill. Closing her eyes, she at last held the young captain a bit closer, and he gladly obeyed her wishes. And when he gently placed his cheek alongside hers, she realized that he was trying to take in her perfume so that he could always remember it, wherever the war might lead him.

Only moments later, it seemed, the band finished playing and the captain released her from his grasp. And then, when at last Brooke opened her eyes, without a word he was gone. Moments later, Greg had his arm hooked through hers, and he was escorting her back to their table . . .

"Soon after that," Chelsea read aloud, *"I asked Greg to bring me home. Being in that officer's arms has somehow stirred a divide within me that I had yet to realize*

was present. For a time, it was like I was dancing with Bill. And then when he left me so suddenly and Greg appeared, all that consumed me was a renewed desire to be in Greg's arms again, and to be guided around the dance floor in that wonderfully awkward way of his. And so we danced once more, before I asked him to take me home. But rather than being able to leave these new and strangely conflicting feelings behind at the dance, it seems that they have followed me home, where they haunt me still, even as I write these words . . ."

With that, Chelsea closed her grandmother's old journal and set it on the coffee table.

"I'm assuming that's the end of the fourth entry?" Brandon asked.

Chelsea nodded.

"Did it upset you?" Brandon asked.

"A little, I guess," Chelsea answered. "I have no way of knowing what the rest of the journal will reveal, but one thing is becoming certain."

"What is that?" Brandon asked.

Before answering, Chelsea gazed at the fire. "Brooke's heart was becoming torn," she said. "And I can also sense that it goes deeper than the mere words that she wrote down. It's as if I can literally feel what was happening to her. Call it a 'woman thing,' if you want, but with the reading of each new entry, I can literally experience her world starting to turn upside down. And I can also sense that it was beginning to scare her."

Brandon nodded. "I know," he answered compassionately. "All of which makes me wonder what happens next."

Suddenly feeling vulnerable, Chelsea edged nearer to him on the sofa.

"I wonder that too," she answered as a charred log slipped farther down in the fireplace grate. Then she turned and looked into his eyes. "But I do know one thing for sure."

"And what's that?" he asked.

At last, Chelsea gave him a little smile.

"I'm really glad that you're taking this journey with me," she answered.

Saying nothing more, Brandon put one arm around her shoulders.

18.

Later the following afternoon, Chelsea sat on her porch, thinking. There was so much more that she wanted to know about Brooke's summer here so long ago, and with each bit of information she gleaned, her curiosity only deepened.

But was she making too much of all this? she wondered. Many people would probably think so. If Brooke did have an affair, of what possible importance could it be now? And why go rummaging around in someone else's past when it might only dredge up more harm than good?

But Chelsea knew the answers to those

questions, and she would not be dissuaded. By asking Chelsea to read her journal, Brooke told her that she wanted her to know what had happened during that final summer. Chelsea had silently vowed to honor her late grandmother's wishes, and so she would. But there was another, perhaps even more important reason to do this.

Since Chelsea had been old enough to remember, Brooke had always suffered a special sort of sadness all her own. Her car crash had been both awful and life changing. But as Chelsea grew older and wiser, she came to suspect that Brooke's accident alone was not the full cause of her sorrow. Although it was only through death that Brooke finally defeated her wheelchair, she had never railed against being in it, either. Instead, she had found ways to continue enjoying her two great loves—cooking and painting. No, Chelsea knew. It was not just the accident or its aftermath that had so distressed Brooke. To a far greater extent, the true culprit had been whatever occurred during her final summer there at Lake Evergreen—the same summer that she described in her journal.

In all the time that Chelsea had known her grandmother, Brooke was never so melancholy as when someone happened to mention her abandoned cottage or when asked why she never returned there. It was not a despair so great that it caused her to break out in tears—at least not that Chelsea had ever seen. Rather, Brooke's reaction was always a sort of great wistfulness, a seemingly huge sense of regret over what might have been. After announcing that she wished to hear of it no more, she would usually wheel herself out onto the porch, where she could paint in solitude. And because of that, the family eventually stopped mentioning Lake Evergreen and the lovely cottage that had been closed up for so long. Indeed, until Chelsea learned that it had been she who had inherited the cottage, the place had almost been wiped from her thoughts.

Chelsea turned in her chair and gazed briefly at the mysterious old journal that lay atop the dining table. *Those pages hold the answers,* she thought. *Brooke wanted someone to know, and she chose me . . .*

Chelsea looked at her watch to see that it was nearly four P.M. She then casually gazed down the shoreline, looking for Brandon. Although his Jeep and float-plane were in evidence, she didn't see him. Exhausted from their wanderings, Dolly and Jeeves lay dead asleep atop a stretch of shaded sand. The lake was calm, with but a few passing pleasure craft, and in a few hours the sun would begin its nightly descent. Then Brandon would come over, and he and Chelsea would explore another excerpt from Brooke's journal.

To her pleasant surprise, Chelsea had become patient regarding the journal. When she had first arrived here, it had been all she could do to keep from devouring it in a single sitting. She still could, of course, should she wish to. But by now she very much enjoyed the idea of waiting for Brandon and sharing the journal with him. She greatly valued his quiet strength and his unbiased viewpoint. Also, he seemed to be her emotional compass, always bringing her back to reality if something in the journal set her emotionally adrift. Moreover, reading only one excerpt at a time allowed her the chance to process what she had learned and to enjoy the anticipation until next time. Although she and Brandon had read only one excerpt together, Chelsea was absolutely convinced that more revelations awaited them.

"A penny for your thoughts!" a voice suddenly said.

Startled, Chelsea swiveled in her chair. Brandon stood on the other side of the screen door, medical bag in hand.

"May I come in?" he asked.

Before beckoning him inside, Chelsea waggled an accusatory index finger at him.

"You know," she said, "you've got to stop doing that! It scares me to death! So, I'll tell you what. Now that I'm pretty sure you're not an ax murderer, you can enter my place unannounced—provided that you grant me the same privilege. Do we have a deal?"

Brandon nodded happily. "Sorry," he answered. "I guess I'm still not used to having a neighbor! Anyway, I've come to tell you that if you want to read some more of Brooke's journal tonight, it'll have to be a bit later than usual. I have to follow up on that baby girl with the flu that I told you about. Her mother just called and asked me to come back out. But I should be home in time for us to read a bit more, if you want. And after that," he added slyly, "you can cook a late dinner for us."

Chelsea nodded. "Okay," she answered. "And yes, I'm eager to read some more of it, too. But I'd rather wait for you."

"I was hoping you'd say that," he answered.

Brandon then looked out at the lake, where his red and white floatplane tugged gently at her anchor. The sky was clear and the winds were light. Lovely flying weather, he realized. As an idea formed in his mind, he smiled again. When he looked back at Chelsea, she realized that something was brewing.

"Okay, out with it," she ordered. "There's no escaping it, Dr. Yale. I know that look by now."

"Come with me," he said simply. "I'd love to have you along for the ride."

"But . . . you're taking the plane, right?" she asked.

The twinkle in Brandon's eye grew brighter. "Yep," he answered.

Chelsea pointed at the floatplane. "That very *little* plane?" she asked rhetorically.

"Do you see another one out there?" he asked.

Oh, God, she thought. *Now what do I do?*

"I don't know . . . ," she answered. "I've never been up in one of those. Are they dangerous?"

"Well," he said, "let me think. The weather is perfect, I've flown this route several times, and I'm an experienced army pilot. No, you're right. We'd probably never make it back alive."

Despite her continued misgivings, Chelsea snorted out a short laugh. She very much wanted to spend time with him. And because this was his first request that they do something together, she felt that she mustn't decline, lest she appear uninterested. But the other part of her—the sensible, city-girl part—was scared silly to think of herself soaring around in some flimsy little airplane over great stretches of relative wilderness.

"What about the woman who asked you to come out?" she asked, secretly hoping that her question might dissuade him. "Won't she think it's odd if I'm tagging along?"

Brandon shook his head. "No," he answered. "I've known her for a long time, and I'm sure that she'll enjoy meeting you. What's the matter? Your life insurance is paid up, isn't it?"

Chelsea scowled. "Very funny," she answered. "All right, damn it. I'll go. But if we both die in a crash, I'll kill you!"

"If we die, I'll let you," Brandon replied. "Now go and grab a jacket. It'll be close to dark by the time we get back, and it can get chilly up there."

Marvelous, Chelsea thought as she went to fetch her leather jacket. *Not only do I get to be petrified, but I'm going to have my butt frozen off, too.* When she returned with her coat, she took another moment to look at Brandon's handsome face. *The hell of it is,* she thought, *he's worth it . . .*

After locking up their cottages, Brandon and Chelsea walked to the end of Brandon's dock, where his aluminum fishing boat lay tied up. Brandon helped Chelsea into the boat, then he too got in, untied it, and rowed them out to the floatplane. On circling around to the passenger side, he opened the door for Chelsea and helped her in. He then paddled around to the pilot's side, tied the boat's rope to the mooring line, unhooked the plane, and clambered up inside with his medical bag.

Although Chelsea found the cockpit to be cramped, there seemed to be no end to the various dials, knobs, and switches laid out before her. Like most people unaccustomed to piloting a plane, her first glimpse of its control systems was hugely daunting. As Brandon secured her seat belt for her, she pointed at the dashboard.

"How in the world does anyone remember what all of these thingamajigs are for?" she asked. "It'd take me a lifetime to understand them all."

Brandon levered open his side window at the bottom to let in some fresh air. "I know it seems confusing," he said. "But once you understand that everything has its own purpose, it all falls into place. And to prove the point, once we're upstairs I'm going to let you fly her."

Chelsea was aghast. "Like hell!" she answered. "No way, no how!"

Brandon laughed. "Let's get up there, and then we'll see. Who knows—you might just change your mind."

"I wouldn't count on that, if I were you," she answered.

Chelsea watched as Brandon fiddled with a few knobs and switches and then turned the ignition key. The motor coughed twice, spat out some dark smoke, and promptly died.

"That was comforting . . . ," Chelsea said.

"No worries," Brandon answered. "Like another female I know, she's sometimes stubborn."

"Ha-ha," Chelsea answered.

Undaunted, Brandon repeated the process. This time the motor roared into life, the whirling propeller immediately becoming little more than a circular, telltale blur. Chelsea was surprised at how loud it was inside the cockpit, and the entire plane vibrated as if angrily demanding an immediate release into the sky. As the reality of actually going flying sank in, Chelsea grabbed the door handle so firmly that her knuckles turned white.

After checking a few of the gauges and setting the flaps, Brandon gave the plane a quick shot of power and then turned her into the wind, simultaneously making sure that they were well clear of the moored fishing boat. As he did, the waves noisily sloshed the plane back and forth a bit, adding to Chelsea's growing distress.

Brandon gave her a comforting look. "Ready?" he asked.

"I guess so . . . ," she answered.

"Okay, then. Here we go."

Chelsea watched Brandon turn the plane a bit more westerly, then he opened up the throttle. As the Cessna gathered speed, the noise from the engine became a deafening roar. Faster and faster they went until Brandon gently lifted the nose, and the floatplane finally slipped the watery bonds of Lake Evergreen.

As they climbed, Chelsea discovered that with the plane angled upward, there was nothing to see out of the windshield but clouds and sky. So she glanced out her side window as the earth and everything upon it grew progressively smaller. Brandon soon leveled off and then circled Lake Evergreen so that Chelsea could get her first bird's-eye view of the lake. It was fairly circular and larger than she had imagined. Climbing the plane again, Brandon set a course for their destination.

Once he reached cruising altitude, Brandon throttled back and let the plane level out again. Now Chelsea could see not only the ground from her side window but also the land and sky stretching out before them. With the throttle reduced, the conditions inside the cockpit became a little quieter.

After making another small course correction, Brandon lifted a set of combination headphones and microphone dangling from a dashboard hook, and he told her to put them on. He also donned a pair.

After flipping a switch on the dashboard, he said, "How's that?"

For the first time since getting into the plane, Chelsea smiled. Not only did the headphones shut out much of the engine noise, she could also hear Brandon much easier.

"Yes!" she answered. "This is better!" As she finally started to relax, she released her grip on the door handle. "So where are we going?" Chelsea asked.

"Toward a lake called Devil's Pond," Brandon answered. "Getting there won't take long."

As they continued toward their destination, Brandon took the opportunity to explain the dials, gauges, and switches. As he did, he found her to be a quick study. He momentarily thought about showing her how to use the controls, then decided that it might be best left for another time. Soon, Devil's Pond loomed up ahead.

Brandon pointed at the lake. "There it is," he said.

Like the time before, he buzzed Claire's trailer to let her know he had arrived. Just as Claire had promised, Pug's truck wasn't in evidence. When Claire started walking toward the lakeshore, Brandon began setting up his landing. With the wind again in his favor, he put the plane into a descent and lined her up for the final approach. Almost before Chelsea knew it, the Cessna's two floats hit the water once, then again, and the plane finally settled down.

As Brandon taxied toward the dock, he looked at Chelsea and asked, "That wasn't so bad, right? It seems that we lived, after all!"

Chelsea couldn't help but smile. "No," she answered, "not bad at all. In fact, it was kind of fun."

"I'm glad to hear you say that," Brandon answered as he cut the motor and they drifted nearer.

Chelsea unfastened her seat belt and removed her headphones. "So who are this woman and child we've come to see?" she asked casually.

"Claire Jennings and her daughter, Rachel," Brandon answered. "Claire's husband is called Pug."

Chelsea's heart skipped a beat. *Pug Jennings?* she thought. *That's the man who caused the trouble in Beauregard's! Oh, God . . . Plus, I never told Brandon about it, because I didn't see any need. . .*

As they coasted closer to the dock, Chelsea reached out and touched Brandon on one arm. He immediately recognized the troubled look on her face.

"What's wrong?" he asked. "Worried about having to fly back home?" Then he laughed a little. "I could ask Claire to drive you back on Pug's Harley, but I can pretty much guarantee that you'd find the experience even scarier than the plane ride."

"No, no," Chelsea answered urgently. "It isn't that at all. But before we get out of the plane, there's something you need to know."

Chelsea quickly explained what had happened at Beauregard's. As her story evolved, Brandon's expression darkened.

"Well," he said, "I certainly wish that you'd told me sooner. But don't worry—Pug isn't here. And besides, Claire isn't like him. But to be on the safe side I'll make this quick, and then we'll get going again."

Just then one of the floats gently bumped the dock, and Claire began securing the plane. Before opening his door, Brandon paused and gazed meaningfully into Chelsea's eyes. His expression was stern but compassionate.

"I'm sorry about what happened back at Beauregard's," he said quietly. "Life up here can be hard, and it sometimes changes folks for the worse. But whenever I'm around, you'll never have to suffer that kind of trouble again, I promise you."

Chelsea found herself deeply affected by his words, his strength, his sudden display of intimacy. He had just promised to protect her, and the tug on her heart was the strongest ever.

Wow . . . , she found herself thinking. *No other man has ever spoken to me quite like that. . .*

Moments later, Brandon and Chelsea were standing on Claire Jennings's ramshackle dock. Chelsea wondered what kept it from collapsing into the lake. Claire's hair had been put up in a scrunchie, and she wore an old housecoat and a pair of dingy Keds.

Brandon gestured first toward Claire, then Chelsea. "Claire Jennings . . . Chelsea Enright," he said. "Chelsea inherited the cottage next to mine. She's here for the summer."

Claire smiled and held out one hand. "Pleased to meetcha," she said.

"And you," Chelsea answered.

While shaking Claire's hand, Chelsea felt some rough calluses, doubtless earned from many hours of hard, physical work. By now, Chelsea realized that living in such an isolated spot presented its own set of unique challenges. Her sympathy for Claire's plight only increased as Claire's eyes enviously poured over Chelsea's clothes and makeup.

Life has been hard for this woman, Chelsea thought. *And I know why . . .*

Eager to see Rachel, Brandon cleared his throat. "So how's the baby?" he asked.

Suddenly jarred free of her reveries, Claire looked back at Brandon and shook her head. "She's still feverish," she answered, "and now she's wheezing a bit. I'm getting scared for her, Brandon."

Brandon nodded. "Let's go, then," he said.

As the three of them neared the trailer, Chelsea scanned the run-down property and became further saddened by what she saw. When she entered the trailer, her overall impression didn't improve much.

"Is Rachel in her crib?" Brandon asked.

Worriedly gathering her worn robe around her, Claire nodded.

"While I go and check on her, why don't you keep Chelsea company?" Brandon said to Claire. "If I need you, I'll holler."

"Okay," Claire answered.

As Brandon walked down the lone hallway with his bag, Claire beckoned Chelsea toward the kitchen dinette set, where they sat down.

"Some coffee?" Claire asked her. "Or somethin' stronger, mebbe?"

"Coffee's fine," Chelsea answered.

While Claire rifled through her cupboards, her embarrassment over not being able to produce two matching coffee cups became palpable. But they were clean, Chelsea realized as Claire poured two steaming cupfuls. Claire put the coffeepot back on the burner, then joined Chelsea at the table. An awkward silence reigned for a time as two women from vastly different worlds each searched for something to say.

"So you inherited the place next to Brandon's," Claire finally said.

"Yes. At first I wasn't sure whether I

wanted to keep it. But then I came up here, and I was hooked."

"So where're you from?" Claire asked.

Chelsea sipped her coffee. "Syracuse," she answered. "Fayetteville, actually."

"I've heard of Syracuse, o' course," Claire answered. "Can't honestly say the same for Fayetteville."

Chelsea gave Claire a little smile. "That's understandable," she said. "Until recently, I'd never heard of Serendipity."

Claire produced a rumpled pack of cigarettes from her night coat. "You mind?" she asked.

Chelsea shook her head. Claire expertly lit a cigarette with an old Zippo, then she lifted her chin and gratefully blew some smoke toward the ceiling. Smoking seemed to calm her, Chelsea noticed. But then Claire's worry over Rachel resurfaced, and she again stared down the hallway.

"Brandon's a great guy," she said absently. "Any woman would be happy to have him."

Chelsea nodded, then took another sip of the strong coffee. "From what little I know of him," she answered, "I think you're right."

As if trying to comfort herself, Claire absently rubbed one arm. "Not long ago," she said, "one of the local girls nearly hooked him. But it ended badly. It wasn't his fault, but he still thinks that it was. Has he told you about it?"

Chelsea very much wanted to hear Claire's story about Brandon. But at the same time, she didn't want to appear too eager. Before replying she took another sip of coffee, then sat back casually in her chair.

"No," she said. "He hasn't. From what I gather, he doesn't talk about himself much."

Claire snorted. "Understatement of the century," she answered. "After what happened, I'm not sure that any woman will ever get that close again. He won't let 'em, you see."

Chelsea knew that she'd be pressing her luck to ask more, but her curiosity won out. "Would you mind telling me about it?" she asked innocently.

As she pondered things, Claire took another luxurious drag on her cigarette.

She seemed to enjoy it so much that Chelsea began wondering if smoking was Claire's only form of refuge.

"Well," she said at last, "I don't suppose that telling you'd hurt anything. It's common knowledge, anyway. Ya see, it all started when—"

Just then they heard a horn blow and the telltale sound of tires crunching down upon the driveway gravel. To Chelsea's horror, she looked out the window to see that Pug had come home. When he exited his battered old truck and saw Brandon's floatplane, his face turned scarlet with rage. Claire's hands immediately flew to her face.

"Oh, good Jesus . . . ," she whispered. "He wasn't supposed to be back so soon!" Then she started trembling all over. "This is gonna be bad . . . ," she whispered. "Pug hates Brandon! Even swore to kill him once! The two of them ain't been face-to-face for nearly three years! God only knows what will happen now!"

Wide-eyed, Claire hurried toward the hallway. "Brandon!" she shouted. "Brandon! Pug's come back!"

When Brandon appeared he was cradling Rachel with one arm and holding his bag with his free hand. The baby was crying loudly, adding to the thick sense of tension. Pug would be inside in mere moments, Chelsea realized. Knowing that her place was beside Brandon, she rose from her chair and hurriedly joined him.

Just then the weathered front door blew open so violently that its lone window nearly shattered. On the other side of the landing stood Pug. He didn't seem drunk, but he was clearly enraged. When he saw Brandon holding his daughter he pointed accusingly at him, and his face took on a twisted, hate-filled expression.

"You son of a bitch!" he shouted. "You just can't stay out of my life, can you?"

He then glared at Claire, causing her to cringe noticeably and to gather her modest housecoat closer, as if it might somehow protect her from her husband's fury.

"I suppose that *you* asked him to come out here!" he shouted at Claire. "Well, I'll deal with you later. Now go and get my daughter back!"

Chelsea watched as Claire obeyed Pug

without question. It was a sad thing to see, causing Chelsea to wonder how long Claire had been under this terrible man's thumb. After Brandon handed Rachel over, Claire took her into the kitchen and put her in her high chair.

Pug walked menacingly closer to Brandon and Chelsea. As he neared, Brandon whispered to Chelsea, "Get behind me. Don't question me, and do it right now."

While Chelsea did as Brandon ordered, Pug took a few more steps. Then he stopped and smiled wickedly at her. As he did, Chelsea suddenly recalled how much he had repulsed her that morning at the diner. When Pug took yet another step, Brandon held his ground.

"Well, hello there, precious," Pug said to Chelsea. "Nice to see you again. I guess that you just can't stay away from me either, huh?"

"Leave her alone, Pug," Brandon said. "I've done all I can here, and we're going to go. But first, you need to know that Rachel should be admitted to the hospital. She's got the beginnings of pneumonia, and in a child it can escalate very quickly.

She needs antibiotics and professional care, neither of which she'll get here."

"Says who?" Pug asked nastily. "You, I suppose? And just why should I listen to you? You're the medical genius who loses people on the table, right?" He then looked at Chelsea again. "Are you sure that you wouldn't like to stay, girlie?" he asked. "After the doc leaves, you and me could have some fun."

Chelsea was scared but also enraged. And although she was trying to control her temper, it was becoming a losing fight. As an idea occurred to her, she stepped to Brandon's left, looked Pug straight in the eyes, and shook her head. She then lifted one hand up above her shoulder.

"You remember the height requirement, don't you, Pug?" she asked. "Well, guess what? You still don't qualify."

His rage escalating sharply, Pug stepped closer yet. As he did, Chelsea sensed Brandon tense up.

"I'd like to pay you for your time," Pug said to Brandon. "Seems only right, don't you think?"

Brandon's eyes narrowed warily. Not

only did Pug have no intention of paying him, he knew, he probably didn't have the money, anyway. *Stay alert,* he thought. *Something's about to happen . . .*

Pug took one more step, which finally brought him to within striking range. To Brandon, his intent was clear. Brandon dropped his bag to the floor and shook his head.

"Don't do it, Pug," he warned. "It won't go well for you."

"Bullshit!" Pug shouted. "I never did believe that crap about you being an army ranger! We both know that you ain't got the stones for it!"

Chelsea watched in fear as Pug formed his right hand into a tight fist. *Please, Brandon,* she thought. *Please tell me that you see it, too . . .*

"Besides, I only want to give you what you got comin'," Pug said. "And I've got it right here, special delivery . . ."

Suddenly, Pug's right fist lashed out at Brandon's face. As it did, Brandon quickly slid forward, directly into the arc of the oncoming blow. He immediately slung one arm under Pug's striking arm and then twisted it upward, wrenching Pug's shoulder to its limits. As Pug cried out in pain, Brandon closed his thumb tightly against the palm of his free hand, then slammed the exposed fist knuckle of his index finger directly into Pug's larynx. Gasping in agony, Pug crashed backward against the nearest wall like a broken doll and then fell straight to the floor.

Transfixed, Chelsea watched Pug desperately gasp for air. His face had gone scarlet again, this time from lack of oxygen. Drool dripped from his mouth and his blank, dazed eyes gazed out at nothing. Brandon went to him. He quickly checked Pug's pulse and looked into his eyes.

"You'll live," he said. "Just relax and breathe, you dumb bastard. If I'd wanted you dead, you would be."

Still awestruck by what Brandon had done, Chelsea watched as Pug tried to marshal his breathing. After a few seconds more he partially recovered but was still unable to stand upright. Reaching out, Brandon grabbed the lapels of Pug's dirty work jacket, then he hauled him to his feet and pulled him close, so close he could smell Pug's fetid breath.

"Now, you listen to me," he ordered. "If you harm Claire or that baby in any way, or if you ever harass Chelsea again, I'll come back here. And trust me, that's not something you want. Are we clear?"

Still gasping, Pug nodded stupidly.

"Good," Brandon said.

At last, Brandon let him go. Totally defeated, Pug again crashed down onto the cheap linoleum floor and lay there. Then Brandon looked over at Claire. Shocked by what had just happened, she was trembling noticeably.

"Use Pug's truck and take Rachel to the Serendipity hospital," Brandon ordered her. There was no sense of compromise in his voice. "And do it right now," he added, "while you still can. I'll call and tell them that I want her held for observation. I'll order some antibiotics for her, then I'll look in on her tomorrow and give you a call. Do you understand?"

Claire nodded nervously.

"Good," Brandon said. Then he turned and looked at Chelsea. "We're leaving," he told her.

After picking up his bag, he took Chelsea by one hand and briskly started leading her from the trailer. On reaching the door, he paused and looked back into Claire's weepy eyes.

"I'm sorry, Claire," he said quietly. "He left me no choice."

"I know," she answered.

Aside from the roar of the floatplane's engine, Brandon and Chelsea's flight back to Lake Evergreen was a quiet one.

19.

Brandon angrily swallowed another belt of bourbon. This was his third stiff drink in an hour, and Chelsea was beginning to worry for him. He had said absolutely nothing during the flight home and little else since angrily making a fire in Chelsea's fireplace. Now he stood before the mantel staring silently into the flames. Deciding to remain quiet, Chelsea waited on the couch.

Outside, darkness had fallen. It was a quiet evening, save for the crackling fire and the rhythmic ticking of Brooke's old mantel clock. Given the sense of tension pervading the living room, even those gentle sounds seemed deafening.

His expression now showing nothing but sadness, at last Brandon turned and joined Chelsea on the couch.

"I'm sorry about what happened back there," he said. "I didn't want to do it, but he left me no choice. And I especially apologize for insisting that you come along. It was stupid of me, it seems."

"Well," she said, "you didn't know about my run-in with Pug until we were already there. That's my fault. And for what it's worth, I thought you were amazing. I'd forgotten about you being an ex-ranger."

Brandon shook his head. "I still am a ranger," he said. "You're never an ex-ranger."

"Okay," Chelsea said. "But you only did what you had to."

Chelsea took a sip of her red wine. Only a short time before the altercation, Brandon had sworn to protect her, and he had. With each passing hour, Chelsea was realizing with ever-greater certainty that Brandon was a rarity among men in this day and age. He was someone who always kept his word, and he seemed to live by a personal code of honor that appeared unshakable.

Even so, she remained concerned about his supposedly troubled past. Jenny had mentioned it that day at the diner. And in her own way, Claire had also alluded to it only hours ago. Despite what she knew about Brandon, Chelsea still didn't fully understand him, and she very much wanted to. She didn't want to pry and perhaps push him away. But clearly, there was something important he hadn't told her, something about which others were aware but that he wasn't willing to discuss with her. In order to truly know him, she had to discover what it was. But she also knew that getting him to talk about it would be difficult.

Despite all that, there was one thing about which Chelsea was certain. Somewhere deep inside Brandon, there existed a dichotomy. When it came to emoting for others, he never failed. But when called upon to express his own feelings, something oftentimes prevented him from doing so. He kept his emotions close and his past even closer. Chelsea knew something else, too. In order to draw him out, she would first have to admit something to him, something that had been growing inside her for some time.

Although Chelsea had thought long and hard about broaching the subject, even now she remained unsure. Given what had happened today, this was either the most opportune time to tell him what was in her heart or the worst. Hoping for the best, she decided to take the leap. It would be an important step for the two of them, she knew, if only he would open up to her, as well. After taking another sip of wine, she sidled a bit closer and looked into his eyes.

"There's something I need to say," she said. "And I hope that you can accept it in the same spirit in which it's given."

"All right," he replied.

"I've come to care about you, Brandon," Chelsea admitted. "Perhaps more than I should, given the brief time that I've known you. I willingly concede that. But if we're going to continue seeing each other this way, I need to know what's troubling you. There's something wrong, I can sense it. You've been badly hurt, and

I think that Pug Jennings is somehow a part of it."

Pausing for a moment, she carefully considered her next words.

"You see," she said, "every time I trust you with the contents of Brooke's private journal, I'm also trusting you with the contents of my heart. One of the greatest needs a woman has is to be able to trust, and I'm no different. As much as it pains me to say it, unless you can be forthright with me, I'm not sure that I can go on like this."

As she watched Brandon's face, she realized that her words had affected him greatly. She now saw a sort of wistfulness there, a kind of acquiescence indicating that he might at last open his heart to her.

"You're right," he said. "I should explain it to you, but it's so hard for me . . . You see, I've never actually *told* the story to anyone before. That might seem hard to believe, but because Serendipity is such a small town, I've never had to. In places so tiny and provincial, bad news travels fast, and it reaches into every corner."

"It's okay," she said quietly. "I think I

understand you well enough to know that whatever happened, you did nothing wrong."

Brandon nodded. "Thank you for that," he said. "I just wish that I could believe it, too." While gathering his thoughts, he took a deep breath.

"Simply put," he said, "Pug holds me responsible for the death of his sister Mallory."

Although Chelsea was surprised, she tried not to show it. "Please go on," she said.

While anxiously rolling his glass between his palms, Brandon paused for several moments.

"Mallory was wonderful," Brandon said. "Blond, effervescent, highly intelligent . . . Everyone loved her, and she was the apple of Pug's eye. For his part, he was a far different person then. He held a steady job working for his father, and his marriage to Claire was good. He had always been something of a drinker, but rarely to excess. And believe it or not, we were once friends. But then Mallory died, and everything changed for him. When he began drinking harder to dull the pain of losing her, the alcohol fueled not only his growing sense of injustice but also his need to blame someone. In the end he chose me, and maybe he was right."

As if trying to summon more strength, Brandon closed his eyes for several moments. Realizing that he was struggling, Chelsea remained quiet. When at last Brandon looked at her again, he shook his head.

"Mallory was only thirty when she passed," he said. "Although she had a degree in advertising, she chose to work for her father, like Pug. They owned a very successful logging company. Mallory ran the office. She knew that she was never going to get rich at it, but she was happy, and that was what mattered most to her."

Brandon took a deep breath. "She died from a hunting accident," he said. "A lot of women up here love to hunt, and she was no exception. One fall day, she and Pug were out pheasant hunting. As it happened, Pug was walking behind her. Just then their dog suddenly flushed a bird, and Pug released the safety lever on his gun. But then he tripped and fell, and the gun went off. The bird shot struck

Mallory in the back of her right shoulder, literally blowing her off her feet. Pug did the right thing by trying to stem the bleeding and rushing her to the hospital, but they were pretty far away.

"She was badly wounded," he added, "and by the time Pug got her to the hospital, she had lost an irretrievable amount of blood. She finished bleeding out on my table, right before my eyes. I did everything I knew to try and save her, but she died before the surgeon could get prepped. I begged him to start working on her anyway, told him that the risk of her dying right there and then far outweighed that of any infection. But he wrongly assumed that she could hang on. In the end, there was nothing that either of us could do."

It was a heart-wrenching tale, Chelsea realized. And given that Mallory had died while technically in Brandon's care, Chelsea now understood why Pug blamed him, wrong as he was to do so. But over the course of Brandon's career, there surely must have been others whom he had lost. It happened to every doctor, especially those who worked in trauma departments. So why, then, was this woman so special? Suspecting that there was more to learn, she reached out and gently touched his hand again.

"But that's not all, is it?" she asked him. "Please, Brandon, I need to know."

This time when he looked into Chelsea's eyes, she saw nothing there but pain.

"Mallory was my fiancée," he said, his voice a near whisper. "I loved her more than life. I would have gladly died in her place that day, if I could have."

Oh, my God . . . , Chelsea thought. *It's no wonder he still grieves . . .*

"We knew each other in high school," he said. "Some time after my army service and my medical training we reconnected, and sparks flew. From that point on, our relationship was a whirlwind. One year later, we were engaged. Eight months after that, she was dead."

Brandon abruptly stood and faced the fire again.

"You can't imagine my horror at seeing her on one of my own ER tables!" he exclaimed, his voice suddenly raw and angry sounding. "She even opened her eyes once and looked up at me. And then she smiled! She actually goddamn *smiled* at me! But when she remembered, an expression of abject horror overcame her face. That was the last time we ever saw each other, and the memory still haunts me. Even now, I have nightmares about it."

As Chelsea watched his tears gather, she desperately wanted to comfort him. But the right words seemed a million miles away, ephemeral, fleeting, impossible to capture and use. Soon Chelsea felt her eyes well up, too. Having at last calmed himself, Brandon again sat down beside her.

"So now you know," he said. "But the story doesn't end there. After Mallory's death, Pug began pickling himself in booze and our friendship died. Then his father passed, Pug inherited the logging business, and due to his drinking he drove it straight into the ground. That put some of the locals out of work, and they resent it to this day. As you might guess, he has few friends left. After the logging business closed, he became a handyman, but he doesn't get much work."

Pausing for a moment, Brandon took another slug of bourbon.

He continued. "It's as if Mallory's death consumed whatever good once existed inside him, leaving him hollow and angry. I wish that things could be different for all of us, but they aren't. I've often thought about selling both my cottage and house and starting over somewhere else. But I still love it here, despite all that's happened. Besides, I could never abandon my patients."

Brandon then reached out and caressed Chelsea's cheek, his touch so light that she hardly felt it.

"And then," he said quietly, "some brash city girl inherits the cottage next door, and in a matter of only a few days my whole life gets upended again. You want the truth, Chelsea, so here it is: You've affected me far more than you know, and I've developed a deep affection for you, too. You were a great surprise, because I never thought that my heart would experience such feelings ever again. Even so, I can't say where our relationship is going. For better or worse, until you came along I was fully mired in the past. And now I feel like I'm being torn between the past and the present. I can't honestly say which is worse, and as of this moment, there's no way for me to know which side will win out. I'm sorry if you were hoping for more, because for now, this is the best I can do."

Just then he remembered something he had once heard, and he shook his head. When next he looked into Chelsea's eyes, a slight smile managed to break through his sadness.

"Réticence entre deux amants peut souvent causer la mort de leur ardeur," Brandon said. *"Et donc, mon amour, peut-être cette erreur jamais subir nous. Pour plutôt que s'exprime dans les chuchotements, son amour devrait être cria joyeusement de sommets."*

Although Chelsea couldn't know what he had just said, it somehow touched her heart, just the same.

"More French . . . ," she said.

"Yes," Brandon answered. "It's something that I heard Jacques Fabienne once say to Margot. I've never forgotten it."

"What does it mean?" Chelsea asked.

Brandon shook his head. "Perhaps someday I'll be ready to tell you, but not yet."

When Chelsea started to protest, he

gently placed two fingers against her lips, stopping her.

"Now then," he said, "do you still want to read some more of Brooke's journal?"

After wiping her eyes again, Chelsea nodded.

20.

As Chelsea crossed the room to retrieve the old journal, she sensed feelings of concern. Not only had Brandon's story affected her deeply, there was no telling what Brooke's next entry might also hold for her. It had already been a momentous night, and she couldn't escape the feeling that there were more revelations to come.

There are so many secrets here at Lake Evergreen, she thought, *both old and new. Things that I never imagined learning but that keep presenting themselves to me just the same. What will I take from*

Brooke's journal this time? Will it be something that I'll enjoy knowing? Or might it be another upsetting disclosure that makes me wish I'd never begun this journey into her past?

After sitting down beside Brandon, she began reading the next entry aloud.

Monday, July 13, 1942, 8 00 P.M.

The day was a quiet one. As I sit upon the couch before my fireplace, my dog, Ike, lies asleep alongside me. So far, my days here at Lake Evergreen have been quiet and comforting. The war sometimes seems a million miles away, as if it isn't happening at all. Much of the time, I relish that sentiment. But then I think about Bill, and I feel guilty about being here in this lovely place where my existence is so peaceful. Sometimes it's almost as if I'm hiding away, like some fugitive who has committed a crime. For despite how much I love being at Lake Evergreen, I cannot escape the feeling that I should be back in Syracuse, again doing all that I can to support the home front. And that the more

I accomplish in that regard, the greater the chance that Bill will survive this war. A silly premise, I know, but there it is . . .

I must also admit that I've become hopelessly torn between these two vastly different worlds. My sense of duty now seems a siren's song, urgently beckoning me homeward. But at the same time, my love for this wonderful place exerts an almost unconquerable hold over me, a grip so tight that it makes me never want to leave. But leave one day I must, no matter how strong the urge to stay. For unlike Lake Evergreen, the real world—the one with bloodied beaches and with far darker waves upon which menacing warships prowl—is being rapidly torn apart by a terrible conflict. And so when I return, I'll do everything in my power to redouble my previous efforts. Then one day my dearest Bill and I will be together again, and all will be right. But until that time comes, I must hold on as best I can. Just as so many other lonely women are doing, while we collectively long for our men to return. . .

On a less somber note, tonight's din-

ner was a simple one. Some escalloped potatoes with a bit of precious ham thrown in, and a few stalks of fresh asparagus from my little victory garden. I finished the meal with another cup of the wonderful coffee that Greg gave me on the first day we met, and I'm rationing it to myself. That's a strange notion, I suppose. That is, to carefully allot myself bits of something that was supposed to have been rationed in the first place but wasn't! Maybe there's some poetic justice in that, I don't know. But what I do know is that Greg would think me silly, and he would likely laugh at me. Either way, his illicit treats are just too good to turn down. His old Packard is gone most afternoons, and my guess is that he's usually off somewhere, taking his landscape photos.

One could have a far worse neighbor. Greg is intelligent, gentle, and kind. And there is of course an artistic side to him, which is something that I've rarely encountered in the other men I've known. That he is one of the handsomest men I have ever seen goes without saying. I still cannot understand why he

has never married, because he must
have to chase women off with a broom—
especially now, when so many of our
men are away, fighting the war. I can al-
most understand how a lonely married
woman might become tempted to . . .

The sudden knocking on Brooke's kitchen door came loudly. When she went to answer it, she saw Greg standing there in the moonlight, a great smile beaming across his handsome face. In one hand he held a cold bottle of champagne, a highly precious commodity these days. Brooke couldn't remember the last time she had tasted some.

"Have you heard the news?" Greg asked her.

"War news?" Brooke asked as she opened the door and let him inside.

"We sank a German submarine today," Greg said. "She was the U-153, the radio said. After she was damaged by one of our submarine chasers, one of our destroyers sank her off the coast of Panama. That might not be huge news, Brooke.

But at least it's *good* news for a change. Is seems that the Nazis aren't the 'supermen' they claim to be!"

On an impulse, Greg put down the champagne and then suddenly took Brooke into his arms, his lips accidentally brushing hers. To her astonishment, Brooke felt a sudden, indescribable torrent of conflicting emotions rush through her. They held one another that way for some time, while gazing silently into each other's eyes. At long last Greg finally let her go, and he stepped back a bit.

"I'm sorry, Brooke," he said apologetically. "I guess I just got carried away. Do you forgive me?"

While trying to comprehend the emotional storm that had overcome her, at first Brooke found no answer. She was trembling a bit, and she guiltily realized that it was not the war news that was causing it but having again been in Greg's arms, instead. *A man who is not your husband,* her heart called out accusingly.

As all these thoughts and more rushed through her mind, she found that her legs were shaking. Not knowing what else to do, out of habit she nervously smoothed the bodice of her dress. To her added surprise, her palms had gone clammy.

"Yes . . . ," she finally said. "Yes, of course I forgive you. After all, it's good news, isn't it . . . ?"

Relieved that she had accepted his apology, Greg smiled again. "Thank you, Brooke," he said. "I promise that sort of thing will never happen again. I guess that not being out there with them makes me more of a newshound than most."

To her continued astonishment, Brooke found herself desperately wanting to again be held in Greg's strong arms. To help hide her feelings, she stared down at the floor. Her breathing had deepened, her heart was hammering, and she felt helpless to control them.

My God, she found herself wondering as she continued to avoid his entrancing gaze, *what is happening to me?* When she at last looked at him, she found it impossible to take her eyes from his.

Smiling again, Greg happily lifted the sweating champagne bottle high. "And besides," he said, "I've been looking for a decent excuse to crack this open. Will you join me?"

Brooke's first impulse was to ask him to leave. But at the same time, the physical and emotional memories of having just been in his arms dictated the opposite. Although she fought the feeling, in the end it was simply too strong to overcome.

"Yes," she finally answered. "That would be nice. We can sit by the fire."

"Do you have any ice and champagne flutes?" Greg asked, smiling. "It would be a shame to drink this wonderful stuff from coffee mugs."

"Sure," she answered.

Greg walked into the living room and sat down on the couch, causing Ike to find a new resting place atop the floor. When Brooke returned with an ice-filled bucket and a pair of leaded flutes, Greg popped and poured the champagne.

With a well-practiced touch, he gently clinked his glass against hers. "Here's to sunken German submarines!" he said. "May there be many more."

Brooke smiled a little. "Yes," she answered softly.

The champagne was excellent, and this time she knew better than to ask how he had acquired it. After taking another sip, she said, "Thank you for this, Greg. It's so good . . . I can't remember when last I had any."

After taking another sip, he smiled back. "It is good, isn't it?" he asked. "There's nothing in the world that dances upon the tongue so enticingly or so ephemerally."

"Are those your words?" she asked.

Greg shook his head. "No," he answered. "They're courtesy of my late father."

They then sat quietly for a time and enjoyed their champagne, the only sounds the crackling fire and the rhythmic ticking of the mantel clock. After a time, Greg lit a Chesterfield. When he finished it, he casually tossed the butt into the fire. He then regarded Brooke strangely, almost as if he were assessing her rather than admiring her. The change in his attitude was obvious, and it piqued her curiosity.

"What is it?" she asked.

"You know," he answered, "I never did

repay you for that wonderful whatchama-callit pie that you gave me the other day."

Brooke shook her head. "Don't be silly," she answered. "The coffee and sugar you gave me were far more valuable. Then there was the dance, and now you bring me champagne, too? It seems to me that *I'm* still in *your* debt."

"Well," he said, "I want to give you something more, anyway. And I know the perfect thing. It will be my honor."

Brooke was puzzled. "What are you talking about?" she asked.

To her surprise, Greg stood up in that torturous way of his and began limping toward the porch. "You'll see," he answered over one shoulder. "I'll be right back." Soon he was out the door and headed back toward his cottage.

While he was gone, Brooke tried to grasp what had just happened to her, but no ready answers came. She was shocked by how her heart had been so swiftly and raggedly torn in two, one part wishing that Greg would never return, and the other desperately wanting to be near him again.

Before she could make any sense of things, he returned bearing a sketch pad and a small cardboard box. He sat beside her again, then opened the box. Inside were some pieces of colored chalk. He then again regarded Brooke in the same odd way as before, his gaze piercing, almost analytic in nature.

"Don't move," he ordered her. "This won't take long, I promise."

As he sketched her, he positioned the pad so that she could watch him work. It began as only a rough outline, but as time went by and his fingers danced lightly over the paper, Brooke could almost feel her form taking shape there. While his talented hand continued to craft her likeness, it was as if he were literally caressing the same parts of her slightly trembling body. She could almost feel his deft fingers upon her as he re-created her lips, her breasts, her thighs. As the sensation grew stronger, she had no choice but to close her eyes and surrender to it completely. To both her fear and her delight, she now shamelessly wanted this man's hands upon her for real. There was no escaping her newfound desires now, despite how much her other half wanted to fight them. Her breathing soon became labored, and she felt a sudden and over-powering need to be taken by him, and by him alone . . .

"Brooke . . . ," she at last heard some-one say. "Brooke, I'm done."

At first she found the struggle to re-turn nearly impossible. But then her eyes opened, and she came back to reality. She looked admiringly at the sketch to find that Greg had not only captured her likeness but somehow the very nature of her illicit desire, as well. It was as if he too had fully undergone all that she had ex-perienced, and he wanted her to know it.

"My God . . . ," she breathed. "It's wonderful . . ."

"Thank you," he answered as he gently set the sketch pad on the coffee table. "Creating a lovely portrait is an easy thing when the subject is so beautiful."

Suddenly more overcome than ever, Brooke again did her best to defeat the new and burgeoning emotions swirling within her. She urgently wanted Greg to leave, yet she also desperately wanted him to stay. As the flickering firelight highlighted his chiseled features, she again found herself wanting to be utterly consumed by this amazing man—this artist, this powerful male presence that had so suddenly and unexpectedly entered her life.

On seeing the change in her, Greg gave Brooke a compassionate look. "Are you all right?" he asked. "You seem a bit pale."

With a rather unsteady hand, Brooke set her glass on the table. "I'm just tired," she answered. "And I'm not used to champagne. I thank you so much for bringing it, and for creating such a lovely likeness of me. But if you don't mind, I need to call it a night."

When Greg innocently patted her on one knee, his touch felt electric. She tried to hide the welcome sensation but wasn't at all certain whether she had succeeded.

"Sure," he said. "Do you mind if I take the rest of the champagne home? That stuff's hard to get, even for a scrounger like me."

"Of course not," Brooke answered.

When Greg smiled again it was as if she were seeing him for the very first time, for the man sitting before her had suddenly become a far different Gregory Butler than the one she had previously known. She now wanted him, and trying to deny it would be a pointless lie.

"Then I'll be going," he said as he stood and picked up the champagne bottle. He then also collected his drawing things, leaving the new sketch on the table for her. "But first," he added, "I'd like to ask you something."

"What is it?" she asked.

"May I paint your portrait while we're both here for the summer?" he asked. "I'd love to do it. Making that brief sketch of you just now gave me the idea."

At first, Brooke didn't know what to say. What she had just experienced had been so unsettling that she wasn't sure whether she wanted to go through anything like that again. Although torn about her decision, at last she relented.

"Well, yes . . . I suppose so," she answered tentatively. "Provided, of course, that you don't mind."

Greg smiled at her. "Mind?" he asked. "Are you serious? It would be my pleasure! I rarely have such beautiful subjects.

And thank you, Brooke. I look forward to starting."

"Well, good night then," Brooke said, her heart nearly breaking at the thought of his leaving.

"And good night to you, too," he answered. While cradling his things in both arms, he limped endearingly out onto the porch and was soon treading his way homeward.

Only moments after Greg's departure, Brooke's conflicting emotions collided yet again with an even greater intensity, and her eyes exploded into tears. She already missed his presence beyond all reason, and she badly wanted him to return.

My God, she thought. *What will become of me now? And of Greg? And, dare I say it, of* us . . . ?

Later, just before she went to bed, she wistfully looked at the framed photograph of Bill that she always kept on her nightstand, no matter where she traveled. It had been with her every day since Bill left, and she had lovingly brought it with her from Syracuse. Normally that picture granted her comfort. But while looking at it now, the only emotion she experienced was overpowering guilt. Before slipping between the sheets she placed the photo facedown atop the table, so that his newly condemning eyes could not look upon her as she slept. Somehow, in the space of less than an hour, her world had changed so vastly, so unexpectedly, that she could no longer bear her husband's gaze.

As she tried crying herself to sleep, she shed what she believed were unrequited tears. But what she didn't know—what she couldn't have known—was that Gregory Butler had experienced the same set of overwhelming emotions this night, as well. And that he, too, was finding sleep impossible to capture.

Momentarily stopping in her reading, Chelsea wiped her teary eyes.

"It is a terrible thing, being this way," she then read aloud to Brandon. *"I feel so guilty and torn, my heart suddenly a jumble of desire, guilt, joy, and sadness. What am I to do now? My conscience says that I should return to Syracuse as soon as*

possible and forget all about this man named Gregory Butler. But my heart is demanding that I stay and discover where all of these newfound feelings may take me. All I know for certain is that I must somehow decide. And although the outcome may have disastrous implications for everything I know and love, and I am quite unsure of where life is now leading me, I feel compelled to follow . . ."

With a sigh, Chelsea closed the old journal and placed it on the coffee table. *The same table where Brooke and Greg shared their champagne, so many years ago,* she thought. *And the exact spot where she first realized her great desire for him. How did their story end, I wonder? And perhaps even more important, am I still sure that I want to know?*

Brandon reached out and comfortingly touched her on one shoulder. "Are you all right?" he asked.

Chelsea shook her head. "I don't suppose that I'll be able to answer that question until we've learned everything that Brooke's journal has to offer," she answered. "Brooke wanted me to read it, but given what we've learned so far, I'm still at a loss to understand why."

"I know that it seems we've discovered the beginnings of an emotional affair," Brandon said. "But we still don't know whether Brooke and Greg ever acted on it."

"I know . . . ," Chelsea answered. When she next looked at him, she realized that it had been many hours since they had last eaten. "You must be ravenous," she said. "But it's a bit late to cook a full meal. I could rustle us up a couple of sand-wiches, if you want."

Brandon nodded. "That'd be good," he answered. "I could use something in my stomach besides alcohol."

At last, Chelsea smiled. "Consider it done," she said. "Is tuna salad okay?"

"Anything . . . ," he answered.

On impulse, she reached out and gen-tly brushed the hair from his forehead. "I'll be right back," she said.

Bearing two plates, Chelsea soon re-turned to the living room. When she reached the sofa, she smiled. Brandon lay fully stretched out, fast asleep and snoring lightly next to the dogs.

After returning the sandwiches to the kitchen, Chelsea tiptoed into her bedroom, found a woolen blanket, and used it to cover Brandon. Then she stood back and again regarded him, thinking. As he lay there in the firelight she took in his dark, wavy hair, his strong face, and his muscular body.

And then, suddenly, something stirred within her. It was a feeling of which, until this very moment, she had been less aware. But now, as she stood looking down at him in the quiet of the night, she at last felt it fully and it swelled her heart nearly to breaking. Totally overcome by it, for several moments she just stood there, watching him sleep.

And there it is, she thought joyously. *Like my dear grandmother, I too am falling in love with the man in the neighboring cottage. And also like Brooke, I've come to realize something else. I want him more than any man I've ever known. Before this moment, I thought I had loved others. But now, as I look down upon Brandon, I realize that I was wrong and that all the others in my life were mere dalliances. This is romantic love as it was meant to be— palpable, alive, overpowering in its intensity. But will Brandon ever be able to fully return my sentiments? Can he in fact ever overcome the loss of his fiancée and find the freedom to love again? Only time will tell, I suppose. And to find out, I must be willing to wait . . .*

Two hours later, Chelsea still found sleep elusive. The moonlight streamed through her bedroom window, coating everything in a slivery sheen, while the passing clouds created ephemeral shadows that glided, ghostlike, across the room. Perhaps her sleeplessness was from knowing that Brandon still dozed before the fireplace. But far more likely, she knew, it was her sudden realization that she had fallen fully and irretrievably in love with him that kept her awake. Just then she heard footsteps. Although they arrived lightly, she knew that they were his.

Turning in bed, she rose up on one elbow and looked toward the double doors that led into the living room. Then she saw him pause near one of the door frames, as if unsure. He looked like some wonderfully carved Greco-Roman relief as the last of the fireplace embers dimly glowed behind his tall silhouette.

"You're awake?" he asked quietly.

Chelsea nodded. "I couldn't sleep," she answered.

"Nor could I," Brandon said. Then silence reigned once more while he carefully considered his next words.

"May I join you?" he asked respectfully.

Suddenly, the tug on Chelsea's heart was far stronger than any before it. *I want him so badly,* she thought. *But is now the time? What would it say about me, about him . . . about . . . us?*

Taking a deep breath, she leaned forward a little. "I'd like that, Brandon," she said at last. "I really would. And I'd be lying to you if I said that I haven't thought about it. I'm just not sure that I'm ready for—"

Before she could finish her sentence, he was moving toward her. He approached quietly, then bent down and looked at her. At last she could clearly see his features, as they too were now highlighted by the full moon. She felt her heart beat even faster.

"You didn't hear me out, city girl," he said. "I just want to hold you."

With shaking hands, Chelsea turned over and pulled down the sheet and comforter on the other side of the bed. Still clothed, Brandon got into bed beside her. As he spooned her from behind, his body took on the shape of hers and she could feel his breath, warm and steady, against the nape of her neck. He felt so right lying there against her, far more so than any man before him.

"Thank . . . you," she heard him whisper as he neared the cusp of sleep.

"You're welcome," she whispered back.

Before closing her eyes, Chelsea took his free hand and held it against her beating heart.

21.

When Brandon awoke, the first thing he saw was Chelsea, sitting on the side of the bed. She was already showered and dressed. In her hands she held a mug of steaming black coffee.

"Hey there," she said quietly.

As Brandon rose up on one elbow, his head started to swim. After taking a deep breath, he ran his fingers back through his hair and then gratefully accepted the mug from Chelsea. The mind-clearing coffee was hot and good. At last he managed a smile. But some of the effects of the bourbon were still with him, and it showed.

"Bless you," he said after again sipping his coffee.

Chelsea smiled. "You're welcome," she answered.

Brandon looked at her apologetically. "So, uh . . . did I do anything inappropriate last night?" he asked. "I mean, I woke up in your bed but I'm still dressed. So unless you redressed me afterward, nothing happened, right?"

"Right."

"Thank God," he said.

Chelsea raised her eyebrows. "You're actually *glad* that nothing happened?" she asked.

"Sure," he answered.

"I don't get it."

Before replying, Brandon set the coffee mug atop the nightstand and gingerly clambered out of bed. "It's simple," he answered with a mischievous smile. "If something more *had* indeed happened, it'd be a crying shame if I couldn't remember it."

This time, Chelsea laughed fully. "I suppose that's true," she answered.

As Brandon stood there before her, with his hair mussed and a telltale five o'clock shadow on his face, Chelsea again felt overcome by his presence. They had slept side by side all night, his body curled up against hers, his breath warm and rhythmic against her neck. When at last she had awakened, it had been all she could do to leave his side and go make coffee.

It's still true, she thought. *The night wasn't playing tricks on me after all. Even in the cold light of day, I love this man. I can't deny it now, can't take my heart back to how it was before. . .*

Brandon turned and looked at the nightstand alarm clock. "Wow . . . ," he said. "It's already nine thirty."

"What time do you have to be at the hospital?" Chelsea asked urgently. "Sorry, but you were sleeping so soundly that I didn't have the heart to wake you."

"It's okay," he answered. "According to the rotation schedule, I'm off today." Then he smiled wryly and rubbed his forehead. "Good thing, too," he added. "So unless somebody requests a house call, the day is mine."

He then stepped closer and looked into Chelsea's eyes, sparking her physical need for him again. She could literally feel his male presence tempting her once more, which made part of her regret that nothing sexual had happened last night.

"So tell me," he said. "Shall we spend the day together?"

While trying to surreptitiously calm her excitement, Chelsea smiled and nodded. "I'd love that," she finally answered. "Do you suppose that we could go to the Blue Rooster and have lunch? I'd love to see it."

Brandon picked up the coffee mug and took another appreciative swallow. Slowly but surely, he was starting to come alive.

"Absolutely," he answered. "But first I've got to go home and clean up. I'm a mess."

"You go and get yourself presentable," Chelsea said. "When you come back, we'll take off."

"Sounds like a plan," he answered.

"Thank you for this," Chelsea said to Brandon.

Happy to be with her, Brandon smiled. "Well, it wasn't like my social schedule was full! And besides, I'm having a good time."

Chelsea happily looked around as she and Brandon sauntered through downtown Serendipity. The weather was nice, with puffy clouds and a light, cooling breeze. The main street was just like Chelsea had expected, with aged brick buildings, narrow sidewalks, and coin-operated parking meters. Their destinations a mystery, cars and pickup trucks bustled back and forth. Seeing Serendipity for the first time made Chelsea wonder just how much, or how little, perhaps, it had changed since her grandmother last visited back in 1942.

Serendipity had no large chain stores or franchise restaurants, it seemed. Instead, Serendipity's much humbler businesses seemed to exude a quaint mom-and-pop quality. It was as if no matter who walked in, he or she would immediately be welcomed as both a customer and a friend.

Chelsea and Brandon soon passed by an old-time barbershop with an honest-to-goodness barber's pole mounted out front, an ancient shoe-repair place that looked as if it were still serving Civil War officers, and an old-fashioned soda shop complete with an awning, a marble counter, and an original soda-mixing machine. Most of the businesses weren't so vintage, but those that were seemed especially welcoming, and their charming ambience put Chelsea at ease.

"Before we go to lunch," she asked Brandon, "is there by chance an art supply store in town?"

Brandon nodded. "The hardware store carries some of that stuff," he answered. "Why?"

"I'd like to paint while I'm up here. I don't need a lot of things—just the basics, to get me started."

"So you paint, eh?" he asked. "Guess that makes sense, you being an art teacher."

"Yeah," Chelsea answered, "although I don't think I'll ever be as good as my grandmother Brooke was. She's the one who first taught me. Plus, I also took some formal studio training in college."

Moments later they made way for a young couple coming in the opposite direction. The wife was pushing a brand-new baby carriage. As they passed, their baby boy looked up at Chelsea and gurgled happily.

Brandon snorted. "That figures," he said.

"What does?" Chelsea asked.

"You being able to instantly attract men of *any* age," he answered.

As Chelsea laughed a bit, her thoughts returned to earlier that day, while Brandon had been freshening up at his cottage. She had called Allistaire Reynolds to request that he arrange for the direct deposit of her checks and for her mail to be forwarded. When Chelsea told him that it was delivered by boat, he had laughed.

Antiques hound that he was, when she eagerly described the wonderful old Chris-Craft she had inherited, she distinctly heard him gasp. Then his lawyerly instincts took over, and he asked her if it was registered and insured. To her mild chagrin, she said that she didn't know. No matter, Allistaire said. Just send him the paperwork that Jacques had given her, and he would take of it.

After buying Chelsea's art supplies and storing them in Brandon's Jeep, they ventured onward. Soon Brandon stopped before a picturesque café.

"So this is it?" Chelsea asked. "It's cute!"

"Yes," Brandon answered. "It certainly is."

When Chelsea had first visited Beauregard's, she was struck by how many of the customers were men. But as she and Brandon entered the Blue Rooster, it became equally clear that the ladies of Serendipity had claimed this place as their own special province. The café was nearly full of women, most of them eagerly chatting away as they picked at their lunches. Chelsea had vacationed in France several years ago, and she had loved it there. To her delight, the Blue Rooster seemed a near-perfect replica of a Parisian café, and it still looked exactly as Brooke had described in her journal.

Brandon shepherded Chelsea to one of the empty booths, where they got comfortable. As she set her purse down beside her, Chelsea smiled broadly.

"This place is absolutely charming!" she said. "It looks like something that belongs on the Left Bank! I would have never guessed . . . How long has it been here?"

"Since the early twenties," Brandon answered. "Like Beauregard's, this too is a family business, but older. Because Quebec lies just across the Saint Lawrence River, there's a lot of French influence around here. The Blue Rooster is still owned by Emily Rousseau, although I don't know for how much longer."

"Why?" Chelsea asked.

"Well," Brandon explained, "Emily's story is a bit like Jenny's. Her father, Henri, owned this place first, and on his death she inherited it. Emily lives in the upstairs apartment. She must be at least eighty by now, and bless her heart, she still works here every day. She was an only child, and her husband's gone. Sadly, they were childless. Emily loves this place so much that I highly doubt she will ever sell, even though she's the last of the line. Once she's gone, God only knows what will happen to it."

Then Brandon looked around the Blue Rooster wistfully, like it was some sort of treasure to be protected and preserved.

"I'm wise enough to know that nothing lasts forever, Chelsea," he said. "Even so, it'd be a crying shame if somebody turned this wonderful spot into a damn Starbucks . . ."

"I would hate to see that, too," Chelsea answered.

Just then a young waitress carrying two glasses of ice water approached their booth. "Hi, Brandon," she said pleasantly. "Who's your friend?"

Brandon gestured toward the waitress. "Missy Tomlinson," he answered, "I'd like you to meet Chelsea Enright. She's from Syracuse and spending her summer out at Lake Evergreen."

After putting down the glasses, Missy held out one hand and Chelsea shook it. "Pleased to meetcha," she said. "So, do you guys know what you'd like for lunch? We have a great special today."

"What is it?" Chelsea asked.

"Truman's Tomato Sandwiches," Missy answered. "They're really good."

Chelsea immediately felt a tingle run up her spine. *Truman's Tomato Sandwiches . . . ?*

The name had made an impact on Brandon, as well. He looked over at Chelsea and said, "How does that sound to you?"

Chelsea finally snapped out of her reverie and nodded. "That sounds great," she answered.

"Okay, then," Brandon said to Missy. "We'll have two of those, and a couple of iced teas. Oh, and would you also bring us some of Emily's deep-fried pickle slices?"

"Good choices," Missy replied. After replacing her pencil over one ear, she began wending her way back toward the kitchen.

Her mouth slightly agape, Chelsea stared blankly at Brandon.

"Yeah, I know," he said. "And the truth is, I never made the connection until just now. Legend has it that Emily started serving them here sometime during World War II. It's always been her little secret where the recipe came from. Anyway, they became so popular that they've stayed on the menu ever since.

"Damn," Brandon added. "The cottage, the journal, the photos . . . and then I bring you here, where something on the menu seems so suggestive of your late grandmother. Do you suppose . . . ?"

Chelsea shook her head. "I've been

doing so much supposing lately that I don't know *what* to think anymore. But it does seem too great a coincidence, especially since we now know that Emily and Brooke knew one another. Do you think that I could meet Emily?"

Brandon give her a wink. "You bet," he answered.

Missy soon returned, bearing a tray with three plates and two glasses of iced tea. The sandwiches were made with dense French bread, thick mayonnaise, and huge heirloom tomato slices. As Missy put them down, she smiled. Finally, she also served a small dishful of seasoned, deep-fried pickle slices.

Chelsea gestured toward her sandwich. "I hear that these are really good," she said to Missy. "Can you tell me how they're made?"

Missy shook her head adamantly. "I wouldn't, even if I could," she answered. "Everybody asks! But the only person who knows is Emily, and she's not talking. To keep the secret safe, she still makes every one of those sandwiches herself."

"Could you please tell her that I'm

here?" Brandon asked. "I'd like to introduce her to Chelsea."

"Sure," Missy answered. "I'll let her know."

As Missy walked away, Chelsea took a bite of her sandwich to find that it was the intriguingly flavored mayonnaise that made it so special. As a final touch, Emily had carefully trimmed off the bread crusts.

"So what's the verdict?" Brandon asked Chelsea in between bites.

Just as Chelsea was about to answer, she saw an elderly woman approaching. She walked with unusual steadiness for one so old. Like Brooke, she had remained rather tall and slim in her twilight years. Her short hair was snow white, her eyes were blue, and her face was deeply etched with both the weight of her life experiences and the natural passage of her years. Along the way, she stopped at several tables to greet her regulars. When Emily finally reached their booth she smiled first at Chelsea, then at Brandon. Her manner seemed comforting, Chelsea thought, much like Brooke's had been.

"Hello, handsome," she said to Brandon, her voice revealing the slightest hint of a French accent. "May I sit down beside you, *mon cher*?"

Brandon immediately slid to one side. "Of course," he said.

Emily sat down and patted his hand. "So how have you been?" she asked.

"I'm fine, Emily, and you?" he answered.

"Oh, I'm all right," Emily answered with a casual gesture of one hand. Then she gave Chelsea a sly wink. "For a woman who's lived so long, that is!"

Chelsea smiled and held out one hand. "I'm Chelsea Enright," she said. "I'm a new friend of Brandon's."

Emily shook her hand. "Pleased to meet you, Chelsea Enright," she said. "I gather that you've never visited the Blue Rooster before today?"

"No," Chelsea answered, "but I love it."

"It's been in the Rousseau family for many decades," Emily said as she looked around lovingly. "My father built it with his own two hands. Sadly, I am the last of us."

As Chelsea searched the old woman's face, she tried imagining Emily as a far younger woman, much the way Brooke had appeared in those old black-and-white photos back at her cottage. Like Brooke, Chelsea concluded, Emily had been attractive in her day.

"So tell me," Chelsea said, "do you ever give out the recipe for these wonderful sandwiches? I'd love to have it."

Emily smiled, then shook her head. "*Non,*" she answered. "It was confided to me long ago by a dear friend who invented it. If I had a nickel for every time someone asked me that, I'd be a wealthy woman! Anyway, I promised her that I would never divulge it."

"I see . . . ," Chelsea said. "She must have been a very good cook."

"The best," Emily answered. "And because I'm French," she added with a smile, "that is a real compliment."

"So in lieu of getting the recipe, may I ask you something else?" Chelsea inquired.

"*Bien sûr,*" Emily answered. "Any friend of Brandon's is a friend of mine."

"Your friend's name was Brooke Bartlett, right?" Chelsea asked quietly.

A look of astonishment conquered Emily's face. "Why, yes . . . ," she said softly. "Yes, it was. But how did you know that?"

"Because I'm her granddaughter," Chelsea answered.

"Oh, my goodness . . . ," Emily whispered. "Can it be . . . ?"

Awestruck, Emily stared quizzically at Chelsea for a time. At last she smiled and nodded slightly.

"I knew that she had a granddaughter," Emily said. "And although it has been such a long time since I've seen Brooke, I can recognize something of her in you. Especially around the eyes . . . And also like Brooke, you are very pretty."

"Thank you," Chelsea answered.

Then Chelsea realized something, and her heart lurched a bit. *Emily doesn't know,* she thought. *And I'm the one who must tell her . . .*

Chelsea reached out and touched the old woman's hand. "I'm sorry to have to say this, Emily," Chelsea said, "but Gram passed away recently."

Emily's eyes widened with shock. Soon after, her wrinkled mouth moved but no words escaped her lips. Then she burst into tears and instinctively covered her face with her palms. Chelsea took up one of the spare napkins lying on the table and handed it to her. As Emily dried her eyes, she did her best to compose herself.

"*Mon Dieu . . . mon Dieu . . . ,*" she whispered. At last she found the strength to gaze back into Chelsea's eyes. "How did Brooke die?" she asked. "Was she ill?"

Chelsea shook her head. "She died peacefully in her sleep," she answered. "A stroke, probably."

Emily sniffed a little, then dabbed at her eyes some more. "I am glad that she didn't suffer," she said. "But I can't believe that she is gone. She still meant a great deal to me."

"And to all of us, as well," Chelsea said.

"Of course," Emily answered. "But how did you know that it was Brooke's recipe?"

Chelsea recounted how she came to be at Lake Evergreen and how she had also inherited Brooke's recipe book. When she finished, Emily nodded.

"I still remember that recipe book," she said. "Brooke and her mother, Gwendolyn, used to come into the café occasionally, where we became great friends. And I oftentimes visited the cottage. One rainy afternoon Brooke was making us lunch, and she hit on the idea of the sandwich.

After naming it, she very graciously let me have the recipe for my use here at the café. In days gone by, I traveled to Syracuse from time to time to visit her, but then Father Time caught up with me and made it difficult."

Pausing for a moment, Emily secured Missy's attention and requested a cup of mint tea. Missy quickly nodded, then headed back toward the kitchen.

"But after her car accident, Brooke never returned here," Emily added. "I of course knew that she had become confined to a wheelchair. Even so, her never revisiting Lake Evergreen always seemed odd to me. With help, she could have certainly returned to her beloved cottage and also here, to my little café," she said, her voice cracking a bit. "And when you consider both how much she loved it up here and our ongoing friendship, her continued refusal to return seems even stranger. After I stopped going to see her, we corresponded and talked on the phone from time to time, but it wasn't the same as being face-to-face. Now she's gone, and along with her went my last chance to say good-bye . . ."

"I'm sorry," Chelsea replied. "We couldn't understand why she never returned here, either. She was equally adamant about keeping the cottage, which in itself is also very strange, because my mother and father have absolutely no interest in it. Whenever we tried asking Brooke about it, a wistful look came over her face. Because the subject always seemed to upset her so much, we eventually stopped asking. But I know for a fact that Brooke still loved her cottage, even though she never saw it again. For my mother and father, it has become little more than a distant memory. Then I inherited it, and I've come to understand how wonderful it is."

Missy soon appeared with Emily's tea. After taking a welcome sip, the old woman sighed.

"In France, we have a saying," she said as she stared sadly at her teacup. *"Plutôt que terminer deux amis, la mort de l'un a une façon de se joindre à eux pour toujours."*

"What does that mean?" Chelsea asked.

"'Rather than parting two old friends,

the death of one has a way of joining them forever,'" Emily answered.

Silence reigned as the three of them sat quietly for a time. Soon, a question occurred to Chelsea. She knew that Emily was still upset, and because of that, she almost left it unsaid. But she very much wondered if Emily could shed any light on something for her, so she finally decided to ask.

"May I inquire about something else?" Chelsea said.

"Of course," Emily answered.

"You also knew a man named Gregory Butler, right?" Chelsea asked.

"*Mais oui,*" she answered. "I knew him well, in fact. Greg and Brooke were dear friends. That's how he and I got acquainted. His cottage stood next to hers. Up until his death a few years ago, he still came in for lunch from time to time. In fact, seeing you and Brandon here together is almost like going back in time and sitting once again across from Brooke and Greg."

At last, Emily managed to let go a little smile. "He was very handsome in those days," she added, "like a movie

star, he was. If memory serves, just before Brooke left for good, he was in the
process of painting her portrait. He was
an excellent artist, you know. And he
never married, which always seemed
strange to me."

"Did you ever meet Bill Bartlett, my
grandfather?" Chelsea asked.

Emily shook her head. "*Non,*" she said.
"It was my understanding that he had
finished his officer's training and had
shipped out. Shortly after that, Brooke
just disappeared."

Chelsea scowled. "What do you mean
disappeared?" she asked.

"*Disappeared* is probably the wrong
word," Emily said, "although that's certainly how it felt to me at the time. During
that summer, Brooke was staying there
alone. Then one day she just packed up
and left far earlier than expected. It was
sometime in mid-August, I think. Later
on I learned from Gregory that she never
said good-bye to him, either, and he
seemed quite saddened by it. That part
of it I never understood—especially when
his cottage was so nearby hers, and it

would have been quite easy for her to properly bid him adieu."

Chelsea took a moment to look quizzically at Brandon, as if he might be able to supply her with some answers. But all he could do was shrug and shake his head.

Chelsea was dying to know more. But yet again she hesitated, because she didn't want to tarnish Emily's memories of Brooke. Even so, Chelsea was sitting across from perhaps the only living person who might be able to help her solve the increasingly beguiling puzzle that was Brooke Bartlett's life. For better or worse, she decided to press forward.

"I have some old photos of Greg and Brooke together," Chelsea said. "And in each one, it seems that they were close. *Very* close, if you know what I mean. Can you shed any light on that? I'm not asking you to violate any confidences. But if there are other things that you know and wouldn't mind sharing, I'd be very much in your debt."

Emily's answer came without hesitation. "*Non,*" she replied. "I do not believe that there was ever anything physical

between them, if that's what you're sug-
gesting. Brooke loved her husband, and
she worried for him day and night. He
died in the war, but Brooke never told me
how. Her heart was very closed about
that, so I didn't press her."

Just then, Emily's countenance sobered even more. "Even so," she added
quietly, "Brooke once told me something
heartfelt, something that made me feel
sorry for her."

"What was that?" Chelsea asked.

Emily sighed. "The war years were hard
times," she answered. "Not just for the
soldiers, but for their women, too. Brooke
told me that she was developing deep
feelings for Greg—feelings against which
she was desperately fighting. But she also
swore that she hadn't acted on them, and
I believed her."

Emily sadly shook her head. "In the
end, only Brooke and Gregory knew," she
said, "and they're both gone now. But if
they *were* truly in love, then why did she
leave so suddenly and never come back?
And why did she not say good-bye to
him? It's a riddle, I grant you. And like

many riddles, its unraveling may prove quite impossible."

Feeling more confused than ever, Chelsea sat back in her booth.

A riddle indeed, she thought. *More and more, it seems, the only answers are to be found in Brooke's journal. . .*

"Is there anything else that you can tell me?" Chelsea asked Emily.

"Just one thing," Emily answered. She then pointed to the vase of flowers standing on the table. Their blossoms were violet, and they resembled daisies.

"Are you familiar with those?" Emily asked.

"No," Chelsea answered. "What about you, Brandon?"

"I see them all over the place in the summertime," he answered. "But I've never known what they're called."

"They're coneflowers," Emily answered, "and they grow wild around here. In honor of Brooke, each day I place them on the café tables. I pay a local boy to go and pick them for me."

Coneflowers . . . ? Chelsea thought. Something about that word was tugging at her mind, she realized. But she couldn't understand why, so she let it go. "That's a lovely gesture," Chelsea said. "But why did you choose coneflowers?"

"They were Brooke's favorite," Emily answered. "I once asked her why, but she refused to say. Then one day when I knew that she was coming in, on a lark I placed a vase full of them on the table that I had reserved for her. I also liked the way they looked and smelled, and so I've been doing it every summer since."

Then Emily became quiet for a time, thinking. After a few more moments, she again summoned Missy to their booth.

"Could you please go and get my book for me?" Emily asked her. "You know the one I mean? It's upstairs, on my night-stand."

"I think so," Missy answered. "The green one, right?"

"Yes," Emily answered.

As Missy scurried away, Emily looked thoughtfully into Chelsea's eyes. "There's something that I want you to have," she said. "Your grandmother gave it to me long ago, just before she left Lake Ever-green for the final time. It was one of her favorite things, and I have cared for it long enough. At long last, the time has come for her granddaughter to possess it."

Missy soon returned. In one hand she carried an old book, which she handed to Emily. Emily rubbed its cover thoughtfully for a time, as if she were saying goodbye to an old friend. When at last she surrendered it to Chelsea, Chelsea saw that it was an old copy of *Leaves of Grass,* by Walt Whitman. Its dark green cover had long since faded and appeared to be made of buckram board.

"Have you read it?" Emily asked Chelsea.

Chelsea shook her head.

"That was Brooke's favorite book," Emily said. "She loved to sit on her cottage porch and peruse it. She was quite fond of claiming that everyone should read it at least once in his or her lifetime. Then one day, to my great surprise she left it to me. You'll notice that there is a slight gap between two of the middling pages. I suggest that you open it there and look inside."

When Chelsea did so, she saw two ancient violet coneflowers had been pressed inside. Fearing that they might fall apart if touched, she left them undisturbed as she gently set the old book atop the table.

"More coneflowers . . . ," she said to Emily. "Did you put them there?"

Emily shook her head. *"Non, ma chère,"* she answered. "They were already there when Brooke first left the book behind for me. Later on I asked Brooke about them, but again she did not answer. She had so many secrets, it seems . . ."

Emily looked into Chelsea's eyes. "And now," she said, "you must forgive this old woman, for I have grown tired. I am very happy to have met you, Chelsea Enright, and I hope that you will return to my humble café. It would be lovely to talk to you some more, I'm sure. And please know that I will say a prayer for the woman whom we both loved so much."

Then she stood. "For now, at least, I must say adieu."

"Good-bye, Emily," Chelsea said. "And thank you."

"Au revoir," Brandon added.

While Emily slowly walked away, Chelsea looked back down at the faded, lifeless coneflowers. They seemed so delicate lying there atop the old book, as if the slightest breeze might easily destroy them.

Secrets pressed inside yet more secrets . . . , she thought.

But where are they all leading me?

22.

Later that night, Brandon was helping Chelsea prepare another dinner recipe from Brooke's journal. As they worked together in the kitchen, she smiled at him. Brandon wasn't much of a cook, and he willingly admitted it. The red and white checked apron he wore seemed to hold more ingredients than did the bowl into which they were supposed to be going. Chelsea found his efforts endearing, and his obvious desire to help drew her even closer to him.

Tonight's selection was something that Brooke had labeled Roosevelt's Roast

Beef, the ingredients for which Brandon and Chelsea had purchased in Serendipity, right after visiting Emily. When Chelsea had chosen the recipe earlier that morning, she saw that Roosevelt's Roast Beef was in fact a baked beef strip loin, with a side recipe for a bourbon-mushroom sauce that sounded wonderful.

While Brandon diced the onions, Chelsea again consulted the recipe book. First, she seasoned the meat on both sides with salt and pepper. With that done, she then placed the roast into the oven at 450° F. Soon after, she began helping Brandon with the bourbon-mushroom sauce, which called for mushrooms, onions, bourbon, and minced garlic. When the roast had cooked for forty-five minutes, she served it along with the sauce, some mashed potatoes, and a green salad.

"My God, Brooke was a wonder in the kitchen," Brandon said admiringly, just before popping another piece of beef into his mouth.

Chelsea smiled. "She was, wasn't she?" she answered. "Especially when you consider that all of the recipes in that book are of her own making."

"For sure," Brandon said. Then he gave Chelsea a sly smile. "And her only grand-daughter's no slouch in the kitchen, either."

Chelsea laughed a little. "Why thank you, Dr. Yale," she said. "Even so, I could have never done it without Brooke's help from the great beyond."

After cleaning up the dishes, Chelsea and Brandon took their coffee, along with Brooke's journal, out onto Chelsea's porch. Dark clouds were gathering, and no boats braved the gray, whitecapped waves. If it rained, Chelsea realized, it would be for the first time since she had come to Lake Evergreen. Brandon picked up the journal and looked at it thoughtfully, wondering what its next entry might tell them.

"May I read it to you, this time?" he asked Chelsea.

"Sure," she answered.

After finding the appropriate page, he gave Chelsea a questioning glance. "It's blotched in places here," he said, "like some of her tears fell on the pages. Are you sure that you want to go on?"

As Chelsea steeled herself, she turned

and cast her eyes across the waves. *More heartache to come?* she wondered.

"Yes, Brandon," she finally answered. "I want to hear it, no matter what."

Just as the first raindrops fell, Brandon began reading aloud:

Wednesday, August 5, 1942, 9:00 P.M.

Two more weeks have passed. I've been crying tonight, and my tears are falling upon these journal pages, even as I write them. Although the reasons for my distress are clear enough, the solution to stopping it remains impossibly elusive. Since I realized my love for Greg, my heart has been in a constant battle with my conscience. I am still smitten with him, while my dear husband trains in the art of war, so as to help save our very way of life.

My God, have I become one of those women about whom I've been so critical, the ones who betray their husbands, despite how much they claim to love them? Because I haven't consummated my love for Greg, I would like to believe that I have yet to join their trai-

torous ranks. Nor can I, if I ever again want to look my husband in the face. But my heart asks, which is the greater trial? A guilt-ridden, illicit physical affair or a long-distance one without sexual intimacy?

I have also become strangely torn about Bill ever coming home, a conflict that until only two weeks ago I believed could have never existed within me. If he doesn't survive, will my feelings for Greg at last be set free? And if Bill does return, how will my heart deal with it? Will I still love him as I once did? Or because of my newfound feelings for Greg, will my ardor wither at the mere sight of my husband? Will my heart then compare one to the other and find one lacking? And if so, which one?

Although I have of course seen Greg since my last journal entry, because the last two weeks have passed rather un-eventfully, I still can't tell how he really feels about me, and the mystery is driv-ing me mad. He has begun painting the portrait he promised me, and it is nearly half-done. We talk casually as he works, his paint and brushes busily creating my likeness while I do my best to sit still. The process is perhaps more arduous for me than it is for him, given that I can't help but wish that it were his fingertips caressing my skin, rather than his brushes caressing the canvas . . .

The slightest possibility that he loves me as I do him makes me shudder with a great fear the likes of which I have never known. While part of me desperately wishes it to be true, the other half of my soul knows that nothing worse could befall the three of us. For unrequited love is, by its very nature, terrible enough. But true, requited love is a self-fulfilling prophecy . . .

I should go back to Syracuse, I know, and try to forget all about this man named Gregory Butler. But in the end, what good would it do? Having just built his cottage, he surely will keep returning to Lake Evergreen for many summers to come. And if so, then what am I to do? If Bill survives the war, am I to never come back here simply because of my unresolved feelings for Greg? Or if I do, would it prove too painful, too guilt-inducing, too selfish?

Either way, what happened today was another step toward what I fear may be inevitable, and it has made my dilemma even more difficult to bear . . .

While struggling to make the climb, Brooke felt some sweat trickle down her forehead, forcing her to again wipe her face with a handkerchief. Greg was several paces ahead of her as he led her up the rather steep mountain trail.

This was no well-established hiking trail, Brooke realized. Heavily strewn with rocks and brush, it was more like some narrow, abandoned goat path than any clearly defined mountain route she had ever seen. All of which jibed with what Greg told her before they set out—that only the locals knew about this path, and that it was seldom used. He had impishly refused to tell her where they were going, saying only that once they arrived, the trek would be worth it. He hadn't climbed this trail since he was a teenager, he had added happily, so it would be like he too were going there for the first time.

It had all started when he had shown

up at her door early that morning, glee-fully holding a wicker picnic basket in one hand. "We're leaving," he had told her, and he wouldn't take no for an an-swer. In the end, Brooke had agreed. Not because she had been eager to make an exhausting slog, but as a way to be close to him. Her guilt had yet again haunted her heart as she made ready to go but she pushed it aside, telling herself that there was in fact nothing wrong with two friends merely going for a walk. But his unex-pected invitation meant far more than that for her, and in her heart she knew it.

After a short drive in Greg's Packard, they had pulled off Schuyler Lane and driven another one hundred yards or so up an even more desolate dirt road. On stopping the car before a barbed wire fence that bore an ominous NO TRESPASSING sign, Greg forced open a ramshackle gate and bade Brooke through it. They then walked across an adjoining field until they reached the base of a small mountain and began climbing upward. Greg had a large-caliber Browning pistol stuck in his belt, and when Brooke asked him why, his one-word answer had been, "Bears."

That had been an hour ago, and Brooke was tiring. So far, the climb had produced few memorable vistas, given that the entire mountainside was heavily laden with trees. Nor could she know how much longer it might take to reach their destination. Plus, the climb had made her tired, and she had been scratched by the brambles. Despite being with Greg, she was nearing the end of her patience.

"How much farther?" Brooke shouted up at him.

Greg laughed. "Just another ten minutes or so," he shouted over his shoulder. "Are you doing okay? I promise that it'll be worth it."

"Ten more minutes I can do," Brooke answered. "But any more than that, and you might have a mutiny on your hands."

"Impossible . . ." Greg laughed. "You forget, my dear, that I'm the one with the gun!"

In the end, Greg's promise proved true. Soon the terrain leveled out, and they were standing at the edge of the woods. Hand in hand, they walked out onto a flat, grassy meadow.

The deep-green field perched atop the

little mountain was lovely. Surrounded on three sides by dense forest, the clear side opposite Brooke and Greg looked north and ended in a vertical cliff. As they neared it, Brooke became ever more impressed by the beauty of this place. At last they reached the cliff's edge, where, still hand in hand, they gazed at the sprawling terrain that stretched out below them.

From where they stood, they could see the silvery ribbon that was the Saint Lawrence River, flowing northeasterly to the sea. Just beyond it lay the green patchwork that was Quebec. It was a dazzling sight, and Brooke realized that Greg had been right—it was indeed worth the climb.

"Is there a name for this place?" Brooke asked.

Greg put down his gun and picnic basket, then he lit a cigarette. "Yes," he answered. "It's called Red Rock Mountain."

"Why 'Red Rock'?" Brooke asked.

Greg smiled at her. "Look around," he answered.

While still standing at the edge of the cliff, Brooke turned and took a closer look at the meadow. She now noticed obscured outcroppings of reddish stone here and there, as if they were hiding in the grass. She had also seen some during her climb. The lovely and unusual rocks seemed familiar, but she couldn't grasp why.

"Still don't understand?" Greg asked.

"I see the pinkish rocks," she answered. "And I recognize them from someplace, but I can't remember where."

Before answering, Greg smiled and sat down on the grass, then bade Brooke to do the same. "In your very own cottage, that's where," he answered.

"Huh?"

"Your *fireplace*," he answered. "The hearth is made of rose quartz. There's a lot of it around here. I suspect that when your father had your cottage built, the contractor suggested it."

While smiling at the realization, Brooke gathered her arms about her knees. "Thank you for this," she said. "As far as I know, I'm the first in our family to come here."

Greg opened the picnic basket and removed a small tablecloth, which he spread out on the grass. He then produced a serving dish, a bottle of red wine, a large chunk of cheese, a loaf of fresh bread, and two wineglasses. Using the knife from his belt sheath, he cut the bread and cheese, then arranged the pieces on the plate. He opened the wine, poured two glassfuls, and handed one to Brooke.

Brooke smiled. "It seems that you've thought of everything," she said.

"The least I could do," he answered, "considering the way I kidnapped you this morning. And besides," he added, "the best things in life are often the simplest." Smiling, he raised his glass. "Here's to 'a jug of wine, a loaf of bread, and thou' . . ."

Brooke smiled and also took a sip of wine. "Another quote from your father?" she asked.

Greg took a final drag on his cigarette, then stubbed it out in the grass. "Nope," he answered. "Omar Khayyám."

They ate and drank in silence for a time as the wind waved the grass to and fro and the clouds raced across the sky. The clouds seemed to travel faster up here, Brooke realized, just as the past two weeks had seemingly done, since her epiphany about Greg. Then she looked at him, thinking.

It was true after all, she realized, as she watched him sitting there in the grass. She did still love him. She had feared that with the passage of time she might not feel the same about him, as if some spell had been cast upon her from which she would suddenly awaken. But that had not happened. She loved this man, and there could be no going back. But she must never consummate her love for Greg, for doing so would forever seal her betrayal and take her heart to a place from which it would likely never return. So far, all of her time spent with Greg could be explained away—at least to her own satisfaction. But if the unthinkable happened, she knew that it would forever tarnish her conscience.

Even so, another part of her wanted it to happen, wanted to willingly give herself over to whatever his eager body might demand from her. She had thought about it over and over again, in the short space of time since her feelings for him had fully burst forth. How he might take her, how she would respond to him, and the illicit, secret favors they would grant to one another. Bill was the only man she had ever been with. But Bill had been gone for a long time, and her body yearned for satisfaction—so much so that the temptation of lying with Greg was nearly more than she could resist. And she knew something else, too. Trying to deny these feelings now, as she sat beside him atop this windblown mountain, would be a monumental lie.

My heart has come to a dreadful place, she thought. *A place so foreign yet familiar. So wrong and yet so exhilarating. So tempting yet so dangerous . . .*

She then watched as Greg again rummaged around in the wicker basket for a few moments. On finding what he wanted, he removed it from the basket and he handed it to Brooke.

It was a copy of Walt Whitman's *Leaves of Grass.* The book's front and rear covers were made from green buckram boards, giving one the impression of grass. Brooke opened it to see that it also included some striking illustrations, in both color and black-and-white. She then thumbed back to the inside cover, where she saw something that Greg had written. It said:

August 5, 1942
For Brooke. May this book bring you
as much pleasure as it has brought me.
Fondly, Gregory Butler

Brooke looked at him and smiled. "I love it," she said. "But you didn't have to do this. I can tell that you've owned it for a while."

Greg nodded. "That's true," he said. "It's the 1940 edition. And yes, I have enjoyed it very much, but I now want you to have it."

While assigning this moment to her memory, Brooke smiled and rubbed her palms over the surface of the book.

"Thank you, Greg," she said. "I'll always treasure it."

"You're welcome," he answered. "Just as I will always treasure the moment I gave it to you."

Greg then lay back on the grass and laced his long fingers beneath his head. The clouds were high and light, and he too noticed that they seemed to cross the sky faster up here. He was wearing the same clothes today as when Brooke had first met him: a tan work shirt, matching pants, and work boots. As he fished around in one pocket for another cigarette, his face took on a look of mild surprise.

"What is it?" Brooke asked.

Greg removed his hand from his pocket and opened it. In his palm there lay a small gathering of coneflower seeds, some of the same group that he had been planting when he first met Brooke.

Greg smiled. "More seeds," he answered. "I'd forgotten that I hadn't planted them all. The ones back at my cottage have already started coming up."

But as he began to replace them in his pocket, Brooke stopped him. "Let's plant them here," she said.

Greg thought for a moment. "But this land isn't ours," he answered, "and we're already trespassing, as it is. I'm not sure that we should—"

"But you said that some of the locals also come here, right?" she protested. "So how is anyone to know who did it?"

Greg grinned. "Why, Mrs. Bartlett," he said. "I never knew that you were so devious."

As Brooke lay down beside him, she grinned in return. "Well, Mr. Butler," she said, "I suppose that's what I get for keeping company with a rogue like you."

But there was more to her request, Brooke knew. Given her unsettled relationship with Greg, she couldn't be entirely sure whether she would ever return to Lake Evergreen, much less to this remote and beautiful spot. And because of that she wanted to mark the place somehow, to tell the world that someone had been here and had planted coneflower seeds where they would likely never reach on their own. And that if those seeds should grow, and the resulting flowers return every spring, then perhaps a part of her time with Greg would go on living here year after year, even if her love for him did not.

As if he had grasped the deeper meaning of her request, he nodded. On sitting up, he dug out a small area of fresh earth with his knife, carefully planted the seeds, and then covered them again. Saying nothing, he then gazed deeply into her eyes.

"Thank you," she said.

"You're welcome," he answered quietly.

And then, as Brooke watched, his expression changed yet again. This time it became one of hunger, a yearning, a need to have something within him satisfied. To Brooke's surprise, he reached out with both hands and gently pinned her to the grass. And then, before she knew it, his mouth was on hers, his arms around her, his body tight alongside her own.

At first she wanted to resist him. But as his kisses deepened and her physical ardor for him was unleashed, she fully responded in kind, holding him, wanting him, running her hands through the blond highlights in his hair. Suddenly there was just the two of them in the world and nothing else. She was becoming lost in him, she knew, but what would happen next? Would he try to possess her right here and now? And if she fought him, would he then force himself upon her, here in a secluded place where there was no one to save her? And perhaps worse yet, was that what she really wanted? Had she become such a stranger to the workings of her own heart that she did not know the answer?

Suddenly, something inside her rebelled and she reluctantly pushed him away. As she did, he did not fight her. Angry and confused, she quickly stood and walked to the edge of the cliff.

My God, she thought. *It's actually happening! And I let it go on . . . What is to become of me?*

At once she began to cry. Not so much out of shame this time, she realized, but confusion. She wanted this man, and yet she didn't. She had loved being in his arms, but at the same time she knew she had just crossed the line, the same forbidden boundary that she had sworn to never traverse. Just then she sensed Greg standing beside her. When she turned to look at him, his expression was contrite. Reaching into a pants pocket, he produced a handkerchief and handed it to her.

"I'm sorry," he said as she dabbed at her eyes. "I just . . . well, you see . . ."

Brooke turned to him. "I know," she answered. "Because I feel it, too. But it must end here, Greg, atop this mountain. I simply cannot betray Bill. With God's grace, he may survive this war. If he does, this will already be hard enough to live with. And much more so if it goes any farther."

"I understand," Greg said. "I really do. And please also realize that this was not my reason for bringing you here. Even so, there's something else that you must know, Brooke."

Then the gaze coming from his gray eyes returned to one of longing, and he was forced to wipe away a tear.

"I love you," he said quietly. "I have since the night that I sketched you. But despite the pain it will cause me to be near you, I will abide by your wishes."

Brooke nodded. "Thank you," she answered. "And please know, my forbidden darling, that I love you, too. But all that can happen in this regard has already taken place on this mountaintop. This may be where our physical ardor began, but it must also be where it ends. So if you truly love me, then promise me, Greg. Promise me that nothing like this will ever happen again."

Although his heart too was breaking, Greg nodded. "If that's what you want," he answered, "then yes, I promise you."

"Thank you," she answered.

On their return to the picnic area, Greg began repacking the basket. As he did, Brooke looked at the recently turned earth beneath which lay Greg's coneflower seeds.

Will they one day burst through the soil? Brooke wondered. *Although I don't know, one thing is for certain. If they do, they'll be the only sign of what just happened here . . .*

"And so, dear diary," Brandon read, *"that is the story of what happened today. My heart is now even more heavily burdened, my physical need for him even stronger after being nearly taken by him, and my guilt now overpowering. And yet, I cannot*

help but look down the beach and search out his cottage in the moonlight, the light coming from behind his windows telling me that he, too, is home alone. Does he still yearn for me as I do him? And if so, will that short stretch of sand be enough to keep our souls separate, as we have promised one another? I do not know. I only know that I am in the grips of the most grievous emotional pain I have ever experienced and that I am totally uncertain of what my future holds."

Having finished the entry, Brandon closed the journal and set it on the table. The rain was coming harder now, and when he looked over at Chelsea he saw tears running down her cheeks. Reaching over, he took one of her hands in his to find that it had gone cold.

"Are you all right?" he asked.

Chelsea sniffed and shook her head. "I don't know," she answered. "But I've learned one more thing about Brooke."

"And what is that?" Brandon asked.

"Why coneflowers became her favorites," she answered softly.

They sat there in silence for a time as

the rain continued its steady drumroll on the old porch roof. Deciding to wait before speaking again, Brandon gave Chelsea all the time she needed. At last, she wiped her eyes and turned to him.

"Do you know where it is?" she asked.

"Where what is?" he replied gently.

"Red Rock Mountain," she said. "Have you been there?"

"Yes," he answered. "When I was younger. For most of the kids around here, going there is a rite of passage."

"Will you take me there one day?" she asked.

"Of course," he answered.

"Thank you," she said.

Chelsea then returned her attention to the gray, restless waves and the incessant sheets of rain that fell upon them.

Love can be so elusive, she thought. *We all speak of it, search for it, cherish it. But in the end, sometimes it leaves us only bemused, baffled, and bewildered. Brooke was so unsure of whether she wanted Greg's advances, yet he was more than willing to shower them on her. And I love a man by whom I would love to be taken but whose past still forbids him to do so. Oh, my dear grandmother! Can we women ever hope to understand our men—these vastly confusing beings with whom our hearts and minds wrestle so endlessly?*

Despite her confusion, Chelsea knew one thing for certain. She was learning to understand her beloved grandmother in ways that she could have never imagined before coming to Lake Evergreen. And because she felt neither betrayed nor disappointed by Brooke's evolving story, her tears were born not from judgment of her grandmother but rather from the great sense of empathy that she now felt for Brooke in her growing plight.

But despite how much Brooke loved Greg, Chelsea thought, *she suddenly abandoned the cottage that very summer and refused to return for the rest of her life. And given that Bill didn't survive, why did you do that, Gram? Why did your story with Greg end? And even more importantly, will Brandon ever embrace me as Greg did you? Or will I, too, one day feel the need to leave and never come back, because being here might prove too painful?*

As Brandon gave Chelsea's hand a gentle squeeze, the best she could do was to close her eyes against her growing tears.

23.

"She is beautiful, *non*?" Jacques Fabienne asked. "Lovely as the day she was
built! And it is lucky for the mademoiselle
that I know how to operate her, because
the owner's manual from so many years
ago is long gone."

Three weeks had passed since Jacques
had hauled the boat into Serendipity for
her reactivation. And now that she was
ready, Jacques smiled proudly again as
he focused his gaze first upon Chelsea,
then Brandon.

"*Beautiful Brooke* truly lives up to her
name, *non*?" he asked.

Brandon, Chelsea, Jacques, and Margot were all standing on Chelsea's dock, looking down at *Beautiful Brooke*. If it was at all possible for a boat to look happy to be back on the water, *Beautiful Brooke* was doing just that. Her mechanics had been reactivated; her woodwork, chrome, and leather had all been polished; and Jacques had even attached a small American flag to the stern flagpole. The light waves caused her to bump restlessly against the dock, as if she were itching to be set loose after so long a respite.

Smiling again, Jacques placed his meaty fists akimbo. "The mademoiselle is very lucky to own such a boat," he said. "I do not believe that there is another like her on all of Lake Evergreen."

Brandon squatted down and surveyed the cockpit controls. "I'll second that," he said. "Wow, is she gorgeous!"

"Do you know how to run her?" Chelsea asked Brandon. "Because I certainly don't!"

"I've driven a lot of boats," Brandon answered, "but this one's a whole different animal." Then he stood and smiled at

Jacques. "So it's a good thing that we have you to show us, *n'est-ce pas?*"

With that, Jacques's barrel chest seem to puff out even farther. "That's true!" he said.

While the others watched, Jacques maneuvered his great bulk down from the dock and into the driver's cockpit, where his sausage-like fingers inserted the key into the ignition. He then eagerly began pointing out the controls.

"As you can see," he said, "one must first put the transmission shift lever into neutral. If the motor is cold, you then grip the choke knob and pull it out about halfway. Then you turn the key and press the 'start' button. Once the motor is running, you . . ."

Eager to learn all she could about her boat, Chelsea listened intently. But although everything Jacques said made sense, Chelsea decided right then and there that she would ask Brandon to drive first, while she rode as a passenger. The day he took her up in his plane, she realized that he seemed to possess an inherent gift for handling machines that she didn't share. Since inheriting the cottage she had been very lucky to have Brandon and Jacques in her life, and she knew it.

Smiling at Chelsea, Margot pulled her aside. "I should stop Jacques from talking so much, but I don't have the heart," she whispered. "If you listen closely, you'll realize that he's starting to repeat himself!"

Chelsea listened for a moment and then laughed. "You're right," she said conspiratorially. "And Brandon is so absorbed that he either doesn't know it, or he doesn't care," she added. She then turned back toward them and she sighed. "Boys and their toys . . . ," she said.

Margot gave Chelsea a wink. "Come with me, would you?" she asked.

"Sure," Chelsea said. "But where are we going?"

"To the truck," Margot answered. "I have something for you."

Chelsea laughed a little. "More food?" she asked.

As the two of them began walking off the dock, Margot smiled. "*Mais oui!*" she said. "Jacques and I are French, after all!"

When they reached the truck, Margot opened the passenger door and retrieved a wicker picnic basket, which she handed to Chelsea. "Voilà!" she said.

"What's inside?" Chelsea asked.

Margot made a nonchalant gesture with one hand. "It's just a little bit of this and a little bit of that," she answered. "There's a bottle of Pinot, some goose-liver pâté, cheese and sausage, and a loaf of bread. Peasant food, but good."

She then turned and looked at Brandon, who was still intently listening to Jacques. "And romantic food, if you understand what I mean," she added coyly.

Chelsea blushed a little. "Yes," she answered. "I do . . ."

At last Brandon and Jacques joined them. "Well, have you learned everything you need to take me for a ride?" Chelsea asked.

"I'd better have," Brandon answered, "or Jacques will have my hide." He then looked at Jacques again. "Before I forget, is there an anchor in the storage compartment?"

Jacques nodded. "Plus a pair of paddles and plenty of stout line with an eye hook at one end. There's also a folding ladder. Everything's brand-new."

"Well done," Brandon answered. He then looked at the picnic basket Chelsea was holding. "And what do you have there?" he asked.

"It's another care package from Margot and Jacques," Chelsea answered. "They must think that I'm starving out here."

Brandon laughed. "Well," he said, "if it comes from them, then whatever's in it must be good."

Jacques respectfully removed the black beret from his head and held it before him with both hands.

"It is time for Margot and me to leave, mademoiselle," he said. "As you requested, I had the bill for the boat work sent directly from the marina to Mr. Reynolds in Syracuse. I so hope that *Beautiful Brooke* meets with your satisfaction."

Chelsea simply couldn't help herself. Despite how little time she had actually spent with them, she had come to love Margot and Jacques. Stepping forward, she gave the huge Frenchman a kiss on one cheek. Almost immediately, Jacques began to blush.

"She's wonderful, Jacques," she said. "Truly. If Brooke knew about this, she would be so pleased." She then turned and looked at Margot. "And thank you so much for the food," she added.

Jacques gave Chelsea a rather sad smile. "If you will permit me, I believe that Madame Brooke does in fact know."

With that, they all said their good-byes. Jacques and Margot got back into their battered truck, and in moments they were gone.

Brandon gave Chelsea a mischievous look. "So what's in the basket?" he asked.

Chelsea grinned back at him. "That's for me to know," she said, "and for you to find out, Dr. Yale."

"And I've got the perfect way," Brandon said. "Let's take *Beautiful Brooke* out and have a picnic supper."

That does indeed sound perfect, Chelsea thought. "All right," she answered. Then she looked at her watch. "But it's almost six, and it'll be dark soon."

Brandon gave her a rather piratical

smile. "Even better," he said. "A perfect excuse to build a bonfire."

"But how will we find our way home?" Chelsea asked.

"I'm a trained army ranger, remember? Now go and put on a swimsuit and a cover-up, and I'll do the same."

Chelsea scowled a little. "Why would I need a swimsuit?" she asked.

"Just trust me," he answered. "Oh, and when you leave your cottage, make sure that all of your lights are on. I'll be doing the same."

This time, Chelsea was really baffled. "Why?" she asked.

"You'll see, city girl," he answered. "And bring along that heavy quilt that's on your bed. Now hurry up and get going."

"All right, all right!" she exclaimed jokingly.

24.

By the time Chelsea returned to the dock, Brandon was already aboard the boat and had her engine running. Chelsea was wearing a black, one-piece swimsuit with a cover-up, and flip-flops, plus she carried a light jacket and the bed quilt. As an afterthought, she'd also brought with her two wineglasses and a corkscrew. When she reached the boat, Brandon gestured for her to place everything onto the backseat and then get in beside him.

"Did you leave all your cottage lights on, like I asked?" he said.

Chelsea nodded as she settled in.

"Yes," she answered. "But it's still a big mystery."

"You'll see," Brandon answered.

As Brandon busied himself with casting off, Chelsea adjusted her sunglasses against the setting sun. Brandon then put the boat in reverse, and he carefully backed her away from the dock. Once they were about ten yards or so from shore, he shifted her into forward, added just a bit of throttle, then consulted the compass and headed north-northwest. At first he went very slowly, causing Chelsea to ask why.

"Aside from her tune-up at the marina, this old motor hasn't come alive in more than fifty years," he said, his voice rising to overcome the sounds of the engine. "I'm going to take it slow for a bit, before I crank up the throttle."

"Where are we going?" Chelsea asked.

"To a little island I know that lies about fifteen minutes away," Brandon answered. "Once I get us up to speed, that is."

"What's it called?" Chelsea asked.

"Spinnaker Isle," he answered.

Chelsea smiled at him. "And is Spinnaker Isle great, Dr. Yale?" she asked.

"Yes," he answered. "Yes, it is."

"And just how many other women have you taken there?" she asked coyly.

The wind ruffling his dark hair, Brandon turned toward her and smiled. "Three hundred and twenty-seven," he said. "You'll make it three hundred and twenty-eight. I'm shooting for an even thousand."

As Chelsea laughed, Brandon gradually applied more throttle until they were at last speeding across the water. Chelsea had never been in a boat this fast, and she immediately loved it. As Brandon again consulted the compass and kept *Beautiful Brooke* on the proper course, Chelsea turned around for a moment and watched their two cottages shrink in the distance.

About ten minutes later, she saw a small spit of wooded land up ahead. As they came closer, she recognized it as an island.

"Is that it?" she asked loudly.

"Yes," Brandon answered. "We'll be there before you know it."

True to his word, soon he was slowing the boat and letting her drift toward shore. When they were at a depth of about shoulder height, he cut the engine and set the anchor. Finally satisfied that the boat was secure, Brandon slipped over the side and then asked Chelsea to hand down the picnic basket, which he held over his head.

"You can bring the rest of the stuff," he said. "And don't get the quilt wet!"

Chelsea gave him a wry look. "So now I know why we needed to wear swim-suits," she said as she gathered up the other things. "But how am I supposed to do this?"

Brandon laughed. "Hold everything over your head, put your butt on the gun-wale, and then slide into the water," he answered.

Unsure, Chelsea looked around for a moment. "What's a 'gun- all'?" she asked.

"The edge of the boat!" he answered laughingly as he turned and began wad-ing toward shore.

Chelsea did as he said, yelping a bit as she slid into the cool water. Soon she had reached the beach, where she took a mo-ment to look around the island. The sandy beach was fairly deep, ending at the edge of a thick stand of maple trees whose founding seeds had somehow reached there long ago. The wind was light, and by now the sun had drifted lower toward the horizon. She felt a bit cold, but not chilly enough to make her shiver.

While Brandon spread the quilt out on the sand, Chelsea began unpacking the picnic basket. At last they sat they sat down together atop the quilt. As Brandon opened the wine, Chelsea looked out at *Beautiful Brooke* tugging at her anchor line.

Wondering something, Chelsea looked quizzically at Brandon. "Why didn't you just run the boat up onto the beach a bit?" she asked. "That would seem easier to me than anchoring it."

Before answering, Brandon poured two glasses of wine. "The answer's simple," he said. "Her hull's made of highly polished mahogany. The sand would have scratched it. And don't you dare run her up on your beach, either. Tomorrow I'll rig up a permanent anchor for you offshore by your cottage because I know that raising and lowering the boat in the boathouse cradle is a real chore for one person."

Chelsea took her first sip of wine. "Why can't I just leave her tied up at my dock?" she asked.

"That's okay during the day, provided you're at home to keep tabs on her," he answered. "But for overnight, she should always be anchored. If a storm comes up, she'll tear loose from the dock and be carried away. It's the same for my plane."

That made sense to Chelsea, and she nodded. *I've learned a great deal since I've been here,* she thought. *And I also have a feeling that there's much more to know about Brandon, Brooke's past, and Lake Evergreen . . .*

"Now then," Brandon said. "Let's get a look at what the Fabiennes supplied us with this time. I don't know about you, but I'm starving!"

He cut up some of the cheese and sausage, sliced the bread, opened the pâté, and handed some of everything to Chelsea before starting in himself. Chelsea liked watching him eat. Although his manners were always good, he was never dainty about it or stood on ceremony, like some of the men she had known in Syracuse. Yet again, she realized, he seemed to be so much in his element here on this sandy beach, with no seeming need to impress her or anyone else.

When they had finished, the sun was already touching the western horizon. It would be dark soon, Chelsea realized, and she was becoming a bit worried about getting home safely. Lake Evergreen wasn't huge, but it was certainly large enough to get lost on. Just then she realized why Brandon had asked her to leave all of her cottage lights lit, and she smiled.

"I just figured it out," she said.

"What?" he asked.

"Why you had us leave all the lights on in our cottages," she said.

Brandon smiled. "Oh, yeah?" he asked while taking another sip of the very good wine. "Why's that?"

"Once we get near enough, they'll serve as beacons and guide us the rest of the way in," she said proudly.

Brandon nodded. "Yeah, but once you see the lights, how can you be sure that the cottages we're heading for will be ours and not somebody else's? If we relied only on that, we could end up way off course. Not to mention anchoring off someone else's beach!"

Chelsea had to admit that she was stumped again. "Okay, wise guy," she said, "so how *do* we know the cottages are ours?"

"Because there are only eighty or so cottages on the entire lake," he said. "And in our area, there are no two so close to each other. So when we return on a reverse course and then see lights that are side by side, they must be ours. Greg Butler once told me that it all goes back to when your great-grandfather divided his lot and sold part of it to Greg."

"Of course . . . ," Chelsea mused. "That makes sense . . ."

Just then Brandon wiped his hands and stood up. "I'll be back in a minute or two," he said.

"Where are you going?" she asked.

"Firewood," he answered simply, then he turned and strode into the woods, the maple trees seeming to immediately engulf him.

With Brandon gone, Chelsea suddenly

became a bit apprehensive. She knew that he would return, of course, but without him by her side she suddenly felt vulnerable and alone, here on this tiny speck of land.

He seems such an important part of my life now, she thought, *whether or not I have a right to feel that way. What would it be like, I wonder, if he were suddenly gone from it?* She looked out across the restless lake once more and then up at the darkening sky. *Losing him, I have come to realize, is something that I never want to experience . . .*

About twenty minutes later Brandon reappeared, his arms loaded down with fallen, dried limbs and logs. He had also collected some desiccated leaves and twigs to use as kindling. After giving her a comforting smile, he began setting a fire. Soon there was a good-size blaze going, doing a respectable job of warding off the encroaching darkness and cold. Just then Chelsea remembered something that Margot had said.

Romantic indeed . . . , she thought.

No sooner had they gotten settled again

than Brandon spied something down the shoreline and he stood back up. Chelsea looked up at him questioningly.

"Where are you going this time?" she asked. "We were just getting comfortable!"

Brandon gave her a wink, then he took off again. When he returned he was carrying a large piece of curved driftwood, which he set down onto the sand.

"Lean back," he said.

As Chelsea did, she found that the arched driftwood against her back felt rather comfortable. Brandon sat beside her, then he gathered up the quilt and put it over them both. As he did, Chelsea snuggled a bit closer to him. They stayed that way for some time as the waves rushed the shore, the fire crackled, and the inky night arrived at last.

Being with Brandon in such a romantic spot, Chelsea couldn't help but feel that the two of them had somehow passed another milestone, and for that she was immensely glad. But as the fire began to fade and the stars became all the brighter for it, her doubts crept in on her again.

How many more such milestones must

there be? she wondered. *Will the wonderful man sitting beside me ever care for me the same way I do for him? He has suffered so much loss. And because of that, am I destined to love him only from afar? Will our relationship never be more physically intimate than two people sitting side by side on the sand? Will there ever be a time when he will take me in his arms, as Greg did Brooke?*

As she let go a slight sigh, Chelsea laid her head on Brandon's shoulder.

25.

"How much farther?" Chelsea shouted.

The climb was tough, and she was becoming tired as she followed Brandon up the trail. He turned and grinned over one shoulder.

"Stop complaining!" he said, laughing. "This was your idea, remember?"

As a trickle of sweat ran annoyingly down her back, Chelsea shook her head. "Don't remind me!" she shouted. "I must have been crazy to suggest this!"

"Maybe!" Brandon answered. "But we're not turning back now!"

Three days had passed since Brandon and Chelsea had visited Spinnaker Isle. Since then it had rained incessantly. While Brandon worked at the hospital, Chelsea busied herself with visiting Jenny Beauregard at the diner for breakfast each morning, perusing her grandmother's copy of *Leaves of Grass,* restocking her grocery shelves, and calling her mother once more. And each evening, she and Brandon shared dinner. One night, Chelsea had taken her first stab at making Brooke's MacArthuroni and Cheese, and it had been wonderful.

Having drinks and dinner with Brandon in the evening was by now a regular occurrence, one that Chelsea greatly enjoyed. Even so, Chelsea decided that she didn't want to read any more of Brooke's journal until she had actually visited the summit of Red Rock Mountain. She believed that going there would make her feel more grounded and better prepare her for whatever the remaining journal entries might reveal. For she now craved a more physical sense of the things Brooke had actually done, as much as Brooke's written words. She needed to visit the place where Brooke and Greg had experienced such an important moment, to feel the same wind, to behold the same sky, and to lie back upon that same soft meadow. She now believed in her heart that doing those things would tell her as much—and perhaps even more—than would the journal. And she would not be dissuaded, no matter how hard the climb to the top of Red Rock might be.

And so for the next three nights, Brandon and Chelsea ate together and then sat before the fire talking, while Dolly and Jeeves dozed at their feet. And each night Chelsea felt her love for him deepen even further. She knew that he cared for her, too. But to her continued dismay, he had yet to say that he loved her.

And that, more than anything else, was what Chelsea wanted. For until then, their blossoming relationship would seem frighteningly breakable to her. Was it only wishful thinking to hope for his love? Perhaps, she realized. Even so, in some ways over the past few days it had been as if they were married, with her cooking dinner while waiting for him to come home. But at the end of each night Brandon had left her and taken her lovely illusion with him.

It was a particularly empty feeling for Chelsea each evening as she watched Brandon saunter back down the moonlit beach to his cottage with Jeeves following along, the waves of Lake Evergreen licking at their feet. All three nights she sat on her porch and watched, waiting patiently for his cottage lights to go out. Maybe she was being silly, but it gave her a measure of peace. And each night she had gone to bed alone, her only company the sweet memory of the time Brandon had held her as she slept. That was the physically closest she had ever been to him, and she yearned for more. More than once she had considered making the first move, hoping that he would respond and at last take her into his arms. But instead she chose to wait and let it be his decision.

If it is to happen, she decided, *then he has to initiate it. Because that's the only way I'll know whether it's real. And if it never happens, then it wasn't meant to be . . .*

Just after midnight on the fourth day, the rain finally stopped. It was a Sunday, and Brandon was finally free to escort her to the top of Red Rock. Chelsea was wearing a blue short-sleeved shirt with its tails tied around her waist, a pair of tan shorts, hiking boots, and an old Yankees ball cap of Brandon's. A ponytail extended from the back of the cap, jauntily swaying to and fro as she hiked along. Despite her growing tiredness, she did her best to trek onward.

A bit later, Brandon stopped and turned around. After a few more paces she caught up to him, breathing heavily. Bending over at the waist, she placed her hands on her knees, trying to recover.

"You okay?" he asked.

Breathing deeply, Chelsea nodded as she stood back up. "Yeah . . . ," she finally said. "But this . . . really takes it out of a girl."

Brandon grinned. "Well, it really takes it out of a *city* girl, it seems," he answered.

Chelsea took a welcome slug of water from her canteen. "Very funny," she said while wiping her mouth. "But how much farther is it, really?"

Brandon turned and pointed. "Look," he said.

Chelsea gazed up the trail to see shards of bright sunlight streaking here and there into the shady woods. "So we've made it?" she asked hopefully.

Brandon nodded. "The meadow is just beyond."

"Thank God," Chelsea answered.

Brandon snorted out a short laugh. "Come on," he said. "We're practically there."

Moments later they stood at the edge of the woods, just as Brooke and Greg had once done. Chelsea gripped Brandon's hand, and this time it was she who led them onward. As they stepped onto the flat, grassy meadow, Chelsea's mouth fell open.

"My God, Brandon," she said with awe. "Just look at it . . ."

Like Chelsea, Brandon stood there quietly, admiring the beautiful scene. When he turned toward her, he smiled knowingly.

"You knew, didn't you?" Chelsea asked. "You knew! I just realized that, because you said that you'd been here before . . ."

"Yes," Brandon answered.

"So why didn't you tell me?"

"Simple," he answered. "I didn't want to ruin the surprise."

The meadow was spectacular. Greg's coneflower seeds had indeed taken root those many years ago, and over the course of the decades the resulting flowers had totally covered the field. So dense were they that they seemed to wave as one with the strong breeze that buffeted this lofty and beautiful place. It was as if a sea of violet had been born here atop the land, its bounty destined to return with every new spring.

So it's true, Chelsea thought as she stood staring at it. *Greg's seeds did thrive here, and Brooke's hope came true after all. Their forbidden love for each other does indeed go on living here year after year, even after each of them has passed from this earth. I know in my heart that Greg's flowers will continue to come up every spring. And yes, they will wither and die each fall. But more will always arise again, both vibrant and new.*

While she stood thinking for a bit longer, a tear came to one eye.

Perhaps that's what Brooke was trying to say in her journal, Chelsea thought. *That although some lovers' ardor may die, it always springs eternal for others . . .*

She then looked skyward, and she smiled.

"I told you it would be worth it," Brandon said.

Chelsea turned around and again admired the meadow. "Were the coneflowers here the first time you visited?" she asked.

Brandon nodded. "Yes," he said. "But since then, they've thrived."

"I wonder if this is the same spot where Brooke and Greg stood," Chelsea mused.

"Perhaps," Brandon answered. "But it doesn't matter. We know that they were once here, just as we now are."

Chelsea nodded. "Yes . . . ," she answered.

"Let's get off our feet for a bit," Brandon suggested.

As they sat down near the cliff's edge, they heard a birdcall come from high above. Looking up, they saw a pair of hawks gracefully riding the wind currents as they hunted for their next meals. Glad for the rest, Chelsea removed her ball cap and freed her hair from its ponytail. As the wind rose again and the flowers waved gracefully, she and Brandon sat in solitude, enjoying the many splendors of this place.

After a time, Chelsea carefully reached into one of her shirt pockets and produced a sheet of tissue paper. As she began to unwrap it, Brandon looked at her quizzically.

"What do you have there?" he asked.

Chelsea finished unwrapping the paper to reveal the two pressed coneflowers that Emily Rousseau had given her the day she and Brandon had visited the Blue Rooster.

"Brooke's dried flowers?" he asked.

"Yes," Chelsea answered.

"Why did you bring them along with us?"

"To be honest, I'm not entirely sure," Chelsea answered. "I was hoping that this field would be filled with the flowers that Greg planted so long ago, and I'm happy that it is. I guess I thought that if there were no flowers here, then I'd scatter these two from Greg and Brooke's days together, here where they made their fateful pact. But now I'm happy to say that there's no need. I'm glad, because I'm not sure that I could have parted with them, anyway."

Just then a thoughtful look overcame

Brandon's face. "May I take one for a few moments?" he asked. "I promise not to harm it."

"Of course," she answered.

Brandon gently lifted one of the delicate old flowers from the tissue and he examined it for a time, thinking. To Chelsea's surprise, he then walked alone to the edge of the cliff and stood there, facing north. Unsure of what to do, Chelsea waited quietly on the grass. After what seemed like an eternity, Brandon finally returned and sat down beside her. Chelsea gently touched him on one arm.

"What is it?" she asked.

"Mallory . . . ," he answered, his voice a near whisper, his teary eyes staring out over the cliff.

"What about her?" Chelsea asked quietly.

"She's gone, Chelsea . . . ," he said, his gaze at last returning to the dried coneflower in his hand.

Still unsure, Chelsea thought for a moment. "Well, yes . . . ," she answered gently. "And I know how much you loved her. But is there something more that you're trying to tell me?"

"The old and the new . . . ," he answered, his voice a new whisper. "Suddenly, after all this time, I've finally realized it. My heart has at last come full circle, and I have you to thank for it."

"What are you saying?" she asked.

"Mallory is gone," he said, "and she's never coming back, despite how much I might wish it. She has become like this dried flower, so colorless and fragile, while you and I sit here among all these new ones, so vibrant and full of life. Life is for the living, Chelsea. And until this very moment when you showed me the dead flowers that your grandmother once treasured, I had forgotten that. To me, you are like one of the new flowers in this field. And Mallory, God rest her soul, is like the dead flower that I hold in my hand. I will never forget Mallory, and in my own way I will always love her. And like with this dead flower, I know now that there was nothing that could have been done to save her. It was her time. She's gone, and like the new flowers surrounding me, you're in my life now."

After replacing the precious coneflower

on the tissue, he looked into Chelsea's eyes.

"I love you, Chelsea," he said at last. "I love you with a passion that I've never felt before, even for Mallory. I love you, and I want you to be mine. I can only hope that one day, you'll feel the same about me."

Chelsea simply couldn't help herself. As tears of joy streamed down her cheeks, she reached out and took his face in her hands.

"Yes . . . yes, my darling," she answered breathlessly. "I do love you. I have for some time now, and I want to be yours, as well . . ."

With that, all of Brandon and Chelsea's suppressed longings finally slipped their shackles. At once Brandon took her into his arms and he kissed her, long and hard, on her lips. As Chelsea felt the heat rising between them, she slowly reclined atop some of the thousands of violet coneflowers, and he followed her down. And when he took her, she experienced a joy that she had never before known— total, unfettered, and overpowering. In

the same place where her grandmother
had resisted her lover, Chelsea now willingly joined with hers. As she did, she
gently dropped her grandmother's dead
coneflowers to the earth. And when her
moment at last arrived fully, she reached
out and blindly grabbed some living ones
in one hand, crushing them in her grip.

26.

Later that evening, Chelsea smiled across her dining table at Brandon. Because the night was breezy, they could easily hear the waves of Lake Evergreen, rushing the sandy shore.

Things were very different between them now. With this afternoon had come a sense of peace and certainty between them that hadn't existed before. The pact had at last been sealed and its wonderful possibilities realized. So too had come the sort of joy and contentment that arrives only when two people fully admit their love for one another. After having

searched for so long, Chelsea at last believed that she had found the right man,
a strong and honorable man who would
protect her at all costs and love her in
return with equal ardor.

Once they'd returned from Red Rock
Mountain, they had again perused
Brooke's old recipe book, choosing a
dish for which Chelsea already had all
of the needed ingredients. Brooke had
named it Bogart's Baked Beans, and it
had been delicious. Using barbecued
baked beans, chopped bacon, red onion,
and cut-up hot dogs, Brooke had succeeded in turning a normally pedestrian
side dish into something rather special.

Smiling, Brandon finished the last of
his dinner and put down his fork. Doing
his best imitation of Humphrey Bogart, he
gazed at Chelsea and said, "Here's looking at you, kid."

Chelsea gave him a confused look.
"Huh?" she asked. "Why are you talking
that way?"

Brandon raised an eyebrow. "You're
kidding, right?" he answered. "Bogart's
Baked Beans; get it?"

"Get what?" Chelsea asked.

"That was a line from *Casablanca,*" Brandon answered. "You know—Humphrey Bogart, Ingrid Bergman, and Peter Lorre . . . You've seen *Casablanca,* right? It's only the most romantic movie of all time."

"Well, yes," Chelsea admitted. "But I don't think I've ever seen any of his other movies."

Brandon shook his head with mischievous disbelief. "Are you kidding?" he asked her. "*To Have and Have Not, The Big Sleep,* or *The Maltese Falcon,* for heaven's sake? Are you actually telling me that none of those ring any bells?"

"Not really," Chelsea admitted with a little laugh.

Brandon shook his head and cast his gaze toward the ceiling. "Dear Lord, I've fallen in love with an uncultured heathen!" he exclaimed. "Well, my dear, we'll just have to remedy your lack of cinematic education over the course of time."

"Okay," Chelsea said with a laugh. "You've got a deal."

For the next few moments they regarded each other happily, each of them knowing that they were just as comfortable with one another during the quiet times, too. It should be like that in a good relationship, Chelsea had always believed. But until now, she had never experienced it. When silence prevailed between two lovers because of contentment, it was a sure sign of happiness. But when it reigned due to tension, it was an omen not to be ignored. And just now, contentment was the order of the day.

Brooke's journal sat on the table near Brandon's elbow. He picked it up and casually thumbed through it before again looking into Chelsea's eyes.

"The stuff that dreams are made of . . . ," he said.

Chelsea smiled. "More Bogart?" she asked.

"Yes," he answered. "But there isn't much left here to read. In fact, it looks like there's only three more entries. Shall we read the next one tonight?"

Chelsea nodded. "Let's take the wine and the journal out onto the porch."

After letting the dogs back in, Brandon joined Chelsea on the porch. He then turned to the next entry and handed the journal to her, whereupon Chelsea began reading aloud:

Tuesday, August 11, 1942, 4:00 P.M.

As I write these words, I can control neither my worry nor my excitement. The two conflicting emotions are running through my veins like adrenaline and tearing my heart in two. As if it might somehow provide an answer to my dilemma, I keep rereading the telegram that arrived a few hours ago. When I first saw it in the dock mailbox I nearly fainted, fearing the worst. But then I realized that anything untoward happening to Bill during his stateside officer's training was unlikely, and I tore open the telegram with abandon and read it. Afterward, I pasted it into this journal as a keepsake.

Chelsea turned the page and saw the World War II–era telegram that Brooke had in fact included. Before attaching it, Brooke had folded it so that it would fit within the confines of the journal. As Chelsea gently unfolded it, she saw that it was heavily wrinkled in its center, where the paste secured it to the page. After gazing at it for a few moments more, she began reading aloud again:

WESTERN UNION:
FRIDAY AUGUST 10 1942 STOP
MRS. BROOKE BARTLETT, 18 SCHUL-
YER LANE, SERENDIPITY, NEW YORK:
OFFICERS TRANING ENDED STOP
HAVE LEFT FORT BENNING FOR SYR-
ACUSE BY TRAIN VIA DELAYING
ROUTE STOP WILL JOIN YOU AT LAKE
EVERGREEN FOR ONE NIGHT ON AU-
GUST 11 STOP THEN MUST RE-
TURN TO SYRACUSE NEXT DAY AND
BOARD TRAIN TO NYC FOR TROOP-
SHIP PASSAGE TO ENGLAND STOP
ALL LOVE STOP BILL

*I can't begin to describe how I feel!
At last Bill and I will be together again,
even if it is for just one night. But despite my happiness, I also worry about
what will happen when he arrives. With
Greg still in my heart, how will I react
when I see my husband? Will my love
for Bill be so strong and sure as always?
Or will my heart shrivel at the mere sight
of him, telling me once and for all that
it is now Greg whom I truly love? Will
Bill's impending visit be the test that finally answers all my burning questions,*

the trial by fire that will forever define what's really in my heart? And if so, what will the verdict be?

The mere thought of such concerns has quickly tempered my joy, and in its place has again risen the terrible sense of guilt that I carry. What will happen when Bill appears here only hours from now? Greg will undoubtedly know without my telling him, because from his cottage he will surely see Bill arrive. My God, what will Greg then do? Will he actually come over, asking to be introduced? Or will he stay at arm's length and not intrude? This scenario hadn't occurred to me, although I now realize that it should have. As a testament to my anguish, my hands are shaking even now, as I write these words. . .

Perhaps I should go to Greg and tell him what is about to happen. But what could I say to him that wouldn't hurt him even more? That Bill is coming tonight, and that I wish Greg to stay away? Is he to be banished like some pariah, even though he has done nothing more sinful than I? I can easily envision the pain in his eyes, should I tell him that.

And like the pain I saw there when I rejected him atop Red Rock Mountain, that is something I never again wish to experience. And so I have resolved to say nothing to him of Bill's impending visit, in hopes that he will be gentleman enough to understand and not come to us. And yet, despite our promise to each other, I still adore him. Can a woman love two men at the same time and not go mad?

Several hours later, while sitting alone in the dark on his porch, Gregory Butler nervously lit his fortieth cigarette of the day. They usually calmed him, but not tonight. He was also rather drunk.

Reaching out, he poured another two fingers of straight gin and then clumsily tossed it back. He needed the alcohol to dull his pain, and he knew that he would need even more of it later, as both the night and his sense of despair deepened.

As twilight had fallen, he heard the unexpected sound of a car approaching Brooke's cottage. When he saw a tall, young army second lieutenant exit the black Lincoln, it was as if someone had poured ice water into his veins. There could be no mistake, he knew. Brooke's husband, Bill, had come to Lake Evergreen.

It all made sense, he realized, and he castigated himself for not having predicted this possibility before now. On the first day they met, Brooke had told him that Bill's officer's training was nearly done. And although Greg understood little about military protocol, he knew that at the end of such training the newly minted "ninety-day wonders," as they were being called, were granted either a furlough or to take their time reporting to active duty by what the army called "a delaying route." Greg couldn't know which option had been granted to Bill, but none of that mattered to him right now.

More than once, he had nearly left his cottage and walked over to meet Brooke's husband. It was more than mere curiosity that tempted him, he knew. Rather, it was an odd, almost macabre wish to put the three of them in the same room, to size up the other man, and perhaps most important of all, to try to gauge Brooke's feelings. But in the end he would not go, because he knew that she would not want it. Despite how much he loved her, this night belonged to Brooke and Bill. If there remained a single shred of decency in him, Greg decided, he would summon the will to stay away, no matter how much it hurt him to do so.

But he also knew that the moment of his greatest anguish was still to come. And that, more than any other reason, was why he sat waiting on his porch. The night was still, the moon was full, and the waves brushed the sandy shore ever so lightly. As Greg took another drag on his cigarette, its lit end glowed brightly for a moment, then faded again.

In an attempt to put Brooke more at ease this night, Greg had purposely left all of his cottage lights off and parked his old Packard on the opposite side of the cottage, to make it appear as if he wasn't home. He couldn't know whether Brooke believed it, but he hoped so. For if Brooke thought he was away, she would have fewer worries this night.

But the worst of it was yet to come, he knew. For when the lights went out in Brooke's cottage, it could mean only one thing. Brooke and Bill were at last in each other's arms, lying on the great sleigh bed in Brooke's bedroom, enjoying each other, wanting each other, and pleasing each other in ways that they had not done for many months. Whereas Brooke had rejected Gregory Butler that day atop Red Rock, she would joyfully take William Bartlett to her bed.

And, as much as it pains me to think so, that is how it should be, Greg thought. *I have no claim on that woman, no matter how much I might love her. Not only did she have every right to turn me away that afternoon atop Red Rock, she was correct to do so. Even so, not even the gin is helping to assuage the terrible pain I feel this night.*

When he again looked over at Brooke's cottage, this time his greatest fears were realized. One by one the interior lights were extinguished, leaving the little house bathed only in moonlight.

And so it is happening, he thought. *But*

from where will I find the strength to endure this?

As he turned and looked out over the waves, his eyes again filled with tears.

Chelsea put down the journal and stared out at the ever-restless lake. Brandon could sense that she was upset, so he remained quiet, allowing her the first word. After picking up the journal and examining the telegram for a time, Brandon put the journal back down again. It was the first time he'd seen an actual telegram such as this one, and he soon found that its existence brought Brooke and Greg's story into much sharper relief for him, just as he believed it had also done for Chelsea.

"That's where the excerpt ends," Chelsea said at last. "So Emily was right. Bill did come here to be with Brooke. And in all certainty they made love."

When she finally turned to look at Brandon, her face was filled with sadness. "I can't help but feel sorry for him," she said quietly.

"For Greg?" Brandon asked.

Chelsea nodded. "And if Greg knew Bill was there, I can't imagine how much pain it must have brought him."

"I know," Brandon said. "But he had no right to her."

"Yes," Chelsea answered. "I know that, too. But the heart wants what it wants, Brandon. That's always been the way of things, and I suppose it always will be."

"And that must have been the night your mother was conceived," Brandon said.

"Yes," Chelsea answered.

"But even now we don't know how your grandfather Bill died," Brandon mused. "Or why Brooke left here so suddenly and never returned. It's still quite the puzzle."

Chelsea nodded again. "In the end, we all just assumed that discussing Bill's death was too painful for her, so we stopped asking."

"Perhaps one of the last two entries will tell us," Brandon said.

"Maybe," Chelsea said. "But that's not what I need just now."

"No?" Brandon asked.

Chelsea stood from her chair. Lifting his chin, she kissed him slowly, languorously.

"No," she whispered. "What I need tonight is you . . ."

As Brandon stood and took her into his arms, she laid her cheek on his shoulder.

27.

"It is good to see you again, *ma chère,*" Emily Rousseau said to Chelsea. "I'm so glad that you called and asked to visit me."

Two days later, Chelsea and Emily were sitting at Emily's dining table, enjoying some mint tea and blueberry scones. Chelsea had called this morning, asking if she could come by. The lunch crowd had come and gone, but Emily's waitresses and chef still remained to clean up and start preparing for tomorrow. Chelsea could occasionally hear noises coming from the floor below, confirming their presence.

After taking another sip of her tea, Emily smiled knowingly. "And unless I'm mistaken," she added, "there is a glow about you that wasn't there the first time we met. That wouldn't have anything to do with your next-door neighbor, would it?"

Chelsea felt herself blushing. "Well, yes," she answered. "As a matter of fact, it does. You're very perceptive."

"We women can sense things that men never see," Emily answered with a smile. "Your grandmother, God rest her soul, no doubt had that same look about her one day. It would have been right after her husband had visited her at the cottage, just before he shipped out for England. Sadly, Bill died. But nine months later, Brooke was blessed with the birth of your mother. Then Brooke was involved in her awful accident, and everything changed for her yet again. That period in her life was a series of drastic ups and downs, poor thing."

"That much I already know," Chelsea said, "although I haven't gotten through the entire journal."

"Well," Emily said, "I can't know what the rest of Brooke's writings might hold for you. More than I am able to offer, no doubt. But when you are done reading it, there is one thing that I would ask of you."

"What is that?" Chelsea said.

"If you learn why Brooke left Lake Evergreen so suddenly that summer and never returned, I would very much appreciate knowing," Emily answered. "I held our friendship so dear, and I could never understand her motives. Years later, during one of my visits to Syracuse, I did ask her why. She apologized but refused to elaborate. Because she was so adamant about it, I respected her privacy from that point on. But if you do learn why, please satisfy this old woman's curiosity and tell me about it, would you?"

Chelsea reached out and patted Emily on the hand. "Of course," she answered. "But the truth is, I was hoping that *you* could tell *me* about that. Was there in fact anyone else who knew her up here and is still among us?"

Emily shook her head. "Not that I know of," she answered. "Even Gregory Butler once told me he did not know why she left so abruptly. He too seemed very hurt by her so sudden and unexplained departure. Perhaps it was because of Bill's death that she went home so abruptly, but that still doesn't explain why she didn't bid either of us adieu or why she never returned. And I know that she very much cared for us both and that she could have had no reason to want to hurt us. All of which makes it only harder to understand."

Disappointed, Chelsea sat back in her chair. Although she liked Emily very much, her hopes about learning more from her were quickly being dashed. She had been optimistic that Emily hadn't told her all she knew the time before, because Brandon had been with her. But even now, Emily had little more to offer regarding Brooke Bartlett's last days at Lake Evergreen.

Chelsea had called Emily that morning asking to see her, and Emily had eagerly agreed. Two days had passed since Chelsea and Brandon had climbed Red Rock Mountain. It had been a momentous day for them, and like any two new and infatuated lovers, they were deliriously happy. Last night they had again made love, more slowly and languorously this time, in Chelsea's old sleigh bed as the moonlight highlighted their naked bodies. It had again been all that the two of them could have hoped for and more. And this time Brandon had stayed the night with Chelsea, and she had awakened in his arms.

But they had read no more of Brooke's journal, largely because Chelsea decided that she first wanted to visit Emily and see if she could shed any more light on why Brooke left Lake Evergreen in the dead of night, never to return. Having spoken to Emily again, it now seemed to Chelsea that the only remaining answers were going to come from Brooke's writings. But there were few entries left to read, leading Chelsea to wonder if the answers would ever surface at all. And so far as Chelsea and her mother knew, once Brooke returned to Syracuse for good, her journal writing had ended.

While taking another sip of her excellent mint tea, Chelsea looked around Emily's five-room apartment. Located above the Blue Rooster, it was a lovely and comfortable place that seemed to suit Emily's needs perfectly. Her only companion was her tricolored cat, Josephine, named after the illustrious wife of Napoleon, who at this moment was so eagerly rubbing her lithe body against Chelsea's shins. There were many old photos in the apartment, most of which were of Emily's long-dead parents. What photos Emily had of Brooke she had already shown to Chelsea, but they had provided no new information. Chelsea was about to give up and leave when another question occurred to her.

"The book you gave me," she said to Emily. "The copy of *Leaves of Grass* with the two coneflowers pressed inside it—when did Brooke give it to you?"

Before answering, Emily took another bite of her scone. "Well," she answered, "in a manner of speaking, she never actually *gave* it to me."

Chelsea shot Emily a questioning look. "What do you mean?" she asked.

"As I told you last time, I was already familiar with the book," Emily answered. "On the same day that your grandmother left here for good, I found the book on the back steps that lead up to this apartment.

Brooke had carefully wrapped it in a paper bag and left it there for me to find. I could be certain that it was hers, because Greg's inscription to her was written on the first page."

Chelsea sat back in her chair, wondering. "And the two coneflowers?" she asked. "Did Brooke give you those at the same time?"

Emily nodded. "Yes," she answered. "They lay under the front cover."

"There was no note?" Chelsea asked.

"No," Emily answered.

"Did you ever ask her why she gave them to you?"

"*Certainement*," Emily answered. "But all she would say about it was that she wanted me to have them for safekeeping. And then she added something that I never quite understood."

Chelsea leaned forward a bit. "And what was that?" she asked.

"That the flowers and the book were important to her," Emily answered. "And so, as a way of keeping them together, I pressed the flowers deeper in the book, and they remained that way until I gave both the book and the flowers to you. When your grandmother gave me the flowers, they appeared to have been picked only hours before."

Chelsea was surprised by that. "They weren't already dried and pressed?" she asked.

"No," Emily said. "I remember that part with certainty. The flowers grew old and dried in my care, not Brooke's."

Chelsea tried to deduce something from that but couldn't. As she again looked around the apartment, another concern struck her.

"Forgive me for asking, Emily," she said, "but what will become of the Blue Rooster when you're gone? It's such a wonderful place . . ."

Emily sighed and shook her head. "As you know," she answered, "there is no one to follow me. I cannot say what will happen here, once I have gone to my reward."

And then, despite the gravity of the subject, she smiled and gave Chelsea a mischievous wink. "But I refuse to worry about it," she said. "Because I know that the moment I start, it will be the beginning of the end. And I plan on living forever!"

Chelsea couldn't help but laugh. She cared for Emily, despite how briefly she had known her. As she thought some more about things, she smiled knowingly.

Coming to Lake Evergreen has enriched me far more than I could have ever imagined, she thought. *In addition to my love for Brandon, I've also met some other wonderful people along the way. Not to mention all of the revelations I've discovered about Brooke and those that might still come. And to think that when Allistaire first told me I had inherited Gram's old cottage, my initial reaction had been to perhaps sell it, without even seeing it first. Then I read Gram's letter, and everything changed . . .*

On noticing the faraway look in Chelsea's eyes, Emily laid one of her old hands atop hers. "What is it, *ma chère*?" she asked.

Chelsea smiled at her. "I was just thinking about how surprising life can be," she said. "Had I not inherited Gram's cottage, you and I would have never met. And I would have been the poorer for it, I assure you."

"As I too would have been, my child," Emily answered. "As I too would have been . . ."

28.

As her lovely old Chris-Craft sliced across the whitecaps of Lake Evergreen, Chelsea smiled. By now she and Brandon had taken *Beautiful Brooke* out several times, and Brandon had patiently taught Chelsea how to operate her. Provided the weather was good, Chelsea now had no qualms about taking her out alone.

Chelsea was about a hundred yards out into the lake and following the westerly shore toward the small cove that sheltered Beauregard's. She had something she wanted to discuss with Jenny, something that she wanted no one else—not even Brandon—to know about yet. Of the people Chelsea had met here, Jenny seemed the most logical one to ask for advice. The day was so lovely that taking the boat to the diner seemed the most enjoyable way to go.

Smiling to herself, Chelsea added a bit more power to the inboard engine and heard its comforting growl strengthen. The old boat bounced a bit as Chelsea cut perpendicularly across the wake of another speedboat, just the way Brandon had taught her. To her delight, the other craft's occupants waved at her and gave her the thumbs-up sign. Because there was no other craft on all of Lake Evergreen quite like *Beautiful Brooke,* whenever Chelsea took her out, there were many eager admirers. Suddenly a bit of spray flew up and over the windshield, splashing Chelsea lightly in the face. Laughing, she wiped her face with one palm and then pulled the bill of her ball cap a bit lower.

While pushing onward toward Beauregard's, Chelsea couldn't help but again think of her late grandmother. From what the Fabiennes had told her, Brooke had also very much enjoyed this boat. Brooke once sat at these very same controls that Chelsea now employed, felt the same wind through her hair and the same sun burnishing her face. Despite how much Chelsea loved the cottage, it was while skippering this boat that she felt closest to Brooke's memory.

The morning had broken bright and clear. Chelsea and Brandon had again awakened together, and Chelsea had made Brandon some breakfast before he headed off to work. At first she had been unsure about how to spend her day, and so she had taken another cup of coffee out onto the porch to sit and think about it. After a time an idea came to her, causing her to smile. *It would take some planning,* she thought, *but it would make me very happy, I'm sure of it.* But she wanted some advice first, and Jenny would be the best one with whom to talk.

As Beauregard's loomed up ahead, Chelsea cut back on the throttle and began guiding *Beautiful Brooke* alongside one of the docks. Jake Branch, Jenny's jack-of-all-trades who worked the docks for her, helped to guide the boat closer until *Beautiful Brooke* gently bumped up against the row of old car tires hanging against the side of the dock. Once the boat was tied up, Chelsea cut the engine.

"You're gettin' a lot better at this, Miss Enright!" Jake said, a wide grin seeming to split his angular face in two. "A regular mistress of the waves, y'are!"

While Jake tied up the boat, Chelsea clambered up from the driver's seat and onto the dock. Jake was a man of about fifty, with a ruddy face and bushy eyebrows. He was dressed in greasy coveralls, and his squat, muscular form was solid as a fire hydrant. He had worked for Jenny for a long time. Among his duties as the docks manager, he pumped gas for both the cars and boats. During the wintertime when the docks were closed, he doubled as a short-order cook.

"Thanks, Jake," Chelsea answered with a smile. "But I'm still glad that you're always here to help guide me in."

After tying up the boat, Jake smiled back at her, his wide smile seemingly as bright as the summer day itself. "Shall I top her off?" he asked.

Chelsea nodded. "Might as well," Chelsea answered. "So tell me, is the boss lady working today?"

While Jake lifted a gas nozzle from one of the pumps, he nodded. "I've never known when she wasn't," he answered wryly.

"See you later," Chelsea said laughingly as she began the short walk to the diner.

It was close to noon, and Beauregard's was about half-full. Buddy Holly was soulfully lamenting something from the jukebox and a handful of regulars were sitting at the booths, tables, and counter. Because Chelsea had visited here several times since her fateful run-in with Pug Jennings, she no longer attracted any undue attention from the patrons. As she approached the counter, she removed her ball cap and freed her hair from its ponytail. When Jenny saw her, she let go a smile nearly as radiant as Jake's had been.

"Well, well," she said. "If it ain't the big-city girl come callin'! What can I getcha?"

Chelsea smiled in return. "A toasted BLT," she said, "and an iced tea. And if you can spare the time, could you join me in one of the booths for a little girl talk?"

"Sure thing," Jenny answered.

After repeating Chelsea's order to the cook—and forcefully adding that it had damned well better be the best BLT he had ever made in his life—Jenny removed her apron and escorted Chelsea to one of the booths that looked out toward the road.

After they got situated, Jenny said, "So what's the big secret? More to do with your grandmother, I s'pose?"

"Well, yes," Chelsea answered. "But that's not the reason I came by."

Jenny leaned back and grinned. "Okay, then," she said. "Lay it on me."

Chelsea had already told Jenny about what had happened at the Jenningses' trailer and how she and Brandon had fallen in love. She then went on to tell Jenny about the last few journal entries that she and Brandon had read and that save for how Emily Rousseau had come to own Brooke's copy of *Leaves of Grass* and the two coneflowers so long ago, the old woman had had nothing more to

add. And there were only two more entries to read, Chelsea also told Jenny, but
she held out little hope that they would
provide all the answers for which she was
looking.

Just then the cook brought Chelsea's
order. As Chelsea bit into her sandwich,
Jenny smiled. "Good?" she asked.

"For sure," Chelsea answered.

"Call it female intuition," Jenny said,
"but I think you still ain't gotten around to
it. So out with it, girl."

In between bites of her sandwich and
sips of iced tea, Chelsea explained her
secret idea to Jenny. The more Chelsea
talked, the more intrigued Jenny became.
When at last Chelsea finished, Jenny
leaned back in the booth, thinking. As
she did, Chelsea thought she could almost see the wheels turning inside Jenny's head.

"So . . . does Brandon have any idea
that you're gonna ask him?" Jenny asked
at last.

Chelsea shook her head. "No," she answered. "And until I fully decide one way
or the other, that's how it's going to stay."

Jenny nodded thoughtfully. "Can't blame you there," she said. "But are you sure about this?"

Chelsea smiled again. "I'm pretty sure, but I don't know how he'll react," she answered. "That's why I came to see you first. You've known him far longer than I have."

Jenny laughed. "Yeah," she said, "but how do you know that—"

"I don't," Chelsea interjected.

"Well," Jenny said, "I think it's a great idea! Are congratulations in order?"

"Not yet," Chelsea answered as she finished the last of her sandwich. "I've still got a lot of thinking to do."

Nodding thoughtfully, Jenny took a deep breath. "If I were you, I'd think long and hard about this," she said. "This would be a life changer, and you'd be giving up a lot. That's often not a such a great idea, even during the best of times. But I must also say that given everything you've told me over the last few weeks, the more I think about it, the more I realize that it's not such a big surprise, after all. If you do it, I wish you luck."

"Thanks, Jenny," Chelsea answered. "I knew that I could count on you."

Jenny snickered a little, then she shook her head.

"The plot thickens . . . ," she answered.

29.

Later that night, Chelsea and Brandon sat on Chelsea's couch, talking. A fire burned in the hearth, and after dinner Chelsea had made some warmed cider laced with blackstrap rum. Brooke's journal lay on the coffee table before them, the flickering firelight dancing prettily across its old cover and binding. As Chelsea sipped her cider, she couldn't help but think about her talk with Jenny that day.

Jenny had been right, Chelsea knew. What she was considering would indeed be a life changer. And that, more than anything else, was why she would wait awhile before approaching Brandon about it.

Given his difficult past, she couldn't be sure about how he would react, and the last thing she desired was to scare him away. And so she would wait and think about it a bit more before asking him. But given their deepening love for each other, she knew that this was something that she wanted, despite how huge a step it would be.

Brandon reached out and picked up the journal. "Are you ready for another excerpt?" he asked, unintentionally breaking Chelsea's train of thought. "Only two more left to go, you know. Only two more chances to solve the riddle of Brooke's last visit here."

As he thought quietly for a time, his expression became more sober. "Will you be all right if we don't?" he asked.

"If we don't . . . what?" Chelsea asked back.

"If we never find the answers that you're looking for," he answered. "Can you live with that?"

Sighing, Chelsea tucked her legs up under herself. "I won't have much choice, will I?" she said. "And maybe that would be for the best, anyway."

"How so?" Brandon asked.

"It depends on what those answers might be," she said. "I don't want to judge Brooke, because whatever happened to her was a long time ago. And for all the time I knew her, she always treated me with the greatest of kindness. That's just the sort of person she was. So I'm having a hard time believing that anything scandalous occurred between her and Greg. But then again, she did seem to leave in a terrible hurry, never to return."

Brandon picked up the old journal. "Only one way to find out," he said.

Chelsea nodded. "Go ahead," she said. "But promise me something first."

"Anything," Brandon answered.

"When you finish reading, be prepared to hold me," Chelsea said with a rather sad smile. "I may end up needing to cry on your shoulder all night."

"My pleasure," Brandon answered.

He then opened the old book, found the appropriate page, and started reading:

Wednesday, August 12, 1942, 2:00 P.M.
Of all the journal entries I have made,
I suspect that his one will be the hard-

est. Bill was here last night; he left just hours ago for Syracuse, to meet the train that will take him to New York City. There, he will board a troopship that will carry him to England. He told me that he believes once the Allies are ready, we will invade France in an attempt to wrest Europe from Nazi domination. Bill still does not know what part he is to play as this most massive and deadly drama in all of human history unfolds. All I know for certain is that I will probably not see him again until the war is over, which will likely be years from now. And that of course assumes not only that he will survive, but that we will also win—two things about which we have no assurances whatsoever. . .

Seeing Bill again was heaven on earth. He looked so handsome in his uniform, with the second lieutenant insignia upon his chest and shoulders. The time passed so quickly that it seemed no sooner had he arrived than he had to leave again. That's just one of the awful things that this war has done to us, I've come to realize. It seems to compress time during those rare in-

stances when we can be together and somehow lengthens it when we are apart. And now, I fear, the time until I see him again will be very long indeed.

And yes, we made love last night. It was a joyous, wonderful union that we both wished could have gone on forever. When at last the dawn light began creeping through the bedroom window we were both still awake, as if a single moment given over to sleep might have somehow robbed us of the brief happiness we were being allowed to share.

I considered going to New York City with him to see him off, but then I decided that the sight of him climbing the gangplank to the ship with all the other men—many of whom will never return— would be more than I could bear. Better to give him one last kiss here in this beautiful place, I decided, before watching him get into his car and drive away.

But as much as I loved seeing Bill again, I must admit that my passion for Greg has already begun bleeding through my façade of faithfulness. I know that Greg was home last night, despite his well-intentioned attempts to make me believe otherwise. I thank God that Greg was somehow able to resist what must have been an almost uncon- querable urge to come by and size Bill up. Men are like that, that's the just the nature of things . . .

So in the end, Bill and Greg never came face-to-face. And yet again I thank God because if they had, I'm not sure that I could have borne it. I was desperately hoping that seeing Bill again would settle my heart once and for all, but it did not. Instead, puzzle- ment seems to rage within my soul more hotly than ever. And so today I find myself only more confused, more torn, and more in love with each of them. Because I will not see Bill again for perhaps as long as several years, I fear that my emotional needs, my phys- ical yearnings, and my wanting to be held in Greg's arms again will do noth- ing but grow, perhaps even to the point that I will no longer be able to control them. Greg and I will see each other soon enough. But I will not go to him. There will be no need, for as sure as I

*know the sun will rise tomorrow, I know
it will be he who comes to me . . .*

When the light knock came upon her
kitchen door, Brooke instinctively knew
that it was Greg. She had been sitting on
her porch, reading and wondering when
he would arrive. As she stood from her
chair and walked into the kitchen, her
throat seemed to dry up and her hands
became damp with perspiration.

When she looked through the screen
at Greg, she was taken aback by what she
saw. He was disheveled and unshaven.
His clothes looked as if he had slept in
them all night, if he had indeed slept at
all. A lit cigarette dangled between his
lips. Before speaking, he spat out the
cigarette and crushed it beneath one
shoe.

"Do you have any coffee made?" he
asked tentatively. "I don't know about
you, but I could surely use it."

Brooke nodded. "I'll make some," she
said as she opened the door for him.

As if it were for the first time, Greg
walked into her kitchen and looked oddly

around. It was like everything seemed different to him now, as if Bill being in this little house last night had irreparably adulterated the sacred place where he had fallen in love with Brooke. As he sat at the dining table, Brooke began brewing the last of the coffee he had given to her.

As the percolator began burbling, Brooke sat down beside Greg. When he looked into her eyes, for the first time ever she saw a sense of pain there that she was quite unable to describe. It was a hurt, a longing to somehow go back in time and erase what had happened here last night. But such pining was of no use, and they both knew it.

"That was him, yesterday, wasn't it?" Greg asked, his voice shaking a bit. "That was Bill."

Brooke closed her eyes and nodded. "Yes," she answered quietly. "His officer's training is over, and he's on his way to Europe."

"Do you still love him?" Greg asked. "Or has your time apart from him changed your heart?"

Brooke wiped away a tear. "I still love

him," she answered. "I know that's hard for you to hear, and I'm sorry."

"And you made love . . . ," he said quietly.

Brooke looked down at her hands. "Yes . . . ," she answered.

Greg closed his eyes for a moment. When he opened them, they too had become shiny with tears.

"Did you look upon him last night the same as you do me?" he asked.

Unsure of Greg's meaning, Brooke shook her head. "What . . . what are you talking about?" she asked.

"When you looked at him, was it the same as when you look at me?" Greg repeated. "Or did it feel different?"

As Brooke considered Greg's question, her expression saddened. "It was different . . . ," she finally answered.

"How so?" he asked.

"I looked upon him with more love than passion," she answered, her own words surprising her. "But I look upon you with more passion than love. God forgive me, but I do."

Greg reached out and took her hands

into his. "And will you ever be able to set that passion for me free?" he asked.

Her previous admission having both startled and frightened her, Brooke began sobbing openly. She abruptly stood from the table and turned her back toward him.

"I don't know!" she fairly shouted. "Can't you see, goddamn it? I just don't know anymore! Why oh why did you have to come into my life now, at the very time when I cannot have you? What is this war doing to us?"

Greg stood and went to her, again taking her hands in his. "It isn't the war that's doing this to us, Brooke," he said quietly. "It's our hearts. War or no war, this would have happened to us anyway, my love. All that was required was for us to meet." Then he turned and looked out her kitchen window. "But I made a promise to you on top of Red Rock Mountain, and I'll do my best to keep it."

"You will?" she asked. Once again, she was finding herself quite unsure of what she really wanted.

"Yes," he answered. "But I don't know if I'll succeed. I just love you too much . . ."

With that, he turned and walked back out the kitchen door. As she watched him go, she knew why he had left so suddenly. He had been about to take her into his arms again, and rather than break his promise to her, he did the only other thing that he could. . .

"Is that the end?" Chelsea asked.

"Yes," Brandon answered as he closed the journal and returned it to the coffee table. "Just one more to go."

"Just one more . . . ," Chelsea said softly. "And then it's over."

Brandon reached out and took her into his arms. "Are you all right?" he asked.

"No," she answered, "but I will be, one way or the other. They suffered, Brandon," she added. "Even now, nearly sixty years later, I can feel their pain. Sadly, that's all love is sometimes. Nothing but disappointment and pain. That's how it was for me, too, before you came into my life. Always searching, but never finding . . ."

"I know, darling," Brandon said. As he felt her body start to shake, he held her closer. "I know . . . ," he said again. "But

I'm here now, and I'm not going any-where."

As he held her in his arms. Brandon looked at the old journal, lying quietly atop the equally old coffee table.

For some of us, is the search for love re-ally nothing but suffering? he wondered. *And if so, then is that all it ever was for Brooke and Greg?*

Holding Chelsea closer yet, he again looked at the old journal, wondering about its final entry.

30.

For Chelsea, the following morning was passing much like the recent ones before it. There had been breakfast with Brandon, and now a few light chores needed to be taken care of. She was in the bathroom, transferring a load of wet wash from her small, stacked washer into the matching dryer below it. Sometimes she hung her wash on a line outside, letting it gather up the natural scent of the evergreen trees as it dried. But today again looked like rain, so she had decided to let her new dryer do the work. Dolly and Jeeves were in the kitchen, fast asleep near the potbellied stove. Just as she was finishing, the wall phone in her kitchen rang, and she went to answer it.

"Hello," she said.

"Chelsea?" someone answered. The male voice seemed familiar, but she couldn't place it.

"Yes . . . ," she said.

"Allistaire Reynolds here," the lawyer said. "How are you doing up there?"

"Oh, hello, Allistaire," Chelsea responded. "Things are just fine. How about you?"

"I'm good too," he answered. "You're getting your mail okay, right?"

"Yes," she said. "And thanks for taking care of that."

"And the registration and proof of insurance for the Chris-Craft came by now, I presume?"

"Yes, those too, thank you."

"God, I'd love to see that boat," he said.

Chelsea laughed a little. "When I come home," she said, "I'll drop by your office and show you a picture." But when

Allistaire didn't answer right away, Chelsea began to wonder what this call was really about.

"Actually," Allistaire said, "I need to see you before that."

"What are you talking about?" she asked, suddenly becoming a bit nervous. "Are my mother and father okay?"

"Oh, yes," he answered. "Nothing like that. But before you come, I must ask you a couple of questions."

"Why?" she asked. "What's this all about?"

"Patience," Allistaire answered. "Now then, have you examined all of the things that your grandmother asked you to?"

His question startled her. "Yes," she said, "but how do you know about them? Did you peek at her letter to me, before I read it that day in your office?"

"Of course not," he said. "But what I really need to know is whether you have in fact looked at everything in its *entirety*."

As far as I know, only the last journal entry remains, Chelsea thought. *Brandon and I are planning on reading it tonight. . .*

"Not entirely," she said. "But by the end of the day, I will have."

"Good," he said. "Can you possibly come to my office tomorrow?"

"I suppose so," she said. "Would it be okay if I brought someone with me?"

Silence reigned again while Allistaire considered his answer. "Who would that be?" he finally asked. "Have you met someone up there?"

"Yes," she answered. "His name is Brandon Yale, and he's a doctor. He owns the cottage next to mine."

Again, there was silence for a time. "Is he trustworthy?" Allistaire asked.

"Yes," she answered. "If he wasn't, I wouldn't ask."

"Then I guess it would be all right," Allistaire answered. "And now for my second question: Have you decided whether to keep the cottage?"

"Yes," she said. "I love it up here."

"All right, then," he said.

"So now can you tell me what this is all about?" she asked.

"Yes," Allistaire answered. "But even I know only a part of it."

"*Which is . . . ?*" Chelsea fairly shouted into the phone.

"I have another envelope for you from your late grandmother," he said.

"*What?*" Chelsea asked.

"It's true," he said. "When you visited the office that day, I actually had *two* envelopes of hers for you in my safekeeping, rather than just the one I gave to you. This second one is also sealed. Brooke brought it to me some four years ago, just before you were about to turn thirty. She said that I was to divulge its existence to you only after you had seen some things at Lake Evergreen. And yes, Chelsea, I am still unaware of what those things are. Would you care to tell me about them? I must say, all of this is becoming 'curiouser and curiouser,' as the saying goes."

Stunned by what she had just heard, Chelsea paused for several moments before answering. "No, Allistaire," she answered. "One day, perhaps, but not yet."

"All right," he said. "But I need to pencil you in for tomorrow. Will noontime be okay?"

"Yes," she answered, "provided Brandon can work his schedule around."

"Then noon it is," he said. "But if your friend can't make it, call me and we'll reschedule."

"I will," Chelsea answered rather absently, her mind still racing. "But, Allistaire . . . ," she said.

"Yes?" he asked.

"What's this all about?"

Allistaire sighed into the phone. "I wish I knew, Chelsea," he said. "You're already privy to far more than I. Either way, my guess is that by the end of our meeting tomorrow, you'll know a lot more."

"Until tomorrow, then," she said.

"Until tomorrow," Allistaire answered, and hung up.

Stunned, Chelsea shakily hung up the phone. She then went and sat at the dining room table, Brooke's journal just inches from her grasp. She suddenly wanted to read the final excerpt even more than ever, and she knew that it would be all she could do to resist doing so until Brandon came home.

Rising from the table, she walked into the living room and stood before Greg's unfinished portrait of Brooke. This time, Brooke's eyes seemed to look straight down at her, as if she were trying to tell her something.

But what? Chelsea wondered as she continued to regard the portrait. *Just when I think that I'm about to learn it all, you do this to me.* As she turned and again looked at the old journal lying so peacefully atop the dining table, she shook her head slightly.

Even now, Gram, you still reach out to me from the grave, Chelsea thought. *But what is it that you're trying to tell me?*

31.

"Well, this is certainly a bolt out of the blue," Brandon said. "Who'd have guessed that Brooke left another letter for you? And yes, I'll be glad to come along with you to Syracuse. I'll fix it tonight. One of the other doctors owes me a favor, anyway."

"Thank you," Chelsea said. "I can't imagine going to Allistaire's office without you."

Frustrated by the news, Chelsea ran one hand through her hair. Rather than being intrigued by Allistaire's phone call, she was clearly upset. She couldn't imagine why there was a second letter from Brooke or why Brooke had wanted her to examine the journal and view all the old photographs before being allowed to read it. Allistaire had done a good job of following Brooke's orders, it seemed, and he had been right about a couple of things. Chelsea was indeed already privy to far more information than he. And by the end of their meeting tomorrow, she too believed that she would know much more about her grandmother's past. Just then she remembered something Allistaire had said over the phone, and it set her to thinking.

Brandon noticed the change in her expression. "Is there something else?" he asked.

Chelsea nodded. "Allistaire said that he had an *envelope* for me," she answered. "He never said anything specifically about a letter."

"Really?" Brandon asked. "An envelope? I guess after you telling me about the first letter, I just assumed . . ."

"So did I," Chelsea said. "But that might not be the case. Anyway, I guess we'll find out tomorrow."

They had eaten dinner at his place and they were sitting on his porch, watching the sun set. All afternoon Chelsea had been highly impatient to read the final entry in Brooke's journal, and it had been all she could do to resist the urge until Brandon had come home.

When she heard him arrive, she had immediately gone over and told him about Allistaire's phone call. Brandon had been as surprised as she, but he said that he wanted to eat dinner before reading the journal. He had suggested that they also take some time and talk first. And now that dinner was over, Chelsea was actually glad that they had waited. She had to admit that she felt calmer and better prepared for whatever lay ahead. She also realized that Brandon had sensed her nervousness, and this had been his way of calming her. Even so, Brooke's old journal still lingered at Chelsea's cottage, its final entry waiting to be read. After the two of them sat in silence for a while longer, at last Chelsea looked over at Brandon.

"It's time . . . ," she said.

"I know," he answered. "But before we

go, you must promise me a couple of things."

"What?" she asked.

"Please let me be the one to read it," he said. "I think that it will be easier for you that way. And if it should become too painful for you, tell me and I'll stop. There's no need for you to suffer through it just because I want to know, too."

Thinking, Chelsea looked out at the waves. Unlike everything else in her world, they never seemed to change.

"All right," she said quietly.

Fifteen minutes later they were seated on Chelsea's couch. Brandon had lit a fire, and a freshly opened bottle of red wine and two glasses sat before them on the coffee table. Brandon picked up the journal and turned to the final entry. As he looked at the pages, he shook his head.

"What's wrong?" Chelsea asked.

"It's barely legible," he answered. "Her tears fell on these last few pages. And her handwriting is extremely poor, as if she had been shaking. Something important happened just before she wrote this, Chelsea."

"Can you make it out?" Chelsea asked hopefully.

"Yes," Brandon answered. "But you'll have to forgive me if it's slow going." With that, he began reading aloud:

Sunday, August 16, 1942, 4:00 A.M.

My hands are shaking terribly as I write these words, and so many of my tears are falling upon the pages that what I record here may be forever lost the very moment it is written. Be that as it may, I feel that I must get my thoughts down now, before I lose my courage.

Three more days have passed, and so much has happened this night that I know my life has been forever changed. Two terrible things have occurred; one was of my making, and the other was not. And I am as desolate over one as I am the other . . .

I have vowed to leave Lake Evergreen immediately after penning these words. And I've decided that before I go, I must collect this journal and whatever photographs I have of me and Greg and hide them somewhere here in the cottage. I simply cannot take them home. For I

*know that I would be compelled to look
at them again, and that would drive a
stake through my heart . . .*

It was nearly midnight as Greg sat on his
porch. The wind was high, causing the
waves of Lake Evergreen to cap strongly.
He had been unable to sleep and had
come out for a cigarette. Since Bill's visit
to Brooke, he had been smoking more
than ever. It helped to calm his nerves,
especially when he thought of Brooke's
and Bill's bodies lying together.

Even so, he was not sorry that he had
gone to see her three mornings ago. He
had desperately wanted to see if there
was any change in her after she had been
with her husband. Would she seem happier? he wondered. Or would she be even
more depressed and torn than before? He
hadn't known the answer, but there was
one thing about which he had been sure.
He had needed to confront her that morning, and nothing could have stopped him.
Especially now that her husband was
gone. And to his great disappointment,
he had gotten his answers.

Despite his jealousy over Bill and Brooke's reunion, in a way he felt sorry for them. To his mind, their time together must have been a form of both pleasure and pain. Pleasure at the mere sight of one another. Pleasure at holding each other, and talking, and laughing, and making love after so long. But he also believed that it must have been torturous for them as well, because it was so fleeting. And because of that, had Bill's visit perhaps proven to be more of a curse than a blessing for Brooke? Only she could provide that answer, Greg knew. But given the promise he had made to her, he daren't ask that question.

His heart was still hers, of that he was certain. And he believed that it always would be, despite the impossible situation in which he and Brooke found themselves. Since falling in love with her, more than once he had considered selling his cottage and going back to New York to live full-time. But he loved it here, and knowing that she would likely return every summer—and that he would not— would surely cause him even greater pain. And so he had resolved not only to stay for the rest of this summer but to also return here each year, just as he knew Brooke would do. And perhaps, given enough time, the two of them could find some sort of harmony.

Just then he smiled lightly. He was still hearing the music, he realized. Brooke's lights remained on and her old record player had been going all evening, which was largely why he had been unable to sleep. She had been playing the same blues record over and over again, and Greg recognized it as the one that Brooke once said was Bill's favorite. As New Orleans blues floated from her cottage toward his, Greg lit another cigarette off his earlier one, wondering why she wasn't asleep.

Just then he heard Brooke's squeaky porch door open and close, causing him to turn his head and look. To his surprise, he saw Brooke coming down the porch stairs. She was wearing only a negligee, and as she descended, her steps seemed wobbly and unsure. She then paused for a moment at the bottom of the stairs, her bare feet in the sand, her eyes cast toward the sky, the moonlight pointing up the delicate folds of her white negligee. Had the scene not been so bizarre, it would have been quite beautiful, Greg realized.

But as Greg watched her, he instinctively knew that something was very wrong. Then to his great horror, he saw her tentatively cross the sandy beach like some unearthly sleepwalker and wade straight out into the high, dark waves of Lake Evergreen. A huge sense of worry rose within Greg as he then saw her strangely pause for a moment, the waves brushing strongly up against her, causing her to sway to and fro in the water. And then, with the moonlight still highlighting part of her lovely form, she again started her trancelike walk and began going even deeper.

Fearing the worst, Greg tore from his porch and ran to her as best his bad foot would allow, his heart in his throat. By the time he reached her she was nearly chest-high in the deadly water. Wasting no time, he slipped one arm beneath her knees, lifted her up, and held her close. He tried to look at her face, but when his eyes met hers, her only response was to begin sobbing uncontrollably and bury her face in his chest.

Deciding not to speak, Greg hurriedly carried Brooke back to the cottage, where he laid her down on the couch before the fireplace. Although the fire had not gone out, he quickly added a couple more logs, ensuring that it would last a good while longer. While turning off the record player, he noticed that a half-consumed bottle of whiskey stood alongside it.

After retrieving a towel from the bathroom, he did the best he could to briskly dry her off and again tried looking into her dazed eyes. To his dismay, Brooke was still crying uncontrollably. In an attempt to calm her, he gently wiped the wet hair away from her face and placed his hands on either side of her head.

"Brooke . . . ," he said gently. "Why did you do that? You could have died . . ."

She had begun shivering strongly, the desperate tears running from her eyes impossible to distinguish from the drops of cold lake water that still lay upon her face. But even now, she did not speak.

Several moments later, she lifted one arm and pointed at the coffee table standing before the couch. When Greg turned to look, he saw a piece of crumpled paper lying there. As he smoothed it out and read it, he quickly understood the reason for Brooke's uncontrollable distress. The piece of paper said:

WESTERN UNION
WU 35 GOVT=WUX WASHINGTON DC
AUG 20 1942
MRS BROOKE BARTLETT 18 SCHUYLER LANE
SERENDIPITY NEW YORK
THE SECRETARY OF WAR DEEPLY REGRETS
TO INFORM YOU THAT YOUR HUSBAND
2/LT BARTLETT, WILLIAM T, DROWNED DURING
TRANSPORT TO ENGLAND AUGUST 15 1942 STOP
TROOP TRANSPORT SHIP SUNK WITH ALL HANDS BY GERMAN U-BOAT STOP
NO SURVIVORS STOP U- BOAT SUNK IN SUBSEQUENT ACTION STOP
CONFIRMING LETTER WILL FOLLOW

JAMES ALEXANDER ULIO ADJUTANT
GENERAL
OF THE ARMY

Greg simply sat there for several moments, speechless.

My God . . . , he thought.

His hand trembling visibly, Greg set the terrible notice back down atop the coffee table.

"Brooke . . . ," he uttered at last.

When she still didn't answer, Greg bent down closer and took her chilled hands into his. They felt dank and lifeless, as if all the vitality she once possessed had been suddenly drained from her.

"I know . . . ," he said quietly. "I saw the telegram. I'm so sorry . . ."

"He's gone," Brooke said at last, her voice so faint he could barely hear her. "Bill's gone . . ."

Not knowing what else to do, Greg put his arms around her and held her close. They remained that way for some time, the only sounds the light crackling of the fire and the rhythmic ticking of Brooke's mantel clock. And then, quite unexpectedly, Brooke lifted her face to his, and she kissed him on the lips.

Startled, Greg tried to sit up. But she held him close and then kissed him once more, longer and more deeply this time. And as she did, he remembered how much he wanted her, needed her, and how he had dreamed of this moment. But now was not the time, he knew. She didn't want him, he realized, as much as she wanted the return of her dead husband. She was in shock, and she needed someone to hold on to while her entire world fell apart. But the longer they embraced, the more he found his willpower weakening. At last he tore himself free of her enticing grasp and sat up.

"Brooke . . . ," he said, his voice suddenly sounding hoarse and unfamiliar. "We can't do this . . . it's wrong, and you're doing it out of grief, rather than love . . ."

To his surprise, Brooke was no longer crying. Her face an unreadable mask, she reached up and placed two fingers against his lips, silencing him. "No more words," she said. "No more waiting . . ."

When she stood from the couch, her

body was no longer shaking, her stance no longer unsteady. After again looking deeply into his eyes, she took his hand and began leading him into her bedroom. And although every fiber of his being told Greg that it was wrong, he found it utterly impossible to resist her.

Two hours later, Brooke sat on the edge of her bed, crying so softly that she could barely be heard. Moonlight filtered in through the bedroom window, its velvety hue highlighting Greg's naked form as he slept soundly. But the moonlight seemed to shine even more brightly upon the terrible deed they had done, upon the shame Brooke felt in her heart, and upon the realization that her beloved husband was dead. The emotions swirling through her were so strong and conflicting that she scarcely knew herself anymore.

They had made love, and she had welcomed it. More than welcomed it, she realized shamefully. It had in fact been she who had demanded it, embraced it, and taken all she could from him in a slow, almost dreamlike coupling. But now, as she sat on the edge of the bed in the moonlight, she understood that Greg had been right. It hadn't really been him she had wanted but the physical memory of Bill, the other man with whom she had slept in this very bed, just four days ago. And as she sat there thinking and crying, she came to some heart-rending conclusions.

She would leave Lake Evergreen this very morning. For facing up to Greg and the terrible thing they had done this night would be far too much for her to bear just now, and she knew it. She would hide the journal, the photos, and the two telegrams somewhere in the cottage, not only because taking them home to Syracuse might one day expose what had happened here, but also because looking at them would be far too painful. If she ever saw them again, they would do nothing but remind her not only of her shame, but also of the man she loved but could not have—the same man now lying asleep in her bed.

Before going she would write him a letter, she decided. One that would hopefully explain what was in her heart as best she could and the real reasons for what had just happened between them. And then she silently vowed to never see him again, no matter how the rest of her life might unfold. For after what had happened here tonight, she knew that being near him again would be far too heartbreaking, too terrible, and too guilt-inducing for her to endure. At last she slipped on her robe and then looked down upon him again, as the moonlight highlighted his handsome features.

Yes, she thought as she stood there looking at him. *The very first time I saw him, I was right. He does look like Errol Flynn. . .*

As fresh tears raced down her cheeks, she left the bedroom.

Two hours later, Greg suddenly started awake to find that he was alone. He held his watch to the moonlight and saw that it was nearly three A.M. After putting his clothes on, he left the bedroom.

The living room seemed to yawn at him as he entered it. The fire had at last gone out, and the air had become cold. The lights were switched off and the terrible death notice still lay on the coffee table, but there was no sign of Brooke. After walking out onto the porch, he saw her standing at the bottom of the porch steps, her bare feet in the sand, her eyes gazing blankly out over the waves.

He quietly opened the door and walked down the steps to join her. But as he looked at her profile, she did not turn toward him. Instead of the warm, loving woman he had made love to only hours before, she now seemed to be made of stone; immobile, cold, and intransigent. As a way to refrain from embracing him again, she had wrapped her arms about herself. When he stepped before her and tried to look directly into her eyes, Brooke shamefully turned her face away.

"We have to talk about this . . . ," Greg said. "Perhaps not now, but eventually. Some important things happened here tonight, Brooke. You know that as well as I do, and I'm worried for you."

Still without looking at him, Brooke shook her head. "No," she said, her voice a near-whisper. "Nothing happened here tonight. Now please go home, I beg of you."

"But, Brooke," he said, "you can't deny what—"

"Go home, Greg," she said, her tone now akin to outright begging. "Go home and leave me alone . . ."

He started to speak again, then thought the better of it. *You're so shattered,* he thought as he looked at her lovely profile, bathed in moonlight. *And you will be this way for a long time. But I can wait for you, because now we have all the time in the world. And so I will obey your wishes and allow you to grieve in your own way and in your own time . . .*

Totally unaware that it would be for the last time in his life, Greg faced Brooke and he looked into her eyes.

"Good night, my love," he said quietly.

While Brooke watched him go, her heart finally reached its limit and it broke irreparably in two.

Two hours later, Brooke was packed and ready to leave. Her journal, photographs, and telegrams had been hidden, and she had penned her good-bye letter.

Before going, she walked into the living room and stood before Greg's unfinished portrait of her. In between sessions she had been keeping it atop the fireplace mantel, where it now rested. For several moments she considered taking it with her, as a reminder both of the man she loved and of the amazing talent he possessed. But in the end she realized that she could not, for the same reasons she could not take her other mementos. After taking a last look at the portrait, she wiped the tears from her eyes and departed her cottage for the final time.

Just one more thing to do . . . , she thought sadly.

On loading her bags and Ike into her car, she removed Greg's letter from her purse and trod across the moonlit beach toward his cottage. She stopped to listen for a few moments and heard nothing. All of the cottage lights were out; the only sounds came from the light breeze streaming through the pines, and the waves as they rushed the sandy shore. After silently climbing the porch steps, she inserted the letter for Greg between the porch door and its frame.

As she came back down the steps, something caught her eye. Near the far side of the little house, she saw the fully grown coneflowers that resulted from the seeds Greg had been planting that first day she met him. They had grown tall, their stems and blossoms swaying slightly in the breeze. Bending down, she plucked two of them and placed them into her purse.

Then she quickly walked back to her waiting car. Before leaving, she turned and looked at her beloved cottage one last time and then toward the restless lake that lay just beyond it. She already knew that she would never return here. She would never again see this wonderful place, swim in that pristine lake, or hear the familiar rustle of the pine trees.

And perhaps even worse, she knew that so long as Greg returned here every summer, she could not. Being so close to him would only reopen all of her wounds and revive the terrible guilt she already felt over what had happened in the cottage she still so loved, but now felt too

ashamed to occupy. Her humiliation totally overpowering, she looked up at the
stars.

"Forgive me, Bill . . . ," she whispered,
her voice cracking. "I have done wrong,
and I accept my penance . . ."

After getting into her car, she started
the engine and quietly departed Lake Evergreen for the last time in her life.

Brandon closed the journal. Like she had
done with the first telegram, Brooke had
folded and pasted the second one into
her old journal as well, and he had read
directly from it. He then turned and looked
at Chelsea. She was crying, and shaking
slightly. Knowing that she needed to be
held, he put his arms around her.

"My God . . . ," Chelsea said, her voice
quivering. "Do you think that Brooke actually tried to—"

"I don't know," Brandon quickly said.

Although he had purposely cut her off,
this tone had been loving rather than
harsh. As he looked into her eyes he saw
her pain there, much the way Greg had
seen the pain in Brooke's eyes that night,

here on this same couch, some sixty-odd years ago.

"People sometimes do strange things when they're in shock," he added softly. "But that doesn't mean that she . . ." Sighing, he searched for the right words.

"There's no point in trying to figure it out, my love," he said. "All that will do is cause you more torment. And besides, is that really how you want to remember her?"

Chelsea dabbed at her eyes with a handkerchief. "No . . . ," she answered quietly. "And like I said before, I will not judge Brooke. I wasn't there, but in some ways I can feel what she was going through—her worry, her pain, her sense of shame over simply having loved someone. And then her guilt over having acted on it, out of such a sudden and overpowering sense of grief. But at least now some of our questions have been answered."

"Such as . . . ?" Brandon asked.

"Well," Chelsea said, "for one thing, I now know why she never returned here. As she said in her journal, the pain of seeing Greg again, coupled with her shame over having been with him, con-spired to keep her away. And I now also know why she never sold this place, too."

"Why?" Brandon asked.

"Don't you see?" Chelsea answered. "Her journal and photos were still hidden here. If some new buyer happened to find them, they would in all likelihood return them to her. And because Brooke lived with my mother she couldn't risk that, so she kept the cottage and willed it to me. But what I still don't understand is why she wanted *me* to learn the story, rather than Lucy. Perhaps whatever Allistaire has to show us tomorrow will answer that."

As Chelsea blankly gazed at the fire, she took another sip of wine. "It's amaz-ing, isn't it?" she asked.

"What is?"

"That like my grandmother, I too would fall in love with the man in the neighbor-ing cottage," she answered quietly.

"Yes," Brandon answered. "But this time, it will have a happier ending."

At last, Chelsea smiled a little. "Prom-ise?" she asked.

"Yes," he answered. "I promise."

But while Brandon thought some more about things, his expression darkened. *She still doesn't fully understand,* he thought. *She is so immersed in Brooke's feelings that she hasn't realized the ramifications for herself. And I must be the one to tell her, because I'm the only other living person who knows the full story. . .*

Brandon turned and looked into her eyes. "I'm sorry to say this, Chelsea," he said. "But you either haven't grasped it or you do in fact realize it and simply don't wish to face things. Either way, I think we should talk about it."

"What are you trying to say?" she asked.

"Well," Brandon said, "the truth is, there's a fifty-fifty chance that Gregory Butler was your grandfather, rather than Bill Bartlett."

For several moments Chelsea simply sat there, speechless and unmoving. Then at last, she buried her face in her hands.

"My God," she whispered. "You're right. Why didn't I see it sooner?"

Brandon smiled a little. "Your focus was on Brooke rather than on yourself.

You loved your grandmother, and you always will. But given that she slept with Greg only four days after being with Bill, you'll probably never know for sure. The real question, I think, is whether you can live with that."

As Chelsea again reached for her wineglass, Brandon noticed that her hands were still shaking. After a time, she nodded.

"I think so . . . ," she answered. "I never knew Bill Bartlett at all. But after reading Gram's journal, I now feel that I know Greg Butler. Either way, it doesn't change who I am."

After thinking for a few more moments, Chelsea sighed. "But now," she said, "all of this raises another equally difficult issue . . ."

"Which is?" Brandon asked.

Chelsea tiredly laid her head upon Brandon's shoulder. "Just how much of this do I tell my mother, if indeed I ever do?" she asked. "She isn't strong, like Brooke was. And she's already had all the bad news she can handle."

"Well," Brandon answered, "that part of it is up to you. I don't know Lucy, so it's impossible for me to advise you about that. But maybe we could remedy that tomorrow, while we're in Syracuse. I'd love to meet your parents, if I could."

Just then, the idea that Chelsea had been thinking about resurfaced in her mind. She wanted to ask Brandon now, but was this the right time? As she sat there with his arms around her she felt safe and warm, despite the unsettling revelation about Brooke and Greg. But at the same time she didn't want to push too hard and frighten him. Because that, she knew, would break her heart irreparably. And then another fear seized her heart.

If asking him does drive him away, would I then be in the same situation as Brooke those many years ago? she wondered. *If Brandon stopped loving me, would I ever again feel right about returning to this wonderful place I've come to love so much?*

Deciding that it was now or never, she sat up a bit and looked questioningly into his eyes.

At once, Brandon noticed the change in her.

"Is there something else?" he asked.

"Yes," she said. "And it has taken some time for me to get up the courage to ask you. So please, Brandon, let me finish what I have to say before you answer."

Brandon nodded. "All right," he said simply.

Hoping against hope, Chelsea poured her heart out to him.

And as she did, Brandon listened patiently.

32.

At a little past noon on the next day, Allistaire Reynolds reached out and heartily shook Brandon's hand. "It's a pleasure to meet you, Dr. Yale," he said. "Any friend of Chelsea's is a friend of mine."

Brandon smiled and sat down beside Chelsea. "I want to express my gratitude for everything you've done for Chelsea," he said. "And please, call me Brandon."

Allistaire smiled and leaned back in his chair. "Thank you," he answered.

He then looked a bit more closely at Brandon, sizing him up. *So this is the man*

Chelsea met up at Lake Evergreen, he thought. *Lucky fellow . . .*

Allistaire then looked at Chelsea. "And how have you been, my dear?" he asked. "From what I can tell, it seems that the great outdoors agrees with you."

Despite her nervousness, Chelsea tried to smile. "It does," she said. "And much to my own surprise, I must admit."

Now that the pleasantries were over, Allistaire's lawyerly persona surfaced in full. Leaning forward, he placed his palms flat atop his desk.

"Please forgive me for asking this, Chelsea," he said. "I mean no disrespect toward Brandon, but are you quite sure that you want him present today? I ask because even I do not know what is contained in the envelope that I am about to give to you. You are my only client in this affair, and I feel it right to make sure."

Chelsea nodded. "I'm quite certain, Allistaire," she answered. Then she turned and gave Brandon a little smile. "In fact," she added, "there's no one in the world I trust more."

"All right, then," Allistaire said. Then he

looked at Brandon again. "No offense," he said.

Brandon nodded. "None taken," he answered. "As you just said, it's your job."

"I have a few questions first," Allistaire said to Chelsea. "Are you still going to keep the cottage?"

"Yes, definitely," she answered.

"Okay," Allistaire said. "I'll get to work on transferring ownership to you. And have you examined *everything* that your late grandmother wanted you to see?" he asked.

"As best I know," she said.

"All right," Allistaire answered. "But I must tell you that all of this is unusual, to say the least. Are you sure that you wouldn't like to tell me what's really going on?"

Chelsea shook her head. "No, Allistaire," she answered. "One day, perhaps. But not now."

"Very well, then," Allistaire said.

He opened a desk drawer and produced a manila envelope. With shaking hands, Chelsea accepted it from Allistaire. Before opening it, she looked over at Brandon and he nodded.

Chelsea opened the envelope and found a smaller one inside, which was addressed to Chelsea in Brooke's familiar handwriting. Chelsea opened the second envelope to find another letter from Brooke. It too had been written in her grandmother's familiar black fountain ink. But this time, the aged handwriting was more difficult to read:

Thursday, February 22, 1994, 4:00 P.M.

Dearest Chelsea,

Hello again, my child. I fully understand that this second letter comes as a shock, but it was necessary. I have written this to you and entrusted it to Allistaire's care because now that you have been to Lake Evergreen and have read my journal, and seen the photographs and the telegrams, you know my story. And I also write this because as you will soon learn, I have two further wishes to ask of you.

I sense that my time left on this earth is growing short, and so I wanted to write this letter now, to ensure that it is placed into Allistaire's safekeeping before something irreversible happens to me. As I write this I am sitting in my wheelchair, on the sunporch of your mother's house. It is a lovely winter's day with crisp, white snow on the ground and crystalline icicles hanging from the eves. As much as I like being here, I cannot help but wish that I could see my beloved cabin just one more time . . .

By now, many of your questions have been answered. But there are some things that you still do not know. As the journal says, for sentimental reasons I did indeed pick two coneflowers from Greg's garden on the morning that I left Lake Evergreen. But on the way home I realized that I could not keep them, for the same reasons that I could not bring with me the journal or the photographs. And so I stopped at a friend's place and I left them on her steps, pressed inside the book that Greg gave to me that day atop Red Rock Mountain. My friend's name was Emily Rousseau, and she still owns and runs a small Serendipity restaurant called the Blue Rooster.

Should you decide to keep the cottage, you may wish to visit her one day.

You now also know why I left the cabin so suddenly and why I never returned. Nor could I sell it, because the new owners might have discovered the tin box that I had hidden and what lay inside it. I willed the cottage to you, rather than to your mother, because of the two of you, Lucy is the far more fragile, brittle, and unforgiving one. Because she never expressed any interest in the cottage, had I willed it to her, she would have likely sold it. And as I have said, I couldn't allow that to happen. And so, my child, I made it yours. I cannot know whether you have decided to sell it or to keep it, or whether your visit there has granted you any additional happiness. Either way, I hope that you will keep the cottage. But should you choose to sell, in this too you have my blessing.

You are probably now also aware of why I took up painting after I left Lake Evergreen for good. If you assume that it was a way of staying "close" to Greg, then you are right. At first I thought that I would simply try it and soon find that I had no talent for it. But to my surprise, I was wrong. And although my humble paintings will never make their mark on the world of art history, I nonetheless enjoyed creating them. But perhaps the very best thing that came out of my growing passion for painting was that you came to love doing it too, and because of that we were able to spend so many happy hours together, as I taught you. I also like to think that Greg's unfinished portrait of me still rests atop the fireplace mantel, rather than your having disposed of it in anger. But if the latter is true, then please know that I understand.

As for the journal, the photos, and the two telegrams, they too are yours to do with as you wish. And should you choose to tell my story to Lucy, you also have my blessing. I know that deciding whether to tell her will be a great quandary for you, and for that I am truly sorry. I cannot offer any advice in that regard, save to say that should you do so, it must be done in the gentlest possible way.

And now for the greatest of all the questions, the one that I'm sure you have already imagined but to which you have no answer. The simple truth is that I cannot tell you which of the two men I loved that summer was your grandfather. Because of the short period of time in between, I learned I was pregnant only after being with both of them. For my own selfish reasons, I always chose to believe that Bill was that man. But the truth of it is that I had never had any right to do so, and I suppose I chose that way of thinking only to ameliorate my guilt over what happened between Greg and me . . . What I did was wrong, I know, and I hope that you can forgive me.

And that, my child, is how I want to go to my final rest. Yes, I loved two men at once, but as I said in my journal, I am still unsure whether a woman can do that without going mad. And oddly enough, knowing which of them fathered Lucy might have perhaps confounded me even more. In the farewell letter I wrote to Greg, I asked that he never try to contact me. And although I can only guess at how much it must have hurt him to grant my wish, he complied, just the same.

In closing, I would make two more requests of you, one of which is conditional upon the other, but neither of which you are obligated to carry out. The first one is I hope you can find it in your heart to forgive me. I know that doing so will be difficult, and that is why I wanted you to read the journal and to see the photographs, rather than simply read another letter from me that told the same story. I hope that you were able to live my story through my words, to feel what I was going through, and to understand that—wrong as it might have been—I did in fact love them both. I realize that I have in some ways left you in limbo, and for that I am truly sorry.

And there is one last thing that I would ask. If you are in fact able to forgive me, would you please revisit my grave and tell me so? I fully understand that I will never know of your decision, but if you can find enough forgiveness in your heart, please do as I ask.

This will be my last communication with you, Chelsea. No more letters, journal pages, or photographs. It is now time for you to chart the rest of your own life's course. I did the best that I could to let someone in our family know the truth about what happened to me during those fateful wartime days, and the one I chose to tell was you. Because, my dear, of all of us, yours is the best, the most receiving, and the most forgiving heart. Stay safe, my child, be well, and may you one day find all the happiness that you rightfully deserve.

All my love,
Brooke

Her eyes brimming over with tears, Chelsea handed the letter to Brandon. By the time he had finished reading it, his eyes had also become shiny. Then he simply nodded at Chelsea and handed the precious letter back to her.

Recognizing their distress, Allistaire tactfully cleared his throat. "I hope that it wasn't too disturbing . . . ," he said.

Chelsea shook her head. "No," she answered, "at least not in the way that you probably mean."

"And I don't suppose that there's any point in my asking to read it?" he inquired.

Again Chelsea shook her head. "No," she answered softly.

"Then our business is concluded?" Allistaire asked.

Before answering, Chelsea looked over at Brandon. When he nodded back at her she felt her heart swell again, just as it had when she first realized she was falling in love with him. *So be it then,* she thought. Her tears at last starting to subside, she took a deep breath and looked back at Allistaire.

"As a matter of fact," she said, "there is something more that you could do on behalf of us both, and we'd like you to get started on it right away. You see, Brandon and I . . ."

As Chelsea made her explanation to Allistaire, he listened quietly. And then, when she had finished, he looked at Brandon again and he smiled.

Lucky fellow, indeed . . . , he thought once more.

33.

"So, Brandon," Adam Enright said, "what gauge shotgun do you use up there for birds? A twelve, I assume?"

Brandon nodded and set down his beer glass. "Yes, that's right," he answered. "Especially for grouse. You need the extra firepower to blast through the leaves and such. And you need a good gun dog."

"And is your setter good?" Adam asked.

Brandon smiled. "The best," he said. "Sometimes I think that Jeeves can suss out a bird from a mile away."

Adam laughed. He was warming up to

Brandon, and it showed. *"Jeeves!"* he said, laughing again. "Christ, but I like that name for a dog! I'm gonna remember that, next time I get a pup."

After taking another sip of wine, Chelsea sat back in her poolside lounge chair and lovingly regarded her parents. Once she and Brandon had left Allistaire's office, she had called Lucy and then Adam, asking if they could do a midafternoon barbecue rather than dinner. Adam had happily agreed, offering to pick up everything they'd need on the way over to Lucy's house. The rib eye steaks, corn on the cob, and cherry pie had all been delicious.

Chelsea had not, however, revealed the real reason why she and Brandon had asked to see Lucy and Adam earlier than planned. The truth was that she wanted plenty of time to revisit Brooke's grave, as Brooke had requested in her final letter. And that, she had wisely decided, was something best left unsaid. The only person she wanted to accompany her to the grave site was Brandon; of that she was abundantly sure.

As the sun slowly crossed the sky and

the wind lightly rippled the swimming pool water, Brandon sat by Chelsea's side at the poolside table. Adam sat across from them, happily nursing a Manhattan and smoking a cigar. Lucy sat beside Adam, diddling with her coffee spoon. Lucy had been rather nervous, and aside from the recent loss of her mother, Chelsea knew why. It wasn't every day that Chelsea presented her not only with a new love interest but also with one about whom she cared so deeply.

Chelsea had known that bringing Brandon along would likely set Lucy's nerves jangling, but that couldn't be avoided. Chelsea also guessed that her decision to remain at Lake Evergreen for the entire summer had caused her mother anguish. Lucy had been making a good show of liking Brandon, and perhaps she genuinely did. But with Lucy it was always hard to tell. Chelsea instinctively also knew that Lucy considered Brandon to be the greatest reason why Chelsea had stayed at Lake Evergreen, and to Lucy's credit she was right. And that would make it more difficult for Lucy to fully accept him, if indeed she ever could.

For his part, Adam liked Brandon the moment he met him. Adam had appreciated the attitude of respect that Brandon exhibited on entering the house and while meeting him and Lucy. That Brandon was a doctor also carried a good deal of weight, Chelsea realized. But the true tipping point had come when Adam learned that Brandon not only hunted and fished but that he also had a deep love for gun dogs. When Brandon told Adam that Jeeves could fetch beers from his refrigerator, Adam had nearly fallen down laughing and then begged Brandon to one day teach his dogs, too.

On the way into Syracuse that morning, Chelsea had told Brandon how her parents would likely act, and she had been right. Her father would be jovial, kind, and welcoming. But Lucy would be brittle, nervous, and more concerned with her own feelings than with actually seeing her daughter again. Chelsea knew full well that with both Brooke and Adam gone from the house, Lucy felt immensely alone. And now that Chelsea had decided to spend the rest of her summer at Lake Evergreen, Lucy had no familial shoulder left upon which to cry, making her sense of isolation finally complete.

Lucy had many friends in whom she could supposedly confide, but Chelsea had always wondered whether they were really the sort to whom her mother could reveal her inner heart. And now, after having been away for weeks, Chelsea believed she had her answer. Despite her many so-called friends, Lucy had only been able to confide in her immediate family, and especially in her mother. And with everyone now gone, Lucy was a lost soul.

Chelsea loved her mother; of that there was no question. But the longer she spent in this house, the more Chelsea understood that going to Lake Evergreen had been the best thing that she could have done—perhaps for both of them.

"And how is that old cottage, really?" Lucy asked. "I can't imagine it being very nice or why you'd actually want to keep it. I must say, you've rather surprised us."

Chelsea took another sip of wine. "The place surprised me too, Mom," she answered. "Actually, it's quite charming. And as for why I've decided to stay there

all summer, well, the most important answer to that is this man sitting right here
beside me."

Lucy immediately realized her gaffe,
and it showed on her face. "Well, of
course, dear," she said. "I didn't mean to
imply that . . . uh, well . . . you know what
I mean . . ."

Chelsea might have pursued that last
remark, but to what end? She and Brandon could have just as easily met with
Allistaire, then visited Brooke's grave and
returned to the lake with her parents none
the wiser. But Chelsea had wanted to see
how her mother was doing. And sadly,
she had gotten her answer. She had also
wanted to take the opportunity for them
to meet Brandon, and that part of the
visit, at least, had been accomplished.

Adam gave Brandon a knowing wink.
"What say us menfolk clean things up
for a change and let the ladies chat?" he
asked.

Understanding Adam's intent, Brandon
agreed, and they started clearing the
table. Chelsea knew that once the men
were in the kitchen, Lucy would start in

with her questions, and she didn't disappoint.

"Honestly, Chelsea," Lucy said in a near-whisper, "are you quite sure about him? He seems intelligent and polite enough. And I understand that he went to Harvard. But at the end of the day, is he really anything more than a glorified country doctor? And where's the wisdom in getting mixed up with the man in the neighboring cabin, for heaven's sake? What if it all goes wrong? Then you'd have to sell the place—which, by the way, is still what I think you should do."

God, Chelsea thought. *Did she really just say, "And where's the wisdom in getting mixed up with the man in the neighboring cabin"? If she only knew the whole truth. And one day, will I be the person who tells her? Gram was right about confiding in Mother. But as of right now, only God knows how to do it . . .*

Remembering that her mother was still grieving, Chelsea did her best to smile. "I love him, Mom," she answered simply. "And he loves me. In today's world, that's not an easy thing to find. And he's more of a man than any of those country club snobs you've pushed at me over the years."

Lucy sighed. "We only want the best for you, dear," she answered.

With that, Chelsea stood, walked around the table, and kissed Lucy on one cheek. "Then be happy for me," she answered. "Because after years of searching, that's what I've got. I know it in my heart, just as sure as I know the sun will rise tomorrow morning."

As if Lucy had been secretly waiting to hear those exact words, her expression quickly changed to one of compassion. Then she did something that surprised even Chelsea. She stood, held her daughter close, and looked lovingly into her eyes.

"The heart wants what it wants," Lucy said, unconsciously echoing Chelsea's words to Brandon of several nights ago. "I once felt the same way about your father, before it all fell apart for us. I know that I've been difficult today, and I'm sorry about that. I also know that I was hard on you about Brandon just now—far harder than I needed to be. But can't you see? I did it on purpose, Chelsea. I had to be sure that it is he who is keeping you up at the lake, rather than me, driving you away from here. And now that I know you're truly in love with him, then I can love him, too."

Then Lucy stood back from Chelsea, and she smiled.

"After all," she added, "I might be getting old, but I still know a good man when I see one."

As Chelsea became unexpectedly overcome, her eyes began to well up. Until this moment, Lucy had never communicated with her so deeply or so honestly. She had been wrong about her mother today, she realized, and Lucy had fooled her. Her mother was in fact starting to heal. While smiling through her tears, Chelsea laughed a little.

"I love you, Mom," she whispered.

"And I love you too," Lucy answered.

At last . . . , Chelsea thought. *And thank you, Mother . . .*

But then Chelsea thought a bit more, and her worries crowded in on her again.

But perhaps your sudden compassion has only made my decision harder, she thought. *Will I decide to tell you everything one day, or will I not? And if I do, will my words only serve to again break your slowly healing heart?*

34.

Chelsea had long believed that Fairlawn Cemetery was a lovely place. Always well-maintained and landscaped, it boasted an abundance of lovely trees, neatly trimmed hedges, and in the summertime a plethora of blooming flowers. After Brandon guided the Explorer through the open wrought iron gates and onto the property, Chelsea told him the directions to Brooke's grave site.

By now the sun was nearing the western horizon, and the cemetery birds had begun warbling their twilight lullabies. Shadows were slowly creeping from the bases of the monuments, their dark lengths stretching across the deep-green grass. Chelsea was glad that there were few visitors about just now, because she wanted her visit to be a very private one.

After a few minutes more, Brandon stopped the Explorer before a neat row of about twenty headstones. The markers backed up to a tall hedge, and in between each of them there grew a lovely white peony bush. As Chelsea had hoped, no other visitors were nearby.

Chelsea and Brandon exited the Explorer and began walking toward one of the larger marble headstones. Someone— presumably Adam or Lucy—had recently placed a pot of fresh, multicolored geraniums on the ground before it. The gravestone read:

Brooke E. Bartlett
RIP
And being loved by another is the most precious gift of all.
1917–1999

With tears in her eyes, Chelsea stepped closer. She was about to open her purse when she felt Brandon silently tugging on her elbow.

She looked questioningly him. "What is it?" she asked.

As Brandon pointed at the headstone lying on the right side of Brooke's, Chelsea drew a quick breath. It read:

Gregory R. Butler
RIP
All the love I had, I gave to you . . .
1916–1994

Stunned, Chelsea wiped her eyes. *My God,* she thought. *So it was here that Greg was laid to rest . . .*

Brandon put one arm around Chelsea's shoulder. "You didn't know?" he asked.

For the moment, Chelsea could only shake her head.

"But you were here at Brooke's burial," Brandon said. "And Greg was interred here before she was."

At last, Chelsea found her voice. "That's true," she said. "And I probably noticed Greg's headstone at the time. But his name meant nothing to me then, so I didn't remember it."

Chelsea closed her eyes for a few moments, thinking. "Until today," she said, "I never understood the inscription that Brooke selected for her stone. Clearly, it's an extension of Greg's. They truly loved each other, didn't they?"

"Yes . . . ," Brandon answered. Just then the wind rose a bit, scattering some early fallen leaves across the ground.

"Before she died, she must have known he was here," he said at last.

"Yes," Chelsea answered. "I can see that now. But how did Greg know that this was where Brooke would be buried? At the time of his interment, Gram had already bought her plot, but her headstone had yet to be laid."

"There are ways," Brandon answered.

Chelsea stood there for a time, looking at the two monuments. Although they were little more than lifeless pieces of carved stone, they had nonetheless accomplished what the two human beings they honored could not do. They had at last reunited two lovers whose single night of passion had separated them for decades. Then Chelsea remembered something that Emily Rousseau had told her, the first time she had visited the Blue Rooster.

"Rather than parting two old friends," Emily had said, *"the death of one has a way of joining them forever . . ."*

Taking Brandon by one arm, Chelsea escorted him closer to the graves. She then opened her purse and removed a tissue. Brandon thought that she was about to wipe her eyes, but he soon knew better. Inside Chelsea's tissue lay the two dried coneflowers that Brooke had picked from Greg's garden, just before leaving Lake Evergreen for the last time. The same two flowers that Brooke had left at Emily's doorstep and that Emily had in turn given to Chelsea, pressed inside Brooke's copy of *Leaves of Grass.*

"So you brought them with you," Brandon said quietly.

"Yes," Chelsea answered, her voice a near-whisper. "I felt that they belonged here with Brooke. But now, I can give one of them to Greg."

With the two old flowers still lying in her hands, Chelsea looked at Brooke's headstone.

"You asked me in your letter if I could

forgive you, Gram," she said. "But there was no need, because there is nothing to forgive. Love is something that each of us strives for, dreams of, clings to, and rejoices in. But who among us can claim to be its master? No, Gram. Love itself is the true master. And we are all powerless in its grasp, just as you were during your last days at Lake Evergreen."

Pausing for a moment, Chelsea wiped her eyes.

"And so, if you can hear me, let your heart be freed at last," she said. "And also know that what I now do, I do in memory of the love you and Greg had for one another."

Stepping forward, with a shaking hand Chelsea first placed one of the fragile coneflowers atop Brooke's headstone and then set the other one on Greg's stone. Backing up, she took Brandon's hand and held it tight.

Almost at once the breeze strengthened noticeably, lifting both coneflowers free of their headstones and comingling them. Twirling and climbing ever higher in the strengthening breeze, at last they broke apart, turned to dust, and were for-ever gone.

Still shaking slightly, Chelsea looked into Brandon's eyes.

"Do you think she heard me?" she asked, barely able to get the words out.

Brandon nodded. "And so did he," he answered.

"Take me home again, Brandon," Chelsea said softly.

"Back to Lucy's house?" he asked.

Chelsea shook her head.

"No," she answered. "Take me back to Lake Evergreen. That's my home now . . ."

Remaining arm in arm, they turned and began the walk back to the car.

35.

"I do!"

Not only did Chelsea Enright say those words with enthusiasm, she meant them.

"In that case, I now pronounce you man and wife!" Father Randall said. He was a tall, broad man with a thick shock of white hair and had been Chelsea's priest since her confirmation.

"And you may now kiss the bride!" he said to Brandon with a wink.

Brandon smiled and gently lifted Chelsea's veil. Throwing caution to the wind, he bent her back deeply beneath him and then kissed her long and hard on the lips.

When at last he swung her upright again, she laughed joyously and then turned to look out over the many rows of happy guests.

It was a crystal-clear late October afternoon in Syracuse. Brandon had asked for her hand one month ago, and Chelsea had immediately accepted. And now that they were married, they were quite possibly the two happiest people on the face of the earth.

Chelsea again looked joyously out over the crowd. Her parents and extended family were in the front row. One of Chelsea's dearest college girlfriends had served as her maid of honor, and one of Brandon's ranger buddies was his best man. Jenny Beauregard sat in the next row back, crying tears of joy. Jacques and Margot Fabienne were two rows behind Chelsea's parents, while Brandon's parents and extended family sat on the other side of the aisle.

To Chelsea's amusement not only was Margot crying, but so too was the ever stalwart Jacques. And Emily Rousseau had ridden down with the Fabiennes, insisting that she could never forgive herself if she missed the wedding of Brooke's only granddaughter. Even Dolly and Jeeves were in attendance, the two of them sitting obediently near one side of the altar. Jeeves wore a black bow tie around his neck, and Dolly wore a white lace scarf.

Chelsea pulled Brandon close and placed her lips to his ear. "We did it, my love," she said.

Brandon smiled back. "Yes, we did," he answered her.

"And now you have to tell me what it means," she said. "There's no getting out of it this time . . ."

Brandon gave her a quizzical look. "Tell you what . . . ?" he asked.

Chelsea laughed a little, then she gently poked the end of his nose. "Oh, how quickly men forget," she answered. Leaving him to ponder the mystery, she turned back toward the joyous crowd.

When at last they left the altar and began the walk back down the aisle, Brandon let go a sharp whistle, causing Dolly and Jeeves to immediately run and join them. As they exited the church, showers of confetti soon filled the air, so much so that some passersby actually began wondering if Syracuse was receiving an early snowfall. Soon after, everyone was on their way to the wedding reception.

The affair took place at Adam's country club, and although Chelsea had protested about the great cost and bother, Adam stubbornly held his ground. He was a well-respected businessman in town, he had argued, and the venue needed to be right. And besides, he only had one daughter to give away.

It was a lovely event with mountains of food and drink, a wonderful band, and an immense wedding cake that looked as if it could have fed twice as many people as the happy throng in attendance. Jacques became quite tipsy on red wine and insisted on singing two songs in his native French. Not to be outdone, Brandon joined him. And as luck would have it, Jenny Beauregard caught Chelsea's bouquet. At last, it was time for Chelsea and Brandon to go. As they made their way to the car, many well-wishers followed them out.

Just then Allistaire Reynolds made his way toward them. As he approached the newlyweds, he smiled. He looked at Chelsea admiringly, then he gave Brandon a firm handshake.

"You're a lucky man," he said. "Should the two of you need anything else, you know where I am. And the best of luck with everything." After Brandon thanked him, Chelsea gave Allistaire a kiss on the cheek that actually made him blush.

Just before Chelsea entered the car, she felt someone touch her arm. She turned to see her mother and father standing there, their eyes filled with tears. Chelsea immediately stopped and embraced each of them once more. As she did, Adam searched her eyes.

"Are you quite sure?" he asked. "Now that you've quit teaching, you could easily come and work for me, you know." Then he smiled a little, remembering. "I'm still immensely willing to assign you absolutely no responsibilities and grossly overpay you for completely ignoring them."

Chelsea laughed. And then, upon seeing the wistful combination of both happiness and sadness in her father's eyes, she reached out one white-gloved hand and touched his cheek.

"You know that I can't . . . ," she said. "My path is set now."

Adam smiled through his tears. "And are the two of you quite certain that you don't want a honeymoon?" he asked. "Lucy and I are very willing to send you anywhere you'd like to go."

"I understand that, Dad," Chelsea answered. "And we do thank you. But you know that we can't right now." Then she saw another disappointed look overcome Adam's face, and she smiled.

"I'll you what, though," she added conspiratorially. "Once we get things settled, we'll gladly accept a belated honeymoon that'll send you and Mom straight to the poorhouse!"

At last, Adam's face lit up. "I'm going to hold you to that, kiddo," he said.

Then Chelsea took her mother into her arms again. Like so many others in the crowd, Lucy was crying tears of happiness. "Are you going to be okay?" Chelsea asked.

Now whenever Lucy smiled, it seemed to come straight from her heart. This was going to take some getting used to, Chelsea happily realized. Lucy reached out and touched her only daughter's cheek.

"Yes, my darling," she said. "I'm going to be fine. Perhaps better than I've ever been. Now go, the two of you, and have a wonderful life."

At last, with both dogs loaded into the same Explorer that Chelsea had driven on her first trip to Lake Evergreen, Chelsea and Brandon waved their final goodbyes and closed the doors. The Explorer was now theirs, a wedding present from Adam. And true to form, Adam had believed that he should have the final word about it. To that end, one of his dealership body shops had mercilessly decorated the entire vehicle with enough paper flowers, streamers, and shoe polish to decorate ten such "going away" vehicles. With a final honk of the horn, Brandon pulled the Explorer away from the curb.

As they left the country club, Chelsea turned around to look. For a time she saw a gaggle of hands waving happily in the air, and then they were gone. She edged a bit closer to Brandon and laid her head on his shoulder.

"Happy?" he asked.

"Yes . . . ," she answered quietly. "More so than at any time in my life." Then she smiled to herself a little. "I'm now Mrs. Chelsea Yale, and you'd better not forget it, buster."

Brandon laughed. "With you and Dolly hanging around all the time, there'll be little chance of that!"

Chelsea snuggled a bit closer. "And now, kind sir, you are obligated to tell me what it means . . ."

Brandon snorted out a short laugh. "What *what* means?" he asked.

"That saying in French," Chelsea answered. "You know, the one you mentioned that night when you finally told me about Mallory. You also said that it was something that you heard Jacques once say to Margot. After you said it in French I asked you what it meant, but you insisted that you weren't ready to tell me. I can only hope that you're ready now."

Brandon nodded, remembering. He had in fact meant those words that night. And yes, he was at last ready for Chelsea to hear them.

"Réticence entre deux amants peut souvent causer la mort de leur ardeur,"

Brandon said. *"Et donc, mon amour, peut-être cette erreur jamais subir nous. Pour plutôt que s'exprime dans les chuchotements, son amour devrait être cria joyeusement de sommets."*

Chelsea turned her head and looked lovingly at her new husband.

"And what does it mean?" she asked.

"'Reticence between two lovers can often cause the death of their ardor,'" Brandon said. "'And so, my love, may that mistake never befall us. For rather than being expressed in whispers, one's love should be shouted joyously from the mountaintops.'"

As she remembered that wonderful day with Brandon atop Red Rock Mountain, Chelsea smiled and edged a bit closer to him.

"I couldn't agree more," she said.

36.

Two days later, it was a cold morning in Serendipity. The sky was still dark and the streetlights remained on, causing the parking meters to cast eerie specters across the concrete sidewalks as Brandon and Chelsea rode along in Brandon's Jeep. Chelsea sat quietly beside Brandon, clutching a plastic zip bag and shivering a bit.

Brandon smiled and handed Chelsea the thermos full of hot coffee he had prepared before leaving.

"Have some of this," he said. "It'll help warm your bones. And besides," he added with a grin, "you've got a big day ahead of you. You'll need to be caffeinated."

Chelsea poured a cup of coffee and took an appreciative sip. Her new husband made the best coffee she had ever tasted. As she breathed, the air leaving her lungs formed telltale little clouds that disappeared as quickly as they came.

"Is that medical advice, Dr. Yale?" she asked.

"Nope," he answered. "Just common sense. In case you haven't already noticed, we're big on that up here."

As she watched Serendipity pass by in the early-morning darkness, Chelsea took another sip of coffee. Brandon was right, she realized. This was going to be a big day, and she knew it. Her only hope was that it would all work out.

A few minutes later, Brandon double-parked the Jeep and left the motor running. "It's going to be all right," he said. Then he pulled her closer and gave her a kiss. "You've done the right thing, I just know it."

Once more, Chelsea glanced tentatively outside. The darkness still seemed ominous, causing her to wish that the sun would soon rise. "I hope you're right . . . ," she said softly.

"Of course I am," Brandon answered. "But you'd best get going. I'm off today, and I'll be back at four to pick you up, just like we planned."

"Okay . . . ," she said.

After giving Brandon another kiss good-bye, she opened the door and got out. As the Jeep disappeared down the dark street, Chelsea suddenly had another moment of uncertainty about her decision. But there was no going back now, and she knew it. While taking a deep breath, she removed a set of keys from her purse, unlocked the door before her, and stepped inside.

Save for having no customers yet, the Blue Rooster looked exactly like it did the first time Brandon had brought Chelsea there. The shiny, black and white checkerboard floor was spotless, and the booths of dark leather lining either side wall still sported gleaming brass rails atop all their seat backs. Wrought iron tables for four with their white lace table-cloths took up the remaining floor space, and the European-style frosted globes that hung from the high ceiling were burning brightly. Then Chelsea smiled a bit through her worry as she again remembered how much this wonderful little place reminded her of a true French café.

Still clutching her plastic bag, Chelsea walked across the dining room floor and toward the kitchen that lay at the far end of the room. As she neared she heard voices, again causing her to smile through her trepidation.

They're already here . . . , she realized.

Pushing open the swinging kitchen doors, Chelsea walked in. The kitchen was like a welcome, comforting world that easily belied the chilly weather outside.

As if her advanced age meant nothing, Emily Rousseau was hard at work preparing some sauce or another. Jean, the French-Canadian chef who had worked for Emily for decades, busied himself with loading some vegetables and chicken parts into a stew pot. The wonderful aroma of fresh baked goods already hung in the air, as did the enticing scent of freshly made coffee. The four uniformed waitresses were also there, chatting among themselves as they loaded service onto trays for the dining room. Just then Chelsea smelled an intriguing aroma, and she smiled.

It's the beginnings of coq au vin, she thought. *Just like my first day at Lake Evergreen, when Jacques and Margot brought some to me...*

Emily was the first to see Chelsea. Throwing her hands into the air, she rushed straight over and hugged her warmly.

"Good morning, my dear!" she said in French. *"I am so glad that you're here at last!"*

Chelsea smiled broadly. "Now, Emily," she said, "you know that over time I'm hoping to learn French from you! But until I get acclimated to working here, you have to oblige me and speak only English! It's already bad enough that I've never done this sort of thing before . . ."

"Do not worry, *ma chère!*" Emily said insistently. "Everything will be just fine! You'll see!"

Then Emily smiled wryly.

"And besides," she added, "you are my boss now, *n'est-ce pas?* So I must do as you say!"

As if she still couldn't believe it, Chelsea looked around the kitchen again. *It's true, after all,* she thought. *I really do own the Blue Rooster. . .*

As the others eagerly gathered around her, Chelsea looked back at Emily and she laughed.

"Well," she said, "I guess you're right. And I want to thank you all for staying on. Without you at my side, this will never work!"

Just then, Claire Jennings tentatively approached Chelsea. The waitress uniform she wore was brand-new, as were the freshly minted tears in her eyes.

"I want to thank you again so much for this job," she said. "Pug and I were practically broke when you called. I promise you that I'll do my best."

Chelsea smiled at her. "I know that you will," she said. "Did you find someone good to look after Rachel?"

Claire nodded. "My mother," she answered.

After putting down her plastic bag, Chelsea took off her coat, gloves, and hat, and again stared into Emily's kind old eyes.

"So . . . where do I begin?" she asked.

After handing Chelsea an apron, Emily put one arm around her shoulders.

"Come, *ma chère,*" she said, "and I will begin teaching you the ways of true French cooking, just as my mother taught them to me so long ago. It may seem confusing at first, but with time, you . . ."

While Chelsea listened to Emily, she smiled. At last, her life had fully begun anew. She had kept ownership of her cottage on Lake Evergreen, and she couldn't possibly envisage a time when she'd ever let it go. She had also unraveled her late grandmother's past, and other than trying to decide whether to tell her mother, her heart was at peace with it. Best of all, she had a new husband whom she loved beyond all reason and who had strongly agreed with her plan to stop teaching, move to Serendipity, and buy the Blue Rooster from Emily.

For her part, Emily had been delighted at the prospect of at last passing down her little café to the only grandchild of her great friend Brooke Bartlett. Brandon had suggested that in return for Emily's guidance she be allowed to continue living upstairs rent-free, and Chelsea had heartily agreed. And besides, Chelsea had realized, for at least the first year or two she would need all the guidance that Emily could give her. It had also been Brandon's idea to hire Claire.

This, then, was the plan that Chelsea and Brandon had explained to Allistaire Reynolds, that same day when she and Brandon had read Brooke's second letter. Allistaire had handled the transaction, Adam had written Chelsea's business plan, and Adam's accountant had performed the due diligence on Emily's books. And it had been Jenny Beauregard's advice that Chelsea had sought out that day when Chelsea visited her by boat.

Shortly after Brandon proposed, Allistaire had also overseen the sale of Chelsea's Syracuse town house and the listing of Brandon's cottage. The cottage hadn't sold yet but it was a highly desirable property, and come spring they would likely have their choice of buyers. They certainly didn't need both cottages, and Chelsea's was by far the more comfortable of the two. The equity from the sale of Chelsea's town house—plus some extra help from her parents—had provided the funds needed for them to buy the Blue Rooster. Chelsea and Brandon would remain in Chelsea's cottage until the weather soon forced them to move into Brandon's house in Serendipity.

Chelsea knew that there would be things about her old life that she would miss. That was just the way of the world whenever a person left one existence and fully embraced another. But she also knew that she already loved her new life far more. And her late grandmother Brooke—the kindly old woman whom Chelsea had loved with all her heart—had been the catalyst that had so unexpectedly set everything in motion that first surprising day in Allistaire's office some five short months ago.

Two hours later, Chelsea's hands and apron had become stained with many of the various ingredients that make French cooking its best. While she wiped the perspiration from her brow, Emily gave her a knowing smile.

"You are doing well," Emily said. "But it is now time for us to discuss the recipe book, *non*?"

"Yes," Chelsea answered. "And I want you to know how much this means to me."

"And to me, as well," Emily answered. "Now, let's see, shall we? Which one shall be first?"

After unzipping the plastic bag she had brought along with her, Chelsea took Brooke's recipe book from it. As a tribute to her late grandmother, Chelsea had decided to add a few of Brooke's recipes to the menu. But the little book contained more than just recipes, she realized. It also held memories of Brooke's life that only she and Brandon fully understood. When she opened the old book, her heart again swelled with everything that Brooke had meant to her, in both life and death.

Thank you, Gram, she thought, *for teaching me so much, and for allowing me to know your secret past. Don't worry about Brandon and me, because we'll always be happy. In the end, we have you to thank for us finding each other.*

As she perused her grandmother's recipes, Chelsea came upon an intriguing one. Smiling, she turned and again looked into Emily's kind old eyes.

"How about Clark Gable's Grapefruit Cake?" she asked.

Emily nodded enthusiastically. *"That sounds marvelous!"* she spontaneously answered in French.

As Chelsea and Emily began assembling the needed ingredients, Chelsea smiled . . .

37.

That same afternoon, Brandon was busily washing his Jeep down near the shoreline of his property when Jeeves suddenly bared his teeth and growled. Jeeves was never wrong, and his insistent warning always meant the same thing.

Someone was coming.

It wasn't Chelsea, Brandon knew, because she was still at the Blue Rooster. As Jeeves snarled and bristled, Brandon dropped his sponge into the bucket of soapy water and turned to discover who it was.

Just then Pug Jennings's old truck

turned off Schuyler Lane and came roaring nearer. Knowing that there was nothing else for it, Brandon stood his ground, hoping at the same time that no one else was following Pug. If Pug was alone and unarmed, Brandon knew that he could handle him. But if Pug had brought any "friends," the situation would be entirely different. As his ranger instincts kicked in, Brandon glumly remembered that his back was to the water.

As Pug drove nearer it appeared that no one was following him, causing Brandon to relax a little. But not too much, because with Pug, one never knew what to expect. Hoping that Pug wasn't drunk again, Brandon grabbed Jeeves by the collar and pulled him aside.

As Pug stopped his truck and shut down the motor, Brandon looked Pug sternly in the face. Pug exited the truck, then he removed the half-consumed cigarette from his mouth and stomped it into the ground. His twisted expression was odd and quite unlike anything Brandon had seen from him before.

For several moments they simply stared at each other like two gunfighters, each man sizing the other one up in that silent, menacing way such men once did. After looking Brandon up and down, Pug started walking nearer.

Brandon held up his free hand. "You can stop right there, Pug," he warned. "I don't know why you're here. But whatever you're selling, I don't want any."

Pug stopped and looked into Brandon's eyes. Then to Brandon's surprise, he lifted his open hands up in a gesture of conciliation.

"I just wanna talk," he said. "You suppose we could do that without tryin' to take each other's heads off, for once?"

"I suppose," Brandon answered warily. "Let's go inside."

Given their history, Brandon didn't really want Pug occupying his cottage. But if Pug wanted to talk, he was willing to listen. As he followed Pug up the porch steps, his mind raced.

Brandon gestured toward two rockers on the porch, and the men sat down. Brandon's nerves were still on edge, and for a time Pug remained cautiously silent, as if he couldn't begin. When he finally turned and looked at Brandon, for the first time in three years Brandon could find no sense of malice in his eyes.

"I wanna apologize," Pug said simply.

Brandon was stunned. *"Apologize . . . ?"* he asked.

Pug nodded. "You taught me one hell of lesson that day, back at my trailer. I needed to have some sense pounded into me, I guess, and apparently you were the right one to do it. And now I'm actually glad that it happened in front of Claire. Took me down a peg or two in her estimation too, and that was somethin' else that I'd been needin', it seems. After Rachel got better, we had a long talk about a lot of things. Or as best I could, after you got done with me . . ."

Then he shook his head and pointed at his throat where Brandon had struck him. "Damn, but that ranger stuff really works. I wasn't right for days . . ."

Unsure of what to say, Brandon thought for a moment. "It was never my intent to harm you permanently, Pug," he finally answered. "But when you took the first swing, I knew I had to put you down."

"I know," Pug said. "Anyway, I haven't had a drop of booze since then, and I know that I'm the better for it. But it was more than just your shellacking and Claire's overdue badgering session that finally set me straight."

"And what was that?" Brandon asked.

Pug stared down at his callused hands. "It was the way you come out and tended to Rachel, despite how you knew I hated you so bad," he answered. "You risked runnin' into me and gettin' a fight started, just so's you could tend to my little girl. That took balls. If you hadn't come, there's no tellin' how bad she might have got."

"Thank you," Brandon said. "But I was just doing my job the best I could."

"And then there's the other thing . . . ," Pug said quietly.

"What other thing?"

"Claire now workin' at the Blue Rooster for you wife," he answered. "When she told me that Chelsea asked her to come and work there, she also said that it was your idea. And so I wanna thank you for that, too. We were about broke when that job turned up, and I have you to thank for it. I just thought that I should do it in person, is all."

And then, as if there was something even more heart wrenching that he wanted to say, Pug again went silent for a time. When at last he looked back at Brandon, his expression had become especially contrite.

"I know somethin' else now, too," he said.

"Yes . . . ?" Brandon said.

"You were also doing your job the best you could when Mallory died," he said, his voice a near whisper. "Just like you did with Rachel. I get that now. But when Mallory died, the booze got in my way and it blinded me. Anyway, I want you to know that I don't feel that way no more. And I'm sorry for the way I treated Chelsea, too. She never done anything to me, and she didn't have that comin'. She must be a good woman, Brandon, 'cause after the way I treated her, she sure as hell had no reason to be kind to us like that."

Then Pug actually smiled a little, and he again rubbed his neck where Brandon had struck him. "But someday I wouldn't mind learnin' that throat thing you used on me . . . ," he said.

Despite his caution, Brandon couldn't help but smile, too. It was small, brief smile, but it was a beginning.

"I did everything that I could for Mallory," Brandon said. "I loved her too. But she's gone now, and you have to accept that. And although it took me a long time to do it, I have."

Pug turned and looked out over the lake. "Then I'm glad for you," he said. "I guess that some of the reason I got so crazy about it all was because she was with me that day, when she got wounded. And it was my gun that went off, you know . . . If I'd got her to the hospital faster, or if I'd been able to stop the bleedin', then maybe she'da had a chance. But I couldn't . . ."

"Like me, you did your best," Brandon said. "That's all *any* man can do."

Pug nodded. "I know that now . . . ," he said.

Pug stood and looked down at Brandon. "I gotta go," he said. "I probably didn't say things very good, but thanks for listenin'."

Brandon nodded. "After Mallory died, I never thought I'd hear myself say this,

Pug," he answered, "but I'm glad that you came."

A questioning look overcame Pug's face. "So we're good, then?" he asked.

"Yes," Brandon answered. "We're good."

"And you'll thank Chelsea for me, too?"

"Of course," Brandon answered.

After shaking Brandon's hand, Pug left the porch and got back into his truck. As Brandon heard its engine fade away in the distance, he shook his head and smiled.

Well, I'll be damned . . .

Then he thought about how his ranger training had ironically helped to bring Pug around, and he smiled again.

Leave no man behind, indeed . . . , he thought.

38.

Chelsea pointed at a painting that hung in Brandon's living room. "What about his one?" she asked. "Do you want to keep it, too?"

Brandon turned and smiled. "I'll bow to your judgment," he said. "After all, you're the one who used to be an art teacher. I'm just a lowly graduate of Harvard Medical School."

Chelsea snorted out a laugh. "Very funny, Dr. Yale. And since you're leaving this one up to me, then yes—I do want to keep it."

"I was hoping you'd say that," Brandon

answered. "So go ahead and add it to the pile."

After taking the painting down from the wall, Chelsea carried it out onto Brandon's porch. There she placed it among the other things from Brandon's cottage that the two of them had selected. They would be moving into the house in Serendipity soon, and because Brandon's cottage had been listed as furnished, they needed to remove those items they wished to keep. It was Monday, the only day of the week that the Blue Rooster was closed.

Although Chelsea knew that this sorting job must be done, she also realized that these were Brandon's things, and she needed to be sensitive. Because of that, she was letting him make most of the decisions. And even though he hadn't actually mentioned how much he appreciated it, she knew that he did.

After placing the painting on the cottage floor, Chelsea paused in her labors to look out at Lake Evergreen. Fall was here, and it had become a time for sweatshirts, woolen gloves, and hot apple cider. Smiling, she turned around and looked adoringly at Brandon while he continued to sort through the living room items. He meant everything to her now, and she loved being married. As she watched him, he carefully removed a blue and white vase from one of the bookcase shelves.

After regarding it for a few moments, he held it up and called out, "What do you think about this?"

Chelsea returned to the living room and gave the vase a discerning look. It was Chinese in style, with a white background and blue painted flowers covering its surface. She quite liked it, and she said so.

"I'm glad," Brandon said. "You remember my telling you that I bought this cottage fully furnished from Greg Butler? Well, although I sold most of his stuff, I did keep a few things. This vase was one of them."

Smiling again, Brandon set the vase down atop one of the sofa end tables. "Maybe we could put it on the mantel of the other cottage," he suggested. "I think it would look nice next to Brooke's unfinished portrait."

Having again been reminded of everything that had happened this summer,

Chelsea smiled and put one arm around Brandon's waist. "I think you're right," she replied. "And I just know that it's something Brooke would have liked, as well."

Just then they heard Dolly and Jeeves scratching at the porch door, begging to be let inside. While pushing up the sleeves of her sweatshirt, Chelsea smiled.

"They must be cold," she said. "I'll go and do the honors."

Brandon gave her a quick kiss on the forehead. "While you're doing that, I'll be in the kitchen, pouring us a couple of bourbons."

"That sounds great," Chelsea said as she headed for the porch.

While Brandon poured the drinks he heard the porch door squeak open and closed and the dogs come bounding inside. Smiling, he opened the refrigerator door and produced a leftover hamburger patty, which he promptly broke in half.

"Hey, guys!" he shouted over one shoulder. "Who wants to eat?" But as the dogs came charging through the living room, Brandon heard a crashing sound.

"What was that?" he called out to Chelsea. "Did something just break?"

When Chelsea didn't respond, he went to the kitchen door and looked across the living room. Chelsea stood near one of the sofa end tables, staring down at what used to be Brandon's Chinese vase.

"Oh, hell," Brandon said as he walked over. "What happened?"

"Jeeves's tail struck it as he ran through the room," Chelsea said. She again looked down to see that it had broken into several jagged pieces. "And by the looks of it," she said, "it can't be repaired."

"My fault," Brandon said. "I'll fetch the broom and dustpan."

Just then something caught Chelsea's eye, causing her to bend over and more closely examine the little mess. "Brandon," she said, "I think you should see this."

Brandon walked back over and squatted down beside her. On the floor there lay what looked like an old envelope, partly hidden beneath two of the larger pieces. When Brandon picked it up, Chelsea saw a look of astonishment conquer his face.

"What is it?" she asked.

Rather at a loss for words, Brandon simply continued to stare at it. Severely yellowed and dog-eared, it was deeply curved lengthwise from having been hidden inside the vase. The envelope was addressed, *"To My Lost Love."* What stunned him the most, however, was not to whom it was addressed but the nature of the handwriting. Brooke had penned this, he was sure of it. Not only was it in her highly recognizable style, it had also been written in black fountain ink.

He handed the envelope to Chelsea. "I think that Brooke wrote this," he said. "And if I weren't saying so myself, I'd never believe it."

As Chelsea looked at the envelope, her eyes widened with surprise. After letting go a deep breath, she looked back at Brandon.

"I think I know what this is," she said. "It's the farewell letter that Brooke wrote to Greg the night she left Lake Evergreen."

Brandon nodded. "Could be," he answered. "The same letter she placed in the porch door frame just before she headed back to Syracuse." Brandon rubbed his forehead, thinking. "After reading it, at some point Greg must have decided to hide it in that old vase. And rather than sell the vase, I kept it, and the letter has been inside it all this time."

"But why would he leave it in the vase when he sold the cottage to you?" Chelsea asked. "It must have meant a great deal to him."

"Good question," Brandon answered. "But maybe not so odd, if you think about it. He had no heirs, and I'm sure that he couldn't bring himself to destroy it. By leaving it hidden in the vase, the letter would not only go on 'living,' but it would probably never be found, as well. And had it not been for Jeeves, all of that would still be the case. Year after year, this letter would have rested on your cottage mantel, alongside Brooke's unfinished portrait."

Then Brandon smiled a little again as he shook his head.

"That would have been very fitting, wouldn't it?" he asked. "Even though we wouldn't have known what we'd done . . ."

Chelsea nodded. By now her hands were trembling a bit, and it was clear that she had been deeply affected by this unexpected discovery.

Brandon looked at the old letter again. "Only God knows how many times Greg reread this over the course of his remaining years," he added. "Hundreds would be my guess. He loved her so much, and he so desperately hoped that she might one day return to him, that he never married."

"Yes . . . ," Chelsea said. "But what will we do with it?"

Thinking, Brandon took a deep breath. "Well, I'd like to read it," he said. "After all, it's the last piece of the puzzle, and finding it was an amazing stroke of luck."

But as he looked back into Chelsea's eyes, he saw some uncertainty there. On recognizing her reticence, he put one arm around her shoulders.

"If you don't want to know what it says, I understand," he said compassionately. "But with your permission, I do. As best we know, it's the last form of communication between Brooke and Greg."

Chelsea looked at the old envelope again, thinking. Suddenly, this letter seemed a good deal different to her than had the journal. Brandon was right—these were in all likelihood Brooke's last words to Greg, but she wasn't sure that she wanted to hear them.

For the most part, over the course of the last few weeks she had come to terms with all of this, and she didn't want that sense of peace to become uprooted again. She was happy with her new life and nothing must disturb that—even including what appeared to be Brooke's final message to Greg. And there was something else holding her back, she realized. Unlike the old journal that Brooke had requested she read, this letter had been privileged correspondence between Brooke and Greg and was never meant to be shared by anyone else. And so, she didn't want to read it. But at the same time, something inside her didn't mind if Brandon did. When she looked back into Brandon's eyes, she shook her head.

"If you want to read it, that's okay," she said. Then she turned and again looked out across the porch and toward the ever-restless waves of Lake Evergreen. "But I can't do it," she added quietly. "At least not now. Maybe I never will."

"I understand," Brandon said.

After kissing her cheek, he left her and walked out onto the porch, where he sat down on one of his old rocking chairs. And then, after also looking out over the lake for a time, he opened the old letter and started reading . . .

A short time later Brandon wiped his tearful eyes and then replaced the letter in its envelope. He then looked out over the lake again, thinking.

My God, he thought. *Chelsea needs to read this . . . but will she ever have the strength to do so?*

When Chelsea saw that he had finished, she finally picked up the two glasses of bourbon and went to join him. By now the wind had risen, the waves had darkened some more, and it had grown colder.

Or maybe now, after learning about the existence of that letter, the world just seems a little colder, she thought. She had come to realize something else, too. Although she knew that Brandon would gladly tell her what the old letter said, she would not ask him.

Just then the wind rose again, winnowing its way among the evergreen trees. And when she reached over and took her husband's hand into hers he squeezed it lightly, telling her that he understood. . .

39.

As the days progressed, the Adirondacks were enjoying a marvelous stretch of Indian summer, allowing those who owned places on the water to swim and boat just a bit longer before the inevitable arrived. Soon the last vestiges of warmth would fade for good, the few remaining leaves would all be gone, and winter would come calling.

Three weeks had passed since Chelsea and Brandon had married, and regarding Brooke's story, it had been a bittersweet time for Chelsea. There was no more of Brooke's journal to read, and in a way that had been comforting. But she missed it, too. Every time she and Brandon had delved further into Brooke's life, Chelsea had acquired an ever-deepening bond with the wonderful grandmother she had so recently lost. On the other hand, her evenings with Brandon were now free of Brooke's request that Chelsea learn what had happened here those many years ago. Now it was just the two of them, and Chelsea treasured each night with him.

Even so, she still had not read the letter that she and Brandon had so unexpectedly found in Brandon's cottage. She was of course curious, but she also didn't need or want anything to upset her perfect little world—no matter how much closer it might make her feel to her late grandmother.

And there was another reason why Chelsea hadn't read the letter, she realized. Unlike the journal, which Brooke requested she read, that letter had been private between Brooke and Greg, and Chelsea still felt uncomfortable about violating that trust. Strangely, she hadn't felt that way about Brandon's reading it, and gentleman that he was, he had said nothing more about it since that fateful afternoon. Since then the old letter had resided inside Brooke's tin box, along with all of her other things from the past.

It was late afternoon and Chelsea was standing on her porch, where she had stationed the easel and the other painting things she had purchased that day when Brandon had taken her into Serendipity to meet Emily Rousseau. She was working on a painting of Lake Evergreen as seen from her porch, and it was coming along well. Dolly and Jeeves lay nearby on the porch floor, sound asleep.

After a time, Chelsea put down her brush and relaxed in one of the porch rockers. It was a rather cloudy and windy day that caused the waves to cap and the trees around her little cottage to bow and sway more deeply than usual. But as happy as she was, Chelsea remained haunted by some worries.

After three weeks of wondering, she was still at odds with herself about whether to tell Brooke's story to Lucy—to say nothing of letting Lucy actually see the old photographs or read the journal for herself. Chelsea knew full well that

Brooke had left the decision in her hands, but she had given Chelsea no inkling of her opinion. Lucy had been stronger and happier when Chelsea and Brandon had visited her and Adam in Syracuse. But although Chelsea had talked to Lucy several times on the phone since then, she remained unsure whether those changes in her mother had persisted. Chelsea hoped so, but she also knew that a few phone calls weren't enough to decide. One always needed to actually face Lucy, to talk to her, to listen to the tone of her voice, in order to take her full measure. And even then, Chelsea knew, one could easily get the wrong impression. That's just how Lucy was.

Brooke had said in her second letter that she had always preferred to think of her husband, Bill, as Lucy's father, and Chelsea knew why. It had been Brooke's sense of shame that had fostered and nurtured that attitude over the years, and Chelsea sympathized.

But because Chelsea's perspective on the matter was different from Brooke's, her feelings differed, too. Chelsea had never known Bill and she had seen very few pictures of him over the years. Un-surprisingly, Gregory Butler now held a more vivid and prominent place in Chelsea's mind and heart, and she was not surprised by that. Reading Brooke's journal and seeing the photos of her and Greg together had provided Chelsea with a sense of familiarity regarding Greg that had always been quite impossible for her to develop about Bill. However, she had not taken sides about which of the two men to call "Grandfather."

When she had asked Brandon his opinion about telling Lucy, he had politely told her that it would be best if she made up her own mind first. Only then, he had added, would he tell her whether or not he agreed. Because this was such a personal matter, he didn't want to color her thinking, he said. That had frustrated Chelsea a bit, but at the same time she understood.

As she reclined in her rocker, Chelsea realized that on the face of things, it all seemed so simple. Tell her mother Brooke's story, and then show her the journal and the photos. But it wasn't that straightforward, and Chelsea knew it. There were only two choices. She could tell Lucy everything and hope for the best, or she and Brandon could carry what they knew to their graves. There could be no in between, no half measures regarding all of this. And if Lucy was devastated by it all, then Chelsea's decision to tell her would be the cause. And could she live with that? she wondered endlessly.

Chelsea sighed. *What to do? What would I want, if I were in my mother's shoes?* Then she thought about it some more, and at last she made a decision.

I would want to know, she thought. *I would want to know it all, no matter where the answers might lead me. And so for better or worse, I will tell her. I think she deserves that, no matter how she might react. . .*

Just then she heard the kitchen screen door open and close. *Brandon,* she thought happily. At once the dogs bounded up from the porch floor and rushed to greet him. Then Chelsea heard Brandon laugh, causing her to smile.

Brandon came onto the porch, gave Chelsea a quick kiss, and sat down beside her. After he and Chelsea exchanged some notes about their respective days, Brandon looked over at Jeeves.

"Jeeves!" Brandon ordered. "Fetch!"

Jeeves let go an energetic, "*Woof!*" and then trotted into Chelsea's kitchen. They soon heard the refrigerator door open and close, whereupon Jeeves promptly reappeared with a cold bottle of beer clamped firmly between his teeth.

Brandon smiled and took the beer from him. "Good boy!" he said. As he twisted the cap free of the bottle, he looked over at Chelsea. "Want one?" he asked.

Chelsea shook her head. "Not yet, thanks," she answered.

After sitting quietly for a time, Chelsea gave Brandon a more serious look. "I've decided," she said simply.

"About Lucy, you mean?" Brandon asked.

Chelsea nodded. "I'm going to tell her," she said. "All I can say is that if I were Lucy, I'd want to know."

"I'm glad," Brandon said. "And now that you've told me, I think you made the right decision. But I've also been giving it some more thought, and I have a suggestion."

"Which is?" Chelsea asked.

"I'd ask her to drive up here and tell her then," he answered. "Plus, when you tell her, it should be just her and you. This will be a very emotional moment for you both. And yes, I know that Brooke's story happened here, which might make hearing it harder for Lucy. But I think that the peacefulness of this place will help."

Again, Chelsea nodded. "Thank you," she said quietly. "What makes you so smart, anyway?"

Brandon gave her a short smile, then he took another sip of his beer. "Have you forgotten already?" he asked. "I'm the Yale guy who went to Harvard! Now then, can I help you with the dinner?"

"Sure," she answered. "How does some MacArthuroni and Cheese sound?"

"Like heaven on earth . . . ," he said.

40.

As Chelsea stood upon the sandy shore, she shuddered slightly.

The sun had begun setting over the far horizon of Lake Evergreen, the lower edge of its fiery sphere seeming to literally descend into the restless waves. Autumn was seeing her last days, and winter would soon be here. Next week, she and Brandon would at last be forced to move into his house in Serendipity.

The breeze coming off the lake felt unusually cool tonight, providing yet another portent of things to come. As was oftentimes the case, it bothered the lake

surface to create the slightest of white-
caps. Chelsea had been standing alone
here for some time, watching those white-
caps endlessly reach and fall, and now
that sunset had come she felt not only
relief but also a clawing sensation of
dread.

Shuddering again, she hunched her
shoulders and gathered her woolen
sweater closer. It was not so much the
early evening's chill that made her shiver
as it was the nature of the task that lay
before her. She had resolved to do this
thing, even though it might desperately
hurt someone she loved very much. For
what felt like the hundredth time today,
she tried to strengthen her resolve.

At last, she had called her mother yesterday and asked her to visit the cottage
for a night or two. Her argument had been
simple but effective. She would be closing the cottage soon, she told Lucy, and
she very much wanted her mother to see
it first. After some hemming and hawing
Lucy had finally agreed and said that she
would come up the following night.

When she felt that the moment was
right, Chelsea would show her mother

the journal and the photographs and explain everything to her. This had been a heart-wrenching decision to make, and although she was determined to go through it, all day today Chelsea had had to keep reinforcing her will. For better or worse, the most important talk that she would ever have with her mother would soon take place. And as much as Chelsea wanted Brandon by her side for this, she had agreed that he should not be present.

At last she turned away from the lake and slowly looked around. Brandon and Jacques had already hauled the dock ashore and boarded up the boathouse windows. *Beautiful Brooke* again lay in her boathouse cradle, beginning her winter's hibernation. Then Chelsea turned and looked at her cottage. She had lit a robust fire, its smoke gently curling free of the chimney only to be lost to the strengthening breeze. The cottage would soon also be locked shut and its windows covered, lending it the same abandoned appearance that it had possessed when Chelsea first arrived there. She also relished watching the evergreen trees for a time, their still-green needles providing a welcome bit of color against the drabness of an encroaching winter.

Taking a deep breath, she closed her eyes and lovingly recorded these images into her memory because she would soon leave this place for the winter and eagerly begin counting off the days and months until her return.

After a time, Chelsea opened her eyes and turned back toward the pristine lake. Not only had she come to love it here, her persona had changed much during these last months. She was a different woman now, and like her love for Brandon, the other changes that had been engendered within her would forever remain a part of her life. She then looked down at her right hand, and she smiled a little. She still carried the short scar that had formed from when Jeeves had bitten her that first eventful day. Like the many other, deeper changes in her, she would also carry that scar for the rest of her life. And that was quite all right.

So much happened here this summer, she thought. *And so much more will happen tonight. But what will come of my decision? I have resolved to tell Brooke's story to my mother, but am I wrong? Will the final result be only that I hurt her? Or has she at last become strong enough to accept the truth?*

She then looked down at the familiar tin box she held, and she lifted its top. It now contained Brooke's journal and telegrams, the old photos, and both of Brooke's letters to Chelsea. Inside too lay Brooke's final letter to Greg.

She didn't know why she had brought the box out here with her. Perhaps holding it close gave her some added degree of courage. Or maybe just feeling it in her hands helped to keep her connection to Brooke alive in her heart. For she would need both those things tonight, and she knew it. Because now, rather than seeming like precious possessions from the past, all of the items in the box felt like little individual threats that conspired against her, trying to rob her of her bravery. As she felt her resolve weaken yet again, her hands began to shake.

Just then she heard a horn blow, and

she turned to see Lucy's Mercedes approaching the cottage. While the car neared, Chelsea closed the box.

She's early, Chelsea realized. *And here I stand, with all of Brooke's secret things in my hands. May God give me strength . . .*

With a worried heart, she went to greet her mother.

41.

When Chelsea reached Lucy's car, Lucy had already removed her two Louis Vuitton suitcases from the trunk and stood waiting for her. Chelsea sighed and shook her head a bit. Even if Lucy was only going somewhere overnight, she always found it quite impossible to travel light. True to form she was overdressed, wearing a navy suit, a matching raincoat, tall heels, and a rather broad hat. It was hardly Lake Evergreen garb, Chelsea thought, but that was Lucy for you. After Chelsea embraced her, Lucy let go a huge sigh of relief.

"My Lord," Lucy said. "This place isn't easy to find, is it?"

Chelsea smiled a little. "I know," she answered. "But it's worth it."

Lucy looked narrowly first at the little cottage and then toward the lake. Before she could comment, the chilly offshore breeze kicked up again, threatening to separate her from her hat. Lucy grabbed its brim and then she shuddered a bit.

"It's colder up here," she said. "And windier. But I guess that's to be expected."

"Yes," Chelsea said. "Fall is finally ending." Still awkwardly holding the tin box in one hand, she picked up the larger of Lucy's two suitcases. "Come inside and I'll make us some hot tea."

Lucy plucked up the other suitcase and began walking with her. "What's the little box about?" she asked.

As if someone had just poured ice water into her veins, it was now Chelsea's turn to shudder. *How stupid of me to be carrying this,* she thought. *But I didn't expect Mother to arrive so early, either.*

"Oh, it's nothing, really," Chelsea answered. "Just a little something that I want to talk to you about later."

On entering the kitchen, Lucy surveyed it judiciously. "It's not so bad as I thought," she said. "But I still don't know how you spent the entire summer up here without going mad from boredom. And where's that handsome new husband of yours?" she asked as she still looked around the kitchen, eying things.

"He has a late shift at the hospital," Chelsea said. "He probably won't be home until about nine." Just then Chelsea felt another chill go through her as she again regretted doing this without him tonight.

Bag still in hand, Chelsea followed Lucy into the living room, where she placed the tin box on one of the sofa end tables. She then carried her mother's bag into the guest room and beckoned for Lucy to join her there. The two women set the expensive luggage atop the bed.

"This is your room," Chelsea said. "I hope it will be okay."

"I'm sure that it will," Lucy answered. "I'm only here for a couple of nights, anyway."

Chelsea couldn't help but look down at the guest room floor, the same floor from beneath which had come Brooke's journal and photos. The same items from the past that had started it all and were now driving her nearly mad with anxiety. When Chelsea continued to simply stand there staring, Lucy gave her a quizzical look.

"Is something wrong?" she asked.

"No . . . no, Mom, of course not," Chelsea finally answered. "Come on, let me show you the rest of the place."

On returning to the living room, Lucy soon noticed the unfinished portrait of Brooke that stood upon the mantel. "And what have we here?" she asked. "It's a very good likeness, I must say. Do you know who painted it?"

Her mind racing, Chelsea tried to gain some time before answering by putting another log on the fire and then needlessly poking at it with one of the hearth tools.

"No," she finally fibbed. "It was there when I arrived."

Lucy stepped a bit nearer. The fire's warmth felt good, she realized.

"This artist certainly knew his business," she added. "It makes me wonder why Mother never mentioned him." Then Lucy stood back from the painting a bit. "And I wouldn't be surprised if there's an interesting story behind it," she added thoughtfully.

With that, Chelsea couldn't help but again glance anxiously at Brooke's old tin box. It lay no more than two feet away from her mother, and she instantly regretted having placed it there. She considered taking it away but then thought better of it. She wasn't ready to tell Lucy about Brooke's story, and moving the box would only invite further interest.

After her short tour, Lucy removed her coat and then accompanied Chelsea out onto the porch. She spied Chelsea's unfinished landscape and walked over to admire it.

"This one's yours?" she asked.

"Yes," Chelsea answered.

"It's good too," she said. "You really do take after your grandmother, you know." She then selected one of the rockers and sat down.

Just then they heard the two dogs begging to come inside. Chelsea opened the porch door and they came bounding in. At once, they happily accosted Lucy.

Lucy smiled and ruffled Dolly's ears. "Hi there!" she said to Dolly. "It's been a while, hasn't it?" Then she looked at Brandon's setter. "And who do we have here?" she asked Chelsea.

"That's Jeeves, the Beer-Fetching Wonder Dog," Chelsea answered. "You remember—Brandon told you and Dad about him during our visit to Syracuse."

"Ah, yes," Lucy answered.

When Lucy reached out and scratched one of Jeeves's ears, he eagerly responded by tilting his head and pressing it harder against Lucy's fingers.

Lucy smiled. "He seems a good dog too," she said. "But I still don't believe all that mumbo jumbo about him fetching beers from the refrigerator."

Chelsea took a seat beside her mother. "Neither did I," she answered, "until Brandon made him do it one night."

"And by the way," Lucy asked, "what's for dinner?"

"I thought we'd have Eisenhower's Eggs Benedict, if that's all right with you."

Lucy screwed up her face. "Huh?" she asked. "Eisenhower what . . . ?"

"Eisenhower's Eggs Benedict," Chelsea answered. "It's one of Gram's war-time recipes. It calls for sausage instead of Canadian bacon, and the sauce is a bit different, too. It's really good. Brandon loves it."

Lucy's expression remained quizzical. "What on earth are you talking about?" she asked. "What wartime recipes?"

And there it is, Chelsea thought before answering. *Another indication of the deep gulf that existed between my mother and my grandmother.* Just then Chelsea remembered something from Brooke's first letter to her, and she nodded slightly. *"Although it will be many years before you become a woman, I already sense that there will grow a strong bond between us—perhaps even greater than the one I already share with your mother . . ."*

"Didn't you ever look at Gram's recipe book?" Chelsea asked. "You know, the same one you gave me that day at the house?"

Lucy shook her head. "No, dear," she answered. "Mom always did the cooking, you know."

Silence took over for a time as these two different women each thought about the one they had so dearly loved and so recently lost. Over the course of the summer it had become abundantly clear to Chelsea that she and Lucy had loved Brooke in very different ways. *Perhaps that's how it always is with daughters and granddaughters,* she thought.

Even so, Chelsea liked to think that Lucy's love for Brooke had been every bit as strong as was her own. But very soon now, Chelsea would tell her mother everything and perhaps destroy that love forever. As she thought about it, another shiver went through her.

"Is something wrong, dear?" Lucy asked.

"No, Mom," she answered. "It's just the chill in the air . . . it gets to me, sometimes."

Chelsea sat quietly for several moments, thinking. Although her mind was made up about telling her mother, there were some things that she wanted to know first. Things that she missed learning about by having spent the entire summer here rather than in Syracuse. Lucy had seemed better that day when Chelsea and Brandon had visited, and she had in her own convoluted way told Chelsea that she approved of Brandon. And Lucy had been extremely happy at Brandon and Chelsea's wedding. But given Lucy's normally fragile state, Chelsea needed to know whether those positive changes she had seen were still present and accounted for. She dearly hoped so, she realized.

"So tell me," she said, "how are you doing these days, Mom? I know that my decision to stay up here all summer was probably hard on you. With Dad and Gram both gone, you must have been lonely."

Before answering, Lucy quietly looked out over the restless waves of Lake Evergreen. And when she at last spoke, she greatly surprised her daughter.

"You know," she said rather absently, her focus still on the waves, "I was wrong about this place. It's really quite lovely here, isn't it? After seeing it for myself, I'm starting to understand why you stayed. I'm still not prepared to say that I could live here that long, but perhaps next summer I could come up and visit you for a few days. Provided, of course, that the two of you think you could put up with me."

Chelsea was stunned. This, again, was a side of her mother that she had never seen. Even when at her beloved house in Syracuse, Lucy had never seemed completely at ease, as if she somehow didn't quite belong there. But Chelsea was starting to realize that here at the cottage, Lucy was different. Like when Chelsea first arrived, Lake Evergreen seemed to be working its spell on her, too. As Chelsea came to realize it, her eyes became shiny with tears. Reaching up, she casually wiped them away before her mother could notice.

"I think that would be great, Mom," she answered. "I'd love to have you here for as long as you'd like."

Lucy smiled at her. "Then it's a date," she said. "And to answer your question about me, I'm doing better, I really am. With your grandmother gone at last, I've had to rely on myself more. I don't mean for physical things and such. No, rather it's about being truly alone for the first time in my life. And although I'm still quite terrible at it, I've even taken up cooking! To be completely frank, when you called me from here to say that you were staying the summer, it worried me. But now it seems that I've adapted to being alone. God knows I'm sorry that your grandmother has left us. But in her absence, I've seemed to developed a sense of peace that I never had before . . . I don't know . . ."

Then she looked over at her daughter again and she smiled. It was such a happy and honest smile that Chelsea didn't completely recognize it, because it was truly the first of its kind from her mother that she had ever seen. Suddenly at a loss for words, Chelsea sat back in her rocker and again briefly closed her eyes against the task that she would soon do.

"So," Lucy said, "is that offer of some hot tea still good? I must say that I could use it."

"Sure," Chelsea said. "English Breakfast or Earl Grey?"

"Earl Grey," Lucy answered. "For my money, it's the only kind there is. And you know what else?" Lucy asked.

"What?" Chelsea answered.

"While you're making the tea, I'm going to take the dogs outside and have a look around. Would that be okay with you?"

"Sure . . . ," Chelsea answered, trying to steady her voice.

"If I'm not back by the time the tea's ready, come give me a shout," Lucy said.

"All right," Chelsea answered.

After Lucy and the dogs left the porch, Chelsea walked back into the living room and again looked up at Brooke's unfinished portrait. She could easily remember the journal entry that mentioned the day Greg had begun painting it and Brooke's inability to sit still. She then also remembered her recent trip to Brooke's grave site and how she had told her grandmother that there was no need for her forgiveness. And how the two ancient coneflowers Chelsea had placed on Greg and Brooke's graves had suddenly, as if by some form of magic, been whisked high into the air, only to comingle and finally be forever lost to the winds.

With Lucy gone, Chelsea took a precious moment to sit down on the couch and again open the tin box. There, each item still waited to be shown, its particular part of the story ready to be told. And then Chelsea noticed Brooke's final letter to Greg, lying on top of the other things.

With trembling fingers, she lifted it from the old box. The envelope was smudged, deeply yellowed, and excessively dog-eared from Greg's repeated readings of its contents over the many years that he had been forced to live without Brooke Bartlett in his life. And then, quite to her own surprise, at last Chelsea removed the letter from its envelope and she began to read it. It said:

My Dearest Darling,

By the time you find this letter, I'll be gone. I know that my leaving will be a great shock to you but it must be this way, and I can only hope that you will understand. As I write these words, it pains me more than I can say to imagine you sitting on your porch and reading this unworthy letter, your eyes brimming over with tears. On seeing that my car was gone, you probably believed that I was simply out running an errand or two. But as you now know, that is not the case. For I have left Lake Evergreen forever, and I have vowed to never return.

What happened between us last night

was at once the most wonderful yet also the most terrible experience of my life. My overpowering guilt is matched only by my deep love for you, and the two conflicting emotions are tearing my heart in two. And so, I must leave here and never return. For seeing you again would not only bring back all of that pain but surely also fuel the great yearning for you in my heart that I am now forced to hope, over time, will finally lessen. For that is how it must now be between us, my love, and as the years go by, I hope that you will be able to see that.

You were right, Greg. Our being together that way was indeed more about my needing someone during my hour of greatest grief rather than trying to seduce you. And would I have kept on walking into those waves, had you not intervened? I don't know, and I probably never will. But it will not be an unpleasant burden, knowing that you may have saved my life . . .

To my great shame, I have experienced the deceit of taking one man to my bed while still desperately mourning the death of another. Although it was wrong of me, I know there is nothing I can to do keep it from happening again, save for leaving here. And so now I will have neither of you. Perhaps that is a fit punishment for what I have done; I don't know. All I know for sure is that the very act of love that I resisted for so long—and which we at last consummated—had the opposite effect with us that it usually does upon two prospective lovers. For rather than join our random hearts, it has in fact separated them forever.

Please do not try to contact me, for my mind is made up about this. Hearing from you in any way will only harm the healing that I must now strive to achieve. But know that I loved you with all my heart, and to my own pain and detriment, I always will. For you see, my love, sometimes in this world there are no answers. There are only choices. And because there is no answer to our dilemma, one of us had to summon up enough courage to make a choice, difficult as it might be.

What we had was brief, I know. Even so, I believe we loved one another more deeply and strongly during our short time at Lake Evergreen than most men and women do during their entire married lives. It is my fervent wish that that sentiment can help to protect your heart from the pain, Greg, and help you to accept my decision, no matter how difficult it will be for you.

Always,
Brooke

Crying fully now, Chelsea carefully refolded the old letter, placed it back into its envelope, and then returned it to the tin box with Brooke's other things.

My God, she thought, *how much she loved him, only to lose him because of that very same ardor. Knowing this story will forever make me closer to her, and also to a man whom I never knew existed and who might well be my grandfather. . .*

But in the end, does any of it really matter? she wondered, tears still streaming down her face. *Perhaps all that matters, despite whatever bits of their pasts our loved ones might leave behind for us, is the here and now, and how each of us chooses to live it. I have become the woman I am largely because of Brooke's love and guidance over the years, rather than because of who my grandfather might or might not have been, his identity clouded by an illicit tryst that occurred decades ago . . .*

And then, as a portion of Brooke's letter to Greg revisited her mind, Chelsea understood something else.

"For you see, my love, sometimes in this world there are no answers," Brooke's letter from so many years ago had said. *"There are only choices. And because there is no answer to our dilemma, one of us had to summon up enough courage to make a choice, difficult as it might be . . ."*

And then, suddenly, Chelsea felt as if Brooke's letter had been intended as much for her as it had been for Greg.

Choices and answers . . . , Chelsea thought. *I've been searching for answers where there are none. Mother's knowing of this would do no good. It would serve no purpose. It would not change who I have become or who my mother is . . . It would make no difference at all, save to cause yet more pain in a woman who is at last starting to heal from a lifetime of in-*

securities. And just like Brooke was forced to do those many years ago, I too must now stop searching for answers and make a difficult choice . . .

Almost as if she were someone else, and before she could yet again surrender to her own self-doubt, Chelsea defiantly stood up. And then, her hands trembling nearly beyond control, she gathered up everything from the little box and she quickly tossed it all into the fire.

At first she simply stood there, quite unbelieving of what she had just done. But as she watched the flames begin to consume those very things she had once deemed so precious, she realized that the die had been forever cast. And for the first time since coming to Lake Evergreen and finding her grandmother's secret treasures, Chelsea's heart and soul felt truly free.

As she leaned her arms against the fireplace mantel, she closed her weary eyes and smiled a little through her tears.

"Hey in there," Lucy suddenly called out as she began ascending the porch steps. "Where are you?"

When Chelsea didn't respond, Lucy

walked on into the living room. As she did, Chelsea was barely able to dry her eyes in time. When Chelsea looked back down at the fire, its flames were quickly relegating all of Brooke's things to ashes. And with their burning, the flames consuming them had grown more vibrant.

As Lucy came to stand alongside Chelsea, she too looked down at the fire. But unlike her daughter, she was unaware of why the blaze had strengthened. As they both stood there watching the dancing flames, Lucy smiled and put one arm around her daughter.

"You know," Lucy said, "now that I've been here at your cottage for a little while, I can understand why you love it so. And somehow, I can sense that a lot of our family's history was created here, can't you?"

Chelsea smiled a little as she watched the last vestiges of Brooke's mementos disappear.

"More than words can say, Mother," she answered quietly. "More than words can say. . . ."

A⁺

AUTHOR
INSIGHTS,
EXTRAS &
MORE . . .

FROM

ROBERT
BARCLAY

AND

WILLIAM MORROW

Reading Group Questions for *More Than Words Can Say*

1. In *More Than Words Can Say,* Chelsea Enright inherits several unexpected items from her late grandmother Brooke and they have a profound effect on her. Have you ever inherited something that was so unexpected or potentially life changing? If so, what sort of effect did that experience have on you?

2. Before going to Lake Evergreen, Chelsea is very doubtful that she will like it there or that she will want to keep the old cottage that she has inherited. However, over the course of time she dis-

covers that she not only loves the lake and the cottage, she is also hungering for a simpler life, and she ends up staying for good. Have you ever wished for a simpler existence in a more rural environment? Conversely, if you live in a rural area, have you ever wished that your life could be more cosmopolitan? Is the grass really greener on the other side of the fence?

3. When Chelsea meets Brandon Yale, she comes to believe that he is a wonderful man, but she also guesses that he has a very troubled past. Only after his violent confrontation with Pug Jennings does Brandon finally open up to Chelsea and tell her his story. Have you ever had a friend or loved one confess a dark secret to you? If so, how did it affect your relationship? Was it for better or for worse?

4. Although Chelsea's lakeside cottage is lovely, it is also quite spartan. The mail is delivered by boat, and the nearest town is some twelve miles away. Additionally, the cottage has no television at

all, nor does Chelsea buy one. Would you enjoy spending an entire summer in such a place? Given all the modern conveniences to which we have become accustomed, would that sense of isolation bore you to tears, or would you find it a welcome relief?

5. After the sudden death of her grandmother, Chelsea decides to go to Lake Evergreen, rather than stay in Syracuse and comfort her distraught mother, as Lucy asks her to do. Which do you think you would have done? Would you have stayed with Lucy and watched over her during her time of grief? Or would you have obeyed the wishes of your late grandmother and gone to Lake Evergreen to unravel the mysteries described in Brooke's letter?

6. Rather than tell Brooke's story to Lucy, Chelsea tosses all of Brooke's mementos into the fire and watches them burn, keeping them a secret forever. Do you believe that this is what you would have done? On the other hand, would your desire to know have been so great,

and your need to inform Lucy been so strong, that you would have shown and told Lucy everything? Like Chelsea, have you ever kept a secret to yourself in order to spare the feelings of a loved one?

7. At the beginning of the book, Chelsea is far from being the outdoors type. But as the book progresses, and she and Brandon become closer, she finds herself doing things that she would never have imagined otherwise. She flies in Brandon's plane, learns to drive Brooke's old speedboat, and hikes all the way to the top of Red Rock Mountain. Have you ever tried new things for the sake of someone you love? If so, did doing these things bring the two of you closer?

8. Near the end of the book, we learn that although Brandon and Pug Jennings have had a very difficult past, it is Brandon's idea to hire Pug's unemployed wife to work with Chelsea at the Blue Rooster. Have you ever performed an unrequited act of kindness for someone

with whom your relationship was deeply troubled? If you have, what sort of effect did it have on the two of you?

9. Although she always believed that she had been happy as an art teacher, Chelsea decides to change direction totally, and she buys the Blue Rooster. Are you happy in your current line of work? Or do you perhaps long to do something different but are unsure about what that might be? Do you believe that you would have the courage and determination to drop everything and start a new life, as Chelsea did?

10. Chelsea also inherits her grandmother's handwritten recipe book. It is filled with original recipes, many of which are named after Allied World War II leaders and famous American movie stars of the 1940s. Have you ever devised an original recipe of your own? If so, did you give it its own name? Have you tried re-creating any of Brooke's recipes found in the back of the book? How were the results?

11. By the end of the book, Emily Rousseau has become not only a good friend to Chelsea but also an important mentor. Sadly, our elderly are oftentimes dismissed as useless rather than being respected for their knowledge. Has an elderly person ever taken the time and care to teach you something of value, something that perhaps only he or she could? Was it a valuable experience? Do you still treasure those memories and the time spent with whoever taught you?

12. Part of Brooke Bartlett's torment stems from the fact that her husband, Bill, is away, training for his future involvement in World War II. Do you have a friend or relative serving in the armed forces who is away at this moment, perhaps even serving in a highly dangerous combat position? If that is the case, as you read the book, did it serve to bring you closer to the character of Brooke Bartlett?

13. As the book progresses, the reader learns about some of the hardships endured during civilian life during World War II, such as the shortages of food, gasoline,

alcohol, etc. Do you believe that we present-day Americans take our relative prosperity and ease of acquiring consumer goods too much for granted?

14. Shortly after their wedding, Chelsea asks Brandon to translate the saying in French that he told her the night he described how Mallory had died. Part of that translation talked about how one's love for another should be "shouted from the mountaintops." Have you ever been so strongly in love that you, too, felt like climbing a mountain and loudly proclaiming your love for the entire world to hear?

More Than Words Can Say
The Story Behind the Book
by Robert Barclay

As I began writing, I knew that I wanted to incorporate some of my own life's experiences into this book, along with an authentic sense of history. "Write about what you know!" is the very good advice that hopeful writers often hear. I already knew about lakeside cottages, fishing, boating, and hiking. What I did not know much about, however, was what civilian life was like in America during World War II, the other time period I hoped to use in the book. Luckily, I was able to get some firsthand knowledge on that score, because both of my parents still carry with them vivid recollections of those days.

During the war, my mother's father was a chicken farmer in upstate New York. Part of his operation was a successful feed store. Although every American was experiencing the rationing of foodstuffs, gasoline, alcohol, etc., because of my grandfather's occupation, my mother's family ate very well—provided one liked a steady diet of chicken and eggs! Even so, acquiring most other things remained as difficult for them as it was for everyone else. My mom has oftentimes told me how the chicken feed was regularly delivered to their farm in gingham bags, and rather than throw the bags away, her mother would reuse them to make dresses for herself and her two older sisters. During those days, one did what one had to.

My father's experience was rather different. A bit too young to be drafted during World War II, he became a likable rogue and literally made his living buying and selling gas ration stamps on the black market. And aside from not having a clubfoot, I am told by my mom that my dad both looked and behaved much like Greg Butler. As I wrote the book, each of my parents continued to give me valuable insight and details into what life was like during World War II and how they dealt with the various hardships of those days.

Sometime around 1966, my mother and father bought a lakeside cottage in Ontario, about a six-hour drive from our home. The cottage was located on a lake called Round Lake, and it is in fact an exact duplicate of the one that Chelsea inherits in the book. Our boathouse, too, was nearly identical to Chelsea's.

This was where my father taught me how to fish, run a speedboat, and fillet and cook walleyes. And not far from the cottage there lies a high outcropping called Red Rock Mountain, where both the climb and the view from the top are virtually identical to those experienced by Chelsea, Brandon, Brooke, and Greg. I can still remember clambering to the top of that peak nearly every time I visited the cabin. And, just like the fireplace hearth in Chelsea's cabin that was made entirely of rose quartz rocks, so too was the fireplace in our cabin, its stones also harvested from the vicinity of Red Rock Mountain.

To my great delight, one day while I was visiting the cottage, a floatplane landed on the lake and then taxied down to the cottage next door, where the pilot exited the plane and tied her up at their dock. Hopelessly intrigued, I couldn't help but wander over and ask about it. The pilot was more than happy to take me for a ride, which immediately sparked my interest in flying. Two years later I got my pilot's license, which helped enable me to describe Brandon's flying experiences in the book.

Like Chelsea's grandmother Brooke, my paternal grandmother, Joyce, was also a gentle, loving, and artistic soul. And like Brooke, Joyce loved to paint. Sadly, I too lost my grandmother around the same time in my life that Chelsea loses Brooke. Since writing *More Than Words Can Say,* I have oftentimes wished that my grandmother had bequeathed to me a secret diary, just as Brooke had done for Chelsea. Sadly, however, that was not the case.

To my great dismay, my parents decided to sell their beloved lakeside cottage in 1985. I can still remember the last time I visited. The windows were boarded up, the boathouse had already been locked and closed, the dock had been pulled ashore, and winter was fast approaching. Knowing that the cottage was being sold, I had gone there to be alone for a few days. I still can remember standing in the living room before that rose quartz fireplace and literally saying good-bye to the place, before I glumly locked the door, put the key in my pocket, and finally drove back home for the last time.

I have often thought that I might inquire about the cottage and try to buy it from whoever owns it now, but the distances involved, and my wife's busy neuropsychology practice, would make visiting there impractical. Therefore, I shelved the idea, much the way each of us is sometimes forced to lovingly stow away their dreams. But who knows? Perhaps someday I will in fact buy back my father's wonderful old cottage. Or maybe at least visit there, in an attempt to relive some of my most cherished memories.

But for now, at least, having incorporated that lovely old place into *More Than Words Can Say* will simply have to do.

Addendum:
A Small Collection of Brooke Bartlett's Personal Recipes from World War II

These recipes come directly from my old, handwritten recipe book that I had with me at Lake Evergreen during the summer of 1942. In some cases I have upgraded them slightly by incorporating a few modern ingredients that we didn't have back then, but they all remain true to the original spirit, I promise you. I hope that you will like them!

Yours,
Brooke Bartlett

Clark Gable's Grapefruit Cake

From the moment I saw Clark Gable roguishly smile at Vivien Leigh in *Gone With the Wind,* he became one of my favorite actors. Rumor had it that he had a weakness for grapefruit cake, so when I invented this particular recipe I decided to name it after him. He also joined the air force and fought in the war. Thankfully, he survived the conflict and returned home to make many more such wonderful movies for us!

Total time: 2 hours 35 minutes
Serves 8–10

Butter, for greasing the pan
2½ cups all-purpose flour
2 cups white sugar
1 teaspoon baking powder
1½ teaspoons baking soda
½ teaspoon salt
3 eggs
1 cup canola oil
½ cup freshly squeezed ruby-red grapefruit juice
½ cup freshly squeezed Florida orange juice
1 banana, mashed
12 ounces sour cream
2 tablespoons orange zest

1 teaspoon grapefruit zest
Glaze sauce (recipe follows)

Rub a large Bundt pan with butter. Preheat the oven to 350° F.

Sift together the flour, sugar, baking powder, baking soda, and salt. Put the mixture into a stand mixer, add the eggs, and mix until combined. Then add the oil; mix until blended. Next add the grapefruit and orange juices and banana and mix until smooth and creamy. Last add the sour cream and zests; mix until just combined and smooth.

Put the cake batter into the prepared pan and bake for 35 to 45 minutes or until a toothpick inserted in the center comes out clean.

When the cake is done, turn the pan onto a serving platter, let stand for about 15 minutes, then poke small holes in the top. I use a straw; be neat about it. Pour glaze sauce on the partially cooled cake. Let cool for about 1 hour and serve. We like it with a scoop of dreamsicle ice cream on the side and a sprig of mint.

VARIATION
This could be a layer cake with cream cheese icing.

Glaze Sauce

¼ **cup grapefruit juice**
2 **cups confectioner's sugar**
1 **tablespoon orange zest**
1 **tablespoon grapefruit zest**
¼ **cup finely chopped pecans**

Mix the juice and sugar until combined. If it is too thick, add more juice, a tablespoon at a time. Stir in the zests and pecans.

Eisenhower's Eggs Benedict

This was an easy one to dream up! My family has always loved eggs Benedict, and we serve it with champagne every Christmas morning. One Christmas long ago I decided to change things up a bit, so I replaced the Canadian bacon with a sausage patty, added the leftover sausage bits from the frying pan to the hollandaise sauce, and then gave everything a good, strong shot of lemon juice. The results were so favorable that my dad promptly dictated that this would be our Christmas morning meal from now on! I hope you enjoy it!

Total time: 45 minutes
Serves 6

Water
½ cup distilled vinegar, divided
12 large eggs
1 tablespoon unsalted butter
12 sausage patties
6 plain English muffins, split
Hollandaise sauce (recipe follows)
1 tablespoon finely chopped fresh chives
    or finely chopped fresh flat-leaf parsley
    leaves

Pour enough water into 2 large skillets to reach a depth of about 3 inches, and divide the vinegar between them. Bring both skillets to a gentle simmer over medium heat. Crack an egg into a cup and carefully slide it into the hot poaching liquid. Quickly repeat with all the eggs. Poach the eggs, turning them occasionally with a spoon, until the whites are firm, or to the desired degree of doneness, about 3 to 5 minutes. Using a slotted spoon, remove the eggs and transfer to a kitchen towel. Lightly dab the eggs with the towel to remove any excess water.

While the eggs are poaching, melt the butter in a large skillet over medium heat. Add the sausage patties and cook until heated through, about a minute on each side.

To serve, toast the English muffin halves and divide them among 6 warmed plates. Top each half with a sausage patty and set an egg on top. Spoon the hollandaise sauce over the eggs and garnish with the chives. Serve immediately.

Hollandaise Sauce

1⅓ cups unsalted butter
2 large egg yolks
2 tablespoons cold water
1 tablespoon strained freshly squeezed lemon
   juice, plus more as needed
1 teaspoon kosher salt
Freshly ground white pepper or a pinch of
   cayenne pepper

In a medium pan, melt the butter over medium-low heat. Remove from the heat and set aside for 5 minutes. Skim and discard the white foam that rises to the surface of the butter. Carefully ladle or pour the clear golden butter into a container with a pouring spout. Take care not to add the milky solids and watery liquid at the bottom of the saucepan. Set the butter aside in a warm spot.

Pour enough water into a medium saucepan to reach a depth of about 2 inches. Bring to a gentle simmer over medium heat.

In a medium heatproof bowl, combine the egg yolks and the cold water. Whisk until the yolks are light and frothy. Place the bowl over the saucepan of simmering water and whisk constantly and vigorously until the yolks are thickened and light, 3 to 4 minutes. (If the eggs begin to scramble or the mixture is cooking very quickly or gets too hot, remove the bowl from the heat and whisk to cool.) Remove the eggs from the heat and whisk for 30 seconds to cool slightly.

Remove the saucepan from the heat and set the bowl over the hot water. Slowly drizzle the butter into the eggs while whisking constantly. Whisk in the lemon juice, salt, and pepper to taste. (If the sauce is very thick, add a few drops of warm water to adjust the consistency so it is creamy and light.) Serve immediately or keep the hollandaise sauce in a small bowl set over warm, but not hot, water, for about 30 minutes or in a warmed thermos for about an hour.

Churchill's Cherry and Cream Cheese Pie

I invented this one snowy afternoon in Syracuse, soon after the bombing of Pearl Harbor. Although the weather was cold that day, once the idea got into my head, I just knew that I had to try it out. This one took a couple of tries before I got it right! In the end it was worth the effort, and it has long since been one of my favorites. As a final touch, I suggest placing a pair of crossed mint leaves on top of the pie.

Total time: 3 hours 10 minutes
Serves 6–8

1 8-ounce package cream cheese, at room temperature
1 14-ounce can sweetened condensed milk
½ cup fresh lemon juice
1 teaspoon vanilla extract
1 9-inch graham cracker crust
1 21-ounce can cherry pie filling, chilled

Either in a stand mixer fitted with the paddle attachment or using a handheld electric mixer, cream the cream cheese until light and fluffy, 3 to 5 minutes. Slowly add the milk, mixing on low speed until well combined. Stir in the lemon juice and vanilla and pour into the crust. Place the pie in the refrigerator for at least 2 hours and up to overnight, until well chilled and set.

Top the pie with the pie filling just before serving.

Roosevelt's Roast

Back when rationing was in effect, it was difficult to acquire all the ingredients for this one, named after FDR. But these days, it's a snap! The trick with this one is the proper preparation of the bourbon-and-mushroom sauce. Don't let it simmer too long, or you'll run the risk of burning it. But do it right, and it will be worthy of serving at the White House!

Total time: 1 hour 35 minutes
Serves 4–6

2 to 3 tablespoons grapeseed oil, for searing
¼ cup coarse sea salt
¼ cup coarse cracked black pepper
1 whole beef strip loin, trimmed with some fat
**   remaining**
Bourbon-mushroom sauce (recipe follows)

Preheat the oven to 300° F.

Add the oil to a sauté pan. Season the meat on all sides with salt and pepper. Sear the meat on all sides, 2 to 3 minutes each side. Place the meat on a sheet tray with a rack. Roast the meat for 30 to 40 minutes. Crank the oven up to 450° F and roast for an additional 15 to 20 minutes until crust forms and meat is nicely colored. When done, allow to rest for 10 minutes before slicing. In a small bowl, reserve the drippings for the bourbon-mushroom sauce.

Bourbon-Mushroom Sauce

5 tablespoons butter
1 tablespoon garlic, minced
1 cup cremini mushrooms, sliced
1 cup onion, finely diced
4 tablespoons all-purpose flour
¼ cup bourbon
3 cups beef stock
Salt
1 tablespoon cracked black pepper
2 tablespoons chopped fresh parsley

In a large saucepan over medium-high heat, add 4 tablespoons of the butter. Add the garlic, mushrooms, and onion and cook for 4 to 5 minutes until nicely browned. Add the remaining ingredients and simmer. Before serving with the beef, add the reserved juice to the mixture.

Bogart's Baked Beans

Named after Humphrey Bogart, this one is especially easy to make. In fact, I threw it together one afternoon while at my parents' house in

Syracuse, largely because I had promised them some sort of dinner and I didn't know what I was going to cook. Plus my father had the car, and I couldn't go grocery shopping! And so, I needed to come up with something that used whatever ingredients I could find that day in my parents' pantry. The result is a recipe that's simple, satisfying, and quick. And like the characters that Bogey oftentimes played on the big screen, it's also colorful and has a flavor all its own.

Total time: 21 minutes
Serves 4

6 cups baked beans
3 slices bacon, chopped into ½-inch pieces
1 medium red onion, finely chopped
¼ cup brown sugar
1 teaspoon coarse black pepper
3–4 cut-up hot dogs
2 tablespoons chopped parsley leaves,
    optional

Preheat the oven to 425° F.

Pour the beans into a casserole dish and place in the oven.

In a small nonstick skillet, cook the bacon over medium-high heat for 2 to 3 minutes. Add the onion and cook for 3 minutes longer.

Slide the beans out of the oven. Scatter the onions and bacon around the beans. Sprinkle the brown sugar and black pepper over the onions and add hot dog pieces.

Bake the beans with the toppings for 10 minutes longer. Garnish the beans with parsley and serve.

MacArthuroni and Cheese

Of all the recipes listed here, this one is the most surefire favorite. I don't know anyone who doesn't like a nice dish of macaroni and cheese! This recipe is especially good, because it's made with two kinds of mushrooms and Gruyère cheese. Just be sure to not skimp on the Gruyère, and use only good-quality mushrooms. During World War II, General MacArthur made his famous pronouncement, "I shall return!" Make this dish correctly, and your guests will "return" repeatedly for second (and maybe even third) helpings!

Total time: 1 hour 30 minutes
Serves 6–8

2 tablespoons unsalted butter
Good olive oil
½ pound shiitake mushrooms, stems removed and caps sliced into ½-inch pieces

½ pound cremini mushrooms, stems removed
   and caps sliced into ½-inch pieces
3 tablespoons cream sherry
Kosher salt
1 pound pasta, such as cavatappi
3 ounces white truffle butter
½ cup all-purpose flour
1 quart whole milk, scalded
12 ounces (4 cups) Gruyère cheese, grated
8 ounces (2½ to 3 cups) extra-sharp cheddar,
   grated
1 teaspoon freshly ground black pepper
½ teaspoon ground nutmeg
2 garlic cloves, chopped
3 tablespoons freshly chopped parsley leaves
1½ cups fresh white bread crumbs

Preheat the oven to 375° F.

Heat the butter and 2 tablespoons of olive oil in a large (12-inch) sauté pan, add the mushrooms, and cook over medium heat for 3 to 5 minutes, until they are tender. Add the sherry and continue to sauté for a few more minutes, until the sherry is absorbed. Set aside.

Bring a large pot of water to a boil and add a splash of olive oil and a pinch of kosher salt. Add the pasta and cook for 6 to 8 minutes, until al dente. Drain well.

While the pasta cooks, melt the truffle butter in a large (4-quart) saucepan and whisk in the flour. Cook for 2 minutes over low heat, stirring constantly with a whisk. Slowly whisk in the hot milk and cook for 2 minutes, stirring constantly with a wooden spoon, until the white sauce is thickened and creamy. Remove from the heat and add the Gruyère, cheddar, 1 tablespoon salt, the pepper, and the nutmeg.

Combine the pasta, sauce, and mushrooms in a large bowl and pour into a 10-by-13-by-2-inch baking dish.

Place the garlic and parsley in the bowl of a food processor fitted with a steel blade and pulse until they're minced. Add the bread crumbs and pulse to combine. Sprinkle the crumbs over the pasta and bake for 35 to 45 minutes, until the sauce is bubbly and the crumbs are golden brown. Serve hot.

Winston's Baked Walleye

I created this recipe for a dear friend during one summer at Lake Evergreen. Because this one has such a strong sentimental meaning for me, I almost didn't include it here. But the recipe is so good that I just had to add it. . .

I prefer to use walleye, but almost any of any kind of fish will do. The secret here is to not bake the fillets too long and risk drying them out. Since the day I came up with this, I have often wished that I had also created a lobster or shrimp cream sauce to go on top of the fish fillets, but I haven't gotten around to that yet. Anyway, this is a good one, and named after Winston Churchill, another of my great heroes. With all that going for it, how could it miss?

Total time: 30 minutes
Serves 4

4 tablespoons (½ stick) unsalted butter
⅔ cup crushed crackers (I use Ritz)
¼ cup (about 1 ounce) grated Parmesan cheese
½ teaspoon dried basil
½ teaspoon dried oregano
¼ teaspoon garlic powder
1 pound walleye, or sole, scrod, perch, or other mild-tasting fish fillets
Lemon wedges

Preheat the oven to 350° F.

Melt the butter in a 9-by-13-inch pan in the oven. While it melts, combine everything else except the fish in a pie pan. Dip each fish fillet in the melted butter, dip each piece in the crumb mixture, and return it to the baking pan. Bake the fillets for 20 to 25 minutes, or until the fish flakes with a fork. Serve with lemon wedges.